THE BIG SHOW

The entire valley grew eerily quiet, just the whispers of the falling snow and the branches rustling slightly in the wind. It seemed as though the birds and other animals had gone silent, anticipating what would happen. The phone beeped, and the comm operator connected him directly to General Mitchell. "Sir, canisters are away."

"Excellent work, Captain. Stand by. I'm ordering the kinetic strike now."

Lex flicked his gaze up into the dark, snow-filled sky, and while he couldn't see them, he imagined the twelve rods of tungsten blasting off from their space-based orbital platform via their rocket motors. They'd plunge toward the atmosphere until gravity accelerated them to thirty-six thousand feet per second as they headed for a collision course with the Earth's crust—or more precisely Fort Levski. Each rod packed all the destructive effects of an Earth-penetrating nuclear weapon.

One rod would wreak havoc.

Twelve would devastate the entire valley . . .

Lex wouldn't have to imagine that part. He and his men had a front-row seat.

NOVELS BY TOM CLANCY

The Hunt for Red October
Red Storm Rising
Patriot Games
The Cardinal of the Kremlin
Clear and Present Danger
The Sum of All Fears
Without Remorse
Debt of Honor
Executive Orders
Rainbow Six
The Bear and the Dragon
Red Rabbit
The Teeth of the Tiger
Dead or Alive
(written with Grant Blackwood)
Against All Enemies
(written with Peter Telep)
Locked On
(written with Mark Greaney)
Threat Vector
(written with Mark Greaney)

SSN: Strategies of Submarine Warfare

NONFICTION

Submarine: A Guided Tour Inside a Nuclear Warship
Armored Cav: A Guided Tour of an Armored Cavalry Regiment
Fighter Wing: A Guided Tour of an Air Force Combat Wing
Marine: A Guided Tour of a Marine Expeditionary Unit
Airborne: A Guided Tour of an Airborne Task Force
Carrier: A Guided Tour of an Aircraft Carrier
Special Forces: A Guided Tour of U.S. Army Special Forces

Into the Storm: A Study in Command
(written with General Fred Franks, Jr., Ret., and Tony Koltz)
Every Man a Tiger
(written with General Chuck Horner, Ret., and Tony Koltz)
Shadow Warriors: Inside the Special Forces
(written with General Carl Stiner, Ret., and Tony Koltz)
Battle Ready
(written with General Tony Zinni, Ret., and Tony Koltz)

Tom Clancy's

ENDWAR®

THE MISSING

WRITTEN BY

PETER TELEP

BERKLEY BOOKS, NEW YORK

THE BERKLEY PUBLISHING GROUP
Published by the Penguin Group
Penguin Group (USA)
375 Hudson Street, New York, New York 10014, USA

USA I Canada I UK I Ireland I Australia I New Zealand I India I South Africa I China

Penguin Books Ltd., Registered Offices: 80 Strand, London WC2R 0RL, England
For more information about the Penguin Group, visit penguin.com.

TOM CLANCY'S ENDWAR®: THE MISSING

A Berkley Book / published by arrangement with Ubisoft Entertainment SARL

For information, address: The Berkley Publishing Group,
a division of Penguin Group (USA),
375 Hudson Street, New York, New York 10014.

ISBN: 978-0-425-26629-8

PUBLISHING HISTORY
Berkley premium edition / September 2013

PRINTED IN THE UNITED STATES OF AMERICA

10 9 8 7 6 5 4 3 2 1

Cover art courtesy of Ubisoft.
Interior text design by Kristin del Rosario.

ALWAYS LEARNING   PEARSON

ACKNOWLEDGMENTS

I'm deeply indebted to a great number of people who have contributed their expertise to this manuscript:

Mr. James Ide, chief warrant officer, U.S. Navy (Ret.), has continued his work as my first reader, researcher, and collaborator—from concept to outline to polished manuscript. He is a true friend and a skilled writer and has kept me honest for many years.

I'm indebted to all the folks at Ubisoft who created the EndWar game, and to everyone else at the company, most notably Mr. Sam Strachman of Ubisoft Paris. Sam has worked with me on several other book projects, including *Ghost Recon: Choke Point*, and offered his keen advice, insights, and terrific sense of humor.

My agent, Mr. John Talbot, and editor, Mr. Tom Colgan, have supported and encouraged me for many years, and I'm truly grateful for yet another project we can share.

Finally, my wife, Nancy, and two lovely daughters, Lauren and Kendall, challenged me to finish this novel before the Mayan calendar ran out (just in case).

Be convinced that to be happy means to be free and that to be free means to be brave. Therefore do not take lightly the perils of war.

—THUCYDIDES (460–395 B.C.)

Only the dead have seen the end of war.

—PLATO (428–348 B.C.)

PRELUDE TO WAR . . .

The unthinkable happens in 2016. A nuclear exchange in the Middle East kills six million people and cripples the world's oil supply. Crude oil prices spike at eight hundred dollars a barrel.

One year later, the threat of worldwide nuclear war is eliminated when the United States and Europe deploy a comprehensive space-based antiballistic missile shield. Russia soon follows with an advanced missile defense system of its own. Intercontinental ballistic missiles are rendered obsolete.

Russia becomes the world's primary supplier of energy and experiences a massive economic boom. With its newfound riches, Russia quickly reestablishes itself as a major superpower and restores her military might.

Western Europe, with the notable exceptions of the U.K. and the Republic of Ireland, unifies to create the European Federation. This new nation is destined to be a formidable twenty-first-century superpower.

In 2020, the United States is on the verge of finishing construction on the *Freedom Star*, a controversial orbital military platform that will upset the balance of world power. The European Federation withdraws from NATO in protest.

Tensions between the European Federation, the United States, and Russia build. Russia invades Canada in an attempt to seize the oil sands and is thwarted by the United States. Smaller scale air, sea, and ground conflicts continue but threaten to escalate into an all-out conflict, sapping the resources of every nation and tearing apart the planet.

The EndWar has begun.

ONE

Major Stephanie Halverson jerked the side stick control-ler, guiding her F-35B Joint Strike Fighter in a hard right turn, the pressure suit tightening around her hips against the agonizing g-forces.

Her pulse raced. Surface-to-air missiles were locking on. Identification: Russian S-500, the latest and most potent mobile SAM system in the world, with radars capable of tracking more than three hundred individual targets and engaging twenty simultaneously.

Screw this, she thought. *I'm breaking radio silence.* "Neptune Command, this is Siren. I've got multiple SAMs inbound! What the hell's going on?"

Earlier in the evening she'd launched from Incirlik Air Base in Turkey, was in-air refueled just prior to leav-ing Turkish airspace, some 200 miles from her target, and had bridged the 720 miles to North Ossetia in the blink of an eye.

"Neptune, this is Siren, do you read me?"

The Sixth Fleet tactical air commander on board the aircraft carrier USS *George H. W. Bush* CVN-77 loitering off the coast of Cyprus did not respond.

Swearing, Halverson released IR flares and clouds of white-hot chaff—countermeasures that might save her from one or two of the missiles, but secondary beeps indicated that more SAMs were being launched.

Jesus God, how many now? Glowing in her Helmet-Mounted Display System were infrared and wireframe representations of the mountain range, the suspected SAM sites below, and the military cargo train about to cross the new bridge towering over the broad expanse of Darial Gorge.

Superimposed against this scene were six inbound missiles, each one's speed and trajectory marked by scrolling numbers beside the yellow squares on her screen.

A proximity alert beeped above the missile warning, and in its cool, emotionless voice, the computer delivered the bad news:

More missiles were now locked on her heat signature. The computer IDed them as Vympel R-84s, two pairs, each with thirty kilograms of HE—enough to easily blast apart her aircraft. The pilots who'd express-mailed them were smiling behind their visors and muttering, "*Do svidaniya.*"

She flicked her glance from the radar scope to a databar indicating that four Sukhoi Su-35 long-range Interceptors bearing 281 degrees were, in fact, streaking toward her. The two lead fighters had fired their Vympels.

She studied the SAMs and the air-to-air missiles, their numbers and ETAs, and held her breath.

The enormity of the moment was almost too much to bear. She was one pilot with ten missiles on her back. She shuddered and thought, *I'm dead.*

But damn it, this wasn't her fault. The mission was supposed to be reconnaissance only, a solo test flight into enemy territory of the AN/AST Radar Warping System and Algorithm (RWSA), along with its associated software. The RWSA's lightning-fast onboard computers were supposed to absorb and amplify an enemy's radar beam and return it at a deflected angle. The idea was based on the planet Mercury's so-called orbital wobble when its orbital line of sight neared the sun. Einstein, in his general relativity theory, deduced that the massive gravitational field of the sun bent Mercury's reflected light beam, tricking an earthbound observer to see the tiny planet along a bearing where it didn't actually exist. Similarly, the new radar warping device was supposed to cause enemy fire control radars to calculate distorted missile/gun firing points in space-time where Halverson did not exist.

In layman's terms, they were supposed to be shooting at her ghost, if they detected her at all. Had Einstein been wrong? Or was this new toy's software just corrupt?

The alarms kept beeping, reminding her that there was a lot more at stake than just one plane and one pilot.

The Radar Warping System was being prepared for

the Joint Strike Force's latest prototype: the X-2A Wraith, a sixth-generation fighter and reconnaissance jet designed by Lockheed Martin's Skunk Works in California. The Wraith was capable of reaching speeds of Mach 6, or nearly 4,600 miles per hour, and Halverson ought to know: She was the Wraith program's chief test pilot. She could never be more proud, because the Wraith was a piece of military hardware that would change the entire scope of the war. No nation could match its speed, stealth, or firepower.

And only a select few knew about it, its coming-out party mere weeks away.

With clouds of expanding chaff blooming behind her fighter, Halverson pulled up hard, panting into a helmet shaped like an insect's head, the oxygen line hissing as her shoulders were pinned to the seat.

Wait a minute.

She thought about what she was flying, her fighter's range of capabilities. She'd almost forgotten this wasn't another prototype like the ones she'd been testing for the past year between combat missions in Europe.

She looked to the train. To the radar scope. To the Russian Interceptors closing in . . .

The F-35B Short Take-Off and Vertical Landing (STOVL) fighter variant could hover like a helicopter via its shift-driven lift fan. The contra-rotating fan with twenty thousand pounds of lift was located just behind the cockpit and built within the fuselage.

That was it. Crazy idea. Insane.

Probably her only hope.

Still no response from Neptune. She knew the protocol. She was on her own now, responsible for doing what was necessary to ensure that her aircraft and its prototype equipment did not fall into enemy hands.

The waning moon flashed across her cockpit as she came around, then shoved the stick forward, diving straight for the maglev train, her speed, distance, and bearing all calculated and displayed against the infrared images of her sensors. The gorge and bridge grew brighter, shifting from a pale green to an almost blue-silver.

Somewhere behind her, two of the SAMs exploded in her chaff, just as she released another cloud, then rolled right, fully inverted, and dove at an even steeper angle, the sky flickering at her shoulders.

She came upright, then glanced down between her legs, the sensors allowing her to stare right through the fuselage at a computer-generated image of the train below.

Throttling up, the Pratt & Whitney afterburning turbofan roaring, she painted the center of the bridge with her laser, then fired—

A single wingtip-mounted Sidewinder exploded away from her jet, tendrils of smoke glistening in saffron light. She had two such laser-guided Sidewinders onboard and could use them to strike hardened targets, as opposed to the usual air-to-air ordnance she carried. Given that this was a recon mission and her load-out was light, she was lucky to have the ability to hit a hardened surface target.

Flying now like an old kamikaze pilot about to swoop down and T-bone the train's lead car, Halverson gasped as the tracks ahead of the train exploded, metal twisting like spaghetti at irregular angles, the maglev train barreling toward the wreckage, its operators already seeing what was happening and slamming on the brakes.

Unfortunate for them.

Between the explosion along the tracks and the heat produced by the train itself, Halverson had just created a secondary and much hotter heat source than her fighter. The S-500s had both infrared and active radar homing (ARH) guidance systems; however, those ARH systems lost their effectiveness the closer the target was.

As the train slowed, so did she, wheeling around to hover and descend beside the first few cars, with Russian troops plastering their faces against the windows in shock and pointing at her. She wasn't cocky, didn't wave. All she could think about were three words: *speed, maneuver, evade.*

The rest of the SAMs came in, striking the still-flaming tracks, now tearing apart the bridge in a near-blinding conflagration that lit up the whole gorge. The snow-capped mountains came alive with shadows and flashes of orange light as broad sections of the bridge tumbled like scaffolding ripped free by a twister, only to crash onto the rocky floor some four hundred meters below.

The train could not stop in time and was heading straight for the shattered tracks and the abyss.

According to Halverson's radar, the Vympels, too, would take this new bait, as all four shifted course toward the SAM explosions, their own ARH systems homing in on the moving train . . .

Halverson drifted back from the gawking Russians, then hit the gas and burst from behind the train, rocketing straight up into the night sky.

Eyes watery, heart still racing, she wouldn't sigh in relief. Not yet.

Those Interceptors were still up there, still had her on their radar—

And not a breath after she leveled off at just a thousand feet above the train, the alarms beeped again.

Two more Vympels. ETA fifteen seconds.

There must've been a third one as well, the one that exploded across her portside wing, the one that had never shown up on the radar, the one that caused her to lean forward against the centrifugal force, flip a panel, and detonate a tiny bomb inside the prototype radar system, effectively destroying it and its software.

Her F-35B was in a flat spin now, and she fought hard with the stick, realizing that no maneuver in the world could save her now.

She thought of her boyfriend, McAllen, the way he'd run his fingers through her long, brown hair. She thought of pizza and the smell of that perfume she loved so much, and she thought about her father, an Air Force pilot like her who'd flown missions in Afghanistan, and of her mother, who'd worked tirelessly at the bank to help support their family. She even remembered Dr. Helena Ragland, director of the Wraith program at Skunk

Works, beaming at her after her first test flight. Halverson's gut felt hollow over letting all of them down.

In the next breath, she released the stick and yanked hard on the black-and-yellow striped handle between her legs, aka the "loud handle."

Here it comes . . .

She screamed against the violent explosion of the canopy shearing off the aircraft—even as she fought against those ugly, chilling feelings of defeat.

She wasn't a quitter, wasn't dead yet. And hell, this wasn't the first time she'd punched out of a jet. She was already a proud member of the Martin-Baker Fan Club, having earned her broken wings in the great white north of Canada at the beginning of the war, when the Russian Federation had attempted to seize the oil sands.

So here it was, déjà vu. The Martin-Baker MK16 ejection seat carried her away from the spinning jet, the straps and padded cuffs locking her to the seat, even as the wind kicked the shit out of her and made her feel like a flaming hardball hurtling out of Fenway Park.

Bang, the drogue chute snapped open, tugged her down, and she began rocking to and fro as the main chute behind the headrest deployed and the seat automatically dropped away from her, drawn off by another chute.

Her helmet's transmitter was active now, her ejection broadcast across the network, with Neptune Command hopefully monitoring her every move despite the silence.

That offered only small relief as she glanced down at the bridge, the maglev train hanging precariously over

the destroyed section of track, the first two cars swinging in midair, the others still hanging on, the fires still
burning around the wreckage.

She couldn't see the automatic thirty-millimeter cannon fire at first, only hear it, only feel the rounds ripping
through her chute. Those Interceptors were equipped with
GSh-30 internal cannons with at least 150 rounds each,
meaning those four pilots had 600 chances to kill her.

Another salvo came in, and she jerked forward, one of
her steering lines severed, a few more lines cut, the chute
partially collapsing, lines getting tangled, and she began
a corkscrewing descent—

Directly toward the train, the troops now pouring
out of the rear cars and fleeing up the tracks, with girders, towers, and decking groaning under the weight and
threatening to collapse. A few suspension cables snapped
like rubber bands pulled to their extremes, whipping
away to crash across the cars and knock several fleeing
troops over the side. They screamed as they plunged into
the gorge.

She was about to detach her main chute and deploy
the reserve when another wave of gunfire came in, the
chute jerking once more . . . and then she was coming
up on the train, seconds away from impact.

She gritted her teeth and reached out with gloved
hands.

TWO

Dr. Helena Ragland was lying in the backseat of an SUV, writhing in pain, her wrists bound by zipper cuffs.

Thirty minutes earlier, she'd been monitoring the test mission over the Caucasus Mountains from her computer station inside the Skunk Works facility, and the moment she'd learned that Halverson had ejected, she'd been called out of the office for a meeting up at Edwards Air Force Base with Lieutenant General Terence Walsh, Deputy Chief of Staff for Intelligence, Surveillance, and Reconnaissance.

Walsh had been a huge proponent of the Wraith program, and he'd flown in from Washington not only to inspect the prototype but to watch a test flight. Halverson's mission failure could not have come at a worse time.

The lieutenant general had been informed of Halverson's ejection and wanted to hear Ragland's explanations. She could rely on the old excuse of her team having to analyze the flight recordings, telemetry, satellite images, and so on to fully understand where the malfunction had occurred, but Walsh deserved better than that. She would be honest with him. Painfully honest. There was nothing obvious that indicated or suggested a malfunction, and she was certain that prior to launch the unit's software was operating flawlessly, as it had during more than a dozen tests here in Palmdale. Halverson should have flown right across the mountains and into North Ossetia without being detected, and again, if she was detected, those SAMs should have been locking on to locations where she'd already been. Something had happened after Halverson had lifted off, something that caused the RWSA's software to indicate systems normal when in fact the unit was not functioning. For a few seconds she'd entertained the preposterous idea of sabotage, but she'd sworn off the notion because of the tremendous security precautions they'd taken at the Skunk Works facility, with all computers being air-gapped and lacking any connection to the outside world. They'd also been exceedingly careful during the F-35B's transfer overseas.

After delivering that frustrating report to the lieutenant general, Ragland would steer Walsh's concerns away from the malfunction and point him squarely toward his downed pilot, their mutual friend, a woman well known by the president of the United States for her bravery under fire. They needed to verify whether Halverson was still alive and send in the Quick Reaction Force (QRF). In point of fact, even as she needed Walsh to think more about Halverson, she needed to forget—otherwise she might break down. She and Halverson had worked closely together for the past year, engineer and pilot, and Ragland had begun to think of the woman as her younger sister, sharing meals and drinks, sharing in the setbacks and triumphs of the program.

And now this.

Yes, it was already a terrible morning. Even the coffee tasted bitter. She reached over to the center console and replaced the steaming cup, then glanced ahead at the highway.

A frantic phone call from her sixteen-year-old daughter had her swearing under her breath. She'd forgotten to give Lacey the pictures she needed for her school project—due today. The pictures were in Ragland's purse.

"Honey, I'm on my way to an important meeting."

"Can't you stop on the way?"

Ragland hesitated. She'd just bowed out of her monthly update briefing with Boeing's Argus project team to focus on the Halverson emergency and could certainly not be late for her meeting with Walsh.

"I want them to know about my father," Lacey snapped.

Ragland tensed. "All right, all right, I'll be there in ten minutes."

Her daughter, her only daughter, the gem of her life, was still struggling with her father's death. Ragland had divorced Steven nearly two years ago. He blamed the Wraith program; she blamed his inability to balance his own medical research with raising a daughter. They used to jokingly refer to their marriage as an episode of *When Scientists Collide*.

Just before the war had broken out, Steven had gone to Paris for a conference and had been killed during the Russian ground invasion. The news was devastating, and the pain in Lacey's eyes only fueled Ragland's desire to complete the Wraith project and put an end to this global conflict.

She reached into her purse and withdrew the old pictures of Steven when he was just a boy. Ironically, Ragland had removed the photos from some old albums and had slipped them into her purse so she wouldn't forget to give them to Lacey. The photos were going to be scanned and become part of Lacey's online portfolio.

Following a quick glance in the rearview mirror, she accelerated, the BMW leaping forward, her anxiety working its way into her foot. She hadn't spent her entire life engineering things that go fast without enjoying a little acceleration herself. Her secret dream was to pilot the X-2A Wraith, bring the jet up to Mach 6, and reach any destination on the planet in less than three hours.

Hypersonic flight powered by scramjet—essentially a single-cycle, four-barrel rocket engine—worked best in a one-to-two-micron atmosphere near space. Once Pratt & Whitney had developed the engine, Ragland had incorporated her modifications to an airframe looking every inch like a matte black manta ray slicing through the air at unbelievable speeds. Oh, how she longed to be a test pilot.

However, that wasn't the path she'd chosen. She had attended UCLA, earning her undergraduate degree in aerospace engineering. Afterward, she'd opted for a radical change of scenery, traveling all the way to MIT for her doctorate in aircraft systems engineering. She'd taught there as an adjunct for a few years but had been lured out of academia by administrators from Skunk Works, the official alias for Lockheed Martin's Advanced Development Programs (ADP). Skunk Works was where all the sexiest pieces of aviation hardware were developed, aircraft like the U-2, SR-71 Blackbird, F-117 Nighthawk, F-22 Raptor, and the F-35 Lightning II that Halverson had flown. Promises of unobstructed research and far less bureaucratic interference since the four branches of the service had come together under the auspices of the Joint Strike Force were too tempting to ignore.

Over the years she'd secured many patents for her employer, most recently the one for the Radar Warping System. While she was readily acknowledged and financially rewarded for the fruits of her engineering prowess, by law, the patents became the intellectual property of the company, and that was fine. The work was immensely rewarding, with the Wraith program now a professional and personal quest. They would get past this setback. They had to. The president himself was a huge proponent of the program. Today he was out in the Mojave Desert, watching some kind of hush-hush drone demo, and the news of Halverson being shot down had no doubt already ruined his day.

She turned off the highway and headed down West Lancaster Boulevard, reaching her three-bedroom home two minutes earlier than promised. Lacey was standing in the driveway, wearing a deep scowl she'd perfected during the last year.

"You always forget," she said as Ragland handed over the photos.

"I'm sorry, honey, I really am. I always have a lot on my mind. Hurry now. Don't miss the bus."

Lacey nodded. "You owe me big-time for this."

Ragland forced a smile, then backed out of the driveway and hurried off.

Within a few minutes, she was on Aerospace Highway, just north of West Avenue F, when, out of nowhere, her Beemer's engine died.

"What now?" she groaned, coasting to the side of the road. She checked the mirror. No cars. The rolling desert hills stretched off for miles.

Cursing, she tried to start the engine again. Nothing. Not even the *click, click* of a dead battery.

She grabbed her smartphone, thumbed it on. No power.

A chill woke at the base of her spine. She got out of the car, shut the door behind her. She spun on her heels, looking for anything, another car on the highway, any sign of power. What was this? An EMP wave? Had the Russians finally gone insane? The nuclear exchange back in 2016 between Iran and Saudi Arabia had crippled the world's oil supply. Did the Russians really believe a nuclear attack on the United States was in their economic best interests?

No, no, no, this wasn't an attack. This was some kind of localized anomaly. Something coming from the base, another test gone awry—but wouldn't she have been notified?

Her breath grew ragged, and then she heard it, a car engine from somewhere to the south. She turned again.

An SUV came barreling toward her. She waved frantically to the driver, who slowed and parked behind her car.

Actually, there were two men, both in their thirties and dressed business casual. Very handsome. She found herself smoothing out her short blond hair and adjusting her glasses.

"Hello there, ma'am. Looks like you've got a bit of a problem," the taller one said, his accent British or Australian, maybe South African.

"Thanks for stopping. Are your phones working?"

The shorter one reached for his, glanced at the screen, and shrugged. "No problem."

"Mind if I borrow it? My battery's dead or something."

"Sure, but we can give you a lift," said the taller one, wriggling his brows.

"Oh, I'm sure you can, but if I could just borrow your phone, I'll have someone from the base pick me up."

"Edwards Air Force Base?" asked the shorter one.

"Yeah."

The taller one took a step toward her. "I'm sorry, Dr. Ragland, but I think you know what this is about. We'll make it as painless as possible." He tipped his head toward the SUV. "Please get in."

"Are you kidding me? Who are you?" she demanded, walking backward toward her car, nearly tripping.

As she turned to grab the door handle, something struck her back and shoulder, the pain excruciating as she turned to them, the Taser dart wires looping back from her shoulder to the pistol clutched in the taller one's hand.

Before she hit the ground they were on her, carrying her back to their vehicle, laying her across the rear seat and binding her wrists behind her back. She could barely talk, her vision blurred by tears.

Oh, yes, she knew what this was about.

The Wraith.

THREE

American Missionary Camp
Amazon Rain Forest
Northeastern Ecuador

"He's on the move," Lex shouted, bolting from beneath the underbrush.

Twenty meters ahead, their target was fleeing through a dense avenue of tagua palms toward the river below.

Captain Mikhail "Lex" Alexandrov and his three-man JSF Marine Corps Raider Team had been tracking this son of a bitch for the past six months, across three different continents, and this was the closest they'd ever come to capturing him.

The baritone and familiar voice of Staff Sergeant Borya, one of Lex's teammates, rattled through his earpiece: "Drone's in the air. Just stay with him, sir."

Their unmanned aerial vehicle (UAV) with infrared sensor was a medium-sized quadcopter that could track their target through the jungle—

But it couldn't look the man in the eye and tell him this was the end of the line. It couldn't let him know that he and his "Forgotten Army" of terrorists were going to pay for the thousands they'd killed.

Yes, the moment the cuffs went on, Lex would tell this guy in both Russian and Spanish that he was unimpressed and that Nestes was lucky he was worth more alive than dead. JSF interrogators would pry out of him everything he knew about his entire network: names, relationships, front companies, communications hubs, weapons transfer points, and current and future operations.

Carlos Nestes might be the leader of the Forgotten Army, but he sure as hell would remember who had captured him.

Soulless *terroristicheskiys* like Nestes came from "failed" states in the Balkans, Africa, and South America. Once a part of the Green Brigade Transnational, a much larger terrorist organization, they had splintered off, recruited drug lords and paramilitary organizations, and even claimed to have the support of factions like Hezbollah and the Taliban.

Lex didn't give a shit about that. They could have connections with a powerful alien race. Point was, if you crossed America, if you crossed the JSF, if you crossed the Marine Corps, you, sir, were going down.

The hard way.

Lex's boots sank three inches into mud that felt like black glue, forcing him off the path and sidestepping down a steeper embankment as the rushing river grew louder. He was bare-handing his M4 carbine, the weapon warm and sticky as he used it now like a tightrope walker's pole for balance. He carefully shifted across the trunk of a fallen palm to bridge a gully formed by run-off. This allowed him to flank Nestes, who was now sliding down the hill, trying to slow his descent, the mud washing up over his jeans and sleeveless T-shirt. He glanced back, long black hair whipping over his eyes, and then he spotted Lex.

Nestes lifted his pistol.

Lex saw the gun flash and heard the report in his head before either actually happened.

He was already diving for the mud, shouting, "Don't waste your time! We've got a drone. You can't run!"

By the time Lex lifted his head to stare back down the hillside, Nestes was gone.

"Borya, where the hell is he?"

"Heading west, paralleling the river, about fifty meters ahead of you now."

"Roger. All three of you move up!" Lex sprang to his feet, swearing as he came around the wooden trunk of another palm, its long pinnate leaves brushing his face. He misjudged the distance and caromed off, his shoulder warming with pain.

Gritting his teeth, he moved across the rise and worked his way farther down, beginning to see the river through the fettered canopy and the shafts of dust-laden light warming the undergrowth. He was sweating like a dog now, his nondescript Raider fatigues soaked, eyes stinging.

As the jungle grew more dense, he reached out with

all of his senses—blue eyes squinting, fingers running across a torn frond as he passed. He noted the muddy tracks winding around a cluster of shrubs. He jerked his head at a sound.

Movement out there, beyond a stand of trees: a flash of Nestes's white shirt.

Lex quickened his pace, homing in on the man as though his brain were now a radar system, prints marked, swinging branches observed, his gaze leaping ahead to predict his target's course. The stench of rotting fronds and mud made him grimace, but he kept on, breathing in a smooth, rhythmic pattern like they'd taught him all those years ago in Quantico, during Officer Candidate School (OCS). He was thirty-three now, but back then, during the good old days when he'd been in his twenties, nobody gave a shit when an American-born guy with a Russian last name wanted to be a Marine. It was a non-issue. But once President Kapalkin and his cronies in Moscow began showing their true colors by manipulating terrorist groups to do their bidding—and after the Russians invaded Poland and parts of Europe—suddenly Lex's colleagues regarded him differently. They loved the idea that he spoke fluent Russian and could work flawlessly behind enemy lines; they hated the idea that maybe, just maybe, blood was thicker than water, and one day he'd turn on the country that had taken in his poor grandparents from Odessa and given them a whole new life in New York. What the hell did they know?

America was Lex's country, but his parents and grandparents deemed it very important that he never lose touch with his roots. Everyone learned English, but no one ever forgot their Russian. His relatives were spread out across the northeast, from Virginia to Pennsylvania to Connecticut and New York, and they too loved their homes, their nation.

But for all of them, that Russian surname was hard to escape when the shit had gone down.

No, the U.S. government had not set up internment camps for Russian Americans like him, but like American-born Muslims after 9/11, they were not treated with the same dignity and respect. Moreover, many of Lex's fellow soldiers never looked at him the same way again. Sure, some would come to his aid and point out how ridiculous their paranoia was, but that didn't help.

Tired of dealing with it, he'd jumped at the chance to join the JSF's new Special Raid Teams Group (SRT) and prove his mettle and loyalty by exploiting his Russian heritage.

Composed of a select few Marines from the 1st Reconnaissance Battalion out of Camp Pendleton and men from the 2nd Reconnaissance Battalion out of Camp Lejeune, the new SRTs were patterned after the original Marine Raiders established by the United States during World War II but disbanded after they had outlived their mission. The old Raiders had been formed to conduct amphibious light infantry warfare behind enemy lines and were some of the United States' first special operations forces to see combat during the war. The new JSF Marine Raiders were charged with the same mission, deploying small teams of operators who could best impersonate the enemy in both Europe and Asia.

For his part, Lex had handpicked his own Raider team, all three Russian Americans like himself, specialists who could walk the streets of St. Petersburg with impunity, manhunters one and all. You either put your faith and trust in them or you didn't. Their record spoke for itself: sixteen high-value targets (HVTs) captured or killed in the last twelve months, even as they were still pursuing Nestes. The Secretary of the Navy himself had congratulated them. It was satisfying to stick it to the doubters and haters.

Lex was even closer to the river now, the mist tickling his nose, the white water partially hidden by curtains of branches and leaves. Once he reached the next tree he stopped, driving himself in tight against the wood, tagua nuts scattered at his feet. He squinted through the trees, waiting.

A slight rustle of leaves sounded overhead, and the water continued beating on the rocky shoreline. A bird squawked. Sweat dripped onto his rifle.

He realized he was panting and tried to muffle his breath. He grew calmer and spoke softly in Russian. "Talk to me, Borya."

The man answered in Russian: "He stopped. Thirty meters southwest of you. He's following the river, keeping about ten meters away."

"Can you cut him off?"

"Yeah, we can. On our way."

Lex lifted his carbine and stared down the ACOG.

He willed himself to grow calm. The gunsight's reticle floated over the hillside, toward an outcropping of moss-covered rocks, then shifted farther down to a tree with some kind of white fungus spread across its trunk like a pair of talons. Lex blinked. Wait a second. That was Nestes, holding tight against the palm. *Got you* . . .

Drawing in a deep breath, Lex shifted aim to the man's arm. *Injure, don't kill*, he reminded himself, but it was hard to hold back when he had the faces of those train victims in Paris in his head, the faces of those children who'd been in Atlanta, and the brutal massacre of all those college kids in Tokyo. Carlos Nestes's face had circulated around the world, his videos gone viral. He'd grown his hair out and been hiding here in the jungle, shadowing an American missionary group, when one of them had spotted him, recognized his face, and given Lex and his men the break they needed.

Now it was time for this bastard to pay. Screw the intel. Screw the deals he'd make. Lex's aim shifted back to Nestes's heart.

He trembled and reminded himself that he was a professional, that he always acted accordingly and in the best interests of the Marine Corps and the United States. No matter what this prick had done, he could not take away Lex's identity, his esprit de corps. Lex should not give in to temptation. He could not.

Letting out a deep breath, he aimed for the man's arm and calculated the distance and bullet drop, rough estimates to be sure. The intel in Nestes's head was too valuable, despite all of the bloodshed. Lex rewound that thought and ordered himself to believe it.

Nestes slowly lifted his head in Lex's direction, squinting. He widened his eyes in recognition.

Lex fired—

But the shot fell wide, tearing a jagged hole in the palm tree as Nestes darted away.

Swearing aloud in Russian, Lex groaned and propelled himself forward, barely minding his step across an obstacle course of moss-and-dew covered roots, his boots sliding, his balance nearly gone before he catapulted off the last one and knifed his way farther ahead, reaching the tree he'd shot, cutting around it, then spotting Nestes as he ducked under several gnarled and low-hanging branches whose surfaces were alive with ants.

"Lex, he's coming toward us," said Borya.

"Roger, let him know he's surrounded."

"Whoa, whoa, whoa, I think he spotted us and he's turning around, coming right at you now!"

Lex hunkered down, tucking himself up against the nearest palm tree, feeling like a jaguar reading his prey. The shrubs just ahead were spanned by thick spiderwebs, the furry beast crawling down toward Lex's leg. Using the muzzle of his carbine, he flicked the spider away—just as Nestes neared him, making a sharp turn toward the river.

"Hold it right there," Lex said, springing up from the tree and training his rifle on Nestes, who came to an abrupt halt about five meters away. He did not turn around, nor did he raise his hands.

Borya had the drone over them now, the rotors humming above the canopy, Nestes's position clearly marked.

"Turn and walk toward me," Lex ordered.

Nestes craned his neck enough to steal a glimpse of Lex, and the second they made eye contact, the son of a bitch took off again, his hair trailing like flames.

"Borya, he's heading straight for the river now. Take the flanks and we'll pin him down there."

Head low, measuring his steps more carefully now, Lex fell in behind the man, the ground turning rocky, the footing precarious, and then, as he pushed through some thick ferns that obscured his entire view, his boots were in the air, no footing at all, and he landed on his rump, the ground dropping away at a forty-five-degree angle and plunging at least fifty meters toward the more level ground at the riverbank.

Even as Lex rode the currents of mud, struggling to sit up, with more mud blasting into his face, he realized that Nestes, too, had made the same error, and was right there, just ahead, arms flailing as he struggled to control his descent.

Lex blinked, the mud blinding him momentarily, and then his boots struck something hard, a large rock that sent him whipping face-forward now down the hillside, the M4 torn out of his grip.

That his combination earpiece/microphone was still attached was a small miracle, he thought, as Borya cried, "Holy shit, boss, are you all right?"

And then nothing, the earpiece flicked away as Lex's

elbow caught once more on a rock and he now logrolled toward the shoreline, covered head to toe in mud.

Each time his body lifted into the air, he groaned, anticipating the next impact on a rock. A kaleidoscope of green-streaked brown filled his eyes, and as the water began to rage in his ears, he finally came to a halt, lying flat on his back, the world still rotating around him.

He stole a quick breath, then wrenched himself up to a seated position. He began spitting out mud and back-handing it from his eyes, and when he turned his head, trying to see anything through all the wetness and dirt, he found a pistol in his face.

"Hello there, comrade," said Nestes in perfect Russian. That wasn't his real name, Lex knew, and he wasn't South American. He'd been born in Kaliningrad. He and his brother, a man who'd gone by the alias of José Nestes and who'd been killed in England, had a Russian father and Peruvian mother.

"I guess you have a conscience," Lex said. "Because I would have pulled the trigger."

"No, I just need you as a hostage to get me out of here."

Lex snorted. "Won't happen."

"Oh, yeah, it will."

"You really—seriously—think you can take me?"

Nestes thought about that, tossing his wet and matted hair out of his eyes. He resembled a savage now, like a character out of literature, gleaming teeth and glistening mud. "Maybe you're right. Maybe it doesn't matter anymore. We're the Forgotten Army, truly forgotten.

The *Ganjin* has changed. We were once partners. Now we're only tools."

"What're you talking about?"

Before the man could answer, the drone came swooping in—

And just as Nestes glanced up, the UAV slammed into his forehead, knocking him off balance.

In that same second, Lex lunged for the man, seizing his wrist with both hands, and then, once in control, he reached up and got his hand around Nestes's pistol, prying it from the man's grip.

As soon as the gun came free, Nestes, in a last-ditch effort, spun around, unscrewing his arm from Lex's grip. As the arm came free, he stumbled back, facing the bubbling, rushing white water behind him, then threw himself in.

As the current swept Nestes away, Lex shuddered with indecision. "Aw, hell . . ."

He dove into the waves.

FOUR

SinoRus Group Oil Exploration Headquarters
Sakhalin Island
North of Japan

She had once been Viktoria Kolosov, born thirty-eight years ago, the daughter of a schoolteacher and a car transporter from Vladivostok, Russia.

And then she was Viktoria Antsyforov, the wife of Nikolai Antsyforov, a doctor who'd died for a corrupt government. She was also the sister of two brothers, one poisoned by radiation like her husband, the other sacrificing himself and his submarine for men who were incapable of gratitude.

But now she was *Snegurochka*. The Snow Maiden. The world's most wanted woman, described by the media as a true sociopath, murdering with cold, cruel efficiency.

The security officer pointing the Uzi in her face assumed he'd just captured her. Was he that stupid?

She knocked his submachine gun away, then drove a knuckle into his eye, a knee into his groin. She wrenched free his weapon and forced him over the catwalk's railing to plunge ten meters to the concrete below.

As his echoing scream rushed up at them, she turned the gun on her other three assailants, spraying them with a hailstorm of rounds as they came charging toward her.

Too bad Fedorovich had given them orders to take her alive, and too bad they were *not* equipped with Tasers or other less-than-lethal measures to subdue her. They might have had more fight in them. She hadn't wanted a bloodbath, but if she had to walk across a carpet of bodies to get the hell out of here, then so be it.

Back up ten minutes ago to the conference room on the other side of this petrochemical processing and recovery plant:

She had just learned that her employers, members of a group called the *Ganjin*, now controlled a member of the Joint Strike Force's high command, and they were about to control General Sergei Izotov, director of the Glavnoje Razvedyvatel'noje Upravlenije (GRU)—the Russian Federation's foreign military intelligence service.

Her handler, Dr. Merpati "Patti" Sukarnoputri, had explained the history of the group thusly:

"*Ganjin* as a concept was born many years ago, back in the 1970s, during the fall of the Communist regime. The movement was the precursor in China toward capitalistic individualism and enabled the beehive mentality of Chinese society to restructure into many hives. The concept prompted Xu Liangyu and Isaac Eisenstein, two classmates at Harvard, to consider how the *Ganjin* could be used to gain control of the world's natural and socio-economic resources."

The *Ganjin*, the Snow Maiden later learned, had plans to undermine the superpowers during this time of war and wreak economic havoc on a global scale so that when the time came, they could take advantage of the weakened economies and, as the Snow Maiden under-stood it, seize control of their governments.

Of course, they had tried to keep that agenda from her. She'd been hired as an assassin and manhunter, promised protection from the Russians, who sought her more than any other government because she, too, had once worked for GRU, knew their secrets, could identify many of their agents, and had told her old bosses in the Russian government in no uncertain terms that she intended to see Moscow burn . . .

But ten minutes ago, in that conference room, she'd learned that her "relationship" with the *Ganjin* was going to become something "so much more." Patti and her boss, Igany Fedorovich, director of SinoRus, had said that China no longer wanted any part of the group, and the "Committee of Five" had split apart. Patti and Fedorovich had a new agenda, one they claimed was meant to foster peace, but in order to get there they needed the Snow Maiden's utmost loyalty.

A five-micromillimeter chip (one-tenth the diameter of a human hair) would be placed into the optical nerve of the Snow Maiden's eye. The chip would capture neu-roimpulses from the brain that embody the experiences, smells, sights, and voice of the implanted person. Once transferred and stored in a computer, those signals would be projected back to her brain via the microchip to be "relived." Using a Remote Monitoring System (RMS), a land-based computer operator would send electromagnetic messages (encoded as signals) to the nervous system, affecting the Snow Maiden's performance. She could be induced to see hallucinations and even hear voices in her head.

Every thought, reaction, hearing, and visual observation would cause a certain neurological potential. Patterns in the brain and its electromagnetic fields would be decoded into thoughts, pictures, and voices.

But most importantly, commands.

Electromagnetic stimulation would change the Snow Maiden's brain waves and affect muscular activity, causing painful muscular cramps experienced as torture if she did not obey.

Obedience brought extreme pleasure, sometimes even orgasm.

Major Alice Dennison of the Joint Strike Force already had a microchip in her eye. Izotov from the GRU was about to have one implanted against his will.

"I don't believe it," the Snow Maiden had cried.

"Silicon and germanium microchips have been around for years," Dennison had said smugly. "They gave way to biochips using strands of DNA in place of wires to latch on to and recognize thousands of genes at a time. Our microchips are the result of that research and the studies done on patients with Alzheimer's and

Parkinson's disease. This is the future, Viktoria, and you'll be a part of it."

"Screw the future, Science Lady. You're not sticking anything in my head."

Flash forward ten minutes, and here she was. They were not happy about her rather rude exit.

They'd confiscated her smartphone before the meeting, but that hardly mattered. There was no one to call, anyway. Patti and her associates had been the Snow Maiden's only true allies in the world. The others from her tenure with the GRU either had been killed or could no longer be trusted because there was a steep bounty on her head, and she'd learned long ago that you could always put a price on friendship.

Alone now, she would do what she always did: fight her way to freedom or die trying. The Russian Federation had kept her under their thumb for many years, used and abused her. They had accomplished that without the use of technology. She'd rather die than allow herself to become a puppet for these eccentric idealists.

She didn't pretend to understand what the cylindrical tanks and network of pipes that resembled the intestines of some colossal mechanical beast were used for; that they stretched out for what seemed like a kilometer within the sweeping walls and vaulted ceiling of the processing plant was useful because the maze of catwalks, ladders, and boxy substations provided plenty of cover. She gathered up two pistols and a second Uzi with extra thirty-two-round magazine. She slung that second machine gun over her shoulder, and then, at the sound of shouts from below, she took off, bounding across the catwalk.

The echoing of her footfalls made her wince, and she considered abandoning her knee-high black leather boots to pad more silently toward the exit on the south end, but once she was outside, the snow and temps hovering around twenty degrees Fahrenheit would put an abrupt end to any barefoot escape.

This was no puppy patrol Fedorovich had hired. Judging from their commands, movements, and weaponry, they were former Army, maybe even Spetsnaz, now able to sell their talents to the highest bidder.

She estimated there were fifteen to twenty of them, based on her observations during her arrival on the island. She'd noted the two guard posts outside the refinery and headquarters buildings, and she'd made certain to remember the others at their posts inside. Years of training as a GRU officer and field operative had become ingrained and second nature, situational awareness always a top priority—especially when trust was at a premium.

Reaching a pair of pipes at the end of the catwalk, she crouched down and listened for a moment as the guards came thumping up the ladders. Four now.

Behind her lay a footbridge, one of four that connected the north and south sides of the plant, narrower but with much higher railings than the catwalks. These were the modern versions of those long and precarious rope bridges she'd crossed in Pakistan, Northern Ireland, and Malaysia while tailing various subjects for her government.

The guards coming up assumed she was heading for that footbridge, and so she pricked up her ears, listening once more as another pair mounted a ladder on the other side of the plant, preparing to cut her off, believing she'd run right into them. They, of course, were unaware of who she actually was, unaware they only had minutes to live.

Before the four guards at the end of the catwalk ever reached the tops of their ladders, the Snow Maiden was already scaling the pipes behind her, utilizing the fittings like rungs of a ladder, reaching the top about three meters above where they elbowed off, connecting with a series of more narrow conduits whose diameters were barely larger than her wrists.

She tucked herself tightly into the groove between the pipes, which were as thick as her own waist. She imagined herself an old Russian Blue, a cat ready to pounce. Fatigue was setting in now, her thoughts beginning to scatter. She gritted her teeth and focused. The four guards came thundering down the catwalk and the other two reached the end of the footbridge to her left.

The leader of the four pointed to the other two, signaling them across the footbridge, while he sent a pair of his men off to the left, down another catwalk intersecting hers. She watched it all unfold. Three pairs, six men in all.

The media was right about her. She would kill all six of them. And she would feel nothing—because forever burning in the back of her mind were the faces of her husband, her brothers, the face of Izotov trying to tell her it was all "unintentional." Now the fury sent a shudder up her back.

They drew closer. She didn't move. The leader and his partner spun back and forth, cursing under their breaths, now within a few meters of the pipes. Neither of them thought to look up—

But one guard on the footbridge, a baby-faced man with the thin voice of a bird, cried, "She's right there!"

When the first pair below lifted their heads, they stared directly into the Snow Maiden's flashing muzzle, no time to even gape before her nine-millimeter rounds stitched jagged lines across their chests, their own shots falling wild as they reflexively squeezed their triggers and fell back to their deaths.

With brass casings clattering loudly across the pipes, she brought the Uzi around, directing it at the guards on the footbridge.

The man who'd spotted her had already hit the deck and propped himself onto his elbows and was returning fire, rounds pinging and sparking off the pipes at her elbows. His covering fire bought his partner a few seconds to come up behind him, adding his rounds to the fray, the onslaught effectively pinning her down. She gasped as the slugs drew closer, the ricocheting relentless, a single round rebounding off three, four, even five surfaces. The Uzi was hot in her grip, the stench of gunpowder so strong that it burned her eyes.

She remembered the other two guards who'd been sent down the intersecting catwalk—no doubt on their way back to her position.

No, she couldn't remain any longer. Her mantra was *shoot and move . . .*

A pause in the fire had her lifting her head a fraction, the Uzi shaking in her hand, and then, damning her fears, she sprang up, sighting the guy on his belly, taking him out with two rounds to the face, while his partner shifted aim. The Snow Maiden's rounds drummed him to his knees. He collapsed sideways to slip off the footbridge and crash onto one of the big tanks below. He slid down the tank's side and into a web of attached ducts, arms and legs snapping against hardened steel.

Her hackles rising at the sound of more guards—in addition to the remaining two—the Snow Maiden cursed and let the Uzi go slack on its sling. She used both hands to pull herself up and across the big pipes. Time to call upon the special forces training she'd received during her early days with the GRU, the many obstacle courses she'd forded, the live-fire gauntlets, the inverted suspension bridges that had her swinging arms-only like a primate. Her courses in covert residency, source recruiting, and source manipulation were a joke when compared to dodging grenades and trying to get a man with knife pried off her back.

She swung her right leg up, hooked her foot over the top of the pipe, and then, working hand over hand, slid herself across the overhanging conduit, driving past a heating duct that sent its warm, metallic breath into her face.

Boots clattered close now. She craned her neck and spotted the two remaining guards below, returning to the main catwalk to check on their fallen comrades. But where were the fresh ones? She could hear them . . .

Realizing she had a chance to come around a much larger pipe and exploit its cover, she reached out and seized the more narrow pipe running parallel to her own.

But that pipe was so hot that she jerked back and groaned, trying to balance herself—just as one of the men behind her shouted.

Her heart sank. They had her.

A second before the gunfire came in, the Snow Maiden looked down. Twelve meters now to the concrete below. With her burned hand, she dug out one of her pistols, and, biting back her scream, she returned fire—

Dropping one of the guards while the second rolled back for cover.

She shot a glance up, toward the highest catwalk, terminating at an exit door to the roof. The ground-floor door on the other side of the plant seemed a world away now, and the sound of those additional guards pouring into the processing plant had her pulling herself up, around, and on top of the pipes so she could reach the next section, checking these first for temperature, then scaling them, swinging across and heading toward that highest walkway.

The guards could not get a good bead on her with all the piping in the way, rounds caroming everywhere and shattering two of the heavy industrial lights, their protective glass covers raining deadly shards across the floor.

By the time she reached the bottom of that final catwalk that would get her on the roof, she saw that at least four more guards had joined the pursuit and were rushing up ladders. Their security force might be a lot larger than she had anticipated, and while that thought chilled her, two other obstacles loomed more terribly in her path:

She was being forced up to the roof—the last place she wanted to be to effect an escape. Once there, where would she go? Jump thirty feet to the parking lot? Second—and this was a fact she'd denied because she was a warrior and refused to give up—the SinoRus Headquarters was located on an island. Fedorovich could alert local authorities to shut down the ferries, ground all the planes and helicopters, even report her appearance to the Russian government. Spetsnaz troops would be en route in seconds . . . If she got away, how long could she hide in the forest before they finally picked up her heat signature?

Cursing away those inescapable facts, she swung up onto the catwalk, stood, grabbed her Uzi, then aimed for the guards ascending the ladders—

Because she was a fighter. Because she didn't give a shit about the facts anymore. Because even if trying to escape made no sense at all and was utterly helpless, she would go down trying. She would make them remember whom they had faced. They could not take her soul. Never.

Suddenly, the door leading to the roof behind her swung open with a rush of snow and frigid night wind, and in charged four more guards, the leader screaming, "Hold fire, Snegurochka! There's nowhere to go! You turn, face me, and raise your arms high above your head."

The Snow Maiden glanced sidelong at him, slowly lifting her hand to rake her fingers through her spiky black hair, her face covered in sweat.

He was an older guard, graying at the temples, definitely former Spetsnaz, the lines of his jaw improbably sharp, his eyes wide and daring her to make a move. He grinned crookedly, teeth yellow as pine.

He'd referred to her by her old code name, but did he know the Russian folklore about the Snow Maiden being the daughter of Spring and Frost, about how she fell in love with a shepherd, which caused her heart to warm, and she melted?

Yes, love would eventually kill her. The love she had for her late husband and brothers had driven her to this. The love she had for revenge, for wanting to see Moscow burn, had already poisoned her thoughts. The love she had for one of her former colleagues, Colonel Pavel Doletskaya, had left her vulnerable.

Maybe she wasn't a fighter after all. Maybe she should surrender to the *Ganjin*. Let them take away the pain. After all, living hurt more than anything now, didn't it? Obedience brought pleasure, and weren't they all slaves to their own desires?

"I said, turn toward me and get your hands in the air." The guard's tone was twice as menacing. He took a step toward her, letting the muzzle of his rifle drift down to her hip. Shoot her in the leg. Make her docile. That was his plan.

The other guards rushed up from the catwalk, and she regarded them with hatred in her eyes. She opened her lips to say something, but there was nothing left.

She glanced down at her Uzi, at the magazine, then flicked her eyes back at the lead guard.

"Snegurochka!" he screamed. "I *will* kill you!"

"No, you won't," she answered.

Then she whirled and leveled her Uzi on him.

FIVE

Caucasus Mountains
Near North Ossetia, Russia

Major Stephanie Halverson landed with a breath-robbing thud on the back of the maglev train's second car, which, along with the wedge-shaped forward car, was dangling off the edge of the burning bridge above Darial Gorge.

The Russian Interceptors streaked overhead as she shuddered against the horrific impact and explosion of her F-35B into a wall of rock, the flames and smoke rising quickly through the shattered bridge.

She seized a thick electrical cable torn free from between the cars, barely catching hold before her chute jerked hard, nearly wrenching her off the train before she cut it away. She was swinging now by one arm, the train groaning and hissing, gases leaking from the damaged cars.

Her grip on the electric cable faltered. She cursed.

And then, to her shock, a Russian troop came crawling across the car above.

They looked at each other. He went for his pistol.

She went for hers.

He was slower.

But the moment she shot him in the head, the car creaked and jerked forward. The troop slid off the top of the car and plunged toward the shadows.

Halverson was about to holster her pistol and try to swing her legs up onto the back of the car when more gunfire ripped into the windows behind her.

Shit. The troops who were outside the train and on the more stable portion of the bridge had spotted her. They were shouting and firing, some laughing, a carnival game of shoot the Yankee pilot who was dangling from a wire.

She looked down at the wavering expanse of snow-covered rock and trees below, her burning jet like a bonfire in the mountains.

An ache formed deep in her gut. She'd once told her old wingman Jake Boyd that a lost plane is a failed mission no matter how you look at it. But when he'd been shot down over Canada and she'd been forced to leave him— only to be killed by the invading Russians—she realized she was wrong. Jake, a man who should've known how she truly felt about him, had lost his plane but their mission was not a failure. He'd fought valiantly to the death. He would be remembered as long as she drew breath.

More shouts from the troops. Two more rounds burrowed into the car not a meter away.

Her gloved hand began to slide down the cable.

"Hold your fire!" came a cry from the bridge. She knew enough Russian to understand the command and assumed the order had come from an officer who'd already seen her capture as a career-advancing opportunity.

But several men ignored him, and the gunfire returned, forcing her to jerk left, raise her pistol again, and return fire as one troop appeared like a scarecrow atop the car, waving his arms as though he were drunk before she shot him in the chest.

And then she saw it: a bottle of vodka jutting from his fist before he fell away. Sure enough, they were all drunk, partying on the train before hell had arrived, and hell hath no fury like a woman shot down.

Her hand slid a little more, and now she was forced to holster the pistol and hang on with both hands. With a groan, she tried to ascend the wire, moving up about a meter—before the damned thing began to pull free from the train, lowering her toward the undercarriage. She tried swinging to and fro to latch on to something. No use. She couldn't reach.

There had to be dozens of them crawling up onto the train now, vying for a front-row seat at the Yankee pilot's demise. They wanted blood, payback, the vodka making them hypercritical of the show. They urged her to try again for the train, swing some more, go for it.

"Somebody shoot him," one cried.

Sexist bastards.

With her helmet on, they didn't know she was a woman, and with her helmet on, her peripheral vision was being cut off. She wanted to tear it off and curse at them, let them see the acid in her eyes.

More gunfire.

She glanced up. A pair had reached the edge of the car and were taking potshots at the wire, hoping to cut it with one lucky shot. This, apparently, was much more fun than just shooting her. More of their comrades gathered behind them, cheering one another on. A fight broke out between two troops, pushing and shoving, and the train began groaning, almost imperceptibly at first, then rising into a crescendo that reverberated up into Halverson's arms.

The drunken fools had put so much weight on the car that it was now threatening to pull the rest of the train over the edge. Two more bridge cables snapped free with booms that sounded like mortar fire.

One cable came down on the troops, their arms raised in sheer terror before they were swatted like flies and whipped into the air, shrieking as they tumbled away.

Halverson fought once more with the wire, dragging herself up as the wind buffeted the cars more violently, the sonic booms of the Interceptors resounding, letting everyone know they were still in the area, still watching.

She looked down again, the snow whipping off the rocky outcroppings along the gorge, the trees bowing to the forces of nature.

A third cable popped on the other side of the bridge, swinging down in a chaotic, almost drug-induced dance, slashing at the fires still raging across the tracks and girders.

"Hey, pilot, come on, we will help!" cried one of the troops. She turned her head, saw him waving to her, and then he tossed down a half-full bottle of vodka that she let bounce off her chest. The troops hooted and guffawed.

I'm asleep, she thought. *We haven't lifted off from Turkey yet and this is a nightmare produced by all the fears lying dormant in my subconscious. That's all this is.*

She laughed bitterly. Here she was trying to intellectualize her way out of the situation, when in fact she had ejected, these troops were here, and she was about to become a prisoner of war if she didn't make the dreaded decision, the one she'd been avoiding from the moment she'd clutched the wire.

Not suicide . . . but a fighting chance, one represented by the small pouch located on the small of her back. Ordinarily she flew without a reserve chute, but there was room in the F-35B's cockpit and seat, and being that this was a test mission, she'd decided matter-of-factly to take one along. Slightly more uncomfortable, yes.

Maybe it wasn't her time to die or be tortured inside some newly built *sharashka* hidden in these mountains.

Freedom was four hundred meters away. Twelve hundred feet.

The train slid forward again, jerking so abruptly that a half dozen men shouting and drinking near the edge were shaken right off. That they'd remained so near was a testament to the alcohol content of their vodka. The officer she'd heard screaming earlier was at it again, trying to evacuate them. He came forward and chanced a look down at her, still barking at the troops, his voice burred with anger, his face leonine, gray hair whipping and glistening in the firelight.

"Hang on," he told her. "We are trying to find a rope. We'll save you!"

Sure you will. So they can pin a medal on your ass.

Halverson gave him the finger and let go.

SIX

After slamming into a jagged rock and getting booted around by the raging current, Lex broke the surface and took in a long and desperate breath.

He'd failed to fully anticipate the river's power, which, for a few seconds, had completely disoriented him, spinning him into a world of dizziness. Despite all the training and his ability to remain calm under fire, he was unnerved, in the clutches of white-water swimmer's remorse, but it was too late to bitch about it. He owned the decision to jump in, and now he had to live—or die—with it.

His paddling was useless against the flow, the river also much deeper than he'd thought, boots not even touching muddy bottom now. His right shoulder was throbbing from where he'd been hammered against the rock. He spat water and tried to look up, through the heavy mist.

The banks were about ten meters apart here, walled in on both sides by towering trees and palms that cast deep bands of shadows across the water. The rafts of stone and larger boulders forming a broken necklace along the shore were deeply eroded and pummeled by the gurgling waves. It was hard to hear much above the hiss—just his breath and the faint gasps escaping his throat as he kicked again, trying to guide himself through the maze.

Twice Lex thought he spotted Nestes through the spray, rising and falling, his head a mere dot against a mottled, boiling sheet of white.

Lex wondered if his men knew where he was, where Nestes had gone, and his answer came in the form of a dark, humming shadow near his head. The UAV hovered above him a moment more, then whirred off ahead, toward, he assumed, Nestes's location.

He blinked—

And was underwater.

As suddenly as that.

The river had curved sharply to the right, the current kicking him sideways and then sucking him down like a vacuum toward the rocks below. He kicked harder, pulling himself up, tanking down air for all of two seconds before the entire river seemed to drop away, as though he were being plucked to safety by a giant hand.

And then he looked down, realizing he was dropping off a small waterfall, no more than a few meters high but enough to send his heart racing.

He was an accomplished swimmer—no Navy SEAL to be sure—but he wanted to believe he could hold his own.

The river had other plans.

He plunged to the bottom, boots hitting hard. He exploited the impact to rebound up and reach the foam so he could breathe again—

But he was still underwater, drawn down again. He couldn't help but panic, cupping his hands and working his way furiously toward the light.

Just as his vision began to narrow, he popped up, shook his head, whirled back, and, panting, took in the falls he'd just descended. His mouth fell open. Between all of the rocks—each one representing a concussion or more serious head wound—and the swirling currents, he was damned lucky to be alive. He paddled hard again, facing forward, the rocks closing in from the shoreline, his palms slapping on more stones to help guide himself around.

The water, when it wasn't shimmering silver and white, took on a deep gray hue, and there was something foreboding about it, those darker sections where there appeared a breach in the choppy waves. He saw one of those shadowy sections now, forming between what looked like a path of boulders used as stepping-stones, with the central stone missing, either washed away or deliberately removed to prevent anyone from crossing.

Lex's fears of the dark water were borne out as he slid off a rocky precipice that simply appeared as one of those black holes in the waves.

He cursed aloud as he went airborne for one, two, three seconds before vanishing into the vortex, this time descending at least a meter farther than the last fall, the turbulence all around him now, battering him like a dozen heavyweight boxers with blows to the head, back, and chest.

He came up again, barely managed a breath, chutes of water blasting into his face. What the hell was he doing? His team could keep the drone on Nestes. He needed to get out of this river before he drowned.

But yes, Nestes would be thinking the same thing, and maybe, just maybe, he didn't have what it took to ride the waves. He'd fight to reach one of the rocks to his right or left, the pools of calmer water like oases lying beside them. He'd wait there until Lex passed, then slip out, back into the jungle—

Where he'd be promptly captured by Lex's men.

Or would he? Maybe Nestes had jumped in because he had help waiting for him at the other end of the river. This had always been part of his escape plan. He'd spent months hiding in this area, shadowing the missionaries, studying the terrain. He had planned and rehearsed multiple escapes. This was Carlos Nestes we were talking about, graduate of Princeton, a boy who'd risen to command an army with a worldwide reach. You couldn't give a bastard like that even an inch.

The reminder of Nestes's cunning had Lex looking back at every tall rock he passed, making sure the man wasn't hiding there.

All right, Lex played through those assumptions

again, wondering how many followers Nestes had left since going underground. How alone was he in the world? He'd lost his brother, and his parents had been killed during a trip to Europe, their plane caught up in an air attack, with a half dozen other civilian transports blown from the sky. He had ice in his veins. There was nothing left to love.

This, of course, was mostly speculation. Lex would have to interrogate the man. He replayed Nestes's last words:

"We're the Forgotten Army, truly forgotten. The Ganjin *has changed. We were once partners. Now we're only tools."*

What was the *Ganjin*? Another terrorist organization? Why wasn't Lex aware of them? And if they were using a group as powerful and sophisticated as the Forgotten Army, then how big were they? And if they were huge—international—then their ability to remain clandestine was staggering, given the scope of the JSF's intelligence efforts since the war had begun.

The current carried Lex swiftly around another turn and drop, and it was all he could do to keep his head up, maintain his breathing, and fight to keep sight of the water ahead.

Wave after wave slapped into his eyes, and when he wasn't blinking away water, he was blowing his nose free. The initial fear that had fanned across his shoulders was giving way to a knot in his stomach because as a Marine Corps captain he sure as hell was used to being in control—not being at the mercy of anyone or anything, this damned river notwithstanding.

He flailed against the current now, putting more muscle into his strokes, grimacing, gritting his teeth, and squinting as far downriver as he could.

Cursing the rapids and his reckless decision to give chase for the nth time, Lex heard the voice of his older sister Oksana ordering him to calm down. *Discipline is remembering what you want,* she'd told him when he used to whine about his homework. Their parents had worked twelve-hour days, his father at the fish market, his mother for a telemarketing firm. Only Oksana was there to help him, to make sure he didn't forget his Russian and did well in school. She'd even been there for him when bullies had followed him home, tried to jump him, and they'd teamed up to scare them all off.

Oksana was the levelheaded one, never raising her voice, never prone to emotional outbursts the way he was. She'd graduated college, attended OCS, and become one of the Army's most decorated AH-80 Blackfoot attack helicopter pilots. She, like Lex, had chosen a career in the service, but hers had been short-lived.

During the Russian invasion of Poland, she'd been called in to provide Close Air Support for three Ghost units on the ground. According to those Ghosts, she'd saved the lives of more than twelve Special Forces operators and thousands of civilians.

The wreckage of her chopper had been carefully inspected, no body found. Days later, after the area around Warsaw had been secured by European and JSF forces, Splinter Cell agents combing the zone for intelligence had learned that before retreating, Russian forces had taken dozens of prisoners, and Lex knew in his heart of hearts that Oksana was one of them. He'd been searching for her ever since. Fourteen months now.

Searching. Coming up empty time and again—despite all of his resources.

There'd been nothing more frustrating.

He'd located, captured, and turned in all of those high-value targets. Traveled the world over. Found clues others had missed. But the one person whose location still eluded him . . . the one person he needed to rescue more than anyone else . . . was somehow out of his reach. Gone. Agonizingly gone.

His deepest pain.

With her memory now fresh in his mind, he screamed as a wave tossed him against a shoulder of rock, sending him careening off to plunge again, and again, off some stair steps of stone and frothing water leading to yet another gauntlet. He lifted his chin to snatch another breath, when, nearly out of sight, just above a series of white caps, he spotted an arm jutting from the water.

Now, instead of becoming a victim of the river, he joined forces with it, pushing himself up and swimming headfirst into the current, freestyle, trying to gain momentum and close in on Nestes.

If jumping into the river was reckless, then swimming hard with the current was even crazier. The rocks were coming up at Lex's face so quickly that it was all instinct now, palms guiding him around before he ever thought about using them, feet kicking harder here and there.

The drone zoomed just above the rocks to his right,

rotors kicking up four columns of haze, the camera pan-ning to record him and his position. He glanced at it, pointed at Nestes, and mouthed the words: *Stay with him!*

Borya, who was operating the drone via the remote, got the message, and the UAV pitched forward and took off once more to stay tight on their prey. If Nestes got a good look at the drone, his morale might crumble. Lex realized he was getting desperate now and that wishful thinking sure as shit wouldn't nab this guy, only Marine Corps tenacity would.

After taking in a long breath, Lex launched back into his freestyle swim, arms firing like pistons, head turning up to steal a quick breath, then back under again.

Between those breaths he noticed the gradual change: the river was widening, the boulders infrequent, the cur-rent increasing dramatically. Those calmer pools of water were beginning to vanish. Any chance Nestes had of breaking off to hit the jungle was gone. Even Lex real-ized with a start that he couldn't paddle himself near the shoreline. They were both committed to the waves.

The river wove sharply to the left, and several low-hanging branches rushed toward him. Lex reached up, grabbed one, but his hand was torn off the wood. He plunged back into the wave, got spun around, then came up, coughing, water filling his nose. His arm throbbed with pain.

For some reason, Borya had the drone back on him again, disobeying orders, and Lex swore and waved him off—

But the UAV would not leave. It kept bobbing up and

down, then swooped in close enough for Lex to grab. What the hell was going on?

The river curved once more, and then it opened up another twenty meters, dappled with long stretches of white caps. A pristine mountain so verdant green that it looked unreal lay dead ahead.

Oddly, though, the river itself was gone beneath the mountain, the image surreal at first, until his brain caught up with his senses.

He stopped breathing and now understood why Borya had kept the drone on him.

Oh my God . . .

Coming close to death was hardly a new experience for Lex.

There'd been that night when he and the boys had blown the Bering Strait Tunnel—the longest railway tunnel in the world, connecting Siberia with Alaska. The bombs had gone off too soon, and they'd almost been crushed by collapsing concrete . . .

There was that power plant in Dukovany that had exploded, right near the Russian fusion core reactor they had been trying to sabotage, and Lex had almost been electrocuted when they'd scaled the lines to rescue three of their comrades . . .

Finally, there'd been that early morning at a Moscow dance club, where he'd caught up with a Chechen terrorist he'd been tracking. The guy had recognized Lex, jumped him in the bathroom, and slashed Lex apart with his knife before Lex finally stopped him. He'd nearly bled out that night . . .

But this? A waterfall?

More than one hundred meters high?

The universe was a cruel bitch.

Borya held the drone at the edge, and Lex had the generous span of three seconds to get into position, imagining he was jumping off the deck of a destroyer in high seas. He held his breath, brought his knees together, tucked his left arm into his chest, and used his right hand to hold his nose.

As the water carried him past the drone, he made the terrible mistake of looking down.

The world was nothing but roaring water haloed in mist. The booming and thundering conveyed such power that he doubted there was a way he could survive. He pictured himself torn to shreds on the rocks below.

But it wasn't over. Not yet. He shot like a bullet through streams of water clustering around him like fiber-optic cables with the uncanny ability to keep him upright, prevent him from spinning like a lost baton.

And then it grew dark, the mist stealing away the light. He took a breath before the lake came up with a horrific vengeance, swallowing him whole in a millisecond, the water rushing up so powerfully that it wrenched up his arms, hands held high above his head.

Crushed or drowned. Take your pick, he thought. Gritting his teeth against the inevitable, he reached out to his sister, his only regret.

Discipline is remembering what you want.

I want to live!

SEVEN

As the Snow Maiden cut loose with her Uzi on the lead guard, the gray-haired man's chest exploding with rounds, she reached into her waistband and seized the pistol, snapping her neck toward the guards coming in from behind.

She squeezed off three rounds at them before running straight over the lead guard's body, toward his three comrades, who were still wrestling with their orders to take her alive. They wanted to kill her, probably could have, knew that if she died they'd be executed themselves. She would save them the stress of that decision.

The Uzi vibrated in her grip as she shot all three at point-blank range, leaping over their bodies to slam into the rooftop door and burst outside.

They'd had her completely surrounded, and in their smugness they'd grown complacent—for just a few seconds, every one of them thinking, *How in the world can she escape now? She's done. It's over. Can someone make more coffee?*

Now they choked on their own caffeinated blood.

Black jeans. Black leather boots. A long-sleeved top with plunging neckline. Yes, she was ready for winter weather. Her fleece jacket was back at the conference room. She hadn't thought about taking it while she was punching Fedorovich in the face and kicking open the door. She stormed along yet another catwalk running across the curved ceiling, her gaze reaching out to the domes of light produced by the floodlights strung along the refinery's perimeter. If there was a catwalk up here, there had to be an exterior ladder leading down to the parking lot.

By the time she reached the end of the walkway, she realized she'd gone the wrong way.

Dead end.

And they knew it, too, three guards running straight for her, two bringing up the rear, one limping, the other clutching his arm.

She'd been cornered at the door. She couldn't believe it was happening again. She was smarter than this. Her thoughts raced. She spun around, gaze probing.

Below were more of those enormous tanks, like alabaster submarines lined up in a dry dock.

Distance to the asphalt: Did it really matter? The drop would kill her, give or take a meter.

She shivered. Noticed her frosty breath. Blinked, tried to focus again.

The tanks. Snow piled across two of them. Maybe enough snow?

The guards were yelling at her, and the first one, a brazen oaf, fired two rounds that ricocheted off the railing just inches from her hand.

"Hey, hold your fire!" she screamed in Russian.

And then she lifted her hands—although she kept a firm grip on her Uzi and pistol.

"Don't move, you crazy bitch!" the first guard hollered back.

Predictably unpredictable. Hadn't they figured her out by now?

When they drew within ten meters, she cried, "It's okay," then dropped her arms and opened fire—

Causing all four to hit the deck.

And in the next second she abandoned both empty weapons, seized the catwalk's ice-cold steel railing, climbed to the top, then launched herself into the air.

Eyes wide, heart trip-hammering in her chest, she fell in a broad arc toward one of the snow-covered tanks.

Her mind emptied of all those extraneous thoughts, the ones never shared or exhibited—the voices of her parents, husband, and brothers; the shuddering guilt over taking so many lives; and that hollow ache of distancing herself from everyone.

It was all physics now. A math game. Forces. Gravity. Impact.

She landed boots first into the snow, then slammed forward, her face crashing through the ice-encrusted top and into the softer powder below.

Her forward momentum took her across the tank, then sliding sideways. She fumbled for anything to stop her fall, but her fingers just dragged against the hard, cold exterior of the tank, and down she went—head first—for another three meters.

Unfortunately, her vantage point above had not allowed her a clear view behind the tanks, and so she had no idea whether she was dive-bombing toward another snowbank or simply the unforgiving asphalt.

One saving grace: Her arms and body created enough friction to slow her descent, so by the time she drifted away from the tank, she wasn't falling with as much velocity and was able to flip around and hit the snow with a heavy thud that knocked her back, onto her rump.

She lay there, breathing, light beams above steaming in the air, and for just a second she didn't move, not wanting to know how badly she'd been hurt.

Voices . . . disembodied voices . . . something about capturing her, they spotted her, she was probably dead, send someone out to the tanks.

She was a little girl now, singing for sick people in the hospital, her brothers whispering in her ears that the suburbs in Vladivostok were so polluted that the air was killing everyone—and that all they were doing was making people happy before they died. She saw herself lying in one of those hospital beds, her body riddled with bullet holes.

She shuddered violently—an electric current of realization taking hold.

Somehow, she was sitting up. Somehow, she was on her feet, and everything worked.

As the pinpricks of cold ripped across her skin, she took off running toward the chain-link fence—and beyond it . . . the forest.

Her knees already hurt. She checked her waist. Second pistol still there. Spare Uzi slung across her back, extra magazine for the submachine gun tucked in beside the pistol.

This was her chance, probably her only chance.

As she hit the fence, it came alive with gunfire, and, without looking back, she knew that fire was coming from the guards still up on the catwalk. Two gunmen. The others rushing down to go after her on the ground.

Their shots were wide, warning shots, and they only urged her on to the top. She slung one leg over, then another, and climbed down halfway before jumping the final meter.

She estimated fifty meters to the tree line.

Her body was conspiring against her now, and she wondered how long she could remain upright. The fall had battered her arms and legs, and the deeper breaths stung. A broken rib? Perhaps two?

Gunfire paralleled her steps.

Muttering a curse, she broke into a sprint, eyes fiery against the pain—

And she reached the first stand of trees within a dozen heartbeats.

She couldn't help it. She had to stop, allow her body some respite. She dropped to the snow, crawled beneath the branches of a tall spruce, then peered out to spy the refinery and a pair of doors to the right of the tanks. Out rushed one, two, three guards. Then two more.

Maybe it was the cold, the lack of sleep, the seemingly helpless situation, but the Snow Maiden glanced down, grimaced, and realized with a shock that she was about to cry.

She had guns. She could do it herself. She'd already vowed not to be captured, to be controlled. The pity party lasted another two breaths before a gear shifted in her mind, and she was back. The fighter.

On her feet now. Sprinting. Keeping tight to the trees, a serpentine path, heading west.

Heading where? No chopper to whisk her away. No speedboat to rush her out to a submarine and deliver her to a safe house at some remote location.

She cursed aloud against the negative thoughts. She'd get to the coast, then lay low. Hide her heat signature, act like her namesake. At night, she'd find shelter, take it by force if she had to. She'd get to the main port, Kholmsk, stow away aboard a cargo ship, and they'd never find her before she reached Vanino, the mainland port across the strait from the island. From there, she could disappear.

Even if they closed the ports, they couldn't do so indefinitely. Yes, she could hide along the coast until those ports were reopened, and then she could stage her plan to stow away. Her chest warmed over the thought. There was hope.

But damn, she had to stop again, the lungs burning, the legs protesting.

Another spruce, right there, its limbs sagging under the weight of snow.

She was back on her knees, wincing through her breaths, shivering now, her lips growing chapped. For some reason she thought of God and remembered the icons and stained glass of the church in Pokrovsky Park she'd attended as a little girl, the pungent scent of incense, the deacon waving the censer in her face.

She closed her eyes. *I assume you've forsaken me. I'm just looking for more time. Maybe time to repent, who knows. Maybe there's a reason I'm still alive, if you'd like to share it . . .*

After a bitter grin that split her chapped lips, causing one of them to bleed, she got back on her feet, heading higher into the foothills that led all the way to the coast.

She ascended for about two minutes, trudging through patches of snow and over ice-slick rocks, pulling herself up through the trees, fighting at times against the incline, her breath coming in short bursts.

The strain was good, though. It emptied her mind, kept her on the task, her senses growing more attuned to the forest. Squirrels scampered across limbs creaking in the breeze. Here and there the wind picked up, coming in a low baritone as though through a cave.

She came over a small rise and stopped. Listened.

A faint thrumming. Then gone.

Shaking her head, she forged on. But there it was again. And again.

Louder now. Helicopters. A pair. Those engines and

rotors were familiar. What had they done? Called in the Spetsnaz? Turned her over to the wolves?

Through the treetops she saw them now:

MIL Mi-24D Hinds or *letayushchiy* tanks, the "flying tank." Big Russian attack helicopters. Room for eight troops aboard each.

A blinding searchlight panned across the forest, cutting a path not two meters from her position, the rotor wash whipping snow into her face.

Those troops would be on the ground any minute now.

Holding back a scream, the Snow Maiden charged off, picturing the heat of thermal cameras washing across her back, the pilots baring their teeth over the red blip moving across their imagers.

Coming up the next rise she slipped and fell, gasped, wanted to break down. No. Fight. She glanced up at the brilliant mantle of stars, the temperature dropping, the rational side of her brain ordering her to surrender.

What were her odds now?

Then again, they never were good. The day she'd left the GRU and gone underground was the day the clock started ticking. Had she really run out of time? No, damn it. No.

She pulled herself back up, brushing the snow from her Uzi, then craned her head toward the choppers hovering behind her, the trees thrashing, the troops fast-roping down into the forest.

If she couldn't draw on hope for motivation, she'd turn now to anger, as she always had, as she'd taught herself over the years. This was no longer an escape. This was an act of revenge against the country that had taken everything from her, and these men were the instruments of that evil.

At the top of the hill she widened her eyes, gaze probing 180 degrees through the forest. A little depression beneath a fallen tree lay five meters ahead; she sprinted for it, tucked herself tightly inside, Uzi held at the ready.

Her breath came through shivers. The commands were faint, but she heard them.

They were coming for her.

Back inside the SinoRus Group conference room from where the Snow Maiden had just escaped, Dr. Merpati "Patti" Sukarnoputri lifted a cup of tea to her lips. Her hand was trembling. The tea had gone cold.

Her colleague Igany Fedorovich, whose eye was swollen, had just spoken on the radio to one of their security team members. The Snow Maiden had escaped into the forest, but the Spetsnaz forces he'd called earlier were already on the scene. They would have her in custody in no time. Patti had argued against calling them in, but Fedorovich had decided on the spot that the Snow Maiden was no longer useful and now a dangerous liability if they couldn't control her.

The American, Major Alice Dennison, with her short, stylish haircut and hauntingly big eyes, was sitting across the table and muttering something to Colonel Pavel Doletskaya, the graying and distinguished former GRU officer she'd rescued from American custody under the guise of a prisoner transfer. Since both were now missing, the Americans would be hunting them. No matter. Dennison and her top secret security clearance had already set into motion a plan against the Joint Strike Force military.

For his part, Doletskaya had been captured in Russia, brought to the United States, and become an informant for the JSF. Dennison had rescued him for the *Ganjin*, who now intended to use him for their intel.

Fedorovich was still holding his pistol on General Sergei Izotov, director of the GRU and a man the Snow Maiden had abducted in Moscow, although President Kapalkin now believed he was taking a leave of absence for personal reasons.

"She'll get away, you know," Izotov blurted out. "She'll kill them all and escape."

"I don't think so," Fedorovich answered. "And now that my security team isn't tied up, we'll escort you out for your surgery, General."

"That won't be necessary," Dennison said, pulling away from Colonel Doletskaya. "We'll take care of him."

The shot rang out so loudly that Patti dropped the teacup onto the floor, where it shattered.

Fedorovich was already slumping in his chair with a bullet hole in his forehead.

Izotov bolted to his feet, his chair slamming into the wall behind him.

Patti could only sit there, in shock, as Major Alice Dennison now turned her pistol on Doletskaya and shot him point-blank in the heart.

"Why?" he cried as he clutched his chest, then collapsed to the floor.

"Major, what are you doing? Where did you get that pistol? What's going on . . . oh my God!" Patti could barely form another sentence as her gaze lifted to the wall behind Fedorovich, now dripping with blood. She glanced to Doletskaya, lying prone, eyes vacant now. Her breath escaped.

"I'm sorry, Patti. You and Igany are the last of the Committee of Five. The old *Ganjin* is dead now. We are a very different organization than the one you created so long ago. We are independent. No single nation can control us."

Patti's thoughts raced and collided until a question finally struck. "If you're not working for us, then who?"

Dennison tugged free a smartphone from her pocket and thumbed a few keys, nodding something to herself. She smiled eerily at Patti, then turned toward the door as it swung open. In stepped a figure, his face cast in shadow until he took Dennison's side.

Patti's breath all but vanished. "No. Not you."

"You're surprised?" he asked. "You knew this was coming, Mum. You knew this a long time ago. You've been living in denial—just like the rest of them."

His face, his name, his position, the audacity of what he was doing utterly overwhelmed her. She could barely think, barely open her mouth to speak before—

Dennison raised her pistol. "I'm sorry," the American said, as though apologizing for the tea being cold. "It's for the best."

The gunshot slammed Patti back into her chair. She looked down, saw the blood, clutched the wound, then faced Dennison, who still wore that absent grin.

Pain radiated in Patti's chest, accompanied by the terrible thought of deceit, the realization that all she had tried to build in her life, both as a member of the *Ganjin* and as a physician and deputy director-general of the World Health Organization, would be poisoned by him. She was out of the chair, on the floor now, trying to breathe, her lungs filling with blood, the fluorescent lights buzzing, Izotov being dragged screaming from the room . . . and then . . .

Just her. And the light growing dimmer, the air vanishing, her limbs turning cold, numb.

But a hot flash of anger ripped through her spine.

No, she could not exact revenge on him. Her time was over. But the Snow Maiden . . .

Patti tried to smile. The Snow Maiden would return. She would tear them apart like an animal.

Clinging to that thought, Patti resigned herself to the darkness.

EIGHT

Caucasus Mountains
Near North Ossetia, Russia

Major Stephanie Halverson had let go of the cable and was plunging away from the Russian officer. She had just issued him a middle-fingered salute.

Now she grinned as he returned the gesture, his face growing small and eclipsed by shadows.

In the next breath her reserve chute snapped open, the cold wind wrenching hard on her harness. She sighed. Good deployment. She reached up, seized the risers, and guided the parachute in a slow turn.

Within a few seconds she was floating away from the burning bridge and maglev train, still tottering over its shattered deck. She glided toward the gorge, the wreckage of her plane blazing in a red-orange slash mark of flames and pennon of black smoke to the east. Beyond, the long walls of dark stone were like monuments of coal lying in the distance. A pang of guilt struck as she thought about the plane, the mission, the countless hours they'd put into the project . . . and then she stiffened in fury as she thought about what could have gone wrong.

She was still lost in that thought when the gunfire came in. From the bridge. The troops still swarming around the train, spilling vodka on each other. Drunken shots by a company or two obviously on their way for a little R&R. This was one show they'd never forget.

The deeper roar of Interceptor engines sounded now, and her heart raced. She needed to get on the ground before those pilots could strafe her.

They wouldn't miss.

She tugged on the risers again, guiding herself more slowly past the twisted girders and sedan-sized chunks of concrete strewn across the talus and scree below, aiming for the serrated line of trees to the north.

The sparks she noted below were rounds ricocheting off the rocks and dirt, tiny eyes flashing, and at least two bullets punched into her chute in muffled pops that did little to compromise its integrity.

A screeching like enormous steel talons on a chalk-board resounded above, echoed off the mountains, and by the time she craned her neck to look back, they were already in the air—the maglev train's first two cars, still attached to each other but broken off from the rest of the train. They soared as if in slow motion, at first nose-diving toward the rock, then beginning to pitch forward into a slow roll.

Three, two, one, they crashed into the gorge, every

window shattering in concert, small explosions popping like fireworks from within the cars as dust, shattered pieces of the undercarriage, and rocks hurled into the air.

She faced forward. *Holy shit*.

One hundred meters now. The trees scrolling up fast, the wind from the north slowing her even more.

Damn it, she was coming up on the forest much too fast. She yanked hard on the risers, aborting her descent for a moment to wheel around—

Just as one of the Interceptors sliced out of the darkness like a glistening scimitar, guns blazing, parallel lines of glowing red fire lit by tracer rounds cutting a few meters to her left before she finished the circle and plunged faster now, running alongside the trees, every gnarled branch promising a broken arm or leg.

She was cursing the pilot now, the chute, the delay, the wind until she held her breath and her boots hit the ground. Suddenly, it was a tug-of-war, a gust now dragging her forward. She broke into a run while simultaneously releasing the chute and charging straight for the nearest cluster of trees near the bottom of a ridge.

Before the Interceptor's pilot could bring his aircraft around for another pass, Halverson was in the forest, helmet off, and out of sight, the air stinging her lungs, the rich, mossy scent enough to make her sneeze. She stole a quick glance up. Chestnut-leaf oaks soared thirty meters, the canopy so dense that the pilots would have to rely on thermals to locate her now.

However, the troops up on the bridge had watched her land, no doubt, so there wasn't much time.

Equipment check. She reached around and felt her back, just above where her reserve chute had been stored. Good. The gear pack Ragland had insisted she carry was still there; it contained a small first-aid/survival kit and one exceedingly useful evasion device in the event that, well, in the event of *this*.

She reached around and tore free the pack from its Velcro straps, dropped it in front of her, and then, at the sound of more Interceptors rumbling overhead, she remembered to check her pistol. Yes, the M9 was still there. She tugged it free from its hip holster, made sure she had a round chambered, then returned the Beretta to its holster.

With hands beginning to shake—if only a little—she slipped out the survival kit stored in a narrow plastic box. She unzipped one of the pockets located just below the left knee on her pressure suit and slid the kit inside. Then she tugged free a second package slightly smaller than a shoe box. She forced back a pair of spring-loaded locks to release the lid.

"All right, baby, it's up to you," she whispered.

Inside, tucked into a bed of gray foam, was a BQ9-5 micro unmanned vehicle (MUV). The drone resembled a miniature version of a Mars rover, with instrument platform, folding antennae, and bulky wheels. Designed to assist downed pilots behind enemy lines, the MUV would both issue a heat signature that mimicked a human's in composition and shape and transmit the standard rescue beacon while traversing enemy terrain at a marching speed of four to six kilometers per hour. The

MUV was a doppelgänger that could demoralize an enemy because when they realized they'd been chasing around a drone, they often abandoned their search efforts. Halverson wished she'd had one back in Canada, when she'd been blown from the sky, when the Russians had stalked her relentlessly, but those were the days when they'd operated on prewar budgets and pilots were a dime a dozen. Since then, with the JSF suffering so many losses, every trained fighter jock was an even more valuable asset. MUVs were one answer to keeping downed pilots alive.

She balled her hands into fists, told herself that the odds were much better this time. There'd been just one automatic signal to the network at the time of her ejection. She had the drone for evasion and escape. In her left hip pocket was an Iridium satellite phone that allowed her a direct link to Neptune Command. Plus, she had a standard secondary beacon she could activate if she were desperate. Yes, that link might eventually be traced, but she had it nonetheless.

She ran through these facts to lift her spirits. Still, the booming of those Interceptors' engines could not be ignored. She'd been shot down in Ossetia, in Russian Federation territory. The situation was as simple—and as potentially deadly—as that.

Halverson removed the drone from its box, and, after tugging off one of her gloves with her teeth, she typed in an activation code on a touchpad located on the MUV's back, between the rear wheels.

While she waited for it to boot up, she unzipped her

left breast pocket and removed a tablet computer no larger than her palm. 3-D maps with street views of the entire region were stored there, and she could read them without having to access the network and maintain security. These were backed up by hardcopy maps stored in another of her pockets in the event the enemy hit the area with a localized EMP wave. She prayed that wouldn't happen because an electromagnetic pulse wave would also bring down the drone.

Her flight path was already stored on the tablet, and she followed it to the bridge, scrolling and zooming with her thumb and index finger until she estimated her current position, about thirty kilometers southwest of Vladikavkaz, the capital city of North Ossetia. Relief warmed her. Nothing but mountainous terrain between her current position and the city. Plenty of cover. She could forge a path adjacent to the two-lane mountain road to the east, using it to get her bearings while remaining hidden in the forest. If the situation got hot, she could even hijack a civilian car, should one come her way. At the same time, though, the Russians could use the highway themselves to swiftly bring in more troops to aid in the ground search. The what-ifs could continue all night. Her mind was set. Plan A was good to go.

She considered a secondary route as she zoomed out to show a wider view of the terrain. Plans B and C began to form, her finger tracing routes through some of the passes but all taking her back to the city. Okay, that was it.

She'd be on the move in less than sixty seconds. Getting swiftly away from her drop zone was important, emphasized during the SERE training she'd received at Fairchild Air Force Base in Washington State, back when she'd been just a "nugget." After her escape from the Russians in Canada, she'd been asked to speak to several classes about her ordeal. Survival, evasion, resistance, and escape (SERE) weren't just words she'd told those nuggets while imploring them to listen carefully and learn as much as they could. They were a difficult bunch to reach, though, self-assured warriors who'd never been shot down and would, of course, live forever.

"So how did you do it?" one pilot asked. "I mean, how did you stay calm and not give up?"

She wanted to tell him that the voice of Jake Boyd, her former wingman, had kept her alive—even though he'd been killed by the Russians. Instead, she answered, "You challenge yourself to embrace the pain. No matter how much they throw at you, you know you can take it. The worse it gets, the more you like it. Sounds insane, but it works. You glare at the enemy and yell, 'Is that all you got, bitch?'"

Now she took a deep breath. Time to see if she could practice what she'd preached.

The Russians would assume she was heading north because any route south would lead to the higher elevations and certain death from any number of causes: exposure, dehydration, even wild animal attack. She had only enough food (energy bars) and water (two eight-ounce canteens) for about two days. So yes, the cities lay to the north, and she had no choice but to head in that direction; however, the Russians might also assume that she would not choose the capital but one of the smaller towns like Mayramadag, Fiagdon, or Dzuarikau, with its natural gas pipeline. She'd attempt to sneak into a less populated area. That made sense—

Which was why she programmed the drone to head off toward the northwest, with its evasion parameters limited to those grids and those small towns to draw any ground teams as far away from her as it could. The drone would take the logical escape path, while she would head into the most highly populated area.

Next, she tugged free the satellite phone, hit the power button, and waited. Green light. Good signal. She placed the call to the Sixth Fleet tactical air commander on board the USS *George H. W. Bush*. "Neptune Command, this is Siren. I'm on the ground, approximately thirty kilometers southwest of Vladikavkaz. As of now, I'm unaware of any ground troops in this area. Moving northeast toward the city, following the mountain road."

"Good to hear your voice, Siren. GPS position marked. We'll get eyes in the sky on you ASAP. No go on the QRF right now. That airspace is hot. We'll get you out, but we'll have to find another way. We're working on it."

"Roger that. Initiating EE protocol, calling every two hours. Appreciate any intel you might have on enemy forces in the area."

"Will do. Godspeed, Siren."

She shut off the satellite phone. JSF encryption notwithstanding, the Russians would pinpoint the signal to her current location. Time to move. She gave the drone an affectionate pat on the back, then picked it up, activated the program, and sent it on its way. After a series of beeps, the drone hummed and rolled forward between the next pair of trees.

Halverson rose, tugged on her glove, drew her pistol, and started up the hill, moving about ten meters, then looking back at her footprints in the snow. She swore. There wasn't time to double back, try to clear the prints, then create a false trail that might lead her pursuers in circles. One of the most ingenious things she'd seen during SERE training was an instructor wearing a pair of stilts whose bottoms imitated deer hooves. Average soldiers would dismiss the tracks, even if the deer's gait was not mimicked exactly. Only experienced trackers would scrutinize the gait and realize the deception. She could use a pair of those right now.

Bottom line: She needed to put distance between herself and this location, and if she could find some stretches devoid of snow, the hard ground would do better to conceal her passage.

She quickened her pace, the gradient increasing, her breath turning ragged and her quads buckling.

A mere ten minutes later, she realized that thirty kilometers of this might kill her. With a curse, she let her thoughts drift away from the terrible exertion to something lighter, the thought that maybe McAllen would drop in out of nowhere like he had back in Canada.

Staff Sergeant Raymond McAllen was a Force Recon Team Leader, call sign "Outlaw One," and he and his men had plucked her from a frozen lake as she'd been about to drown while fleeing from the Spetsnaz on her tail.

Since then, they'd had a tumultuous relationship—stealing what time they could to have ridiculously good sex but failing to ever talk, really talk about themselves, who they were, what they wanted. She couldn't surrender to him because she knew—hell, they both knew—that they were only together to ease the pain. He'd joked that maybe if the war ended and they both were discharged, they could finally become a real couple instead of dropping in on each other unexpectedly to spend long, lazy weekends at hotels. He was about to transfer from Force Recon to the SRT Group, aka Marine Raiders, and was excited about that the last time they'd spoken.

She shuddered with the desire to call him now and tell him she was all right. She hadn't been able to discuss the mission, but he knew she was overseas and flying, and every time she did that, he pleaded with her to send word. If he pulled enough strings and pried enough, he might learn that she'd been shot down, and she didn't want to put him through that. So . . . she would stay alive and prove to that silly jarhead that she was just as tough as him. He'd say he already knew that, but deep down, she knew he had his doubts.

"Always look at the path just ahead. Never look back. Never look at how high you must climb," her father had once told her. "Stay focused. Stay on track."

However, temptation got the best of her, and she gaped at the endless labyrinth of trees and long spines of rock jutting from the ridges. Was it getting colder? The wind whistled now through the branches. Her nose was running.

What was that? She stopped. Listened. Her pulse leapt forward. Distant pops and booms, the Interceptors still up there, somewhere. Next came a tiny voice, almost imperceptible, up on the bridge. Then . . . her breath. So thick in the air. Lips dry. She looked at the pistol and nodded.

Something warmed the back of her neck. A sense. A premonition. A sound?

She spun back, her gaze reaching into the pockets of darkness collecting around the trunks and a path snaking off toward and morphing into the trees. She lifted the pistol, braced it with both gloved hands. Her breath grew more shallow until finally, she stopped breathing altogether. Every sense reached forward, a prickling sensation in her shoulders now.

Three more seconds passed.

Then she sighed. Cursed.

The paranoia might do her in before the mountains did.

She took a step—

Just as a man's raspy voice came from behind, the words in Russian but she understood them:

"Don't move . . . otherwise I'll shoot you."

Halverson closed her eyes.

And her heart sank.

NINE

Lex was trapped at the bottom of the falls, pounded ceaselessly by millions of gallons of water. He had no sense of up or down, and he clawed uselessly for anything to latch on to, a rock, something that he could use to find his way up—wherever that was. Flashes of light appeared through all the turbulence, and he literally screamed for his life as he fought toward those flashes . . .

With the abruptness of a switch being thrown, the water grew calm. Sunbeams flickered across the surface, just a few meters above. He kicked hard. Reached the light.

Shocker: He wasn't dead.

The first breath stung. The second was better; the third had him thinking, *I might walk away from this.*

Blinking hard, he finally caught sight of the falls and gasped.

Curtains of white water were forever closing around a glimmering rock face. The branches were like balconies hanging low on both sides to form an amphitheater in the middle of the jungle. It was beautiful and deadly and heart-stopping . . . and all he could do was curse in awe.

That he'd survived was pure fate and had little to do with his training. Well, yes, he could hold his breath for a while, but he could have easily been thrown onto those piles of rocks forming concentric rings at the waterfall's base.

He began to laugh, still dumbfounded. Apparently, his karma was still good, fate was not exactly an enemy, and the universe had tossed an old jarhead a bone.

After a few seconds, his thoughts turned back to the mission, to Nestes. He scanned the lake, just a broad pool ringed in by more stones and washing out toward calmer waters ahead. No bodies breaking the surface, nothing washed up on the shore.

He paddled toward the nearest rock, just as the drone came thrumming overhead. After a quick glance at the UAV, he kept on, back to his freestyle until he could stand.

Backhanding water out of his eyes, Lex trudged toward the shoreline, his boots like blocks of concrete, his arms sore and feeling torn from the sockets, then glued back. He reached a long, flat boulder and took a seat to catch his breath. He glanced up, shielding his face with a palm, then let his eyes follow the zigzagging pattern of trees along the shore, in search of a body. Nothing. Where was that bastard? Had he, too, survived the fall and escaped? *Bastard!*

Behind him, the jungle grew alive with the hoots and hollers of monkeys. Lex shifted around as Borya, Vlad, and Slava came out of the jungle near the base of the waterfall and picked their way toward him.

Staff Sergeant Borya had just turned thirty and was the oldest of the three. With hair the color of gunpowder and a cherubic face that would turn a deep crimson after he'd had his third beer, he was well liked among all Marine Raiders because he was a tactician and numbers man. Situational awareness was his middle name.

Vlad was the staff sergeant from Buryatia, a semiautonomous republic located within Russia's borders directly north of Mongolia. His narrow eyes and skin suggested he was more Chinese or Mongol than Russian. Like Lex, he'd been born in the United States, Alaska to be precise. He'd been raised in Fairbanks and left to join the Marines at the tender age of eighteen. His Russian was the best on the team, and he could mimic several different dialects. He also took great pleasure in rattling the team's bones with his predictions of doom and gloom on every mission.

Slava, well, what could Lex say? Every Marine Corps Raider team needed a secret weapon, and Lex had certainly found his. Slava looked like an old Soviet weight lifter who ate bowls of broken glass for breakfast and washed them down with a half gallon of gasoline. He had a reputation for being overly aggressive and politically incorrect around anyone ranked higher than captain. He was, admittedly, difficult to navigate around during conversations, but having him on the team was like bringing a nuclear bomb to a knife fight. Lex always felt certain that if it came down to it, Slava would be the last man standing, long after the rest of them had perished.

"Any sign of him?" Borya called as he neared Lex, unfazed by what had just happened.

Before Lex could answer, Vlad was all over the question: "Nestes is long gone—and, boss, you nearly bought it chasing this scumbag. What the hell, man? Aren't we getting tired of this? Is the guy really worth it?"

"Shut up," cried Slava, turning a menacing stare on Vlad. "When I find him, I'll break him in half, and I will feed you the pieces!"

Lex sighed. They were at it again—comrades in arms and at each other's throats. Lex got wearily to his feet. "Gentlemen, in case you haven't noticed, I'm alive." He pointed at the harrowing waterfall. "I survived that shit. And thanks, yeah, I'm okay."

Slava threw up a hand. "You survived because you are a Marine."

Lex grinned. "No doubt." He faced Borya. "You kept the drone on him as he went over the falls?"

"Absolutely. But he just vanished. Never saw him come out in the lake like you did."

"Then he's still here," said Lex. "I want this shoreline searched. All of it. Try thermals. Let's move out."

"Boss, I'll get the drone up near the rocks, where we can't go," said Borya.

Lex nodded. "Do it. And hey, I lost my earpiece. Let me have the radio."

Borya tugged free the team radio from his hip pocket, tossed it to Lex, then moved off, his eyes riveted to the drone's remote, now balanced in his hands.

Lex cleared his throat. "Mother Hawk, this is Green Raider Actual, over."

"Actual, this is Mother Hawk, go ahead."

"We've tracked the Tango to this location. It's a huge waterfall. Searching for him now. Have the QRF ready to go. May need to boogie soon, over."

"Roger that, Actual. QRF is already Oscar Mike, ETA five minutes your location."

"Roger that, Mother Hawk. Hold 'em back till I call. Actual, out."

As Lex turned back toward the falls, Borya was already waving him over and pointing to his remote. The drone hovered over the rocks below the falls, drifting just a meter or two away from disaster and fighting to remain aloft in the mist. Lex hustled over and arrived breathlessly at Borya's side. He squinted at the remote's screen as Borya zoomed in with the drone's camera, the image blurry and then coming into focus:

A hand jutted out between two rocks.

Lex glanced away from the remote to the drone, noted the location, then returned the radio to Borya. "Keep eyes on me."

"Watch your step, boss."

Holding his breath, Lex dove into the lake, swimming hard toward the falls. He reached the edge of the rocks, then hauled himself up, balancing perilously atop the largest stone. The rocks were slick, and he had about three meters to go to reach the hand. Tensing and extending his arms for balance, he set off, slipping twice before slapping his palms on the rock just above the fingers.

He'd expected to find Nestes's body or perhaps the unconscious man lying behind the boulders, but his discovery was decidedly more grisly—

Nestes's arm had been torn off at the elbow and the appendage had landed here, the blood drained, the skin waterlogged and swollen, its once healthy pink color faded to a bluish gray. Lex could only imagine what had happened to the rest of the man's body. He must have landed amid a group of jagged, semisubmerged rocks and been killed outright, his torso and appendages shredded by the force of the horrendous current and boulders.

Lex reached down toward the arm.

A finger twitched.

Shit! He almost fell back off the rocks.

Regaining his balance, Lex took a moment to compose himself, looking away from the arm and probing the rocks for more of the man's body, but the billowing mist camouflaged most of the immediate area.

Grimacing, he reached down and removed the thing from between rocks, then worked his way back to the lake and returned to the shore.

Borya cocked a brow at Lex's find. Slava nodded and grinned. Vlad smirked and rolled his eyes.

Lex placed the arm on the rocks, then shook his head. "I'm disappointed. Higher really wanted this guy alive."

"Come on, boss, we all wanted him dead," said Slava.

"I was being sarcastic," said Lex.

"Oh." Slava lifted the arm and shoved it toward Vlad. "Are you hungry?"

"Guys, settle down. We need to get this thing on ice, get it shipped off to the lab, and confirm it's him."

"Oh, it's him," said Borya. "See the scar on the fore-arm?" Borya traced the three-centimeter line running just above the wrist. "It matches Nestes's description."

"That's a pretty small scar to wind up in his dossier," said Vlad. "Doesn't mean much."

"Or maybe it does," said Lex, using his fingers to probe around the scar. "There's something in there beneath the skin. Microchip. Something."

"Let's cut it out," said Slava.

Lex shook his head. "Evidence for the lab."

"He's tagged?" asked Borya.

"Damn right he is," said Lex.

Borya frowned. "I don't get it. He's actual, he's the commander. You only tag your underlings."

"I know, but I got the impression he was no longer in charge. He mentioned a name. The *Ganjin*. You guys ever hear of it?"

They shook their heads.

"Me neither. And that's what scares me."

"What was that word you used?" Slava asked.

"I said *scared*. But I get the point. We're Marines, never scared. But think about it. We've been at this game

a long time. We've got intel assets all over the world—
NSA, CIA, Third Echelon's Splinter Cells. We know all
the players, even the new guys on the block. They haven't
been able to hide from us—"

"Until now," said Vlad.

Lex bared his teeth, then motioned for the radio. He
thumbed the mike and took a long, exhausted breath.
"Mother Hawk, this is Green Raider Actual. We have
the Tango—or at least a piece of the Tango. Need time
now to locate the rest of his body."

"Roger that, Actual. QRF still inbound, over."

"Mother Hawk, abort QRF for now. Repeat: Abort
QRF. Return on my signal." Lex glanced down at the
arm. "Borya, get me a poncho to wrap this thing up.
Slava, Vlad? Get back on the rocks. Find me the rest
of him."

His men nodded and hustled off.

While Borya dug out the poncho, Lex regarded the
tree line, imagining a one-armed man spying them from
behind the broadest trunk. No. No way. Impossible.

Borya handed him the poncho and said, "I'm glad it's
finally over."

"Over? Are you kidding?"

Borya sighed. "I guess you're right, boss. Apparently—
after chasing this bastard all over the planet—we're just
getting started . . ."

TEN

Forest on Sakhalin Island
North of Japan

Most Spetsnaz troops were strong proponents of edged weapons for clandestine operations. The average troop carried on his person several knives: a knife-bayonet for his submachine gun; a combat knife; an all-purpose "survival" knife; and an all-purpose clasp knife, hidden knife, or fling knife. A few of the more creative ones kept small neck knives sheathed and hanging from pieces of paracord tucked just under their uniforms.

However, the blades that concerned the Snow Maiden most were the combat knives, and right now she had an overpowering desire to have one clutched in her grip.

The Katran-3 was the most popular among Spetsnaz operators, having a top blade for sawing wood or metal and a bilateral guard and steel tang. The handle was usually covered in leather or any number of Russian military polymers. Troops most commonly carried them on their right side, at either the hip or waist.

The troop standing not a meter from where the Snow Maiden lay hidden in the depression beneath the tree carried his Katran-3 at the hip.

His eyes told the story and even offered a spoiler of the ending: He was going to die.

He'd realized only at the last second that he'd just been relieved of his knife and that a woman was on him. His rifle was tugged from his grip while the knife sank deeply into his neck, just above his clavicle. She caught him as he fell back to the snow, fumbling for his pistol, which she also removed.

While he lay there, convulsing, gurgling up his own blood, she searched him, found his secondary blade (a small survival knife), then took it and his assault rifle, a newly designed Izhmash AN-99. She abandoned the Uzi and dragged him to the depression, where she tucked him into the snow, out of sight. He was still bleeding, his breath shallow, eyes pleading.

With the new rifle slung over her shoulder and a knife in each of her bloody hands, she took off running.

That one was for her husband, Nikolai. The next would be for her brothers. Now *she* was the hunter.

She kept on, heading west, the moonlight in her face now. After sprinting for about thirty meters, she ducked around the next tree and dropped to her knees. She closed her eyes, pictured the two drop zones where the Spetsnaz had fast-roped in, noted her own position, then predicted how they would fan out to try to envelop her.

She needed to penetrate their forward line, then double back to pick them off one at a time.

The plan was sound.

The plan did not, however, account for dogs, at least three German shepherds trained at the new Central Military School on the outskirts of Moscow. She'd known one of their trainers, had brought him in for a case she'd been working on years ago, the murder of a lieutenant colonel by one of his own men over a drug deal that had gone bad. Nasty business.

The dogs were barking and picking up her scent.

A wave of panic struck low in her gut and flooded up to choke off her breath. She quickened her pace, thought she heard the footfalls rushing up behind her, heard the bark.

She turned, coming face-to-face with the dog as it leapt into the air.

He went for her neck. She went for the dog's, driving both blades home before the shepherd could sink its teeth into her flesh. They both fell back, into the snow. The animal released a strangled cry as she rolled over, ripped out the blades, and scrambled back to her feet.

She felt worse about killing the dog than any man, the guilt much more palpable. Poor thing. She left it there, shaking and whimpering.

Ten, maybe twelve trees later, as a wave of nausea was coming on, the other two dogs were behind her, barking, gaining.

She swore. The dogs had already sounded the alarm and given up her location. She could try to kill them silently, but while she was on one, the other would tear her to shreds.

She dropped the survival knife, stuck the combat knife into the nearest tree, then turned back and leveled the assault rifle on the clearing behind her.

I'm sorry.

Wishing she could close her eyes, she fired—

Just two rounds, each finding a dog's head, both dropping hard and fast to the snow, tremors ripping through their paws. Bile found the back of her throat as she fetched the combat knife, shoved the rifle around on its sling, and broke once more into a sprint.

Keep moving.

The choppers, once hovering on the periphery, now closed in, searchlights panning across the canopy ahead like the probes of some alien ships, the harsh light causing her to squint.

Next came the wind-whipped snow flushing through the forest as the Hinds descended, and the Snow Maiden searched in vain for another avenue around the lights.

At the next tree, she took a hard left, stumbling over exposed roots, caught herself, then kept on, observing how the slope rose much more steeply to her left—

And there up near the top was an outcropping whose higher left side would make for an excellent sniper's perch—or at the very least provide temporary cover.

"Daddy, why do people have to die?"

She groaned away the voice in her head and dug in deep, prying herself up the slope, some of the lower branches serving as levers to drive her forward.

Those pilots hadn't seen her take this turn, and maybe their thermal imagers weren't picking her up as well because her own body temperature had dropped a little and the dogs were still giving off heat. She couldn't be sure about that. All she knew was they'd turned off, but the shouts of troops converging on the clearing where she'd killed the two dogs were louder.

Highly motivated by those sounds, she set her teeth and dipped into her reserves, reaching the outcropping with her last breath, every sinew blown in her quads, her hamstrings on fire. She crawled onto the broad, icy rock, some ten meters long, four meters wide, shifting on her elbows toward a lip like the gunwale on an attack boat.

She settled down, watching as two troops appeared in the distance, one pointing to her tracks, the other slashing across the snow with his flashlight.

They turned and started up the hill.

What she wouldn't give for a silenced rifle right now.

She lined up the first shot, had the flashlight bearer's head centered in her reticle.

Crack. He jerked back, the flashlight airborne, his arms waving spasmodically before he hit the ice.

The second one dove to the snow, landing exactly where she'd anticipated he would.

Her second round rendered him inert before he could raise his rifle.

She might as well have launched a flare. The shouts came not a breath later.

Closer now.

Getting shakily to her feet, she hesitated, looked over

the path, then stepped gingerly across the rock, its surface reflecting moonlight like glass. She inched toward a
section where she could reach a branch and haul herself
back onto the slope.

Her boot had just left the stone when she heard him.

Coming through the trees, making little effort to
conceal his advance.

She shoved herself behind the nearest trunk and realized, *oh my God*, he was right there, just on the other
side, his breath wafting around the branches.

Stiffening, she took in the longest breath she could
and held it.

"I know you're right there," he said softly. "Let's
make this very easy. The whole mountain is surrounded.
Turn yourself in to me right now, and I promise you
won't be hurt."

She rolled the combat knife around in her palm.

"I'm going to come around the tree now. Put your
hands in the air."

Instead, she came around the tree, driving her blade
up beneath his chin and up into his head, the gun torn
from his grip even as she drove her knee into his groin:
three moves at once, three points of attack she'd prac-
ticed and executed so many times that she dreamed
about them, arms and legs working on muscle memory—
no conscious effort—death blows delivered quietly, efficiently, perfunctorily.

He had quite an ego, this one. He'd managed to get
close to her, only to relish in that triumph and decide he
could capture her alive. That he'd approached so carelessly

was his first mistake. That he'd tried to negotiate a deal was his second. That he'd announced his intentions to come around the tree confirmed that he'd forgotten his training and succumbed to the adrenaline rush of the moment. She set him on the ground, stabbed him once more in the heart, then got to work, rifling through his pockets and small pack, digging out everything she needed.

Her hands were shaking so badly she almost didn't finish. It was the cold. Not nerves. Just the cold.

Within a minute it was all set and she was out of there, the flames small at first but beginning to rise.

By the time she reached the top of the slope, the ammo she'd removed from the troop's magazine and spread across his chest was beginning to cook off, shots ringing out wildly, sounding as though she were in a gunfight with several men. The racket and the flames would, she hoped, draw both the troops and the choppers back to the hill—

While she slipped over the top and began a hair-raising descent, leaning back toward the snow at her shoulders, the incline feeling like forty-five degrees, the trees like bumpers in some weird antique pinball machine.

Into the nightmare she slid.

The canopy grew so dense that it fully eclipsed the moonlight, and for a few moments she could barely see the trees rushing up until a pair neared her so quickly that she barely had time to shift aside, tripped and flew through the air, landing face-first in the snow.

She dragged herself up, cheeks stinging, hands feeling as though they'd crack off. She forced herself to go on, staggering down the hillside, trying to slow her steps.

Legs burning, she reached the bottom where during the summer months a small creek wove a lazy S-pattern through the ravine, the creek now frozen solid, the boulders crowned by snow rising like vertebrae along its shoreline.

This was a crossroads of sorts. The creek ran north-south between the mountains, and she could follow along the banks for a hundred meters or more (either north or south), then make a break back to the west.

She squinted north toward the trees, then south, both paths wandering into blurry silhouettes that promised neither capture nor escape.

Which way?

Her pursuers would, of course, predict she'd simply forded the creek and hustled straight up the next slope—so maybe this was it, a moment to truly lose them. That is, until they brought the choppers back around.

Swearing off her indecision, she headed south, following the bank, stretches of smaller stones and gravel crunching under her boots, the surface less slippery and allowing her to pick up the pace.

Her nose was running again, the tip so cold that her eyes began to tear. Still running, she cupped a hand over her face and breathed hard, the effort and the temperature stealing away her focus again, transporting her to that winter day when she'd been eight and waiting outside her school for her father. She'd sat there on the curb for nearly two hours . . . no gloves, the winter coat too small on her, the hat and scarf forgotten at home that morning.

The car had broken down, and when her father finally

arrived, he was so sorry that he'd cried. He'd asked her how she'd stayed warm. She'd pulled the coat over her head, and remaining that way, in the itchy darkness, she'd told herself stories.

Her favorite was the tale of the Snow Maiden.

She stopped and shuddered herself back to the moment. Turning her head, she frowned. The whomping of the helicopters sounded different. One had broken off and cut across the forest and was behind her now, the searchlight tracing along the creek until it suddenly panned over her, moved off, then returned, as though plugging into her back.

Spotted.

In a maneuver she deemed entirely reckless, the pilot pitched forward and descended until his main rotor was skimming the treetops, shaving off a few.

"You on the ground! Remain where you are! We have this perimeter closed off! You cannot escape!" came a voice from the Hind's loudspeaker.

The Snow Maiden turned and stared directly into their blinding light, lifted her assault rifle, and opened fire, rounds glancing off the fuselage and bulletproof canopy—

The pilot pitched left and pulled off, the spotlight gone, the troops shouting from the top of the mountain now.

Time to break. She sprinted from the creek, staggering up the next slope, the snow nearly reaching her calves.

She fell. Slid back down. Screamed. Got up. Ascended again.

The second part of her escape plan had just taken hold

in the back of her mind. She would slip across to the mainland, vanish—

And then defect to the United States.

That's right. She had valuable intel for the Americans. They needed to know about the *Ganjin*, about Major Alice Dennison's involvement, and about how General Izotov would soon be operating for them. The Americans would be her new friends. They would offer her immunity, a new home, a new life . . .

But that new dream was quickly vanishing as behind her, at least six Spetsnaz came charging across the bank. She reached the nearest tree, got behind it, leveled her rifle—

"Don't," came a voice from behind, not a meter away.

Slowly, she glanced over her shoulder at the troop staring at her, wide-eyed.

He pressed his rifle into her head.

Even as she considered several counterattacks, the other six troops were at the foot of the slope, rifles trained on her, the Hind arcing around to bring its searchlight to bear.

The snow turned to glistening white diamonds, the Spetsnaz tilting their helmeted heads against the rotor wash.

With a gasp, she let the rifle fall into the sling and lifted her palms. She shook violently now.

"That's a good girl," cried the troop behind her. "I want you to know how proud I am to capture the world's most wanted terrorist." He stepped around to face her. "Yes . . . we know *exactly* who you are."

ELEVEN

Caucasus Mountains
Near North Ossetia, Russia

The irony did not go unnoticed by Major Stephanie Halverson. She'd flown into Russian airspace to test a new radar system. The system had failed. She'd been shot out of the sky, ejected, hung from a maglev train teetering off a shattered bridge, and parachuted down from there to safety, and she had, after all of that, still survived to tell the tale—

Only to be captured now by some local yokel pointing a hunting rifle at her?

The universe had a twisted sense of humor.

She sighed. The man holding her at bay was in his thirties, with a thick beard, black woolen cap pulled down over his ears, and heavy Soviet-era parka buttoned tightly at his neck. His jeans were tucked into his calf-high boots, and one side of his face shone in the moonlight, all ruddy cheeks and curls snaking around his neck. He was a full head taller than Halverson, perhaps twice as wide, but he was probably wearing several layers.

She had her hands in the air, the pistol still in her grip, but at least they were facing each other now.

"I saw you come from the bridge," he said. "Your jet crashed back there, yes?"

"If you don't lower your gun, when the Spetsnaz get here, I'll tell them you were trying to take me prisoner," she said.

Or at least she *thought* she'd said.

Her Russian was "okay." She'd been studying the language every day since the war had broken out, but her instructors said she still had a lot to learn.

Indeed . . . because the man looked at her funny, then reared back his head. "You're going to tell the Spetsnaz what?"

She turned up the steel in her voice: "I don't have time for this. Lower your weapon."

"You're not Russian, are you?"

She spaced her words for effect: "Let me go. I won't ask again."

He took a step toward her and spoke in perfect English. "Are you an American?"

Knowing her reaction might give her away, Halverson bit her lip, her eyes flicking up to the sky as the Interceptors came around for yet another pass, the shouts still echoing down from the bridge—her mind now filling with images of those troops working their way down the mountainside to capture her.

Yes, his English surprised the hell out of her, but she wouldn't fall for his ploy . . .

"No, I'm not an American," she insisted in Russian, a few breaths away from bolting.

He shook his head and continued to speak in English. "No more lies."

"Who are you?" she asked in Russian.

"My name is Aslan," he answered in English. "Do you want help or not?"

"Help?" Halverson caught herself. Damn it, she'd just spoken in English—

Which immediately had him lowering his rifle.

"You *are* an American. They'll capture and torture you."

Slowly, she lowered her hands, and then, her eyes never leaving him, she slid the pistol back into her holster, then showed him her palms once more.

"What're you doing out here? Why do you want to help me?" she asked.

"We have a mutual enemy."

"You're not Russian?"

"Chechen. Come on. I'll get you up this mountain."

He started away from her. She remained. He glanced back. "You have to trust me."

"How do you know English?"

"I went to school in California for many years before I came back to my homeland. Now either you come with me, or you die. They'll bring dogs, and you won't stand a chance."

Repressing a shudder, Halverson fell in behind him,

and he led her through the forest, working hard and fast toward the north.

"My father was killed by the Russians back in 2004. They called him and his friends terrorists, but all they wanted was freedom for our people and our country. You had your American revolution and we wanted ours. My father fought to drive the Russians out of Chechnya and have the UN recognize our independence."

"I'm sorry to hear that."

"They meant well, but their methods were questionable."

"What do you mean?"

He hesitated. "They took over a school in Beslan, held it hostage for three days until the Russians came in with tanks and other heavy weapons. My father was killed. Nearly two hundred children were killed."

"Oh my God."

"Yes. And the Russian government lied about everything."

Halverson shook her head. "You can't go your whole life chasing revenge."

"I already am. And I won't stop."

She groped for something to say, then thought better of it. They climbed in silence for several moments, and then Halverson blurted out, "Stephanie."

"What?"

"You never asked my name."

"Okay, Stephanie."

Silence again. This time Halverson succumbed to it and concentrated on the path ahead.

* * *

About twenty minutes later, with the approach of helicopters quickening their steps and Halverson ready to
give up trying to match his gait, they neared a more
rocky portion of the mountain, the trees giving way here
and there to ice-covered faces of stone, and just ten
meters ahead appeared a shallow crevice. As they drew
closer, the opening became a narrow and easily dismissed entrance to a cave.

"What is this?" she asked.

"Big rocks," he said.

She rolled her eyes and followed him inside, where he
grabbed a flashlight hanging from a hook drilled into
the stone.

"Your place?" she asked.

"Not really," he said. "I just work here."

He led her down a tunnel no more than two meters
wide, ducking in places, the air growing warmer, a dense,
musty scent filling her nose.

"I'm going to Vladikavkaz," she said.

"And what will you do there? Try to get a job?"

She smirked. "I thought I'd catch a flight home."

"Are you serious?"

"Pretty much."

"You'll never make it."

"Actually, I was feeling pretty good about my chances
until you came along."

"Are you serious?" he asked.

"You think I'm alone?"

Before he could answer, the tunnel ended in a wider antechamber shielded by a broad iron gate that he unlocked after fishing out an oversized ring of keys. The chamber led toward a cave about half the size of a football field and nearly four meters high, dim lights mounted to the walls exposing the room's breadth, with hundreds of pallets of crated and boxed materials stored in neat rows that stretched off into the darkness.

"What the hell?" she gasped.

"There's a much wider tunnel on the other side," he said, pointing. "That's where we bring in the forklifts and transfer the shipments."

"Shipments of what?"

He answered her in a deadpan: "Bathing suits and stuffed animals."

Halverson crossed to the nearest box, losing her breath as she read the label: FGM-148 Javelin. She glanced back at him. "Are you fucking kidding me?"

"Those aren't bathing suits?"

"You can joke about this?" Halverson rushed to the next crate, and then to the next, and the next. Portable missile launchers, assault rifles, grenades, mortars— some the property of the Joint Strike Force of the United States of America, others belonging to the Russians, the European Federation, and South Africa. She stood back. "You guys are Chechens?"

"We have allies in Turkey, Syria, Iran, and Uzbekistan."

"And this is a weapons depot?"

"No, this is a cave with big boxes."

Her frown deepened. "You're the only one guarding this place?"

He laughed under his breath. "Take a look." He pointed toward the ceiling, from where hung multiple cameras and remote-operated 5.56-millimeter machine guns with suppressors fitted to their barrels. "There were also guards back by the gate, but you didn't see them, did you? We have an operations center on the other side of the cave. We like to keep a low profile."

Halverson narrowed her gaze on him. "You shouldn't have taken me here."

"You'd rather be outside? I told you, they'll bring the dogs."

"You're not letting me go. And you're not Chechen militants. I know who you are. Forgotten Army, right?"

"Not really. Not anymore."

"What does that mean?"

"It means we've been forgotten. The *Ganjin* has changed. We're not true partners anymore."

"*Ganjin*? Partners? What're you talking about?"

"It doesn't matter. Like I said, we have a mutual enemy, and I'll take care of you. We'll let them search the mountain, and then I'll get you down into the city. You can ride along with one of our shipments."

"Why should I believe you?"

He came up and suddenly clutched her by the shoulders. "Because this is not an accident." He shoved her behind one of the crates, away from the cameras. "Because we need each other. Because you're going to help me escape."

"You?"

"Yes."

"I don't understand."

"You will."

TWELVE

SinoRus Group Oil Exploration Headquarters
Sakhalin Island
North of Japan

Christopher said she would enjoy the killing.

He had been right.

Major Alice Dennison had never felt such great pleasure as she had after putting a bullet in Colonel Dolets
kaya's chest. Shooting Fedorovich and Patti and watching
them die took her breath away.

She wanted more . . .

She wanted to feel that excitement coiling around her
spine again and again, even more so now as Christopher
led her into the back of the helicopter, buckled her into
the rich leather seat, then leaned over and shoved his
tongue down her throat. She wanted to rip off her clothes
and make love to him before they even took off.

His Sikorsky S-76C++ was a luxury helicopter with an
open passenger and pilot interior that Dennison loved.

She liked to watch the pilot and co-pilot go about their business when she wasn't watching TV or sipping on a cocktail from the well-stocked bar. Christopher knew how to treat women right, and nothing made her feel warmer than to make him happy. Why had this once seemed so demeaning and sexist to her?

He pulled away as she grabbed his crotch and cried, "Not now, my love."

She pouted. "All right."

They donned their headphones with attached mikes, and he linked his to his smartphone.

While he took a call, she stared through the window at the refinery, the colossal tanks and pipes blurring into a single dot and fading into the darkness like a lighthouse while they headed out to sea.

She thought about Colonel Pavel Doletskaya. How she'd interrogated him after he'd been captured in Moscow. How he'd gotten into her head. How she thought she might be controlled by someone. How he knew things about her that were impossible to know.

And how she'd fallen in love with him—even though she knew he was obsessively devoted to the Snow Maiden, who had in turn crushed his heart.

Why did she feel nothing now? Was the chip capable of erasing her feelings? And why did knowing the chip was in her optic nerve no longer bother her?

She could ask Christopher, but she knew he'd offer only quieting words, tell her not to trouble herself. She glanced back at him, his silky blond hair hanging in his eyes, his jaw angular and firm—an extension of his personality. A curious boy still lurked in his eyes, the crow's-feet and graying temples vanishing in the light of his passion and commitment. She listened to him speak, forceful and commanding, his South African accent rising and falling in a magnificent lilt:

"Then I'll make myself perfectly clear. I need positive confirmation that the Spetsnaz have captured her, not suppositions. No, I don't care what you have to do. All right. Call me when you have it."

"What's wrong?" she asked.

"Those fools Fedorovich hired . . . don't worry about it . . ."

"What about all the bodies?"

"It's all taken care of."

Dennison smiled tightly. "I'm sorry about her."

His brow tightened. "Patti?"

"No, Viktoria. She's a terrible loss, isn't she."

"We don't need her."

"Did you like her?"

"What do you mean?"

"You know . . . in that way. She has very long legs. She seemed very athletic. We could have both made you happy."

He smiled and clutched her chin. "You're more than enough."

"More than your diamond mines and real estate investments? More than all your homes and your yacht and your aviation companies?"

"Of course. History has made it clear: A man's empire is nothing without a woman at his side."

Suddenly, he had a pistol in his hand and pointed it at her head. "If I killed you right now, would you care?"

She felt absolutely no fear, only love for him. "If doing that made you happy, then I would be happy."

He lowered the gun and shook his head. "I've waited all my life for somebody like you—because I've fought with every woman I've ever known. And now that I have you—"

"What? You don't want me?"

"No, I, uh, I just need to get used to you."

"Haven't I done well? I told you about the *Ganjin*, about Dr. Ragland and what I could about the X-2A Wraith project, and I've delivered all the other information you requested."

"You have."

"Then what else can I do?"

"Nothing else yet."

"Are we going back home to South Africa?"

His brows came together. "Why are you asking so many questions?"

"So I can prepare to make you happy."

"Prepare?"

"Yes, if we're going back home, I can make some arrangements."

"Some of those memories you have . . . I keep forgetting how real they are to you."

"They're not real?"

He put a finger to her lips. "Yes, they are. Anyway, no worries now. We need to stop in Tokyo for a little while."

"All right. Will your friends with the Bilderberg Group be even more pleased with your work now?"

"You're back to the questions, huh?"

"I can't help it. I need to know if you're happy. It's like a compulsion. I can't control it. It makes me feel so good."

"I understand," he said. "Do you even know who they are? I know you've heard me mention them."

"I did some research, but what I found seemed confusing. I don't understand why some people are afraid of you."

"They're only afraid of change." He took her hands in his own. "Imagine, if you will, some of the world's greatest thinkers from politics, finance, industry, labor, education, and communications. Not just the richest people in the world but some of the smartest. Put them in a room once a year and have them talk about the world, about the human condition, about how we can all live more happily and productively—without the boundaries and prejudices of nationalism. Ever since the bombs were dropped on Saudi Arabia and the Russians become the dominant oil suppliers, we've been working toward stability. The *Ganjin* threatened to destabilize the global economy even more, so that's why my colleagues charged me with seizing control of the organization and redirecting its efforts toward our mutual goals. The Committee of Five . . . they were once good people, but they lost their way. Do you understand?"

Her eyes lit. "The Bilderberg Group controls the world."

He grinned, as though her statement sounded ridiculous. "I prefer the word *influence*."

"Okay. So . . . Mr. Christopher Theron, leader of the *Ganjin*, member of the Bilderberg Group, can I *influence* you into pouring me a drink?"

"Absolutely."

"And when we get to Tokyo, will there be time for us?"

"Of course."

His smartphone flashed.

She made a face as he turned away, broke their grasp, and read his message. His expression soured.

"What is it?" she asked.

"An interesting turn of events. You told me they were testing a radar system for the Wraith over North Ossetia."

"That's correct. I wish I could tell you more about the system, but my clearance wouldn't allow me to get in."

"Yes, you told me. Well, the Russians shot down that pilot. We'd put some of our allies on alert in that area, and it seems one of them got lucky. He has the pilot."

"Major Stephanie Halverson?"

"You know her?"

"Yes, I'm sorry I never mentioned her name. I didn't think it was important. She's one of the best."

"Then this is fantastic news. We need her. In fact, we need her more than the Snow Maiden."

"You're a man who gets what he wants."

"Because I work hard."

"No, because you're so damned hot." Her hand went for his crotch once more—

But then his phone rang and she sighed.

"Yes? You have him on the line?" he asked. "Okay, put him through. Hello? Yes, Colonel, it's good to hear your voice. So you've confirmed on the network that they've just picked her up. Excellent. I assume they'll transfer her directly to Moscow? What do you mean, you're not sure? Well, update me immediately when you find out. Yes, I will. Thank you."

"Who was that?"

"One of our Russian friends. They've captured Ms. Antsyforov in the woods outside the refinery."

"Are you worried? She has intel that could damage us."

"Maybe, but I doubt anyone will believe her. Either way, I'll take care of the problem."

"Good." Dennison smiled. "Now you promised me a drink."

"Vodka, right?"

She had to think about it. She'd hated vodka. Why did she like it now?

THIRTEEN

Situation Room
West Wing, White House
Washington, D.C.

The Situation Room was a five-thousand-square-foot command-and-control center located in the basement of the West Wing. Three principal conference rooms served as the centerpiece, with a breakout room for small group meetings, a private room so the president could make calls to other heads of state, and the main watch floor with its cocoon of computer terminals where more than two thousand pieces of information were "fused" or analyzed each day.

President David Becerra leaned back in his chair at the head of the crowded conference table and waved his palms. "All right, everyone settle down."

The national security advisor, the deputy for home-land security, and the White House chief of staff were present, seated according to their seniority, along with the secretary of state, the Joint Chiefs, and the deputy director of the Situation Room itself.

To Becerra's right, on the table opposite the vice president, glowed the holographic image of General Scott Mitchell, commander of the Joint Strike Force, the man who had just announced that Dr. Helena Ragland was missing. It'd been Mitchell who'd reached Becerra out in the Mojave to inform him of this and tell him that Major Stephanie Halverson had been shot down over the Caucasus Mountains. Today's meeting was about *three* missing women, each in their own way vital to national security.

"General, I need to ask: Is Ragland's disappearance related to Dennison's?"

"Sir, we can't confirm that. If you'd like my off-the-record opinion, Major Dennison is an impeccable officer with a flawless record. I just can't explain why she made this unauthorized prisoner transfer of Doletskaya. And it's clear she went to great lengths to do this, falsifying orders and doing an expert job of covering her tracks. The trail goes cold right here in Tampa."

"Was she being blackmailed? Manipulated in some way?"

"I've had Splinter Cells investigating that, but thus far there's been no indication from her father, other family members, or friends of any problem. I have Ghost teams searching for them. I can assure you we *will* find her."

"Okay. What else do we know about Ragland?"

"Quite a bit. That trail's hot. We just got some new intel from sources inside Moscow. They're telling us

Ragland was kidnapped by Spetsnaz forces and is being transferred to their headquarters at Fort Levski, Bulgaria."

A screen behind the general glowed to life, showing a satellite map of the area with wireframe overlays. The camera zoomed in on the mountainous region around the fort, then continued farther to reveal a pair of six-meter-tall, heavily reinforced ballistic pocket doors built into the side of a mountain overlooking a broad and heavily populated military base. Databars along the sides provided intel regarding troop numbers, assets, and current operations.

"The Spetsnaz HQ is a heavily defended facility located behind those doors and buried deep within the mountain," Mitchell added. "It's arguably one of the most secure and heavily defended locations the Russians have."

"So a rescue attempt is impossible," said Becerra.

A knowing grin rose on the general's lips. "Sir, my Ghost teams are tied up all over the world right now—with at least two on the mission to find Dennison. However, this is a perfect operation for our new Marine Corps Raiders. These guys are Russian American operators. They look, act, speak, and even smell like Spetsnaz. I'd like to deploy a team to go after Dr. Ragland. Unfortunately, the Bulgarians won't offer any help at all, with the prime minister now answering to Moscow."

Becerra took in a long, slow breath. Sending American service personnel into harm's way was not something he took lightly.

And this wasn't just harm's way.

This was the belly of the beast.

As the son of a Marine Corps sergeant and a reservist himself before getting into politics, Becerra had a keen and intimate understanding of "going downrange," of having his own boots on the ground, of feeling his hackles rise while on patrol. And he'd met with the families of those lost, listened to their stories and wiped away their tears. There was no greater sense of responsibility—and no greater pain—than saying yes. Go. Fight. Protect our way of life. Thank you.

Becerra studied the tactical map of Fort Levski once more, the sheer number of surface-to-air missiles and advanced early warning radar systems making him shake his head. "General, do those Marines really stand a chance?"

"Sir, the team I have in mind is led by Captain Mikhail Alexandrov."

That name sounded very familiar. "He was just in Ecuador, wasn't he?" Becerra asked. "I just read a report about his operation to capture Nestes."

"Yes, they recovered the man's arm. Nothing else. But we're presuming he's dead. The remains are at the lab now. Point is, Lex is a very capable operator. He'll get in there. He'll get Ragland."

Becerra looked to the vice president and the Joint Chiefs; their expressions said they concurred with Mitchell.

"General, a moment please." Becerra rose and met the gazes of Roberta Santiago, national security advisor, and Mark Hellenberg, chief of staff. All three moved to the breakout room, where Hellenberg shut the door after them.

"Look, I don't want to insult Mitchell, but, Roberta, how good is the intel we have on Ragland's location? I'm not sending Marines into hell unless I know beyond a shadow of a doubt that she's there."

Santiago brushed an errant wisp of gray hair from her face, then shrugged and consulted her tablet computer. "It looks good, sir, straight from Third Echelon. We've got two Splinter Cells inside Moscow."

"Mark, the fact that they were able to kidnap her on American soil doesn't bode well for us."

"No, sir, it does not. Should I call Zynski in here?"

Becerra shook his head. He'd deliberately left the director of homeland security out of the conversation because he knew Tom Zynski well; the man would want to fall on his sword for this failure, and Becerra didn't want that. "Look, we don't need this issue politicized—"

"Sir," Santiago interrupted. "The bureau has already launched their investigation, and we'll need to cooperate with them fully. Ragland's abductors might have very well been American citizens working for the Russians, which would work in our favor. The point is we don't know enough to comment on any of this, so I suggest we continue to gather information."

Becerra nodded. "Stall."

"Gather information," Santiago said with a wink.

"We'll accept full responsibility for this—but only after we know exactly what happened."

"Sir," Hellenberg said. "If they break Ragland and she talks, she can give them a lot. The Wraith and Argus projects will change the game. We need to move quickly."

"All right. I'll sign that order. We'll send in those Marines to get her."

They returned to the conference room and took their seats; Becerra shared his decision with Mitchell, then added, "What are we doing to recover Major Halverson?"

"Everything we can, sir," said Mitchell. "But it's difficult. The QRF could not get in there. The Russians have Interceptors in the air and ground troops scouring the area now."

"We're not leaving my girl."

"Hell no, sir. I've spoken to our colleagues at the NSA and Third Echelon, and they've got a man in Grozny, guy named Thomas Voeckler who's worked with my Ghost teams before. We'll contact him, see if he can link up with Halverson on the ground and get her out of there."

"That's it? One man? Not a team?" asked Becerra. "Can't we drop in some SEALs?"

"Sir, she was shot down near Darial Gorge, not far from Vladikavkaz, one of the most populated cites in the North Caucasus. Halverson was testing in that area because of the sheer number of new radar stations. What I'm saying is, the place is very hot. Sending a Ghost or SEAL team in there at this point would not be advisable. Voeckler's already on the ground and the closest man we've got to her location. He has field operatives within the city he can use to get her out. I think this is our best course of action."

"Well that makes me feel a little better. I'd like to send her a personal message," said Becerra.

Halverson had been on the front lines during the outbreak of the war, and her heroism had left Becerra breathless. He'd made a point to thank her personally then, and he'd do so now. The country owed her a lot, and he hoped that a message from him might lift her morale. He could only imagine what she must be going through, trying to evade capture in the snow-covered mountains.

Becerra rose from his chair. "Now then, ladies and gentlemen, I leave you with this painful reminder: We have a security leak. I want it found."

Nearly seven thousand miles away from the White House, in a helicopter bound for Tokyo, Christopher Theron took a phone call.

The man on the other end was brief: "It's all set, sir, and confirmed with our operatives in Moscow. The American Splinter Cell operatives there have taken the bait and passed it on to the White House."

"And what about Ragland? Where is she now?"

FOURTEEN

Submarine
Identification: Unknown
Location: Unknown

After cuffing Dr. Helena Ragland and slamming her into the back of the SUV the had stopped for her on the highway, the two men with accents drove her to Palmdale Regional Medical Center.

Behind the emergency department sat an ambulance marked with American Medical Response logos. Out of sight from prying eyes, she was gagged and transferred to the back of the truck, where inside the shorter man gave her an injection of something that left her lethargic.

She didn't remember much. A sign that indicated she was in Long Beach. Being loaded into a wheelchair, taken along a dock, pushed onto a boat, a yacht, nice boat.

And then the blindfold. The earplugs.

She focused on time, trying to calculate how long it'd

been from the point of capture. The math swirled in her head, followed by tears as she thought about her daughter.

Oh, God, they were going to torture her for intel on the Wraith. Would she talk?

Was a hypersonic plane worth her life? How deep was her loyalty to her country? She'd never been forced to consider these questions.

Hours—or what felt so—passed. She must've fallen asleep. She awoke to movement, her chair rolling now, then awkward shoving, men carrying her, the bobbing sensation, and the distinctive odor of amines mixed with sweat, lubricants, and something else . . .

This was a submarine; it had to be, and submarines, like spacecraft, had a need to sustain human metabolism by removing exhaled CO_2 and replacing metabolized O_2 using a line of oxidizing compounds with biological chemicals such as amines, thiols, and carbonyls. Hypersonic pilots and submariners couldn't just open a window to catch a breath of fresh air. Wraith pilots dealt with the same issue and resolved them in much the same way.

Muffled noises came through her earplugs. Then the sound of an engine—and she knew engines.

Diesel. That was the other smell. Diesel fuel.

And then she was back in the wheelchair. Rolled, lifted, placed on a mattress. Felt thin. No give, no box spring. Hard, flat support.

Before she could guess at more, the gag and blindfold were removed, as were the earplugs.

The light was blinding, and her ears sore. Her mouth was sticky and dry, lips cracked.

She squinted in the dim light. Her eyes wouldn't focus for a moment, and then, as her ears began to pop, she gasped.

They'd taken her to a tiny room whose hatch visually confirmed she was onboard a submarine, perhaps in the captain's quarters. The bulkhead creaked. She could feel her inner organs subtly pressing upward into her lower lungs. The sub was diving.

She turned her head—

And there he was, hovering over her, the tall, handsome man who'd spoken to her near the car. "Dr. Ragland, we're sorry we put you through this. I wish there were another way."

Her reply came out slurred, and she barely recognized her own voice. She tugged against the zipper cuffs, tried to stand, and realized her legs were bound as well.

He drew his head back, seeming to understand the four-letter word she'd attempted to use. "I know you're upset. But rest assured you're safe now."

"Who are you?" Her voice was working a little better now, her anger diluting the drugs.

"My name is Werner. And if you haven't already surmised, you're onboard a submarine."

"Why?"

"I told you . . . you know why."

"You want information."

"Of course."

She closed her eyes and braced herself. "You work for Moscow?"

He chuckled. "No."

She eyed him, confused. "Then who are you people?"

"You shouldn't worry about that."

Ragland fought against the tears and lost. The drugs, the stress, and the constraints had chipped away her will. She'd crumpled too easily. Now they would think they could get anything out of her.

Werner crouched down and faced her, putting his hand on her cheek. "We've no interest in killing you."

"Well, I've no interest in a submarine ride."

"Once you've told us everything we need to know, we plan to reunite the new-and-improved you with your daughter."

"So you'll shoot more drugs into me, and I'll talk."

"You're very strong-willed, and you have an eidetic memory. Even with the drugs, no matter how hard we try, you won't tell us everything."

"So you'll hurt me."

He shook his head and stood. "They're bringing you something to eat. And black coffee, yes?"

"You want me to betray my country."

He thought a moment, then answered, "You won't think of it that way."

"What do you mean?"

"Rest easy now. You've been through a lot."

"Obviously you know who I am. And obviously you know that given my position, my government will stop at nothing to find us. And they will."

"Not this submarine. She's the latest in air-independent propulsion technology, built with HY-100 austenitic non-magnetic steel—"

Ragland snorted. "Wow, I'm impressed."

"And she's coated with a metamaterial developed by one of my companies. She's undetectable by your P-3C Orion ASW patrol planes with their magnetic anomaly detection booms or active sonar."

Damn, materials like that did exist, but despite them the submarine could still have a significant weakness . . .

Ragland knew that most navies operated subs with conventional diesel-electric propulsion. Diesel-powered generators charged battery banks, which then drove an electric motor connected to a propeller.

Since the 1940s there had been numerous attempts to develop a power generation system that was independent of external air. The period between battery charges varied from several hours to one or two days, depending on the power requirements and the nature of the mission.

Fuel cell technology (LOX and hydrogen) to supplement conventional diesel-electric systems extended the underwater endurance to two weeks or more. She was familiar with all of this because the space community also used energy production mechanisms that were air independent, and they relied almost entirely on photovoltaic arrays for electricity generation, with limited emergency backup power from alcohol fuel cells.

Of course, she didn't share any of that with him, but

she did ask, "Is your cloaking material a decoupler or an absorber?"

He beamed. "I assumed you know something about all this. We've been researching broadband passive wave-guides for the past ten years. We're able to redirect acoustic energy around the submarine. And to answer your question, our coating combines both effects, but it acts by redirecting rather than absorbing incident energy."

"Ideal cloak coatings, in theory, remove the radiated noise and reduce or eliminate sonar strength."

"Exactly."

"And here I am, admiring the technology that ensures I'll never be found," she said, tasting the bitter irony.

"That's where you're wrong again. When we're finished with you, you'll be released. You'll go home, back to your daughter, and you won't have any information you can tell them about us. Trust me, this is a win-win situation for everyone, and our enemies are mutual."

"You haven't proven that."

"We will."

"And by the way, your coating is flawed."

He cocked a brow in disbelief. "Really?"

She nodded.

"You're not going to tell me why or how?"

"That'll just be another fact you'll pry out of me."

He shrugged. "We'll see." He opened the hatch and left.

Whoever this organization was, they could not afford or did not have access to a nuclear submarine, which made all the difference in the world. Ragland had already estimated that a diesel-electric submarine like this one could remain submerged for at least two weeks without snorkeling, after which time it would have to surface to purge the interior atmosphere of contaminants and to extend the use of its limited LOX and hydrogen supply by using its diesels to recharge batteries.

And that was when the sub would be most vulnerable, despite the cloaked coating and the crew's best intentions to remain hidden.

She shut her eyes against fresh tears. She wondered how Lacey was doing with her project, if she'd heard the news of her mother's disappearance, and how she was reacting to it. Ragland couldn't bear the thought of her baby in pain.

OhmyGod.

"*You'll go home, back to your daughter,*" he'd said.

They knew about Lacey.

They knew.

And why were these bastards so confident she'd talk?

Was it because they'd abducted Lacey and would threaten to kill her?

FIFTEEN

Dassault Falcon 7X
Speed: Mach 0.80
Destination: Unknown

The Snow Maiden glared at the handcuffs, then spread her legs once more, trying to stretch them against the tension of the ankle cuffs.

Losing this much control was a shock to the system, and her emotions leapt from utter despair to sheer anger, arcing like an electrical current that left her tense one second and gasping the next.

During her tenure with the GRU, she'd never been captured. There'd been a few close calls—operations within the borders of the United States—but she'd managed to ghost her way out of the country before the FBI or CIA knew what had hit them.

The pair of Spetsnaz officers charged with her transfer had buckled her into the jet's rich leather seat, but it was hardly comfortable; the chain extending between her wrists and the ankle cuffs allowed only a few inches of movement.

She threw her head back and closed her eyes. This was President Kapalkin's personal transport, one of the many large-cabin business jets he'd purchased with taxpayers' money and the reason why they'd had to wait so long in Vladivostok. After they'd plucked her off Sakhalin Island, they'd flown her straight to her hometown, and for a moment, she thought they'd kidnapped friends and relatives from her past to use as bargaining chips during her interrogation. No, the city was just a transfer point.

Captured. She still couldn't reconcile with that. This was someone else's nightmare, that of a poorly skilled operative who'd left a hot trail and made one too many mistakes. This wasn't her. She'd grown so confident, so bold over the years that a moment like this was . . . she couldn't find the words.

She tried to reassure herself that it had been a good fight, a good run while it had lasted, even though she'd been unable to stand back and watch Moscow burn. She'd told herself never to trust anyone, and she'd never swayed—until she'd met Patti and the *Ganjin*. They'd paid her well, told her what she wanted to hear, and her plan was to use them to help bring down the Russian Federation. But their relationship had made her too soft, and they saw what a danger a rogue operative like her could be.

And now here she was, trying to give herself some credit, even though it was all about to end.

Kapalkin was flying her straight to Moscow, where

she'd be stripped, dragged before him, and thrown to her knees. The president would raise his muscular arms and whip her until she bled. This brand of barbarism was well within his reach. She'd been forced to help his administration cover up the deaths of several prostitutes who'd been tortured, raped, and murdered. The task had turned her stomach, but she'd kept her focus on the larger picture of taking down not only him but the entire government. She'd fought against the desire to expose him right then and there, but she'd had to be patient— another regret she could add to the long list . . .

Yes, Kapalkin would spend hours torturing her, if only because she'd made him look foolish before the Americans and the rest of the world. She'd double-crossed him during the Canadian invasion, temporarily joining forces with the Green Brigade Transnational terrorists, and forced him to seek help from the Americans when she'd threatened to detonate suitcase nukes and destroy the Canadian reserves. She grinned to herself. She'd betrayed the Russians by using her relationship with the terrorists, and once that was finished, she'd betrayed the terrorists as well and murdered their leader, Green Vox.

And all of this was the result of her association with the *Ganjin*. They had become her true employers—

Until now.

In her business, everyone betrayed everyone. Eventually. Why had she forgotten that?

She shivered as she once more thought of Kapalkin, of his hand raised high above his head, the venom in his eyes. He was an avid swimmer, she recalled, which kept him in excellent shape for a man nearly sixty. She envisioned drowning him now. Watching his eyes bulge. Watching his eyes go vague. The gurgling screams drifting off into silence.

A flicker of light shone in her peripheral vision. There, outside, were the lights of another aircraft, and she looked across the cabin to spot another pair of lights off the jet's wing. Fighter escort. She was precious cargo.

She fantasized about a rescue attempt, the *Ganjin* having second thoughts, sending some mercenary squadron of fighters to shoot down the escort, electronically disable the president's jet, with another pilot hacking into the controls and taking control of the aircraft to fly her to some remote airbase in Siberia, where she'd be returned to them—

And fitted with one of their chips.

Some rescue.

When she'd joined the GRU, she'd had to sign a series of legal documents allowing the government to place a chip in the back of her head that would allow them to both track and "terminate her operations," should her loyalty be called into question.

But with every piece of technology came a thriving black market of hardware, software, and hackers who could render useless and/or have removed from one's person such "inconveniences." While Izotov had warned her that tampering with the chip would result in certain death, the hacker who'd removed hers had scoffed at that, completing the entire operation without removing the expertly rolled joint from his lips. He'd even offered her a twenty percent discount on a tattoo if she wanted to stick around . . .

She raised her head as the officer with snowy white hair, the one she'd recognized from her days with the GRU, although she couldn't remember his surname, rose from his seat at the front of the cabin, drifted back, and attached a tablet computer to the seat in front of her.

"What's this?" she asked.

"You have a call."

A data box appeared and maximized. A small green light warmed to life atop the device.

And for just a moment, she stopped breathing.

President Kapalkin sat in the library of his mansion, walled in by rows of leather-bound first editions and dressed in a black T-shirt, his eyes heavy with sleep. He'd obviously been roused from slumber to learn of her capture and direct her transfer. What his weary eyes could not convey, his mouth did as he flashed a broad-toothed, ridiculously white smile.

"I thought you'd call sooner," she snapped, before he could launch into his bloated tirade of gloating.

"Hello, Colonel," he began, rasping through his grin. "We've been looking for you for a very long time."

She returned her best sarcastic smile. "Yes, I seem to recall all those fools you sent after me—the German especially. And if I remember correctly, oh, yes, that's right, I killed them all." Her last had come through clenched teeth, and she found herself fighting against the cuffs.

"What happened to you, Snegurochka? What happened to the beautiful woman I used to know, the best GRU operative we ever had, the pride of the motherland?"

"I was never any of those things. You have no idea who I am, and you never will."

"Oh, I think you're mistaken. I think we're going to spend a lot of time together—getting to know each other, as you say . . ."

She snorted.

He went on: "General Izotov told me that you hold us responsible for the deaths of your husband and brothers. You know that's not true."

"Your administration authorized that project. You covered up the mistakes, the leak. You keep denying responsibility!"

"Viktoria, please. Nothing will change the past. Let's talk about your future."

She laughed bitterly. "Maybe we should talk about yours . . . and what little time you have left."

He leaned back in his chair and began to chuckle. "You're such a remarkable woman. Even in the face of certain interrogation, torture, and death, you can still make threats."

"No, this is a promise. You have no idea what's about to happen. You're just a fey little man, and when the war's over, you'll be long since forgotten."

Kapalkin leaned forward. "Viktoria, you're a woman I've never taken more seriously—so let's be honest now."

"Absolutely," she said, widening her eyes. "The people I work for are much more powerful than you, the

Americans, or the Europeans. Your government is about to collapse, and you don't even know it."

"Have they fed you?" he asked.

"What?"

"You're not dehydrated? Hallucinating?"

"Listen to me, and listen carefully. When I get to Moscow, I want to make a deal. I'll hand you my employers, I'll tell you everything they have in mind, in exchange for my freedom."

He sighed and set his elbows on the desk, fingers steepled until he suddenly smote his fist on the hardwood and cried, "Do you know what I'm going to do to you? Do you have any idea?"

"You won't get your chance. Moscow will be under attack, and the motherland will be in ruins before you ever get near me."

"You sound pathetic now. And it's sad."

"Where's General Izotov?"

"That's none of your concern."

"He's been on personal leave. He used the excuse of his sister's cancer to take some time off, did he not?"

"So you've hacked into his smartphone and are detailing his personal life to me. Am I supposed to be impressed?"

"Listen to me, you stubborn bastard. Izotov wasn't on leave. I brought him to Sakhalin Island."

"That's interesting—because I just spoke to the general, and he'll be returning to work tomorrow. He's never left Moscow."

"That's what they wanted you to believe, but he's not working for you—"

"Don't belittle yourself any more."

"Shut up and listen to me, old man!"

"Please—"

"Get your people to the SinoRus refinery. He was there!"

"I'm so sorry, Viktoria, but I can't bear to see you like this."

"I told you, I'll hand you my employers. You have no idea what's going on here."

He leaned forward, and his eyes narrowed to slits. "Oh, I know exactly what's going on. This is a woman begging for her life, grasping at any story she can use to buy time. Good-bye, Colonel."

"Wait!"

The screen went blank.

And the officer returned and removed the tablet. He cocked a brow and said, "Would you like some peanuts or a warm towel?"

She glared and cursed at him.

He shrugged, smiled tightly, and headed back up the aisle.

Maybe it was a misstep, trying to bargain with Kapalkin, but if the *Ganjin* controlled Dennison and Izotov, and, perhaps, key players within the European Federation, then their ambitions might become much more aggressive.

"Hey, don't you remember me?" she shouted to the officer.

He turned back to face her. "Does it really matter?"

"Yes."

"I have orders not to speak to you unless absolutely necessary."

"Answer the question."

"Shut up. Otherwise, I'll gag you. The rest of the trip will be very unpleasant."

"I remember you."

"Shut up."

She hoisted her brows. "I was on the committee that vetted you for this job, you asshole. I know all about your service career, your wife's death, the son with Down's syndrome. I've seen your entire record, and back then I thought you were someone who might bring change, someone who might eventually earn the president's ear. But here you are, just an ass-kisser."

"What do you want?"

"When we land, you let me go."

He shrugged. "Okay."

"And in exchange, I'll tell the truth about your wife."

His tone suddenly darkened. "What do you mean?"

She repressed a chill. Maybe he would buy the lie. Maybe she could soften him up just enough.

"The president didn't want you to know the truth."

The officer, whose surname finally came to her—Gorelov—shot from his seat and stormed to her. "What are you talking about?"

The Snow Maiden braced herself. *Here we go . . .*

SIXTEEN

Grozny
Capital City
Chechen Republic, Russia

Thomas Voeckler reached the end of the chain-link fence, his shoulder brushing against a rickety pole.

There, across the street, lay a bombed-out six-story apartment complex draped in nearly a meter of snow. The building's south wall presented at least three separate openings through which Basayev, aka "the Bear," could escape.

Voeckler continued to ignore the buzzing smartphone in his pocket and sprinted after the man, who, when he wasn't smuggling arms through the mountainous North Caucasus region, was a semiprofessional bodybuilder running a small gym—or, rather, a front operation for recruiting soldiers for the Forgotten Army.

On behalf of the NSA, of Third Echelon (the subbranch that supervised him), and of the U.S. government,

Voeckler, a once-reluctant Splinter Cell operative, had been shadowing the Bear for nearly ten days, trying to find the location of his arms warehouse. The weapons moved from the Black Sea to somewhere in the Caucasus Mountains. It was there, in that treacherous and remote region, that the terrorists expertly concealed their trail, storing the weapons, sitting on them, and then making their transfers at random times and using random routes. One such shipment was discovered in the city of Vladikavkaz by an informant who'd told Voeckler that he, too, believed the terrorists had a cache hidden somewhere in the mountains. From Vladikavkaz, the shipment had moved on to Grozny and out to the Caspian Sea. Initial intel confirmed that the Bear directed this operation from his Grozny apartment; consequently, Voeckler had started his investigation there.

While he'd been exceedingly careful not to get too close, the Bear had left his meager apartment in the middle of the night, and Voeckler, who'd been alerted by the sensors he'd placed on the man's door and car, had been forced to move in. Something was going down, and there was no way in hell he'd miss it. He'd even entertained the thought that the Bear would drive out into the mountains and lead him directly to the cache.

But God damn it, Voeckler had been spotted.

And the big Bear had launched his two-hundred-fifty-pound frame like a cannonball across the snow and vanished down the street, only to be picked up seconds later by Voeckler.

So this was it. If Voeckler didn't take the man right

here, right now, the entire operation was finished. Basayev the Bear would disappear into the forest, and within hours he'd completely dismantle his smuggling operation, go underground for a few months, then resurface somewhere else. Just another inconvenience for a man like him.

Voeckler wouldn't let that happen. He swore to himself and drove on, across the broken pavement polished to a sheen by patches of ice and plowed snow, his boots giving way.

Just ahead, the Bear was swallowed by the largest of the gaping holes blown into the left corner of the apartment, his tracks in the snow shimmering in the light of a single halogen on the corner, a heat haze rising above to swirl in the icy wind.

Voeckler wove a bending path around piles of concrete and into the utter and frozen darkness.

He stopped and tried to silence his ragged breath. His nose was running, but he dared not sniffle.

Time to listen. Let his eyes adjust.

He thought of his trident goggles tucked inside the pack sitting in his car. Night-vision, thermal, electromagnetic, and electronically enhanced systems were all at his disposal, but he'd been observing the Bear on foot, waiting for the man to get in his own car, when the plan had gone south.

Now Voeckler found himself standing in a bedroom, a few pieces of abandoned furniture shoved against one wall, their surfaces dusted by concrete, while a snowdrift rose behind him.

Many of the tenements on this street had been lying in decay for more than two decades, victims of wars past, while the northern part of the city had suffered more recent and horrifying damage. Spetsnaz troops had invaded not a month prior and slaughtered nearly one thousand people who were "suspected terrorists or those aiding and abetting terrorists."

For their part, Third Echelon preferred a more civil and sophisticated approach, the scalpel versus the hatchet. The Forgotten Army had launched several attacks on JSF forward supply depots in Poland and Ukraine, escaping with man-portable surface-to-air missiles sent down to the Black Sea. Without question, the JSF had keen interest in recovering the stolen weapons and terminating those responsible—but instead of sending in the butchers, they'd sent in the surgeon—

Who'd unfortunately screwed up.

Footfalls shattered the silence. Where? There, outside the room, a hallway, narrow, more debris piled in the way. He nearly tripped, heard a door slam, went for it, right turn, racing across another room, a kitchen? Another door. Back into another hallway, this one between apartments—

And there he was at the far end, a silhouette in a knee-length woolen coat, turning to face Voeckler.

The Bear lifted his arm.

Voeckler's Glock 21 had been fitted with a suppressor and cracked like a toy gun.

The Bear's pistol boomed like a cannon, the echo resounding through the skeletal building as Voeckler hit the floor and returned fire, squeezing off three rounds that struck the door swinging open just as the Bear bolted away.

Voeckler gritted his teeth, cursed, and sprang to his feet. He charged across the broken concrete floor and wrenched the door out of the way—

To glimpse an intersecting hallway with a dim puddle of light at the far end where a door hung half off. The ceiling here was partially collapsed, trusses exposed like open fractures, bits of insulation and drywall blown free.

To his right, the hall jogged off into darkness.

Silence again. Which way?

Voeckler took in a long breath through his nose. Thanks to his brother George, who'd also been a Splinter Cell, he'd learned to study his subjects down to the very last detail. He could tell you the Bear's favorite drink (Grey Goose vodka) and the kind of music he liked (American alternative), and he could describe in detail the subtle blend of bergamot, jasmine, musk, and oak moss that composed the man's Siberian Barber No. 3 Russian cologne, the scent of which now indicated that the Bear had turned left, toward the light.

Voeckler shifted forward, holding his Glock tightly in both hands. He activated the pistol's viridian green laser sight, the beam cutting through dust motes and peeling back the shadows.

He reached the open door, swung right, holding his breath, saw only the shattered window and another streetlight leaning at a fifty-degree angle in the wind.

The Bear was clever all right. He'd assumed he

couldn't win a straight chase against a man nearly half his size, so it was stop and go. Wait, listen, charge.

Yes, he and his people were cunning. No doubt about that. They were a largely Muslim ethnic group that had lived for centuries in the mountainous North Caucasus region. For the past two hundred years, they'd fought against Russian rule. During the Second World War, then–Soviet leader Joseph Stalin believed that the Bear's forefathers were working with the Nazis. Stalin deported the entire population to Kazakhstan and Siberia. Tens of thousands of Chechens died, and the survivors were allowed to return home only after Stalin's death. Oppression, misery, and death were the Bear's heritage.

On the contrary, Voeckler had been raised in the cushy suburbs of central Florida, where he had attended Florida State University and had terrorized the institution's psychology, political science, and English departments, finally earning his English degree and then going on to flunk out of graduate school in spectacularly underwhelming fashion. His career possibilities had included pizza delivery, apartment maintenance, and camp counselor, while his brother George had joined the Marines and gone on to become a Splinter Cell operative. George had pulled all the strings to get Thomas a shot at becoming an operative, but at the time, becoming a Splinter Cell was George's dream, not Thomas's. In the beginning, Thomas knew that the only reason he'd been hired by Third Echelon was that he and George were twins, and having an agent be in more than one place at the same time was a useful ploy. Thomas had gone along for the ride, and for his brother's sake, he'd tried to behave as professionally as possible, but his heart was never in it.

However, George's death at the hands of a man named Heinrich Haussler, an agent of the Bundesnachrichtendienst (the German federal intelligence service) changed everything. Haussler had been hired by the Russians to bring in the Snow Maiden, even as George, Thomas, and a Ghost team were charged with the same. George had sacrificed himself to save the team, and losing his brother made Thomas realize that he could be more than his past, that he could live up to his brother's dream for him, that he could live an extraordinary life and really commit to helping others instead of wallowing in self-pity.

So now he was Thomas Voeckler, Splinter Cell.

Ready to capture this man. Ready to make this happen. The streetlight groaned in the wind. He glanced at it once more—

But then the door swung back toward him.

He dodged to the right, came around, and raised his pistol at the Bear, who drove forward like a linebacker, straight into Voeckler's chest, knocking him onto the unforgiving floor.

With his head rebounding off the concrete and the wind knocked out of him, Voeckler barely felt the pistol slip from his grip.

He stared up into the man's eyes, gleaming like a pair of jewels, as gloved fingers slid around his throat and began to cut off his air. Below the man's eyes lay ruddy, scarred cheeks and a beard like frieze carpet, dense curls wired with gray.

"Who are you?" the big man groaned in Russian.

Voeckler tried to respond against the man's grip.

Seeing this, the Bear removed one hand and placed his pistol to Voeckler's head.

"All right, talk to me."

Voeckler answered him in Russian, "I'm your contact from Baku. Why did you run from me?"

"You're not from Baku."

"The guy from Sudan? The one you trusted? He's dead. They sent me to contact you. I tried, but you ran."

With a deep frown, the Bear drew back and removed the pistol from Voeckler's head. "Why did you shadow me? You know the protocol. Didn't they contact you about the train crash over the gorge?"

"They did. But I had to be sure, first."

"Why didn't you just call me by name? I wouldn't have run."

"I didn't know that. And they didn't tell me your name. They only gave me the address."

"Fools."

Seeing that his ploy had worked, Voeckler was done with this conversation. He wrenched himself forward, driving the heel of his palm into the man's nose while reaching out with the other hand to seize the Bear's pistol.

Voeckler ignored the fact that he'd failed Third Echelon's training program three times.

He ignored the fact that hand-to-hand combat was arguably his weakest skill.

And he ignored the fact that while he'd regained the element of surprise, the Bear's grip on the pistol seemed unbreakable.

The gun went off, a round blasting into the ruptured ceiling, as Voeckler went for the gun with both hands now, driving a knee into the Bear's groin.

They screamed nearly in unison, the Bear trying to gain control of his weapon, latching his free hand around one of Voeckler's wrists and tugging it back and away.

Another round shattered glass behind them, and the gunfire was sure to draw the locals, hard-faced laborers who knew the Bear, had accepted his many gifts, and would, at the very least, defend him if not join his group.

Voeckler tore one hand free from the man's grip and punched him in the face three times, targeting each eye, then his nose again—

Just as the Bear turned the gun around, now inches away from getting a clean shot at Voeckler's head.

He wouldn't die like this, no. His brother, who was looking down on them, knew what he'd do to finish this fight, and Voeckler strained to hear his brother's words.

The Bear emitted a groan that sounded like it came from the very pit of his belly. Suddenly, he broke free—

Leveled his weapon on Voeckler, who knocked the man's arm away at the same time he fired.

In the next breath, Voeckler spotted his own pistol—

And so did the Bear.

Voeckler lunged for the weapon—but he faked the move, drawing quickly back as the Bear kept falling forward. Now Voeckler's brother, George, would have been proud. Voeckler exploited the misdirection to both wrench free the Bear's gun and deliver a roundhouse to the man's jaw.

The barrel-chested thug fell backward, onto his rump. He lay there for a moment, sprawled out, wheezing. He cursed at Voeckler and said, "You're an American, aren't you?"

Voeckler kept the man's weapon trained on him, even as he picked up his own pistol, then shifted forward. "I want the GPS coordinates of your warehouse in the mountains."

"You'll get shit, Yankee spy."

The smartphone in Voeckler's pocket vibrated again.

"All right, big boy, time to get up. You're coming with me."

"Not tonight."

A man shouted somewhere outside the building. Two more shouts reverberated off the cracked windows.

"Maybe ten men," said the Bear, glancing off toward the hallway. "Maybe more. And you're going to take me prisoner?" He smiled, his teeth stained with blood.

"The coordinates. *Now.* You've got three seconds. Don't assume I have a conscience—because I don't."

"You Americans are weak, full of guilt and dicked around by politicians."

"You're out of time," said Voeckler.

The Bear smiled and shrugged.

"Then fuck you." Voeckler fired point-blank into the Bear's head.

A second later, Voeckler was out the door, sprinting down the hallway, as the Bear's associates came bursting into the building.

He reached the apartment's front door, banged it open, then hightailed across the street toward a towering pile of rubble that had once been another tenement, now a snow-capped jigsaw puzzle of concrete. He hustled toward the alley on the right, then hunkered down in the shadows to catch his breath. He checked his phone:

TERMINATE OP.
DOWNED JSF PILOT NEAR DARIAL GORGE.
FIND AND EVACUATE. MORE INTEL TO COME.
MOVE OUT.

SEVENTEEN

Mi-8AMTSh Gunship
En Route to Balkan Mountains
Bulgaria

Lex and his men had jammed to capacity their load-out bags and had transported their weary butts out to the aircraft carrier USS *George H. W. Bush* CVN-77, operating in the Mediterranean Sea. From there, they'd boarded an attack helicopter with its camouflage pattern fuselage and Russian Federation insignia. Despite its appearance, the chopper was owned and operated by the JSF and armed with Shturm-V anti-tank guided missiles, eighty-millimeter unguided rockets, PKT machine guns, and twin-barreled twenty-three-millimeter automatic cannons. The rocket pods on either side of the gunship could deliver a devastating barrage of firepower that would buckle the knees and crush the spirits of dismounts on the ground.

The team was dressed like Spetsnaz airborne troops in unmarked black utilities and chest plates. They each fielded an HGU 55/P ballistic helmet, MBU 12 oxygen mask, tactical goggles, Aerox VIII O_2 regulator, Twin 53 bailout bottle assemblies, flight suits and gloves, and high-altitude altimeters. The MC-5 parachute rig was a bulky addition but tended to come in handy if they chose to actually survive their High Altitude Low Opening (HALO) jump.

Once on the ground, they'd strip off their jump gear and don their regular helmets. As an added precaution, they were being flown in by Russian American pilots. Lex had quipped that if the fuel for the chopper could've been bought in Russia, the brass would've done so.

Despite those measures, a few of their weapons might betray their true identities. Given the nature of the mission (one-way, suicidal, pick your adjective), Lex had requested from General Mitchell some more "creative" choices. The old Ghost leader had procured the usual Spetsnaz Izhmash AN-99 assault rifles, but he'd also come through with some sleek ordnance manufactured using Metal Storm technology that involved having rounds stacked inside a barrel and electronically fired in any number, sequence, and rate for markedly improved lethality. The L12-7 heat-seeking grenades shaped like small missiles were a prerequisite for a mission like this, as were their SAVs: situational awareness visors hidden within their Spetsnaz helmets and linked to their comm systems. The SAVs were a "down-and-dirty" version of the Cross-Coms used by Ghost Recon teams and were linked to tiny cameras mounted on their weapons and helmets.

Make no mistake, they had all the tools they needed. Now it was just a question of execution.

Lex sat across from his men, their faces partially hidden behind their masks, only their eyes visible through their clear goggles.

Borya had a tablet computer in his hand, one glove removed so he could work the touch screen. Lex knew he was going over the schematics of the Spetsnaz headquarters and layout of the army base. That was just like him. Anyone could squeeze a trigger. Borya would tell you why it was being squeezed, describe the political and historical purposes behind such an engagement, and calculate one of at least three opportune moments when said trigger should be operated and how that kill contributed to the overall battle. He did this not to justify his actions or somehow make himself feel better. He truly enjoyed the statistics of warfare on both the strategic and tactical levels.

Vlad sat beside Borya. The shorter man's eyes were closed, but he wasn't sleeping. He didn't call himself a Buddhist, but he was a huge proponent of meditating before every mission, much to the chagrin of Slava, who thought it was pointless and hardly as beneficial as hydrating and carbing up to keep your head clear and your hands ready to snap necks.

Consequently, while his colleague was lost in thought, Slava had his free ear filled with an earbud and was no doubt listening to his "electro-thrash" metal that sounded to Lex like chainsaws and barking dogs. The lumberjack of a man tapped his boot and slowly nodded.

Like the millions of combatants who'd come before them, from the ancient battle of Sumer and Elam to the current confrontation between the superpowers, everyone dealt with prefight jitters in his own way, and for his part, Lex liked to misdirect his thoughts and had decided to turn the chopper ride into a second debrief of the mission in Ecuador.

He keyed his microphone. "Hey, guys, if you'll listen up, I've got some intel to share."

"We're getting a raise?" asked Slava.

Lex chuckled. "I thought you did this for the glory."

"That and the great food," Slava answered.

"Nice. Well, this isn't about more money or better food. It's about Nestes."

"He's alive?" asked Slava.

"He's not alive, you Cossack," said Vlad.

"They get something on the chip?" Borya asked.

"The lab took DNA from the arm and matched it to José Nestes, who you remember was our guy Carlos's brother and the leader of the Forgotten Army before he was killed in the U.K. Interpol found and processed his body, so we had that DNA to work with."

"Got any better surprises, boss?" asked Slava. "Whose arm could we have found?"

"I know, but you always need to confirm these things." Lex consulted his own tablet computer and reviewed the reports. "The arm did have a surgically implanted microchip and a flat microbattery rechargeable through the skin. So the lab fired up the battery and monitored the immediate area for any form of RF energy."

"They find any?" asked Borya.

"Hell, yeah they did. They picked up some RF bursts

and identified the IP address of the transmitter along with the address of the recipient encoded in the transmission."

"Somebody had Nestes on a leash," concluded Slava.

"Exactly," said Lex. "So after decryption, the lab determined the chip was transmitting GPS tracking data to a known Russian military satellite node."

"So this *Ganjin* thing you were talking about is a Russian group?" asked Vlad. "No big surprise there. They've been exploiting the Green Brigade and these Forgotten Army guys since the beginning of the war."

"Yes, they have," said Lex. "And it gets better. A lab report that just came in a few hours ago indicates that they've found extra pathways etched into the chip, making space to install additional hidden program routines."

"I've read about that," said Borya. "Harks back to electronics being shipped into one country with chips that already contain spyware so the sellers can eavesdrop on the buyers."

"You could make that comparison," said Lex. "So anyway, they've IDed several computer routing addresses to known international submarine cable gateways: the South American-1 gateway in Punta Carnero, Ecuador, and its sister gateway in Fortaleza, Brazil."

"So Nestes was talking to submarine commanders?" asked Slava. "What the hell is that about?"

"I didn't get that part either until I read up on it," Lex admitted. "But check it out: Over ninety percent of the world's computer communications travel at the speed of light, along fiber-optic cables running through our oceans."

"I thought it was all wireless," said Borya.

"Me, too," answered Lex. "But it's not. So it turns out that Fortaleza in Brazil is a strategic gateway with many paths into the United States and continuing paths into Europe."

"Oh, I get it now," said Slava. "They can track the transmissions along the cables back to their origination or destination."

"That's exactly right," Lex told him, then once again read from his report. "The lab's identified the South Atlantic Express gateway connecting Fortaleza with Cape Town, South Africa, via the mid-Atlantic gateway in Jamestown, the port capital of the U.K.-owned South Atlantic island of St. Helena. I've sent you all copies of this doc so you can see the cable map they've created."

"So what're they getting at?" asked Borya.

"Report says that these specific gateways form an obvious communication pathway seemingly terminating in South Africa. However, the purpose and significance of these clandestine piggyback communication addresses has yet to be determined."

"Don't you hate when they do that?" Vlad asked. "They tease you with some significant findings—that turn out to be inconclusive."

"Actually, I think we can draw some useful conclusions from all of this: If this chip design was in Nestes's arm, there might be more in other operatives, and if they're all following the same fiber-optic lines of communication—"

"Then maybe we can locate their signals and track

every single one of them," said Borya. "Use their own comms against them."

"That's the plan. The NSA's supercomputers are already monitoring all traffic along the South American and South Atlantic digital highway using the word *Ganjin* as its primary search key."

"Boss, you're telling us all this because we'll be back on mission, right?" asked Vlad.

"I think so—"

"Which means you don't believe we're going to die horrible and grisly deaths when we get to Fort Levski," Vlad added.

"You listen to me. All of you," Lex began. "We're going to Fort Levski, we're gonna get Ragland, and we're gonna get the hell out. That'll go down by the numbers. Then when we get back, we'll start tracking and taking out these Forgotten Army *Ganjin* bastards all over the world."

"Hoo-ah!" they boomed.

"Now sit tight, gentlemen. We'll be in range soon . . ."

Lex smiled behind his mask, and then, taking Borya's cue, he brought up the headquarters blueprints on his computer.

They had three different plans for penetrating the facility.

All of them required balls of steel.

EIGHTEEN

Forgotten Army Weapons Depot
Caucasus Mountains
Near North Ossetia, Russia

Halverson walked with Aslan down an aisle of crates stacked neatly on their wooden pallets and piled over three meters high. The place was a Walmart of weapons, with labels in multiple languages. The ones in English sent pangs of anger into her gut. How had these bastards gained access? Was someone on the inside shipping them weapons? And why hadn't she heard about this? Was the JSF covering it all up?

With those questions still burning, she followed the American-educated Chechen toward a pair of tunnels that appeared freshly cut in the rock. He still wouldn't elaborate on what he'd told her—about her helping him to escape—but he'd instructed her to remain quiet as they took the smaller of the tunnels and reached a steel gate bolted directly to the cave walls like the first one.

Two men in their twenties dressed similarly to Aslan and armed with AK-47s stood there, and Aslan offered them a curt nod and said, "I'm taking her to Brandenburg."

Without a word, one man turned back to the gate, secured with a chain and key lock. He wrestled with both, then allowed them through. Halverson spied the thick cables running along the floor to her left as they shifted into another cave about the size of her apartment back in Palmdale, although the ceiling was barely two meters high.

Positioned along three walls were portable tables and chairs, behind which sat bearded men whose faces were cast in the dim light of flat screens. Satellite maps of the region, along with e-mail lists, and various other documents, the text of which Halverson could not quite see, scrolled and panned into view. She counted eight men in all, with three wearing headsets and muttering softly into their microphones. Another bank of screens to the left displayed security camera images of both the warehouse and several exterior entrances revealed through thermal images and night-vision lenses. More heavy cables snaked behind the men, running up through a hole drilled in the ceiling that she assumed reached the surface, where they no doubt had set up a system of camouflaged communications dishes.

One of the chairs swiveled toward her to reveal a gaunt-faced blond woman with brilliant blue eyes. She came out of the chair, rising to a full six feet or better. Her lean frame barely held up her heavy woolen coat.

She coughed loudly, then smiled and said, "You're a very lucky woman."

That accent . . . Australian? British?

"And you're wondering where I'm from. Don't worry about it. My name is Joanna Brandenburg, and this is my little mom-and-pop weapons supply house. You'll have to forgive my appearance. I've been under the weather these past two weeks. Some kind of stomach virus, it's terrible."

Halverson kept her hand on her pistol.

Brandenburg noticed that and said, "If I were you, I'd want to shoot me, too."

Halverson opened her mouth, then thought better of it.

"Come on, you wanted to say something?" She paused, waiting for an answer, and when she didn't get one, she continued in a kind of singsong that seemed to amuse her: "You think we're terrorists. You think we're horrible people. You think we stole all those weapons to kill innocent people, but you have no idea the kinds of horrors your government has brought on us. Americans, Russians, Europeans—all conspiring to destroy the world."

"Are you joking? They want oil, money, and power. That's all they want."

As Halverson took a step back, two guards were on her, one removing her pistol, the other zipper-cuffing her hands behind her back. They continued searching her, removing everything she had: remote to the drone, satellite phone, conventional beacon, everything—her lifelines to the JSF gone.

She glared at Aslan, who said, "As I told you, we have a common enemy. But we know you won't trust us, so this is a necessary evil."

"At this point I'm unsure who's worse," she spat. "The Spetsnaz don't play games. They don't pretend to be your friend."

"It's okay, my dear," said Brandenburg, clutching Halverson's chin a moment before she jerked her head away. "We're going to take very good care of you. No interrogation. No torture. Hell, I've even got a bottle of Château Puisserguier Saint-Chinian Blanc I'll share with you."

Halverson stared, dumbfounded. "You have no questions?"

"We already know enough."

"Really."

"Your name is Major Stephanie Halverson. You're an American pilot with the Joint Strike Force. You've been flying a new hypersonic jet called the X-2A Wraith, and you came here to North Ossetia to test a new radar system for the plane. You were shot down because the system malfunctioned."

Halverson's blood iced up, her chest tightened, and she could barely breathe. "That information is classified, compartmentalized."

"Oh, I just Googled it," Brandenburg said, turning back to her men, who broke out in raucous laughter.

"Who are you people?"

"Like I said, don't worry about anything. Aslan? Please take her to her quarters and be sure she has everything she needs."

Aslan nodded and led Halverson back out of the cave.

"What the hell?" she stage-whispered.

"Shhh, not now," he warned. "Go along."

They passed through the connecting tunnel, then walked back across the warehouse and into yet another passageway that likewise broadened into a loading station, with ten or more gas-powered forklifts lined up and the black void of another exit on the far end. To her right sat an area cordoned off by a chain-link fence, where hundreds of boxes of ammunition buckled the thin metal shelves aligning the walls. Aslan guided her to this area, opened the gate with a key, then led her to a single cot set up alongside a stack of empty wooden crates that someone had converted into a makeshift desk with several pens, notebooks, and flashlights scattered across it.

"What the hell's going on here?" asked Halverson.

Aslan glanced up at the camera on the ceiling, swiveling to face them. He turned his back to the camera, winked, and said, "You'll be safe. That's all I can tell you." Then he mouthed the words *I'll come back for you later.*

She watched him go, then lowered herself painfully to the cot, her wrists already sore, the cave's humidity beginning to seep into her bones.

Shit, they didn't have a course for this in SERE school, did they? Here's what to do if while escaping from the enemy you get saved by terrorists who may or may not be your friends and who somehow inexplicably know all about you and your mission, security clearances notwithstanding.

Brandenburg was clearly not a Chechen, maybe an Australian or South African directing these Chechens with unprecedented access to the JSF's operations.

Conclusion? There was a huge breach in security. Absolutely gaping. A mole inside the JSF, to be sure. If they knew all about her mission, then maybe they were responsible for the malfunction? Had spies inside Skunk Works sabotaged the radar system? Maybe they'd taken it out from the ground with a directed-energy weapon? Their comm equipment appeared sophisticated, and they certainly had access to ordnance from around the globe.

Less than five minutes later Aslan returned with a sandwich and an apple. "It's just plain peanut butter—but it's a luxury for us." He removed her zipper cuffs, and she rubbed her wrists and glanced up to find him holding her at gunpoint. "Just eat, okay?"

She dove into the sandwich and between bites said, "I assume they'll ransom me. They'll tell the JSF that they'll kill me if their colleagues aren't released from some CIA black site, right?"

He made a face, wriggled his brows, flicked his glance up to the camera. "I know you'll be safe with us."

She nodded, threw down the sandwich, and in the next breath was on him, knocking him onto his back, one hand seizing his wrist, trying to keep the pistol away, the other latching around his throat. "I need my satellite phone," she whispered in his ear.

He groaned and whispered, "I know. Don't worry."

Suddenly, she no longer believed him —and she realized she had a chance right here, right now, to make her break . . .

She dug nails into his neck, and he gagged, fought harder, and she was about to choke him to death and seize his weapon when the gate slammed open behind her, and two men seized her arms and ripped her away.

She would have killed him. There was no trust, no matter what he said now. If he needed her so much, then he'd better prove it.

The guards shouted at Aslan for his incompetence, and they zipper-cuffed Halverson and shoved her back onto the cot.

Rubbing his neck, Aslan fell in behind them, leering at her before he left.

Either he'd come through, or maybe she'd get another chance to kill him.

She grimaced at the sandwich lying on the cave floor, then shut her eyes and shuddered through her next breath. A few seconds later, a bolt of anger sent her to her feet and she screamed, "Brandenburg! I want to talk to you!"

NINETEEN

Unlike the town of Levski, located in central northern Bulgaria, Fort Levski had been constructed farther south in a valley surrounded by the Balkan Mountains. As the Dassault Falcon 7X made its final approach toward the army base's runway, the asphalt flickering in the predawn light, the Snow Maiden glanced through a window and stiffened as she realized they hadn't taken her to Moscow, no, but to a remote headquarters where she'd never be heard from again.

The infamous stories of interrogations that took place at the fort were a powerful emetic, the stuff of nightmares, the barbarism knowing no bounds. Some of the interrogators had taken their cues from history instead of technology, drawing upon the medieval instead of the medical, employing torture devices like heretic's forks jammed into prisoners' necks and racks to pull them apart. Acid, hot oil, and other chemicals were applied or imbibed, while teeth and fingernails littered the floors. The interrogators studied techniques used by the drug gangs, such as crucifixions and the use of oil drums to cook prisoners alive. A few of those sadistic bastards knew exactly where to place cuts along the body to prolong the bleeding process. Branding and waterboarding were sometimes considered too civilized, and electrocution was dismissed by a few as too mundane.

These stories were not the products of imaginative NCOs assigned as prison guards. As a GRU operative charged with questioning captives, the Snow Maiden had been there, seen the carnage for herself, and Kapalkin knew of her experiences. He'd sent her to Fort Levski and the Spetsnaz headquarters to frighten her before he proceeded to slowly, systematically, break her down. The psychological torture would run concurrently with the physical and draw upon all aspects of her life— her childhood, brothers, husband, everything . . .

If the interrogators were really good at it, and if it pleased the president, they would keep her alive for months, years even, until her voice and mind condensed into the head of a pin and finally . . . vanished.

Those few who knew what went on at the fort had code named the place *черная гора*, or the "Black Mountain."

She would not leave this place alive.

Her eyes closed involuntarily, and she hung her head and fought off the shivers.

In just a few minutes they were on the ground and taxiing along the runway. A voice rose from the front of the cabin:

"I'm sorry I couldn't be more helpful," said Gorelov, the officer she'd helped to vet a lifetime ago. "It's too bad your story is bullshit. The government had nothing to do with my wife's death—but it seems the government will have everything to do with yours."

She was going numb already, his words echoing away before they ever seemed discernible.

With her breath shortening, he dragged her out of the chair and shoved her forward, the chains clanging, her feet dragging, what little fight she had left remaining on the seat.

What the hell was wrong with her? Why was she surrendering so easily? They had her body, but they did not have her mind. Her spirit was still her own.

But this was the Black Mountain. You did not return from here. No one ever did . . .

In the mountains overlooking the runway, unseen by anyone near or within the base, were four sets of eyes . . .

Lex lowered his binoculars, his breath hanging in the air. He turned to Slava. "It's a prisoner transfer, but this can't be Ragland, can it?"

The man shook his head. "She wouldn't be arriving. Intel indicated she's already here."

"Agreed."

"Then who's this?" asked Vlad.

Lex lifted his binoculars once more. "I don't know. Can't zoom in close enough to get a steady image."

"You want to put up the drone?" asked Vlad.

"Negative. Prisoner will be long gone before the drone gets within range."

Borya cleared his throat. "Nothing on the network, boss. Federation comm traffic is absolutely silent about this."

"That's interesting," Lex said. "Must be a real high-value target down there."

How do you want to die? the Snow Maiden asked herself as she climbed down the stairs and placed boots onto the tarmac. *Wallowing or fighting?*

Billowing waves of heat from the jet's engines washed over her between bursts of the frigid morning air. Despite the harsh smell of jet fuel, she could already detect the forest, the hint of pine in the air, an odor that reminded her of the island, of her race through that forest.

They'd brought two squads of men to accompany her back up the mountain, and she paused a moment to let her gaze play over the base from her all-too-brief vantage point.

All right. Information is power. Think. Think. She knew the order of battle for Fort Levski by heart:

The seven-hundred-acre fort was home to three thousand Russian soldiers and a contingent of airmen from the 102nd Military Base located in Gyumri. Battle-readiness assessment was something she'd provided to her superiors countless times as a GRU officer.

Now, applying her own experience and understanding of the Russian soldier mentality, she ticked off her mental checklist.

At any given time, eighty percent of the base's seventy-four tanks would be operational, as well as twelve of the seventeen infantry fighting vehicles and ninety-two percent of the 148 armored personnel carriers.

Seventy-nine of the eighty-four artillery pieces could be brought to bear.

Fifteen of the eighteen MiG-29 fighters and all three batteries of the S-300 anti-aircraft missiles would also be good to go.

Preventive maintenance and parts procurement were not high priorities in the Russian army; however, what remained and qualified as battle-ready represented a formidable if not aging force to any foe.

The base's architects had chosen to cluster administrative offices and personnel housing together, farthest from the runways, at the opposite side of the base, and while this was understandable, it weakened base security. The Americans had learned that lesson the hard way in Pearl Harbor.

To the west rose enormous concrete pylons that each supported pairs of satellite dishes drawing shadows that eclipsed the paved service roads and the conical fuel drums behind them.

Another hundred meters back lay the electrified perimeter fence crowned with coils of barbed wire, motion detectors, and cameras, and connecting a string of guard towers manned by at least four personnel, two of which were snipers.

She counted ten towers. And those tiny pinpricks hovering between them were not birds; they were micro unmanned aerial vehicles providing secondary sets of eyes and ears to base security officers in the event the towers, main gate checkpoint, and secondary gate checkpoints were taken out. That the entire area could be observed from any number of the federation's spy satellites once they came into range was another fact she couldn't ignore. And while she couldn't see them, she knew there were more snipers' nests hidden in the mountains surrounding the base.

The Spetsnaz Guard Brigades underground headquarters complex was built into the cliffs in the southeast corner. A lone dirt road wove a tortuous path up the heavily forested mountain, ran for several kilometers along a treacherous cliff without guard rails, and terminated several hundred meters above the valley, where a pair of heavily reinforced blast doors on tracks had been constructed on the outside of the main cave entrance. A checkpoint manned by ten or more troops was situated just outside the doors and a smaller secondary entrance for pedestrians on the right side.

The HQ's security and relationship to the army base was a wild card and difficult to assess at this point. Were the Russian regulars and the Spetsnaz working together? Operations within and conducted by special forces were not shared with senior commanders on the base. She wondered if a single-prisoner escape would wind up on the network with those in the valley. Such an escape would be a huge embarrassment to the Spetsnaz. Perhaps their egos and commitment to compartmentalization would render them vulnerable.

Now that that was the old Snegurochka. Never giving up hope. Already plotting her escape despite the utter futility of it all.

Before she could scan the base any further, they lifted her into the back of an idling Ural-4320 6×6 truck whose flatbed was covered by an olive drab tarpaulin. That a few of their hands had found her ass was no mistake, the bastards. She grimaced at the stench of diesel fumes filling her nose as Gorelov levered himself inside and collapsed beside her.

"Welcome home," he said grimly.

With the rear tarp tied open, the truck lurched forward, and they left the tarmac, turning around toward the southeast and the mountains.

The president's jet turned and taxied away. She lifted her gaze farther out toward the fighters queued up outside a line of Quonset hangars whose curved roofs rose like speed bumps across the valley. Behind them hung a broad expanse of gray-bellied clouds promising afternoon snow.

Sensing his gaze on her, she turned to Gorelov and lifted her voice: "I wish you believed me about your wife."

"You think I'm that pathetic?"

"Obviously."

"Well, then, Colonel, you're a terrible judge of character,

which strikes me as odd, given your past. I always assumed you were a student of human psychology."

"More a study in . . ."

"You're finally right about something."

She hardened her tone. "Did you love your wife?"

"What kind of a question is that?"

"Did you?"

"I'm letting you talk because I find it amusing, but soon you'll be answering questions, not posing them."

"What do you want to know? Should I tell you about the nuclear accident in Estonia that wound up killing my husband and brother? Or about how the president helped administrators cover it all up? Should I give you the encryption code so you can read the documents and confirm that I've got irrefutable proof of this? Are these the kinds of questions you'll ask? Or would you like me to discuss all the illegal assassinations I've committed on behalf of your president? Or maybe how General Izotov ordered me to stage my own death and go underground to penetrate the Green Brigade Transnational?"

"Why are you saying all this?"

"Because we both know it's all bullshit. The only reason I'm here is that the president wants to make an example out of me, and when you see what they do, you need to decide if these people are your blood brothers, if this is what you call honor and duty and allegiance to the motherland . . . or are you just a spineless little man being directed by animals?"

He leaned in close and spoke through his teeth. "You can stay out of my head."

"I was just like you—brainwashed into thinking that their orders were always in the best interest of the federation. But they're not. Kapalkin worships money and power and nothing else. What he does is only in the best interests of his political cronies, not the country. Trust me on this. And watch what they do to me. You watch."

"I won't be around. I'm not your interrogator. I'm only in charge of your transfer."

"Then don't forget. Don't forget about me. General Izotov doesn't work for the motherland. And if I'm right, he's going to do what I never could. The government is going to collapse . . ."

"All right, no more crazy talk now, otherwise the gag."

She leaned in closer to him. "Please. Think about it."

He frowned and glanced away.

She took in a deep breath and tried to suppress the urge to rub her eyes. A moment later, the truck lurched and bounced as they left the paved road, with rooster tails of dust rising from the rear wheels.

For nearly thirty minutes they rumbled through dense forest, the grade increasing to nearly fifteen percent by the time they reached the cliff access, turned, and now wove their way parallel to the summit.

Within another fifteen minutes they neared the checkpoint. The truck stopped, and the Snow Maiden's pulse mounted as guards came around the back of the truck to inspect the cargo. She locked gazes with one man, whose jaw fell open.

Her likeness had circulated around the country . . .

around the globe, for that matter. Pictures with the long dark locks, then the spiked haircut, her face more curvaceous, then gaunt as she'd gone underground. Her skin once soft, now weathered and worn like the truck's tires.

She turned back to Gorelov. "Open my shackles. Let me run for it. Let them gun me down. Let me go out with some dignity."

"What about the men you killed back on Sakhalin Island—and all the others? Did they die with dignity?"

She pursed her lips.

The truck jerked forward, and the deep reverberations of the reinforced doors sliding open boomed across the mountain as they drove past them and into a long tunnel festooned by pipes, cables, air ducts, and other assorted electrical and plumbing equipment, along with strings of halogen lights. This was the two-lane passage to the headquarters' main entrance burrowed nearly half a kilometer into the mountainside.

The last time she'd been here she'd been sitting in the back of a Mercedes with General Izotov, and she trembled as she remembered the awkward sex they'd had in that backseat. He was a pig she had manipulated to get everything she wanted out of him, and the ploy had worked for a while.

While this was the Black Mountain, they were taking her to its darkest place, dubbed the "Deep Campus," where the prison and interrogation chambers were located.

Designed in a series of concentric circles through which ran a central elevator system with six separate lifts, the headquarters was nearly five hundred meters in diameter, with seven distinct levels: motor pool, command and control, intelligence, research and development, housing and hospital, weapons storage, and confinement and interrogation. The facility was designed to withstand a nuclear strike, bunker-buster bombs, and even a kinetic bombardment from the Joint Strike Force's "Rods from God," those telephone-pole-sized tungsten projectiles that wreaked total devastation by knifing through the atmosphere and slamming into the earth.

The headquarters was similar to the Americans' nuclear bunkers designed for their president and government officials. Walls of concrete and steel, along with the facility's tremendous depth, afforded it a high probability of survival, and the officers the Snow Maiden had met during her first visit had boasted about that. They'd be the future of the Russian government or even the future of the human race. She remembered thinking that if those arrogant warmongers were the future, then she didn't want to live.

The air grew colder as they neared the end of the tunnel, the truck stopped, and troops opened the tailgate and hopped out. Once again, they carried her off the truck and set her down, chains clanging as she followed Gorelov to the main lift doors with guards posted outside each, along with electronic eyes like the antennae of insects jutting from the ceiling.

Gorelov was accompanied by only two troops from the group now, the rest falling back to the truck. He placed his palm on a biometric security scanner, where his index finger was pricked for a blood sample, his pulse was taken, his retina scanned. Five seconds later, the lift doors hissed open, and they filed inside, the interior ten meters square, a service elevator used for moving heavy equipment.

Descending all the way down to level seven would take nearly sixty seconds, she remembered. After about thirty, she turned and faced the three men, their hands going for their sidearms.

She broke into laughter, feeling like a witch in the old-school chains and ready to enter a Salem, Massachusetts, courtroom. "What do you think I can do?"

Gorelov narrowed his gaze. "We know what you're capable of."

"Even with these chains?"

He nodded.

"I wanted to give you one last chance to release me."

Gorelov smirked. "Or what?"

"It's your conscience."

He leaned in toward her ear. "I think we can handle the guilt . . ."

"What did you say?"

He leaned in closer. "You heard me."

The Snow Maiden had not planned to bite off his earlobe.

It just happened.

She clamped down with her teeth, pulled back, and the lump of flesh tore off in her mouth, warm blood oozing.

He screamed and the guards moved in, literally throwing her across the elevator, where she hit the wall, tripped, and collapsed onto her side.

The lift doors opened. She rolled up and spat. The earlobe arced in the air and landed on the boots of a captain in full dress uniform who'd been waiting for a ride.

He looked down at his shoes, eyes widening. Then his gaze traveled from her to Gorelov and he screamed, "Get us a medic right now!"

TWENTY

Vladikavkaz
Capital City
Republic of North Ossetia–Alania
Russia

With trembling hands, Thomas Voeckler had left Grozny and traveled west on Highway M29 toward Vladikavkaz. He'd stopped once at a small petrol station to refuel the fifteen-year-old M-class Mercedes loaned to him by Rykov, a field operative he'd recruited in Grozny. For a few seconds while holding that pump nozzle, Voeckler had suffered a terrible flashback, reliving that moment when he'd looked into the Bear's eyes a second before the gun cracked. At that time, he'd been motivated by sheer anger, but now, with time to reflect, he had trouble believing what he'd done. George had always said the job was about gathering information, not murder.

The drive from one capital city to the next took just under an hour, but once he reached the outskirts, he noticed a military checkpoint set up on Highway P296, with early-morning commuters being stopped, inspected, and shown photographs. He slowed and called Third Echelon to verify. The news was not good. Checkpoints had been established at all the major roads leading in and out of the city, part of the military's operation to capture the downed pilot, no doubt.

They had the pilot's last known GPS coordinates, as provided to them by the Sixth Fleet tactical air commander. She'd landed in the mountains approximately thirty kilometers southwest of Vladikavkaz and northwest of Darial Gorge. She'd reported that she was moving northeast toward the city, following the mountain road IDed on Voeckler's computer as A301.

Another, much more comprehensive update appeared in his e-mail client, and Voeckler nearly ran his car off the road when he read the downed pilot's name: Major Stephanie Halverson, call sign "Siren."

There was reciprocity in the universe, and this proved it. Voeckler owed his life to this very woman. During their operation to capture the Snow Maiden, when he and George had been attached to that Ghost Recon team, they'd been pinned down by Russian Ka-65 Howlers near the Royal Military Academy in Sandhurst, just southwest of London. Halverson had swooped in, blown the shit out of those Russians in that chopper, and saved all of their lives.

Well, there it was. This wasn't a mission anymore. He was personally invested, and he gritted his teeth and vowed to bring her home. He would do whatever it took. Lines would be crossed. Damage would be done.

More bad news, though. Halverson was supposed to initiate something those fighter jocks called EE protocol and was supposed to update hcr GPS every two hours.

She'd contacted the tactical air commander only once. After that, her beacon had gone silent. She'd sent out a decoy drone, but intel indicated the Russians had already found and deactivated it.

A new text popped up on his smartphone:

THEY'RE IN THE BUILDING! COMING FOR ME! THEY
KNOW ABOUT THE CAR!

Voeckler pulled the Mercedes off the road and fired back a text to Rykov:

GET OUT OF THERE.

Something flashed in the rearview mirror. A car had pulled up behind him, doors opening, men getting out, reaching into the pockets of their long coats. He studied their faces: unshaven, a few deep scars, hard men who'd lived hard lives—men highly susceptible to recruitment in terrorist organizations, men whose "roadside assistance" consisted of a little air in the tires and a bullet to the head.

Voeckler threw the Mercedes in gear and screeched back onto the highway, barreling toward the checkpoint ahead. Two battered APCs parked in a V shape blocked the road. To the left lay a dirt path onto which two soldiers were waving the cars they'd already screened, with another pair holding rifles at the ready.

His heart racing, Voeckler neared the line of cars, five deep, and his pursuers rolled up behind him. Once more, doors opened, and the men got out, hands in their pockets.

He willed himself to remain calm, assess the situation.

Okay, two men, one driver.

He glanced at the soldiers. Two had broken off from the checkpoint, with one moving down the line of cars and another shouting for the men to return to their vehicle.

Voeckler clutched the wheel.

The soldiers rushed past Voeckler's car and confronted the two thugs. The taller one gesticulated wildly as he spoke, pointing several times at Voeckler's car. They were feeding this grunt some BS story in order to have Voeckler removed from his car and searched.

No problem. Voeckler had returned his gear pack to the dead drop in Grozny, so they wouldn't find any equipment that would betray his identity. His passport and paperwork for the car were perfect. He was unarmed, planning to gear up at the second dead drop in Vladikavkaz.

It was his word against theirs, and they were local thugs.

Bracing himself and taking in a long, hard breath, Voeckler suddenly climbed out of his car and marched back toward the group.

"Sir, these men are following me! I think they're going to rob me!" Voeckler cried.

"Get back in your car," ordered the soldier, a boy no more than twenty.

The other soldier, whose unshaven face showed signs of graying, lifted his voice and said, "They claim you stole this car from them."

"You can search me. I have all the paperwork for this car. And I'm unarmed." Voeckler pointed to their pockets. "What about them?"

The older soldier stepped back and leveled his rifle on the men, while the younger one ordered the driver out of the car.

The driver cursed and refused.

Eyes widening in fury, the young soldier began to scream and shove his rifle in the man's face.

The other two thugs began yelling, as did the older soldier.

Voeckler stopped breathing—

And he saw it happen in his mind's eye a second before it did:

The two thugs drew their pistols and shot the older soldier point-blank in the face.

As the younger one turned to them, they fired four more rounds, striking him in the face and neck, his gunfire going wild as he crashed onto the asphalt.

Voeckler was already coming around his car, ready to duck for cover, when the remaining two soldiers at the checkpoint ran forward, ducked behind Voeckler's car, and began trading fire with the thugs who'd charged behind their own vehicle. One slid forward and opened a rear door—

And that was when Voeckler saw his chance. He dove for his door, jumped into the still-idling car, threw it in gear, and rolled the wheel, steering himself out of line and barreling straight toward the unmanned roadblock. He rumbled down into the embankment, around the trucks, then floored it, racing back onto the road.

He stole a look in the mirror—just as the rear window shattered.

TWENTY-ONE

Ivanovskaya Square
Near the Kremlin Armory
Moscow

President Kapalkin ordered his security team to clear the area of tourists so that he and General Izotov could have a long moment to themselves.

Izotov greeted him with a firm handshake. "Good morning, Mr. President, it's good to be back, but I have to ask, why are we meeting here?" He lifted his hand and regarded the square with a frown, the dome and tall columns of the former Kremlin Senate building and now the president's home rising behind them.

Kapalkin did not answer. They walked a little farther, the skeletal trees to their left shuddering in the wind.

Finally, Kapalkin smiled tightly and paused near the poles and ornate chain fence encompassing the concrete pedestal and hulking form of the Tsar Cannon. Weighing nearly thirty-nine tons, it was the largest cannon in the world (though technically it was a stylized mortar because of the low ratio between its caliber and the length of its bronze-cast barrel). Eight brackets attached that massive, green-tinged barrel to a cast-iron gun carriage with reliefs of figured friezes, vegetation ornaments, memorial inscriptions, and an equestrian image of Tsar Feodor Ioannovich that complemented the rich ornamentation on the weapon's wheels. It was as much a work of art as it was a killing machine.

Before the cannon's pedestal sat four cast-iron projectiles stacked in a pyramid, each weighing one ton—too heavy for the cannon to have fired but interesting nonetheless.

Kapalkin ran his fingers over the cold chain, then suddenly clutched it. "I thought we should get some fresh air."

Izotov tugged at the collar of his woolen overcoat. "It's cold."

"I've had a chill in my bones for several days now," Kapalkin admitted.

"It'll pass."

"I hope so. How is your sister?"

"She's doing better now. Still a long journey ahead. The radiation treatments have been difficult."

Kapalkin had confirmed via his agents that Izotov had visited his sibling. "Sometimes the cure is worse than the disease."

The general nodded, his gaze lengthening in thought. "At least her children are grown now. She's been thankful for that. It's difficult to sit there and watch someone you've known your entire life begin to wither away . . ."

"I understand. I'll admit, though, that I was concerned because you didn't take your guards."

Izotov smiled. "I hate them." He seemed utterly calm and unreadable.

"I know, but the Euros and Americans have people trying to get to us every day—not to mention the terrorists, whether we're working with them or not. Your safety has to come first."

"Of course."

Kapalkin stared up at the cannon. He thought a moment, then said, "Sergei, I was thinking this morning that we've known each other for nearly thirty years now."

"Has it been that long?"

Kapalkin nodded. "You've always been my friend, even during these past few years, when our jobs have divided us."

"It's just politics. Nothing personal, right?"

They chuckled briefly, and then Kapalkin stared hard into the man's eyes. He gestured to the cannon. "I brought you here because yes, I wanted to get some air, but this is my favorite place in the Kremlin—and do you know why?"

"No."

"Because it reminds me of you. You've always been solid. Stable. Formidable. My big gun, as our enemies might say."

Izotov studied the cannon a moment, then faced him

and said, "Nothing's changed. I'm here for you, Mr. President. Whatever you need."

"I need you to submit to a full interrogation, including a polygraph exam."

For the first time in their conversation, Izotov reacted, but his frown seemed mild, almost forced. "Is this because of my leave?"

"It's because we've captured Snegurochka."

Again, Kapalkin expected a much larger reaction from the general—a burning hatred he knew was there; however, Izotov simply cocked a brow and said, "That's great news."

"Yes, but she's made accusations about you."

Izotov smirked. "She'll say anything now that we have her."

"I agree."

"But you don't trust me."

Kapalkin put a hand on the man's shoulder. "I don't trust our enemies. Perhaps they've gotten to you, and you don't even know it."

Izotov glanced up, his gaze now falling upon the secret police in their long black coats stationed around them, watching him. His tone hardened: "Mr. President, I'm at your service. I'll submit to any and all interrogations. My loyalty is unquestionable, and I'll prove that to you and to the interrogators. I don't know what that terrorist traitor has told you, but rest assured you can take my word over hers, as the director of the GRU, and as your friend."

"Of course. This is just a formality, but I would hope you would do the same, were you in my position."

"I would. And I'm hoping that after this is over, you'll allow me to question our prisoner myself."

"I cautioned you against a relationship with her, and now look what it's come to . . ."

"A mistake, yes. Let me make things right."

"No, I'll be questioning her."

"Where is she now?"

"Fort Levski."

"Why not here?"

"I sent her to the darkest hole I could find." Kapalkin turned away from the cannon and gestured to Izotov that they begin to walk. "What she did to us during the Canadian invasion is inexcusable, and she'll be punished for that—for everything."

"We're responsible," said Izotov.

Kapalkin froze. "What do you mean?"

"When I met her, she was a beautiful young woman. I think we just asked too much of her. We turned her into a succubus."

"Well, she's a demon, all right, a demon who bit the hand that fed her. We both had a special affinity for her. But that's over now."

Izotov nodded. "When do you leave?"

"I'm flying to Bulgaria this evening."

"Very well."

Kapalkin stopped as the security teams moved in. "Once again, Sergei, I'm sorry about this."

Izotov smiled, and a weird light came into his eyes. He strolled off with the security team as Kapalkin watched them go. He was about to leave, but then he chanced a final look back at the cannon.

A chill wove up his spine. He dismissed it and hurried back toward his office.

TWENTY-TWO

Seychelles Archipelago
East of Mainland Africa

Christopher Theron stood on the forward deck of his 370-foot-long motor yacht, *DreamRunner*. Life wasn't just good. It was damned near spectacular. In his hand was a warm mug of coffee made from Indonesian kopi luwak beans—the most expensive in the world. He took a long sip, then turned his head. Silhouette Island lay off to the west, with its five peaks jutting up into a powder blue horizon.

"Can I warm you up, Mr. Theron?"

He turned back toward his chief stewardess, Deborah, as curvaceous as the carafe she held. "Thank you, my dear, I'm fine." She beamed at him, then retreated as Theron sighed into the breeze. *Never sleep with the help.*

He enjoyed these moments alone on the yacht, from where he conducted all of his business, surrounded by his loyal crew of twelve. He'd personally interviewed and hired them from all over the world, stolen them from other crews to be honest, but now he'd assembled some of the most proficient stewardesses, deckhands, engineers, and chefs that money could buy. By treating them with the utmost respect and paying them nearly double what they'd earned at their previous jobs, he'd created a staff whose devotion was nothing short of remarkable. His captain and co-captain had been with him for more than ten years now, as had his bodyguards—two martial arts experts he'd found in the Philippines. They considered themselves a family—

The family he'd never had.

A long life of hard work to rise from his humble beginnings in that Cape Town orphanage had led to a level of success now fully alive before him, the yacht's sweeping lines and aft helipad representing the kind of power he'd only dreamed of as a child. He'd thrown parties for more than a hundred people on the yacht, and no one had ever felt cramped or less than pampered. His hardcover library had more than ten thousand volumes. His flat-screen televisions spanned entire walls. His dance floor had a glass roof and was situated below the swimming pool so while you were dancing, you could look up and admire all the bikini-clad mermaids. His chefs prepared meals found only in the world's finest five-star restaurants. He had people who did nothing else but scour the world, searching for the "very best" of everything and offering it to him.

But now, nearly two decades later and like other men

of his stature, he'd grown bored with his excesses. So when the war had begun, he was, like everyone else, appalled by the terrible loss of life and contamination of the Middle East oil supplies . . . but then, like many others, he began to see opportunity in the ashes. The Bilderberg Group had charged him with looking for ways to secure the entire Indian Ocean theater of operations— part of a much larger and more complicated effort to manipulate the Euros, the Americans, and the Russians to benefit the group's investments and long-term plans toward reestablishing stability. Seizing control of the *Ganjin* was Theron's first major step in accomplishing his task. The second step was to capture Ragland. He lifted his head, closed his eyes, and imagined thousands of hypersonic aircraft like manta rays streaking across the sky.

"I didn't hear you climb out of bed," Dennison said, sliding her arm across his shoulders.

"I didn't hear you come up behind," he answered with a shudder as he snapped open his eyes.

"You made me a spy."

"Yes, I did." He leaned in close and gave her a gentle kiss on the cheek.

She beamed, her nipples hardening beneath her white silk robe.

"What are you staring at?" she asked.

He grinned and gave her another kiss.

"So, when do I get a chance to show you what I've done?" She eyed him like a schoolgirl begging for attention.

He sighed. "Very soon."

"Good. I'm all ready on my end."

"So you've said."

"What about General Izotov?" she asked.

"They're going to interrogate him."

"Are you worried?"

"No."

She ran her hand down, beneath his own robe and across his chest. "Does anything ever bother you?"

"Yes, your hand."

"You don't like it?"

"I like it too much."

She wriggled her brows. "Good. But why do you seem so far away?"

"I'm still thinking about our problem."

Dennison's expression soured. *"Her."*

He shrugged.

"I should've killed the bitch when I had the chance."

"You never had the chance."

"Before you got there."

"You had orders."

She smiled. "I wanted to make you happy."

He put his hand on her cheek. "It's all right. We have Ragland. We have a pilot for the Wraith."

"And we have each other."

His smartphone vibrated: incoming message.

"Always the phone," she groaned.

"A necessary evil," he said, shoving his empty coffee cup into her hands. "I'll meet you below in a minute."

She reached down and flashed him her breast, glanced salaciously at him, then sashayed away.

He checked the phone. Encrypted message from Werner aboard the submarine. ETA: approximately twenty-one days. No issues thus far.

Just as he finished reading, a phone call came in from one of his operatives in Moscow.

"He's in the interrogation room now."

"Are you sure?"

"Yes, I'm the interrogator."

"Excellent. Where is she?"

"He says they've taken her to Fort Levski, the Spetsnaz headquarters there."

"We have a man there, don't we?"

"As a matter of fact, we do."

TWENTY-THREE

Mountains near Spetsnaz Headquarters
Fort Levski
Bulgaria

If he hadn't been deep in the heart of enemy territory, Lex would've better appreciated the rich, pine-scented beauty of the Balkan Mountains—from the heavily forested slopes with snow-brushed trees to the deep ravines drawing delicate lines across them. A pale-yellow sun filtered down through the gathering clouds to cast a thousand beams that coruscated from the army base's guard towers, comm dishes, and aircraft hangars.

A front was moving in, with heavy snow predicted before sunset. Leave it to the weather to tamper with an expertly planned rescue operation. Well, "expertly planned" was being generous. If the weather didn't cause an issue, something else would. Lex mused that he and his Raiders had long ago pissed off the gods by overstocking hell with fresh souls, and those immortals were still exacting their revenge, one mission at a time.

"Boss, I can't lie to you," Vlad began, beginning to shake his head. "We've pulled off some crazy shit in our day, but now that we're looking this devil in the face, I'm just gonna say it—this can't be done."

Lex shifted closer to the tree beneath which they'd established their forward observation post. He glanced up from his tablet computer. "They've got the place pretty well guarded," he said matter-of-factly.

"Are you kidding me? Our plans are shit. If it all goes south, we still don't have enough charges to blow those blast doors, they've got twice as many guards up there as we estimated, and the base is like Fort Knox. Plus they've got drones all over the fence line. I think we'd have a better chance of breaking into the White House and kidnapping the president . . ."

"Hey, you didn't like my idea of the officer's tour. We could've got all dressed up, with all the fanfare and fake IDs, and strolled around the place like VIPs. Maybe insult some of those bastards, check the dust on top of the computers, and generally bust their balls. Would've been good times . . ."

"Yeah, until one of us screwed up, said the wrong thing, and they'd already have us in their prison—"

"Which is why we're here, dressed like Spetsnaz grunts instead of the big boys."

Vlad sighed loudly for effect. "We don't need enemy uniforms or munitions. We need a miracle."

Slava crawled up on his hands and knees and scowled at Vlad. "Hey, Sergeant. I have some tissues if you want to cry."

"Hey, dude, this shit goes south, you're the biggest target we got."

"I welcome the fight."

Borya arrived at Lex's side, out of breath. He dropped to his hands and knees. "Coming in from the north is our best bet," he said. "Just mapped it out. Need to run camouflage all the way, though. Better slow than sorry, I guess."

Lex accepted Borya's tablet and studied the three-dimensional map drawn for them by the drone he'd sent forward to scout their path. The UAV had concealed itself by keeping tight to the trees and mimicking the passage of birds in the area, its heat source equally minimal. The locations of every Spetsnaz wireless security hub constructed within the trees was marked, along with the bunkers and snipers' nests. All positions matched those they'd pinpointed via their initial satellite photos. No surprises.

Yet.

"You take measurements on the blast doors and check them against our gear?" Lex asked.

"I did. We got about twenty meters to spare."

"Perfect."

"Security up top?"

"Sorry, boss, I was getting a little too close to those bunkers. I got a little nervous and pulled back before I could get a good look. Hopefully it's what we think."

"No worries. We'll scout it for ourselves when we get there. Let's get ready."

They all drew back from the tree, opened their gear packs, and withdrew their optical camouflage ponchos with attached hoods. The garments were constructed of a specially engineered metamaterial that mirrored the current operating environment. Fitted just behind the neck was the system's featherweight microprocessor that constantly read and interpreted the background, displaying a near-perfect image that concealed the operator; however, the system worked best when motionless and created a constant blur during movement as the microprocessor struggled to catch up. The faster you moved, the greater the blur, which was why Borya had remarked that they'd best wear the ponchos but move more slowly. Optical camouflage uniforms and blankets were first fielded by the JSF's Ghost Teams, then reached wider distribution to other special forces units like the Raiders.

As an added bonus, these newer ponchos had been fitted with an inner layer made of twenty rings of a material able to dissipate and channel heat to evade FLIR/thermal detection. This technology was based on principles of transformation optics and involved materials able to bend light around something rather than through it. Combine this brand of tech with the Raiders' reputed tenacity, and maybe they didn't need one of Vlad's miracles. Maybe all they needed were the guts to pull it off . . .

"All right. I need to update higher," Lex said, tugging free the satellite phone from his web gear. He plugged in the numbers, waited, then got the comm operator. They spoke in Russian. "This is Deep Raider Actual, over."

"Go ahead, Actual."

"Advancing on target area. Should be in position by eighteen hundred hours local, over."

"Roger that. Eighteen hundred hours. Relaying to Fleet QRF and Standoff Ops Command per your request, over."

"Roger. We'll check in again when in position. Deep Raider Actual, out."

"What're the chances of them picking up the signal?" asked Slava.

"Pretty good. But by the time they break the encryption code, we'll be having our second round of beers."

Slava flashed a crooked grin.

"Move out," Lex ordered.

The team left the tree, looking for all the world like four men made of water, their disembodied faces floating in midair and drawing Lex's grin. He put Slava on point, and he pulled up the rear, slipping down his situational awareness visor so the map overlay would appear in his head-up display. He marked their positions and all the contact points Borya had scouted.

They moved quite deliberately, pausing when they could between trees to allow the camouflage to grow steady. They would remain well outside the perimeter, meaning it would take them most of the day to reach the summit of the southeastern mountain overlooking the base.

After hiking for just fifteen minutes, Lex sensed something in the trees behind him.

He called for a halt, got down, and scanned the area with his binoculars. They'd begun to ascend a steeper part of the mountain where jagged seams of rock erupted randomly, with piles of talus and scree lying below them, the stones worn smooth by erosion.

Movement. He zoomed in.

Aw, shit . . .

"Mission brief only included that short paragraph on wildlife in the area," said Borya, lowering his voice and studying the mountainside with his own binoculars.

"What do we got? Yeti or sasquatch?" stage-whispered Slava, reaching into his web gear.

"No," Lex said. "Those guys already work for the Marines. These guys don't."

"How many you got?" asked Borya.

"I count five," said Lex with a groan.

"Me, too," Borya agreed. "*Canis lupus*. They look hungry."

"The hunting of men is better," said Slava, having a glance for himself. "But for now we hunt wolves."

Lex scanned the rest of the mountainside, then paused on a ledge, where all five gray wolves were staring back at him. "Look at that," he said. "They're stalking us. Careful not to come in too close. Not yet. Waiting for the right time."

"Maybe we can turn them into Marines, too, huh?" asked Slava.

The largest wolf began moving in slow, calculated

steps, its head lowered, eyes wide, shoulder blades visible. Its ears stood straight up. The others fell in behind it.

Slava came up beside Lex, who put out his arm to block the man. "Can't take the risk."

"We can't let 'em get closer."

"Our suppressors are too loud. The snipers down there will hear the clicks."

"Eaten alive by wolves," Vlad said, shaking his head beside Lex. "I didn't see this coming."

Slava drew his oversized Ka-Bar from its sheath, its surface coated black to avoid reflections. "Let's draw them in, then finish them."

"Oh, you think you can kill them quietly?" asked Vlad. "Dude, I've seen you in a fight. You are *loud*."

Lex sighed deeply in thought. "Enough." With a hand signal, he ordered the team forward.

"What's the plan?" asked Borya.

"Just watch them. And keep moving."

They shoved the Snow Maiden into the padded cell. She lay in utter darkness for a long moment . . .

Then she sat up and glanced around, waiting for her eyes to adjust.

Her breath vanished.

They finally had her. After all these years . . .

Before she could contemplate that further, the door whipped open and in came Gorelov, his ear bandaged, his fist raised high above his head.

She didn't flinch. "You taste good."

His swearing sounded more like a growl from a diseased animal as he dropped to his knees and was about to deliver a roundhouse.

What was he thinking? Had he lost too much blood? Had he suffered an acute and sudden case of amnesia? He'd forgotten who she was?

Time for his wake-up call.

She still had control of her knees, and before he could touch her, she slid around, tucked those knees into her chest, then booted him away with such force that he went staggering back, across the cell, toward the open door, where a silhouette appeared—

She didn't hear the Taser above all the screaming, but she writhed hard against the pain now coursing through her body, a knifing pain that struck sharply at first like a pair of daggers, then felt strangely numb around the edges, her muscles vibrating involuntarily, her teeth clenched. Even her hair seemed to hurt.

Her blood sugar was now being converted to lactic acid because her muscles were doing so much work. The charge was also disrupting the impulses that controlled her muscle movement, causing her to lose control of her body. She knew the science behind these Less Than Lethal (LTL) weapons quite well and had both employed them and been a victim of them before.

Experience didn't change that fact that it hurt like a bitch . . .

With her vision going blurry, she caught sight of another Spetsnaz officer in uniform, a lieutenant colonel with a white crew cut and eyebrows so fair and narrow that he resembled an albino. Behind him appeared two security men who dragged Gorelov out of the cell.

The lieutenant colonel got down on his haunches and stared at her for a moment. What might have been a smile seemed to rise from the deep plains of his face. "Colonel Viktoria Antsyforov."

He'd pronounced her name so slowly, so deliberately that it sounded as though he'd been rehearsing the moment all morning.

She grinned and demolished his expectations of her. "Who the fuck are you?"

A hand went to his mouth. "Please . . . let's be civil here. We're so thrilled to have you as our guest. Seriously."

"And I'm so happy to be here." Her eyes grew to the diameter of a madwoman's as she fought off the muscle spasms and lingering pain of the Taser.

"I'm Lieutenant Colonel Osin."

"Excellent. I outrank you. I now order you to become my bitch."

He ignored her and forged on: "I've just been put in charge of your well-being until the president gets here. Are you well?"

"I feel spectacular."

"Good—"

"But a word to the wise: You'd best not break your new toy until Daddy comes home."

He grinned. "I've always wanted to meet you."

"Well, now I'd like to meat you, too. But I spell that with an *A*. Go ahead, you think about it for a while."

"This must be disastrous for your ego."

"As was your last sexual experience."

He laughed under his breath. "You haven't lost your wit, but really, what happened to the great Snegurochka? Before you apparently died, they were still talking about some of your early missions . . ."

"So much for operational security."

"The Americans call you the world's most wanted woman."

"Did I misread that? I thought it was most desirable."

"Please, my dear, you're nothing to look at now. Ragged. Blood on your chin. Boots and bravado are all you have left."

"They're all I need."

He got to his feet. "Well then, Snow Maiden, you sit here and relish in past glories. You think about what's to come. I'm sure that will keep you entertained."

"I need a bathroom."

He considered that, then crossed to the exit. "I don't care." He slammed shut the door.

She screamed after him, then sat up, damning the jingling sound made by the chains—a sound that was driving her mad.

A shiver took hold. She hadn't been lying and really did need to relieve herself. She forced her legs together and clenched against the urge.

After about five minutes, a moment of weakness seized her, as it had during the jet ride, and she began to weep.

But then she stopped, listening intently to the faintest hum coming from the ceiling. She struggled to her feet, crossed to the cell's corner, and squinted up into the gloom, where the tiny camera swiveled down to face her.

She glared back.

TWENTY-FOUR

Outskirts of Vladikavkaz
Capital City
Republic of North Ossetia–Alania
Russia

Thomas Voeckler jerked the wheel and turned left, heading south, away from the city, past an extensive stretch of farmland and toward the mountains breaking through the morning fog.

There were only two men pursuing him now: the driver and one other thug who repeatedly hung out the passenger-side window and took potshots at him with an AK, aiming for his rear tires.

When the first tire blew out, Voeckler accelerated and saw what he had to do, steering wildly for a dirt path that vanished into the foothills.

The Mercedes limped its way across the gravel, then dug in deep, fishtailing across a looser section of rock, and then Voeckler came over a hump and the path leveled off. The car began to slide again, the flat tire flapping loudly. This joyride would end soon.

He squinted ahead, the path vanishing back down into a valley of pine and oak trees too narrow to permit a car. Well, there it was.

Voeckler didn't think about it. He immediately bailed out, hitting the ground and rolling as the Mercedes coasted down toward the trees.

He came up, darted across the path to be on the passenger side of the pursuing car, then hunkered down beside a tree, his hand itching for a pistol that was sitting back at the second dead drop in Vladikavkaz, the one he'd been forced to abandon because of the Bear and his cronies.

So here he was, Mr. Thomas Voeckler, a man who'd gone from scrub jobs to Splinter Cell operative, a man entrusted with hunting down America's enemies, a man who now had nothing but his bare hands to take on these men. He could grab a branch, a rock, perhaps even beat one of them to death with his shoe.

Then again, he could run, hide. But he had a mission, a pilot who needed him the way he'd needed her. That was priority. He couldn't keep looking over his shoulder. Not now.

The two Chechen idiots came rumbling up the path, and as they neared Voeckler's position—

He sprang at them, reaching into the open window and yanking the thug's AK-47 right out of his hands.

The driver floored it, racing down the mountain and realizing too late that he was rumbling straight for the rear of Voeckler's Mercedes, the car now wedged between two trees.

Voeckler sprinted after them, reaching the top of the rise and looking down as they made impact, the driver leaping out a few seconds before to stumble back and fire a few poorly aimed shots with a pistol, the rounds thumping off the trees to Voeckler's left.

The passenger forced open his door and turned back, lifting a pistol in Voeckler's direction.

Voeckler jammed down the AK's trigger, firing off a six-round burst that hammered the thug back into his door and down to the bed of pine needles.

Before he could swing his rifle toward the second thug, a much louder roar than either of their cars resounded from behind him, and he instinctively dove back into the trees, belly flopping onto the dirt.

With his knees and elbows sore from the impact, he came around a tree to spy one of the old APCs from the checkpoint.

Wait, no, it wasn't one of those but an Army 6×6 with an open flatbed carrying six troops that suddenly dismounted as the truck ground to a squealing halt.

That the remaining thug took on seven Russian troops was a testament to his supreme stupidity.

His pistol sounded like a barking poodle against the roar of the troops' AN-94s, those weapons shredding him and the car before he had time to scream or curse at them.

In the next breath, Voeckler warmed with relief.

In the following breath he panicked.

All he'd done was trade one set of bad guys for another, only their numbers had now tripled.

An officer shouted to the men to fan out and search the area.

The squad hustled off, leaving a kid of no more than eighteen behind the wheel to watch the truck. Voeckler waited until the troops had disappeared into the forest, until the shouts of orders had grown faint and the chirping of birds resumed. He braced himself, then left the tree, shifting around the truck, avoiding the side mirrors whose reflections would betray him. He'd slung the AK-47 over his shoulder and removed his belt.

He needed the truck. The driver stood in the way. Time to remove the obstacle. That was all he should have considered.

But this kid didn't deserve to die. He'd probably had a shitty life as it was, growing up in a war-torn nation, no video games or hooking up with hot girls or Burger King or 3-D movie players. He was driving a truck in the Army. Wasn't his fault he had terrible timing. Or maybe it was just his fate. Voeckler tightened the belt between his hands and drew closer.

He froze. Shit, he just couldn't do it. Sure, he needed a vehicle, but maybe one a little less conspicuous.

Did that really matter now?

For a second, he envisioned himself strangling the kid, listening to him gasp before he went limp in the seat. Voeckler trembled with indecision. Where was the ice-cold killer who had put a bullet in the Bear's head? Where was he now?

The door opened suddenly, and Voeckler dropped to the deck and shoved himself beneath the truck.

Breathing loudly, the kid marched over to the nearest tree, unzipped, and began to pee, groaning as the steam rose.

When he turned around, the expression on his face switched from utter contentment to wide-eyed shock.

Voeckler let go of the belt, reached back for the rifle, and waited—

As another troop marched up to the driver and began shouting at him for not manning the truck, for pissing like a dog on the tree, and for his general insubordination that had now earned him extreme punishment. Hazing or *dedovshchina* was still a huge problem in all branches of the Russian Federation military. Voeckler had recruited a young man as field agent who, after the mission, was conscripted in the Army and then had committed suicide because he couldn't bear the torture.

Consequently, this moment was entirely unsurprising to Voeckler. The other troop grabbed the driver by the neck and shoved him back against a tree, fishing into the kid's pockets with his other hand to produce a pack of smokes. He released the driver, and they both paused to each have a cigarette, suddenly best friends again, the entire assault staged by the troop who'd just wanted a smoke.

They stood, muttering to each other, laughing over something Voeckler couldn't quite hear.

A fairly loud humming erupted from Voeckler's chest.

Oh, no. His smartphone was tucked tightly into his

coat's inner breast pocket. He'd forgotten to turn off the vibration.

"Did you hear that?" asked the driver.

"No," said the other troop.

"Was that your phone?"

Another vibration. Voeckler reached into his pocket and switched off the device. Too late.

They started toward the truck.

Voeckler adjusted his grip on the AK. He held his breath. Waited. Their boots were right there, less than a meter away.

Neither man moved.

If they were speaking, they were mouthing their words so as not to alert Voeckler.

The banging in Voeckler's ears grew louder, his heart running wild, out of control.

He brought his teeth together . . .

And then . . . a face. The kid's. "He's here!"

Wincing, Voeckler shot him in the head, then kept on firing, hitting the other soldier in the legs until he could drag himself far enough out of the truck to finish the job, firing three more shots into the troop's chest before he could draw his sidearm.

Knowing he had the better part of fifteen seconds to get the hell out of there, Voeckler bounded for the cab, hopped in, and threw the truck into reverse, wheeling around in the clearing to maneuver the beast back onto the path.

Not a second after he straightened out the wheel, automatic weapons fire ripped across the 6×6's tailgate.

He checked the rearview mirror: The gunfire had come from the troop he'd just shot, the guy still alive and clutching his pistol with both hands. Voeckler cursed over his error: He should have collected their weapons before leaping into the truck.

Nothing he could do about that now, so he floored it and reached the road before any of the other troops could get a bead on him. He continued to head south, digging into his pocket for the smartphone and checking his messages. No update yet on the pilot. He was to proceed toward her last known coordinates, hoping to intercept her as she headed north toward the city. He needed to ditch the truck ASAP, but the farther south he headed, the more rural the landscape became, power lines vanishing, just a two-lane highway wandering deeper into the wilderness.

He checked his current GPS coordinates against Halverson's, saw he was about five kilometers northeast, and then searched ahead for a place to abandon the truck. Within a kilometer he saw an embankment to the right, pulled off, and realized he could send the truck down the hill, where it wouldn't be spotted from the road. After searching the cab for anything useful and grabbing a flashlight, along with an old Makarov and several extra magazines, he sent the old 6×6 on a bouncing roller-coaster ride into the dirt.

Satisfied, he took off jogging for the tree line. Once in he was tucked tightly into the undergrowth, he contacted Third Echelon and updated his status, requesting that the dead drop gear be airlifted to him in the mountains. They'd use a private chopper, and he'd home in on the gear bag's beacon. The request would be granted.

But no, he didn't want back up yet.

Yes, he would find her.

TWENTY-FIVE

Forgotten Army Weapons Depot
Caucasus Mountains
Near North Ossetia, Russia

There were no childhood traumas or father issues that haunted the dreams of Major Stephanie Halverson. No deep-rooted psychological neuroses that still required decades of therapy to resolve.

Instead, her nightmares were filled with visions of those she'd lost or had watched die, most of them from the Canadian invasion—Jake, the wingman she'd almost fallen in love with, lying there on the ice, she shoving a pistol into his hand, he assuring her he'd be all right. But then the nightmare would twist into the unreal, and he'd be screaming at her, accusing her of abandoning him.

Next to him stood a boy named Joey whose farmhouse Halverson had reached after ejecting. She'd sought help from the family, who in turn were killed by the

Russians, as was the boy—even after she'd tried to save him.

The dreams would come, yes, but she would force them away, remind herself that Jake died while keeping a promise to his country. That boy was victim of an invasion; she was not responsible for his death. These images were manifestations of her guilt, of the pain she felt over their loss, but she needed to move on with her life.

The nightmares always ended the same:

She would stand on that frozen lake where she'd been rescued, arms folded over her chest, looking at the decisions of her past—

Until the ice broke, and she plunged into the near-freezing water, struggling for breath . . .

Then closing her eyes and dying before she bolted awake.

She did it again. Cursed. Looked around. What the hell?

Was she awake yet? Or was she dreaming about having a nightmare?

No, this was real. The here and now. Her back hurt and her neck felt as though it'd been clamped in a vise. Her vision seemed to melt into something gray and blue, finally materializing into a chain-link fence, the cave, the cot, the ammunition on those metal shelves.

She remembered screaming for Brandenburg, balling her hands into fists and demanding to know exactly what they planned to do with her. Would they ransom her as she suspected?

She'd shouted for a few minutes, but Brandenburg

had ignored her. Then hours had passed. Aslan had not returned, and so Halverson had fallen back onto the cot, lying uncomfortably on her side, and had drifted off into that deeply troubled sleep.

She was about to rub grit from her eyes but instead cursed the zipper cuffs. Her wrists were sore now, probably bleeding.

Aslan finally returned with two bored-looking guards. His gaze instructed her to remain silent. She was too groggy to argue. He removed her cuffs, and next came the glorious relief of bringing her arms in front of her torso where they belonged. Now her shoulders protested. She sighed through the mixture of stiffness, pain, and relief.

"We have an area where you can clean up," he said. "Come with us."

"Thank you," she answered, her voice sounding younger, thinner, barely there.

He led her toward the back of the cave, down another tunnel and into another cavern where bright light and a sudden blast of icy wind had her lifting her palms toward the source: an exit to the surface wide enough to permit a car. To her right lay several four-wheel-drive pickup trucks, old beaters from the 1990s, their flatbeds covered by tarps. A third pickup was being loaded by four men transferring crates from a pallet balanced on a small forklift. She couldn't read the labels on those crates, but judging from their shape and size, she assumed they were rocket launchers or rifles.

Aslan continued toward the loading area and a

secondary tunnel within which stood, to her surprise, one of those tall, portable toilets, the kind used at country fairs and construction sites, the ones that smelled so inviting. Next to that abomination was a sink rescued from some blown-up apartment, its cabinet battered and scorched. A garden hose snaked down from a large water bottle suspended from the toilet and was draped into the sink. Indoor plumbing. A cracked mirror had been duct-taped to the side of the toilet for the men to shave.

"Five-star accommodations," she muttered.

The guards took up positions on either side of the tunnel, and Aslan escorted her toward the portable toilet. He flicked a glance over his shoulder and then shoved something into her hand—the satellite phone.

His eyes widened, he nodded emphatically, and then he turned back to the guards.

She stepped into the toilet, shut the door, and with trembling fingers, thumbed on the phone, opting this time to send a text and update her position. They were close to one of the exits, much closer to the surface, and she received two green bars indicating the phone had acquired a weak link to the satellite and was on the network.

But then she froze, realizing that Brandenburg and her people should be able to intercept the call—or at the very least discover that a satellite phone signal had been sent from their position.

Too late now. However, if Aslan had a plan to escape, they'd best act on it soon. Very soon.

"Neptune Command, this is Siren, over," she whispered.

"Go ahead, Siren."

"I'm in the mountains, captured by the Forgotten Army. They have a weapons depot in the caves, my current position. Send QRF if possible, over."

"Roger that, Siren. NSA has an agent in your area. He'll contact you."

"Thanks, just get me out of here. Siren, out."

A faint commotion outside began just as she pocketed the phone, then pushed open the door to find Aslan standing over one of the guards, pulling a knife out of the man's neck. The other guard lay beside him in a bloody heap.

"We're leaving now," he said curtly. "Did you contact your people?"

"Yes!"

"Are they coming?"

"I hope so . . ."

He held a remote detonator high enough for her to see, the LED burning green.

"What is that?"

"What do you think?" He slammed down his thumb. Red light.

She gaped as he faced the men still loading the pickup truck, lifted his arm, and now there was a pistol locked in his grip. He fired four rounds, dropping the entire team—

Just as a series of concussions rocked through the cave, followed by a much louder chorus of booms that began opening cracks in the cave's ceiling, with debris tumbling down.

At the same time, a much deeper rumble shook through the place, like the slow, low roll of a timpani drum, the reverberations finding their way into Halverson's chest. As she rushed to catch up with Aslan, two massive blasts, much closer than the others, had her screaming, "What did you do?"

He faced her and pointed to the lead pickup truck. "Get in there, now!"

Four more men came running into the tunnel, but Aslan was already swinging up a rifle snatched from one of his victims. He jammed down the trigger—even as they returned fire.

The cave behind them collapsed with a hissing of dust and booming of rock smashing down, layer upon layer, as even more significant thunder shook the entire mountain, the ground feeling spongy and unstable.

Halverson glanced up, just as a massive chunk of stone dropped not two meters away from the truck. She climbed into the cab as Aslan ripped open the door, hopped in, and seized the key, starting the truck and throwing it in gear before he even shut his door.

"I thought I was supposed to help," she said, dumbfounded. "Looks like you got it figured out!"

"I'll try to get us off the mountain, but she has spotters everywhere. They'll know where we are. We won't last long without your help."

"We should've gone at night."

"No time. They were planning to move you."

"Well, it is what it is . . ."

Aslan steered them toward the cave exit, rolling straight up a rocky road that spilled into the forest. She stole a look back, where she noticed several sets of camouflage netting rolled up but used to conceal the exit from gunships. The maw between those nets was exhaling dense clouds of smoke and dust.

"For the past month I've been wiring the entire place to blow," Aslan said, his voice still shaky. "Then you came. And I knew the time was right."

"Why?"

"Because our message has been lost. And because I am my father's son."

Halverson checked the side-view mirror, where billowing black smoke formed a long chute that began rising high above the mountain, like an old Wild West smoke signal beckoning everyone and his mother to come over and have a look at the Chechen and American pilot trying to escape. "Oh, God, you really did it, didn't you . . ."

Aslan smiled grimly. "Why not?"

She dragged her palms across her face. "We could've done this quietly. You turned it into a fiasco. And you destroyed property that belonged to the United States."

"You don't understand what they planned to do with those weapons. You don't know how many people I just saved."

"Well, here's hoping you add two more to the list."

Just ahead lay a tree with a black band tied around the trunk. Aslan took a hard left, and they rumbled across a dry riverbed, bouncing over the rocks.

After a moment, she blurted out, "I'm sorry."

"Look, I don't expect you to get it. Just listen to me. She'll assume we'll take one of the shipping trails. We won't. It's going to get a little bumpy."

"You think she's still alive?"

"I couldn't plant a charge in her quarters, but I've been slowly poisoning her. I thought she'd be dead by now."

"Oh, this just keeps getting better."

"Shut up and listen to me. She has six observation posts on the mountain. Two men in each. They'll come after us."

"How? We blew up the trucks, right?"

He took a deep breath, stole a look over his shoulder. "Shit, here they are."

She checked the mirror. Two men on dirt bikes with rifles slung over their shoulders came flying up and over a rise, both airborne for a second, engines buzzing before slamming hard onto the riverbed. The lead man's rear tire spun out for a second before he recovered and accelerated, his partner falling in behind him.

"Shit, Aslan, if you knew they were coming, why didn't you hook us up with more rifles and grenades?"

"I did my best in the time I had. The charges were more powerful than I thought . . . Now get to work!" He shoved the rifle into her hands.

She braced herself, then guided the AK through the open window and hung outside, arm braced across the doorsill, trying to level the gun on the lead biker.

Seeing this, he suddenly broke right, leaving his

colleague vulnerable. Halverson slammed down the trigger—just as the truck rebounded over a rut and her bead went wide, shredding pinecones that showered the riverbed.

She swore and shouted for Aslan to find a more level path, even as the lead biker now came up alongside them, checking the trail, gripping the handlebars with one hand, then reaching into his hip holster to draw his pistol.

But Aslan was faster, shoving his own pistol toward the man and firing four rounds, one of which hit the biker in the neck, and suddenly he had both hands on the wound and lost control, falling backward off the bike like a surfer being crushed by a wave. The motorcycle twisted forward, then dropped and launched into the air, boomeranging across the trail to smash into a tree and snap in half.

"Nice! One more!" shouted Halverson.

"Three more!" he corrected.

She craned her neck. "God damn it!"

Another pair had joined the party, and Halverson shoved herself a little farther outside the truck, balancing precariously on the window. Her teeth set in exertion, she lifted the rifle once more, fighting for a clean shot.

The moment she opened fire, all three bikers scattered, the first two veering right, the third swinging left. She kept her bead on that third one and got him—two rounds to the shoulder that punched him off the bike. If the bullets didn't kill him, the fall had, his bare head rebounding off the stones.

Her satellite phone vibrated in her pocket, and she pulled herself back inside and answered.

"Major Halverson?"

"Yeah, who is this?"

"My name's Thomas Voeckler. They sent me to get you out."

"Where are you?"

"Just north. Uploading my GPS now."

"You got an APC? A gunship? What do you got?"

Voeckler wasn't sure how to answer Major Halverson as he crouched near the pair of pines, smelling the fires and spotting the black smoke coiling up over the treetops. What was going on up there?

He winced and replied, "Uh, right now, it's just me, but I'll get you out of there!"

"Just you? Jesus Christ, we're in a truck, heading down the mountain. Got three guys on dirt bikes following. I hope you're heavily armed!"

Voeckler eyed the Makarov in his other hand, thought of the AK slung over his shoulder. "Yeah, okay. Right. What's with the fire?"

"Forgotten Army had a weapons cache up there. We blew the shit out of it!"

A chill struck hard across his shoulders. "You did what?"

"We blew it up!"

He closed his eyes. "Are you kidding me? I've been trying to locate that cache!"

"Well, I found it. We'll link up with you shortly. Halverson, out!"

Voeckler couldn't believe what he'd just heard. After all his hard work, Halverson had unwittingly accomplished his mission. What kind of cruel fate was that?

Then again, he'd head back to Langley with two feathers in his cap instead of one. The Bear's smuggling operation was gone, as was the man. All Voeckler needed to do now was smuggle Halverson out of the county.

The thrumming of gunships sent his gaze skyward, through the canopy—

And there they were, a mechanized flock of three Mi-24s with camouflage-pattern fuselages, each carrying at least eight troops determined to ruin his day.

TWENTY-SIX

Mountains near Spetsnaz Headquarters
Fort Levski
Bulgaria

The wolves were still tracking Lex and his men, the hunters now the hunted, and Lex was concerned about the team's attention being divided between the enemy sniper and observation posts and the hungry pack behind them.

As they moved into a much denser stretch of forest, with the nearest Spetsnaz sniper's nest some thirty meters below, Lex called for a halt and gathered the team. "Gentlemen, when in combat they say the best medicine is fire superiority."

"Hell, yeah," said Borya.

"Well, that old saying gets me thinking—"

"About fire superiority?" asked Slava. "Because all you gotta do, boss, is give the order."

"No, big guy, I'm talking about medicine."

"Boss, can we talk instead about the wolves?" asked Vlad.

"We are," said Lex. "Here's the deal. We each have an MRE, right?"

They nodded, and Slava tapped his pack where his Meal, Ready to Eat was stored. The packaged high-carb, high-calorie entreé and dessert were the lifesaver of many combatants. Admittedly, MREs were hardly gourmet restaurant food, but the military had come a long way in improving the taste and nutritional value of grunt chow, keeping warriors fueled and alive when the op sent them thousands of miles away from the nearest Pizza Hut or Mickey D's.

Lex went on: "So we have our MREs, and we also have some nitro, epi, and morphine in our med packs."

Borya grinned crookedly. "I like it, boss. We inject the pain meds into the food, leave it behind as bait for the wolves, they eat the stuff and get all loopy. Nice."

"That sounds great. Except for one problem—"

They all faced Vlad, who added, "If we blow all our food and drugs on them, what happens if one of us gets hit?"

"We take it like a man," said Slava.

Vlad's tone hardened. "I'm serious. We need those drugs."

As Lex thought about Vlad's concerns, Borya tossed out another question:

"Hey, boss, what if the drugs kill the wolves?"

"You're going to worry about that?" asked Slava.

"Look, I'm an animal lover," Lex said. "I hang out

with you smelly bastards, right? But this is a chance we'll have to take. It's them or us. I don't think we'll kill 'em, though. I think we'll be able to lose them. Vlad, tell you what. You give us your MRE, but you hang on to your pain meds for the team. Good compromise?"

He nodded.

"Then let's get to work."

They gathered up the MREs, tore open the packets, and began injecting the meat loaf, garlic herb chicken, and boneless pork ribs with the various medications. They even shoved in some aspirins and acetaminophen for good measure.

"Spread out the packets," Lex instructed. "We don't want the dominant male eating everything."

"Boss, what if this just whips them into a frenzy?" asked Vlad.

"Then one of us will have to sacrifice himself for the team," Lex said, gesturing for them to move out.

While he didn't look back, he imagined Vlad's expression and how the sergeant was shaking his head.

"Keep on keeping us honest," Lex called back to him.

An abrupt rustling from behind had Borya waving them forward and mouthing, *"Here they come!"*

They jogged away toward the next cluster of trees, their breaths even heavier in the deeper shade, the ground turning harder. They ducked and faced the area where they'd left the bait.

One by one the wolves entered, then darted straight for the packets, two of them fighting over one pack while the others dropped to all fours and ate.

"Let's get the hell out of here," Lex said, giving Borya a hand signal to take point.

Lex fell in behind his assistant, thumping hard and fast through the forest, the pine needles and stones grinding under his feet. He nearly lost it on a patch of ice and began to fall backward, but Slava's forearm was there, driving him up to catch his balance.

"Whoa, thanks," Lex said.

"You're getting old, boss."

"No, just a boot malfunction."

"Oh, okay," Slava answered, chuckling through his reply.

"Hey, that looks good," Lex said, pointing to a depression in the mountainside beneath a narrow ridge. The south side of the ridge was piled high with ice and snow, forming a natural lean-to. "We'll hole up there and send out the drone."

"Sounds good," said Slava, hustling up ahead of Lex.

Once the team slipped into the cover of the depression, Borya reached into a hip holster. He withdrew the UAV and tossed it away like a Frisbee, its quadrotors automatically firing up to launch it through the trees. The remote/touch screen attached to his left forearm showed two camera images, along with a third box displaying a map overlay of the drone's course and the previously marked enemy positions.

"Send it back to the wolves," said Lex.

"En route," answered Borya.

They watched as the UAV flitted around the branches, using a combination of Borya's input and obstacle sensors so that if Borya took his finger off the touch screen, the drone would switch to autopilot and maneuver itself, deftly avoiding the three-dimensional gauntlet of canopy.

Two of the wolves were lying down, their limbs twitching involuntarily.

"Feeling no pain now," Lex remarked.

Borya shifted the UAV up for a wider shot, but none of the others were visible.

"Where they'd go?" asked Lex.

"Uh, boss?" called Vlad. "We got a problem."

Lex turned his head to come face-to-face with three of the wolves, no more than five, six meters away. They'd come around the snowbank to ambush the team, the largest one lowering his head, baring his teeth, and beginning to growl . . .

"You were worried about killing them?" Slava asked Borya. The burly man reached back and drew his knife. "This will not be pretty."

Four men abruptly entered the Snow Maiden's cell. She glanced up through the blinding shaft of light coming in from the open cell door. It took a moment, but they finally came into full view: three baby-faced guards who gaped at her like she was a Hollywood celebrity, along with an older man dressed in a black uniform. A thick shock of gray hair, along with a closely cropped beard seemed unfamiliar to her, but his eyes . . . there was something about his eyes.

"We've been ordered to clean you up," he said, a trace of sadness in his tone.

"And how do you feel about that?"

"If it were up to me, you would be drugged, docile. But the president wants you untouched. No drugs, no more Taser, nothing. So . . . either you will cooperate and enjoy a hot shower, perhaps your last, or we'll simply leave you in here." He sniffed several times and grimaced. "You've soiled yourself. It's disgusting. Wouldn't you like to clean up?"

"Yes."

"Then you'll come with us? Willingly? Quietly?"

She nodded, her gaze flicking to the Tasers clutched in the hands of the other three. "But why are they armed if you're not going to hurt me?"

"They won't be used, but if their lives are endangered, we'll have no choice."

"You'll have to answer to the president for that."

"And I will. But let's not go there. Let's be civilized."

His smile was weak, pathetic really, but it was the first time in a very long while that anyone had showed even a modicum of kindness. "I'm ready," she said.

Two of them helped her to her feet, and she followed the old man out through the door, the awestruck guards pulling up the rear. She'd been too distracted to get a good look at the curving hallway outside the cell when they'd brought her here, so now it was time to refresh her memory and draw the mental map.

The walls were constructed of heavy concrete buffed

smooth and painted gray, the ceiling crisscrossed by pipes, with banks of LED lights glowing along the corners. Not much effort had been made to make the facility aesthetically pleasing; it was all pure function, like the bowels of a Russian tank or submarine.

She counted twenty-five footsteps to the next door, where a guard placed his hand on the biometric control station mounted to the wall, and the door clunked open.

Inside was a large shower and toilet area, the tile an industrial white that left her squinting. The old man shoved a heavy key into her shackles, opening the ankles first, then moving up to the wrists.

"Now, this is the moment where you try to escape, and if you do, you sacrifice the shower, and I take you back there to wallow in your own piss."

"Where would I run?" she asked.

"Exactly. Now, while you're here, you will be watched." He gestured to the cameras hidden behind black domes on the ceiling. "Over there, you'll find a bar of soap and a towel. Please don't try to kill yourself or do anything else. A clean prisoner's uniform is in the locker to your left."

"Are you religious?" she suddenly asked him.

"That's none of your business."

"Will God forgive you for your sins?"

"What're you talking about?"

"I've been through a lot. I've been having trouble remembering people, places. I didn't recognize you at first, but now it's come to me."

"Just take your shower." He turned abruptly and slammed the door behind her.

His name was Dr. Anton Halitov, a medical doctor and chief interrogator for the Spetsnaz for more than twenty years. They called this place the Black Mountain primarily because of him. They said he'd tortured more than a thousand prisoners. They said he'd extracted information from JSF captives when no one else could. He'd even managed to turn the leaders of several Middle East terror groups against each other.

Expert on pain. Delivering and relieving.

But this man, who'd spent countless hours listening to human suffering while turning cold eyes away from the agony he created, this man who some claimed had turned torture into an art form because of his success rate, had changed. His voice was different. The gray hair and beard were new. He seemed broken. The titanium box that protected his heart had been smashed open. He felt something.

And that intrigued her.

Wincing, she slid off her blouse and pants and pried her feet out of the boots. She realized there was no way to avoid the cameras and simply ignored them, prying off her panties and grimacing as she let them fall to the tile. She moved quickly to the showerhead, turned on the water, and waited. The warm spray finally came, grew hot, and she groaned as she began washing her battered body. There were too many new bruises to count, and the places that ached far outnumbered the ones that didn't. She frowned as she took in each new wound, trying to remember where she might have acquired it: The fight back at the refinery? The chase through the woods? The struggle when they'd finally wrestled her into the shackles?

Still clutching the bar of soap, she collapsed on her rump, pulled her knees into her chest, and sat there in the spray, realizing that Halitov was probably right: This would be the last shower of her life.

And now she ached for something much greater than the physical relief. She wanted to let God know that it was okay, that she understood she would burn in the fires of hell and that he shouldn't feel guilty about that. Lying to him now about being repentant, about how she really did deserve a second chance, would only prove how selfish and pathetic she really was, and so she would face the end bravely, admitting her wrongdoing, accepting the punishment, and understanding that there was no reason to weep.

The snow melted, but every year it would return.

Deep down, though, there was one regret, a longing that scared her to the core, one she kept repressed because she knew it would weaken her.

She wept again, damn it, then gave up, surrendered to the feeling and fully admitted it to herself. If only she could have shared her blood, brought a child into the world, taught her how to be a woman—

If only there were someone who would remember her. With love.

* * *

From his desk terminal on level one in the command-and-control center, Lieutenant Colonel Viktor Osin watched the Snow Maiden huddling in the shower.

He'd already reported her arrival to Christopher Theron, using his skills as a signals and intelligence officer to encrypt and conceal his transmission to the man. That signal report had just earned him enough money to retire early, and his next one, updating Theron on the woman's status, would ensure that said retirement would be lavish. Absolutely lavish. His earlier work for the Bilderberg Group had been lucrative; however, Theron and his associates were, according to the rumors, making big plans and paying operatives double for their efforts. Osin was grateful he'd been contacted all those years ago and gone to work for these people. He was not a peon, cog in the wheel, or simple statistic for the Russian military. He was his own man, and he'd exploited his position and intellect to secure himself a life the government would never provide him.

After all, if he hadn't been working for the group since he was a junior officer, he would have wound up like the Snow Maiden, turning openly on them, then captured, tortured, and murdered.

It was sad, really, what they'd do to her. She'd been a proud and terribly efficient officer, better than he ever was. His stint with the GRU as an operative had lasted no more than a year before he'd been forced back into the Spetsnaz to play with computers instead of guns.

She had some long legs, this Snow Maiden, this rogue spy that the president wanted protected. He longed to go down there now and have his way with her, listen to her curse him in that smoky, contralto voice, feel her scratch his back.

He shuddered and switched off the feed as the next message reached his tablet computer.

Theron was calling for his update?

No, this was a report from North Ossetia, from the mountains where Brandenburg was directing the arms shipments. His eyes widened as he read the news.

TWENTY-SEVEN

**Forgotten Army Weapons Depot
Caucasus Mountains
Near North Ossetia, Russia**

Halverson's gunfire ricocheted off the dirt bike's engine before she finally struck the driver in the left leg.

But this only enraged him. He sped up, bringing his bike less than a meter from the tailgate, then reached for his holster and came up with his pistol.

Before she could shoot him, rounds pinged off the windowsill and door, driving her back into the cab as another of the three bikers still pursuing them freed his sidearm and cut loose.

"You have an automatic rifle," cried Aslan, keeping a white-knuckled grip on the wheel. "Can you please kill those bastards!"

"I'm trying!" She turned back, leaned once more out the window, and opened fire, her bead sweeping from left to right to finally make contact, booting one of the bikers off his ride, the engine racing before the machine spun and crashed into the rocks.

"Got him!"

"That's a start," Aslan grunted.

Cursing him under her breath, Halverson ejected a magazine and drove a fresh one home. She chambered a round, held her breath, then three, two, one, she was hanging back outside the truck, screaming to gain more courage and firing madly, intent on emptying the mag into these two fools.

It was glorious. The first biker swallowed her incoming and toppled sideways, forcing his partner to drive right over him and get thrown from his bike in a surreal arc like a Hollywood stuntman who gaped as he realized his inflatable mattress had been removed. He hit the riverbed and rolled, limbs snapping and twisting at weird angles, the trauma lost in a dust cloud wafting up from the truck's rear wheels.

As she ducked back into the truck, she heard both her phone ringing and the whomping of helicopters. "That's my QRF," she shouted to Aslan.

"Your what?"

"Quick Reaction Force. Help's on the way!"

He glanced up through the windshield. "I don't think so."

She did likewise. Mi-24s. Was the QRF flying undercover in Russian helos? If so, why wasn't she notified? With those questions still hanging, she answered the phone, the voice on the other end sounding breathless:

"It's Voeckler. I'm at the bottom of the hill. I can see you coming down. I'm on your right side."

"Do you see the choppers?"

"Yeah."

"Are they ours?"

"Negative."

"Shit!"

"Just pick me up!"

"So we're saving *you*, huh?"

He'd already hung up. She swore as the Mi-24s passed overhead, moving back toward the mountain—

But then one broke off, banking hard to come back for them. "Oh, man, you'd better hurry," she cried.

"Three more choppers," Aslan said stoically, stealing a quick look through his open window and cocking his thumb skyward. "This is . . . this is maybe what I thought would happen . . ."

"So that's it?"

He faced her. "I'm a Chechen. It's not over." With that he brought the truck up beside Voeckler, pulled to a halt, and began to open his door.

"Why are you getting out?" Halverson demanded.

"Yeah, why?" added Voeckler, his shaggy hair and scruffy beard covered in dirt.

Aslan left the cab and crossed to the truck's tailgate, where he began unbuttoning the tarp covering the flatbed.

Halverson stormed out of the cab and was a half second away from screaming at him—

When she caught a glimpse of what was lying beneath that tarp. "Holy shit. Bathing suits? Really?"

He snorted. "I wasn't totally unprepared."

"You have Javelins?" asked Voeckler, his mouth falling open as he, too, stared slack-jawed at the two crates of launchers. "Wait, did these come from the mountain? If they did, then they're evidence, and we can't—"

"The hell we can't," said Aslan. "You either help or run—because if we don't take out those choppers, our story ends here."

Voeckler didn't waste time mulling that over. One look back at the Mi-24s was all the convincing he needed. He hopped up onto the flatbed. "Okay, let me ask you something, asshole, whoever you are, have you ever fired one of these?"

Aslan scowled at him. "What do you think?"

Voeckler looked to Halverson. "What about you?"

"I'm a fighter pilot. We don't play with missiles that small."

He smirked and began opening one of the crates. "Better move our asses. The refrigeration component has to cool the system to get the thermal views online. Takes thirty seconds or more. Might take less time in this cold . . ."

"Fifteen seconds," said Aslan. "We've already tested."

"I see I'm in good hands," Halverson said, now helping Voeckler open the crate. "I didn't know you spies got to play with this stuff."

"We train with all kinds of toys when we're hanging out at Fort Benning. Oh, and before I forget, thanks."

"For what?"

"Nothing much. Just saving my life. Sandhurst. Ghost Team. Russian Ka-65 . . . ring a bell?"

"You were down there?"

"Hell, yeah, I was. Come to return the favor."

"Well, goddamn, Mr. Voeckler, I'm impressed."

He gave her the once-over with wolf's eyes. "So am I."

Her snort sent him hopping down from the truck. He hoisted the big launcher onto his shoulder.

Aslan took up a position on the other side of the truck, the launcher appearing like a dumbbell lying across his shoulder.

"Back blast is minimal," said Voeckler. "But if I were you, I'd get behind those trees."

As Halverson ran toward the trees he'd indicated with his thumb, Aslan shouted, "Here they come. Line of sight. Remember!"

The booming of both helicopters and rotor wash tearing across the trees like multiple tornadoes drove Halverson down to her knees, shielding her eyes—

And in the next breath, she heard the missiles fire, one after the other, the flashes and hiss rising above the intense rotor wash.

While the Javelin was primarily deployed as an anti-tank missile, able to launch straight up and make a top-down attack on armored vehicles, hitting them where they were most vulnerable, the system could also be set for direct-attack mode against hardened targets and airborne threats.

Halverson followed the contrails, squinting now in

the direction of the choppers, just as the HEAT war-heads exploded, their shaped charges creating streams of superplastically deformed metal formed from trumpet-shaped metallic liners. This high velocity particle stream easily penetrated the Mi-24s' fuselages and detonated in clouds of blazing debris—tail rotors sheared off, canopies bursting outward, flaming bodies tumbling across the sky—

While the thunderclaps of the explosions echoed over the mountainside. Next came fireballs as their fuel tanks ignited, both helos drawing red-orange slash marks across the sky as they plunged. The next gust of wind brought the stench of the explosions to Halverson, the burning rubber, melting glass, and flaming fuel coming in a blast wave.

Then, in the distance, the chaotic drumming of debris crashing down through the trees began, thousands of chopper parts falling in a hailstorm, along with the larger sections of fuselage that barreled through the trees, shredding limbs and branches and ka-thudding with secondary explosions across the forest floor.

Aslan and Voeckler threw their empty launchers onto the ground, and Halverson sprang from the trees and joined them—all three leaping back into the cab.

"Two for two," said Voeckler, baring his teeth.

"Still one more back there," said Aslan. "But he's turning tail now, heading back to the mountain!"

"Thank God," said Halverson.

"Get us back down to the highway," Voeckler told Aslan.

The Chechen recoiled. "Are you crazy? We'll be in plain sight."

"No," said Voeckler. "My contacts will be waiting for us. You've made a really loud and really unfortunate exit, but I'm going to make sure we do the rest of this quietly." He put a finger to his lips.

"Good luck with that," said Aslan.

"What about my QRF?" Halverson asked Voeckler.

"I think they've been trying to keep your spirits up," he said. "According to my intel, I'm the only rescue you got. They can't send in any air assets. Way too risky."

"Bullshit." She got back on the satellite phone, but Voeckler tore the phone from her hands.

"Forget it," he said. "Listen to me. I'm here to get you out."

"How?"

"Trust me."

She tipped her head toward Aslan. "What about him? He saved me back there."

"Hey, you can come," Voeckler told Aslan. "In exchange for information, right?"

The Chechen made a face. "I know how the game is played. Everyone has a price."

"Oh, I'm not playing any games," said Voeckler. "If you say no, I shoot you in the head. That's how I define operational security. And if you don't believe me, you can go back to Grozny and talk to your friend the Bear. He might not say much with that bullet in his head."

"You killed him?" asked Aslan, sounding half-surprised, half-impressed.

"It wasn't the plan. But he wasn't very cooperative."

"I see. Well, if I don't have a choice here, then why bother asking?"

"Thought I'd be polite."

"Well, that's nice of you. I'll seek political asylum in the United States. I'll get that in exchange for information."

"That's your deal. I can't make any promises. You come along, you don't give us any trouble, and I'm okay with it."

"I'll vouch for him," said Halverson, but then she faced him and said, "Are you sure you want to leave your country? You might never come back."

"I can't stay here anymore. They'll find me."

"As long as you're sure," said Halverson. "Now how far to the road?"

"From here? About fifteen minutes," he said.

Voeckler began typing furiously on his smartphone. "Okay, okay, I've pulled off a real long shot here, but I think it'll all work out."

"What?" she demanded.

"You'll see in fifteen minutes. But right now, I have bad news. We need to ditch the truck. Too big a heat source. We hike the rest of the way on foot."

"I knew you were going to say that," said Aslan. He pulled over, and they all climbed out. Halverson gathered up the remaining ammo and rifle.

"This way," said Aslan. But suddenly he froze and shaded his brow from the sun—

Just as a pair of fighter jets soared across the sky, toward the mountain.

Halverson studied them intently. "Interceptors. Not ours. Javelins must've instigated them."

Voeckler cocked a thumb over his shoulder. "Let's go."

The hike took nearly an hour, with more air traffic screaming overhead and sending Halverson's pulse racing.

As they neared the paved highway, visible now through an uneven fence of trees and underbrush, Voeckler paused to fire off several texts on his smartphone, then instructed them to wait. Aslan ventured off toward a few trees to relieve himself. Halverson took the opportunity to speak privately with Voeckler:

"He's a good guy, really. Born into a terrible situation. We can help him."

"I don't care. My job is to get you out. He comes, he comes . . ."

"Where are we going?"

"Back to the city. To the airport. We need to move fast." Voeckler checked his phone again. "They're here."

He started forward toward the trees, and she followed. "You better wait for a minute," he said.

"I thought these guys were friends."

"Uh, yeah, let's be sure." He took off.

Aslan came up at her shoulder. "What's happening?"

"His contacts are down on the road. He's checking them out first . . ."

"Do you trust this man?"

"Why wouldn't I?"

"There's something about him. He's an operative for your country, but he seems out of place in the job."

"You get that, too, huh?"

He nodded, then released a loud sigh. "Me, on the other hand, I look and act like a terrorist."

"I wasn't going to say that."

"You didn't have to."

Voeckler appeared ahead, waving them on. They jogged after him, then slowed to descend a rocky foothill toward the road whose paved surface and dotted lines seemed strange after spending so many hours in the dense forest. Off in the embankment idled two white cars with blue stripes and overhead lights, police units to be sure, with Cyrillic insignia painted across their hoods and doors.

"Well, what do you think of this shit?" she asked Aslan. "VIP escort."

"I think your friend is better connected than I thought."

Voeckler instructed Halverson to climb into the first car, then ordered Aslan into the second. Halverson hesitated when she heard that.

Aslan shook his head. "No, I stay with her."

"No, you do what I say—"

"Because you plan to screw me over."

"No, because if anything goes down, I need you to be the decoy. You help me, I help you. Both cars are going straight to the airport. You come with us, otherwise I'll leave you here and you can fend for yourself."

"It's okay," Halverson told him. "I'll make sure nothing happens to you. Please."

Aslan thought it over. "Give me the rifle."

Halverson glanced to Voeckler, who nodded. She handed over the AK.

Aslan gave them both an appraising glance, then said, "Okay, let's go."

Once Halverson and Voeckler were in the lead car's backseat, she glanced over her shoulder in Aslan's direction. "You were telling the truth, weren't you?"

"Yeah, I'll save his sorry ass because his intel might be valuable. If he's been working with the Forgotten Army for a long time, then he might have some information on the *Ganjin*."

"What did you say?" Halverson asked, remembering the conversation she'd had with Aslan when they'd first met:

"*The* Ganjin *has changed*," he'd said.

"I said there's a group called the *Ganjin*," Voeckler repeated. "We're not sure who they are, but they've linked up with or taken over the Forgotten Army. Marines in Ecuador provided the intel."

"Aslan mentioned that name once."

"Good. Then he *is* worth something."

Halverson nodded then stole a glimpse at the driver, a young, clean-shaven man in a dark blue police uniform. "Hey, he doesn't speak English, does he?"

"Of course not, we're fine."

"Where the hell did you find these guys?"

"Simple tradecraft. Even a knucklehead like me can set this up. One of the first things you do when operating in a foreign country is pay off a couple of cops—but you've got to pick them very carefully, lean on the ones that need the money the most, either the underpaid rookies or the ones nearing retirement. You know, the ones who are cynical and bitter and want to get back at the system for screwing them over for thirty years. You study these guys, then make your move. These particular cops, though, they were a little iffy since they're not exactly my field operatives but a colleague's, so I made some big promises. My bosses won't be happy. The bribes will probably come out of my salary."

"I'll pay you back," she said.

"No worries. You already did." He checked his smartphone again. "Our jet is already en route to the airport."

"You really think we'll make it past the checkpoints?"

"There are three between here and the airport. I've already got that covered."

"Thanks. Can I ask you something? You're a strange man to figure out. You don't seem like—"

"I know. My brother got me into this. After he died, I promised myself that I'd give it a chance. It's grown on me, but I've heard it before: I just don't seem like an ops officer. I look like I should be selling tacos."

"What do I look like?"

"Like an old English teacher who flunked me, but hotter."

"Really?"

"Sort of. I'm just being polite. If someone would've

asked me about you two days ago, I would've told them you were an angel. That hasn't changed."

She fidgeted in her seat. "Whoa, sincere awkward moment."

He glanced at her and grinned wearily. "I'm not hitting on you. I'm just happy to finally meet you." He offered his hand.

She took it. "Well, then, yes, it's nice to meet you, Mr. Voeckler."

He winked. "We've got a plane to catch."

TWENTY-EIGHT

Mountains near Spetsnaz Headquarters
Fort Levski
Bulgaria

Lex's breath shortened as he clutched Slava's arm and whispered, "I appreciate it, big guy, but hold back."

"Boss, there's no other way."

"Hey, check it out," said Borya.

The lead wolf who'd been baring his teeth, only seconds away from attacking the team, suddenly dropped on all fours and laid his head on his paws. The other two lingered behind him for a few seconds, and then they, too, lowered themselves to the snow and just lay there, their heads hanging strangely, their eyes going vacant.

"Whoa. I guess it just took a little longer for these guys," said Vlad.

"And they just took a year off my life," Lex said. "Borya, send the drone up to the summit now."

"Roger that."

"The rest of you, back off slowly."

They eased out of the depression, and Lex never took his gaze off the wolves until they were clear.

"Now we can get back to business," he told his men.

Quickening their pace, they climbed around the back side of the ridge, hoisting themselves up a small ledge, then ascending a deep furrow cut into the earth by last spring's melting snow. At the top, Vlad neared Lex and said, "We took care of five wolves. What about the other nine hundred and ninety-five? We don't have anything to spare for them."

"Sergeant, what do you know about the power of positive thinking?"

Vlad frowned, took a long breath, then finally answered, "All right, boss, I get it. Just trying to keep us honest, like you always say."

"You ain't happy unless you're complaining, right?"

"Yeah. I'm not afraid to die. I just don't want to go out doing something stupid."

"Trust me, bro, I can appreciate that."

They hiked for the rest of the day, the grade increasing steadily until in some sections they were sidestepping up the mountain across patches of ice, toeing through pockets of snow, and booting over beds of pine needles. Borya kept the drone thirty meters ahead, having set a series of visual alarms on the remote to warn him should the UAV encounter any targets/obstacles. Slava and Vlad brought up the rear, ever wary of more wolves or abominable snowmen that might pick up their trail. They took note of four more observation posts—tiny nests of concrete draped with camouflage nets, each manned by two Spetsnaz troops whose faces were glued to their tablet computers.

By the time they reached the summit overlooking the blast doors below and the rest of Fort Levski, the temperature had dropped fifteen degrees and snow was beginning to fall. Lex flicked his gaze to the last dregs of sunlight breaking through the clouds, then shifted up on his elbows toward the edge of the cliff. There, he and the rest of the team had taken up positions in the shade of tall pines and hidden beneath their optical camouflage to once more reconnoiter the base.

Staring through his binoculars, Borya began a verbal inventory on all of the heavy artillery, the surface-to-air missile launchers, and the aircraft and armored personnel carriers, while Lex plugged this data into his tablet computer, positions being noted and verified against the most recent set of satellite photographs. Higher had requested up-to-the-minute intel on the base, and they'd get it, but alas, no one could control the weather, which was rapidly taking a turn for the worse, meaning their exfiltration could prove, in a word, interesting.

"Guard towers, Tu-3 Vulture drones, and pretty much everything else looks the same," said Borya. "They haven't beefed up security."

"Good news for us," added Vlad.

"Let's get the ropes, anchors, and belays in place," Lex ordered.

Once they'd established two lines for scaling down the mountainside, Lex gave a hand signal, and they fell back into the darkness of the forest, gathering beneath a pine tree where Lex pulled up a satellite photo of their position and began to create a glowing red overlay using his index finger. He held up his tablet. "Our current position is here."

"I'm good to go with the micros and camera bypasses," said Borya. "Just tested the systems. Drone verifies four cameras."

"Excellent," said Lex. "My laser cutter team good to go?"

Vlad and Slava nodded. "You give us ninety seconds, we'll get you in."

Lex grinned. "Good. Is it time to rock 'n' roll?"

"Hoo-ah," they all grunted.

With a curt nod, Lex put Borya on point. They hiked carefully away from the ledge for about fifty meters, toward the perimeter of what Lex's map indicated was the "motion detection zone."

Borya was already on the problem, launching the team's micro UAVs. The palm-sized Hummingbird 3-A advanced prototypes were small and light enough not to trip the motion detectors emplaced by Spetsnaz security forces, and even if they did, signal officers would dismiss the trigger as a bird or some other natural occurrence. The UAVs would fly to the camera positions and, using a specialized infrared radiation source of the necessary spectrum, they would blind the motion sensors so the team could move in. While in theory their optical camouflage ponchos with heat-dampening technology should be enough to fool those motion trackers, Lex wasn't taking any chances.

Borya checked his tablet. "Should be neutralized in five, four, three, two . . . we're clear, sir. Good to go."

They jogged forward, coming up behind the first of the four camera stations built directly into a broad oak. The Spetsnaz had done a fine job disguising their security measures, but when you had something to protect, it was pretty damned clear that recon points would be in place, and it had taken the signals and intel folks back home only a few hours to locate all four positions based on their wireless signals.

Tricking the cameras in place was a rudimentary job for Borya, one he could probably do while simultaneously playing video games and eating a B.M.T. from Subway. He was able to hack into each camera's transmission and replace it with a digital loop replete with natural forest sounds since the signal also included an audio surveillance track. His finger danced over the tablet's screen, then he faced Lex and said, "Clear for entry."

"Vlad? Slava? You're up," Lex ordered.

The two men took off running.

Borya shifted up beside Lex and hunkered down. "So far, so good. By the numbers."

"Don't jinx it."

"Did you call higher to verify?"

"I'm waiting till the last minute."

"Sometimes operational security can get you killed."

Lex grinned. "I'm a gambling man."

The microphone and attached boom mike clipped to Lex's ear gave a short vibration, followed by Slava's voice: "Deep Raider Actual, I'm on the first one. Vlad's on the second. Start the clock."

"Roger that. Do it right."

Slava took great pride in how quickly he could manipulate his laser cutter, but the grating they had to cut through was particularly thick.

"Weather's not getting any better," Borya remarked, his helmet now covered in snow.

"I hear that." Lex glanced up at the sky. "Platform should be in range by now."

"Sir, can I be honest with you?" Borya asked.

Lex winced. "Can I get back to you in twenty-four hours?"

Borya frowned. "At the risk of sounding like Vlad, I'm, uh, shall we say, concerned."

"When we got this mission, part of me was asking, hey, have you completed your bucket list yet? You know what I'm saying?"

"These ops are scary and fun—all at the same time. But this one's just, aw, man, I don't know."

"Relax. I want you worried."

"Sir?"

"Sometimes we get too complacent, right?"

"Right, sir."

Slava and Vlad came running back. "They were all out of Diet Coke, so I got you root beer instead," the former gasped. "And by the way, eighty-seven seconds."

"Outstanding. Sensors blocked, cameras bypassed,

grating compromised," Lex said. "Time: seventeen forty-one hours. We're early." He took a deep breath. "Get the canisters ready. It's time to drop some quarters into this slot machine and pull the lever. You guys feeling lucky?"

They all grinned and slipped off their packs. Meanwhile, Lex called back to higher: "This is Deep Raider Actual. We're in position and ready to initiate phase one, over."

"Roger that," came the comm operator's voice. "Fleet QRF and Standoff Ops Command indicate slight weather delay. Request you remain in position until we're clear to go."

"Understood. Please remind them we've only got about a thirty-minute window on the platform, over."

"Will do."

"Deep Raider Actual, standing by, out." Lex shook his head at the others. "Hurry up and wait."

Each of his men now gripped a pair of aerosol canisters filled with Kolokol-7, an incapacitating agent derived from the prior Kolokol-1 synthetic opioid and in part a derivative of fentanyl.

Getting into the complex and multileveled facility and battling their way past the guards and biometric security systems all the way down to the interrogation and confinement level had seemed well-nigh impossible. Lex had played out that scenario a hundred different times—

And then an idea had struck him: If they couldn't break into the place, maybe they could flush everyone out like ants—or at least as many as they could. He'd begun researching the facility's ventilation system, its defenses against airborne containments, and tried to learn what he could about hazmat inventories. Since this was an underground headquarters in what the Russians had deemed friendly territory, the odds were against every officer being fully equipped with personal hazmat gear. Sure, some masks would be available, but it was safe to assume there wouldn't be enough for everyone— and not everyone would get to a mask in time.

Here, well above the HQ entrance, were two air shafts that fed fresh air into the underground complex. A pair of three-ton pumps sucked the air down the meter-wide conduits running from the cliff top through the headquarters' center, where the pumps redirected airflow to feeder vents radiating spokelike to the office and living spaces surrounding the central pumping station. The base's engineers had recognized this vulnerability and had camouflaged the shafts within the trees, as well as protecting them with heavy grating and with electronic surveillance monitored by their people on the command-and-control level. Moreover, they'd anticipated enemies trying to gain entrance from above and had placed more protective grating within each shaft, staggering them every twenty meters or so, meaning it would take a few days of absolutely silent cutting for the team to use the air shafts to gain entrance into the headquarters. Too slow, too many risks of being caught.

Lex had gone over the plan and several variations of it with both his senior officers and with General Mitchell. He'd had to reassure the general the gas would not inadvertently harm Dr. Ragland. And then, of course, came the elephant-in-the-room question: What if flushing them out worked but they still couldn't find Ragland? What if they somehow managed to keep her inside, despite the gas?

Lex hoped it didn't come to that, but if it did, they were prepared to "go deep." He took a seat beside the team, and they huddled beneath the tree, watching the snow pile up around them.

Lieutenant Colonel Osin was about to leave his station and head back to his quarters for the night when a call came in from Christopher Theron. Osin tapped a touchpad, enveloping his station in a soundproof cocoon used when receiving ultrasensitive communications.

"Colonel, it's my understanding that you've been a loyal member of our group for many years now," the man began, sans any introductions or happy talk.

"That's right, sir."

"And I'm able to call you right there inside the Guard Brigade headquarters with impunity."

"I'm very good at what I do, sir."

"Excellent. Then you'll take care of a problem for me."

"I've been well compensated to solve problems."

"Good. President Kapalkin is on his way there to interrogate Colonel Antsyforov."

"That's correct, sir. His ETA is one hour, twenty-seven minutes from now."

"Yes, that's unfortunate. You see, that woman has information that could compromise our operations."

"If they believe her."

"Kapalkin is a shrewd man. He'll investigate all possibilities, which could make things difficult for us. At any rate, the Americans have sent a rescue team to your location."

"The Americans? They've come to rescue her?"

"No, they're after someone else they believe is being held there. Make no mistake: An attack will come soon."

"I see. Are you suggesting that the Snow Maiden is, shall we say, killed in the attack?"

"I'm saying go down there and kill the bitch."

Osin grimaced. "Of course. But what's our cover story? If they link her murder back to me—"

"That's your issue. Not mine."

Theron's reply gave Osin pause.

Serious pause.

He'd worked hard for these people and appreciated how they'd helped him rise above his mechanical life. But now here was Theron revealing his true colors, revealing that perhaps Osin had been wrong about himself, that he *was* just a cog in the wheel, just a peon working for a group that had made him believe he wasn't.

He tensed, his breath growing short, then finally answered, "Of course, I'll take care of her. When would you like this done?"

"Immediately."

"Okay. But what about the attack? Should I notify my people here?"

"Absolutely not. Perhaps the Americans will get lucky and take out the president himself."

Osin swallowed over the enormity of what would happen—and how he might be caught in the middle of it. "Sir, once I terminate the Snow Maiden, I'd like your permission to evacuate."

"Excellent idea. You're too valuable to lose. Take care of her, then get out."

Osin rose from his desk. "On my way, sir."

As he strode toward the elevator, he balled his hands into fists, then placed a palm on his sidearm.

A life of obedience. Cog. Peon. Was this him?

TWENTY-NINE

Hawker 400XP Business Jet
En Route to Incirlik Air Base
Turkey

Halverson threw her head back on the seat as the jet reached cruise altitude. She glanced across the cabin at Voeckler, who lifted his glass of Aberfeldy 21 and toasted her. She beamed, lifting her own glass of spring water, having declined the single malt scotch. She'd save the drinking for when she finally reached California.

Two seats behind sat Aslan, mouth open, snoring away. It'd been a long day for the Chechen. He'd saved her life, but as he slept back there, a boy hiding behind all that hair and the beard, she wondered just how many people he'd killed before he'd found his conscience. He was still, and might always be, a terrorist. His father's son. But he'd done right by her, and she would do everything within her power to see that he was treated fairly.

Their trip to the airport via the police had gone off

without a hitch, much to Halverson's amazement. Given the recent circumstances of her life, she would've bet against a routine car ride. They'd been summarily waved through each checkpoint, everyone paid off to keep his mouth shut, his memory erased.

Halverson had been laughing as she'd climbed aboard their waiting jet, more dumbstruck than anything else, flashes of memory striking like tumbling glass—the ejection, hanging from the train, the taunting Russians as they took potshots at her, the release and descent into the gorge, the smell of those caves . . .

She took another sip of water, and as she set it down, her satellite phone rang, the number unrecognizable. A woman's voice: "Major Halverson? I have President Becerra for you."

"You do? I mean, uh, okay, yeah." Halverson lost her breath.

"Major Halverson?"

"Yes, I'm here, Mr. President."

"And thank God for that. We've been holding our collective breath over here, praying for your rescue."

"Thank you, sir. I feel pretty good about that myself."

He chuckled under his breath.

She went on: "And if I can say, the man who helped save me, Aslan, he defected from the Forgotten Army. He's seeking asylum in the U.S. Whatever you can do to help, I'd deeply appreciate it. I'd be dead already if it weren't for him. Please, sir . . ."

"I'll take care of it."

"Thank you so much."

"Now, Major, I've been following your tests with the Wraith program. Outstanding job."

"I appreciate that, sir. I'm ready to get back to work. Something went wrong with that radar system, and you can be damned sure we'll figure out what it was. Once we get the Wraith fully operational, I promise you, she'll change the scope of the entire war."

"I know that. But after what you've just been through, I'd say a little R & R is the best medicine."

"You know me, sir. I'll lose my mind if I don't keep working."

"I understand. But unfortunately we've had to put the project on hold."

"Because of my crash? Or a budget cut? Not another budget cut? Really?"

"While you were testing the radar, Dr. Ragland was taken by Spetsnaz forces."

"Oh my God, are you kidding me? How? She was in Palmdale."

"The intelligence people are still looking for answers. Good news is we caught a break through our operatives in Moscow. They're holding her at Fort Levski, and we have a Marine Raider team down there. Soon as the weather clears, they plan to get her out."

Halverson's thoughts leapt forward. "Fort Levski. That's in Bulgaria. I'm an hour away. Sir, who's backing up that team? Sixth Fleet? Request permission to join their QRF. You know I can fly anything they got—rotor, fixed-wing, you name it. All I need is a plane and a target, sir. I can tell this pilot to divert course right now."

"Major, you haven't even been debriefed."

"Sir, with all due respect, debrief me right now! Let me go out there. She's my friend. We worked on this project together. It was our baby. And if I can help, I need to do that. I need to be there."

"I know how you feel. I've lost too many friends over the years, but after what you've been through—"

"Sir, I *need* to go."

Silence on the other end. Then, suddenly: "You know, if you weren't such a fine pilot, I'd turn you down in a heartbeat. But this is a very complicated mission, and, well, I bet they could use you."

Halverson shifted forward in her seat. "Yes, they could, sir. Thank you."

"I didn't say yes. And I don't want to force you on the mission commander."

"General Mitchell?"

"That's right."

"He knows my work. He'll be glad to have me. Please, sir, I'm literally begging you. Make this happen."

He hesitated a moment more, then sighed and said, "All right, I'll talk to Mitchell, but you'll probably have to submit to a quick preflight physical."

"No problem. You won't regret this."

"Get with your pilot. Figure out where you're going to put down and update us. I'll get a plane out to you."

"Outstanding, sir."

"Just come back in one piece."

"Just a walk in the park."

"You fighter jocks have been saying that for a hundred years, but get serious now. You're going to Fort Levski. Spetsnaz headquarters."

"Perfect. We'll embarrass the Russians even more when we get in there and get her out."

"I like your attitude, Major."

"Yes, sir."

"This country needs more war heroes. This country could use a war hero like you in politics."

She laughed. "That's the best joke I've heard all year."

"Mark my words, Stephanie. Why do you think I've taken such an interest in you?"

She sobered. "You're serious?"

"You've served your country as a warrior, but you can do even more."

"That sounds crazy."

"Look, I never thought I'd be a politician, but here I am. Just get back home, and we'll talk all about it . . ."

She shook her head in shock. "Yes, sir. Thank you, sir."

THIRTY

Spetsnaz Headquarters
Fort Levski
Bulgaria

Lex shifted a little closer to the pine tree and swatted snow off his tablet computer's screen. "Intel coming out of Moscow still confirms that Ragland is here. All we need is the order to go."

"What happens if we miss the window?" asked Vlad.

"We won't," said Lex.

"Hypothetically speaking," Vlad forged on. "There wasn't any mention of that in the briefing or the docs."

"I deliberately left that out."

"You did?"

"That's right," Lex confessed. "We're doing this no matter what."

All three men looked at him.

He hardened his tone. "Does anyone have a problem with that?"

"No backup, no problem," said Slava.

A window suddenly appeared in Lex's head-up display, with a beeping tone from the comm operator. He accepted the call. "Deep Raider Actual, you are clear to move out."

"Roger that," Lex said. "Gentlemen, this is it. On your feet. Let's rock!"

With his heart already hammering, Lex fell in behind the others, sprinting through the forest and back to the ventilation shafts. There, they set down the gas and donned their masks, and then, after checking that each man's gear was good to go, they popped open the Kolokol-7 and dropped four canisters down each shaft, the hissing and whirring of the fans drawing in the chemicals confirming to Lex that in just a few minutes, the entire complex would be filled with the powerful opioid.

Lex exchanged a hand signal with Slava: They were set at both shafts.

They wove their way across the pine needles and broken carpet of snow, returning to the cliff, and once out of the contamination zone, with the wind blowing away from them, they peeled off their masks. While Borya and Vlad assembled their Spetsnaz VSS Vintorez medium-range sniper rifles, Lex brought his satellite phone to his ear.

The entire valley grew eerily quiet, just the whispers of the falling snow and the branches rustling slightly in the wind. It seemed as though the birds and other animals had gone silent, anticipating what would happen. The phone beeped, and the comm operator connected him directly to General Mitchell. "Sir, canisters are away."

"Excellent work, Captain. Stand by. I'm ordering the kinetic strike now."

Lex flicked his gaze up into the dark, snow-filled sky, and while he couldn't see them, he imagined the twelve rods of tungsten blasting off from their space-based orbital platform via their rocket motors. They'd plunge toward the atmosphere until gravity accelerated them to thirty-six thousand feet per second as they headed for a collision course with the Earth's crust—or more precisely Fort Levski. Each rod packed all the destructive effects of an Earth-penetrating nuclear weapon.

One rod would wreak havoc.

Twelve would devastate the entire valley . . .

Lex wouldn't have to imagine that part. He and his men had a front-row seat.

A Klaxon blared from somewhere below, followed by more alarms from the base—an air raid warning that began to drone loudly across the mountainside. The base's Voronezh-class radar was capable of monitoring more than five hundred targets at a single time at distances extending to 3,725 miles. Lex knew that Fort Levski's radar operators were, at the moment, shitting their boxers.

At the same time, pilots scrambled to their MiG-29s. Troops rushed out of the barracks toward their APCs, while more crews charged toward a convoy of Cockroaches now rolling out of three hangars, the hulking infantry fighting vehicles equipped with fifty-seven-millimeter autocannons linked to state-of-the-art fire control computers that made the guns deadly accurate against low-flying airborne threats. Lex counted twelve in those lines. The artillery pieces were left unmanned, but all three batteries of the old S-300 anti-aircraft missiles were coming online, rocket tubes tilting up off their TELs or transporter erector launchers and rising into the sky.

Borya crouched down beside Lex, staring at the intel Mitchell was sending them: a radar image of the incoming rods glowing on Lex's tablet. The picture shifted to a computer animation showing the rods burning through the atmosphere and bearing down on their location.

"Twenty seconds," said Borya.

"Everybody fall back from the ledge, mask up, and brace for impact!" Lex cried.

Lieutenant Colonel Osin ordered the guards aside and rushed into the Snow Maiden's cell.

Still bound in her shackles, she bolted to her feet, looking much more animated than their first meeting. She was dressed now in standard orange prisoner utilities with numbers stenciled on the sleeves and breast but still wearing her knee-high boots.

"What's going on?" she demanded, staring at the gas mask covering his face, the second one in his left hand.

"We need to evacuate now," he said, tugging the gas mask over her face. "The base is under attack. Airborne contaminants. Come with me."

As he shoved her forward, the two guards turned and blocked their exit, they, too, having donned their gas masks.

"Sir, you can't move the prisoner without authorization. I'm sorry, sir."

Osin shot the young man in the neck with his suppressed pistol. He shot the second guard point-blank in the head before that young man could reach for his sidearm.

No turning back now . . .

"What the hell? Are you saving me?" the Snow Maiden asked, her voice muffled by the mask.

"We're getting out of here together," he told her.

But saving her wasn't exactly his plan.

On his way down to the interrogation level, Osin had reflected on Theron's order, on how the man had no regard for what happened to him. Yes, Osin was valuable, but it had taken Theron too much time to recognize that. The man's inability to fully think through his decisions deeply troubled Osin. Was this the kind of leader the Bilderberg Group could fully trust?

Gritting his teeth in frustration, Osin had decided that killing the Snow Maiden was not the answer. Rescuing her and using her to blackmail Theron seemed much more audacious and interesting. Yes, the time had come for bold and creative thinking on his part. Twenty years as a peon and spy would finally come to an end. He'd never get a chance like this again. Not in his lifetime. And Theron wasn't the only bidder. He could even turn over the Snow Maiden to the Americans or the

Forgotten Army for a price. Keeping her alive put him in control. He had the power. He could even negotiate a deal with her, a little payback for the rescue.

Fuck you, Theron.

He shoved her past the dead guards and into the hallway, toward the duty desk a dozen meters away, just as the two junior officers who'd been manning their stations came charging into the hallway, shouting, "Halt!"

One clutched his throat and fell before Osin needed to shoot him, a victim of the gas now pouring in from the ventilation grills lining the ceiling. The second drew his weapon—

But Osin dropped him with a two-round burst, chest and right cheek.

"I can't run!" shouted the Snow Maiden. "Get me out of these chains!"

"Only the legs," Osin corrected, then shoved her forward, the chains clanging as they reached the end of the hall, where Osin rifled through the duty desk. In a drawer below the terminal he found several sets of keys, one of which should belong to her shackles. The other set was locked in the command-and-control center.

He fumbled through the keys, cursing as he tried several on her shackles until the lock finally turned.

The moment those shackles fell off her ankles, the entire facility shook as though it were being excavated by a giant backhoe, the force so strong that it knocked both of them to the floor, the walls sounding as though they were caving in, the lights flashing, the deep reverberations coming straight through their torsos. Then, as the ground continued to rumble so violently that neither of them dared move, Osin knew what was happening, and he wondered if the Americans had changed their plans . . .

This wasn't a "rescue" operation but an attempt to terminate their POW.

Or maybe Theron had been wrong about them. Maybe they knew the Snow Maiden was here, and this was their mission to kill her, with him squarely in their way.

A glimmer woke in the gray-black sheet of clouds, the tinniest of flashes over the fort's communications dishes lying in silhouette like palms cupped toward the sky.

Next came a strange rush, like air blowing across the top of a deep-throated bottle.

And then the first of twelve impacts ripped into the ground with a force so sudden and loud that it drove Lex and his men back onto their rumps.

As the tremendous earthquake continued, sounding like a million bass drums being hammered by enraged musicians, Lex rolled forward onto his hands and knees. Borya had patched them into the night-vision security cameras around the base, and Lex picked up his tablet and watched the devastation unfold in a phosphorescent glow.

The first rod struck the ground a few meters south of the main comm dishes, and the ground heaved as though the blast had come from within, cracking the concrete pylons and sending all four dishes plummeting to smash like fragile flowers across the service roads, metal peeling back like petals and jutting into the earth. The radar station buildings below the dishes were lifted into the air and flipped over like pancakes, the men inside given instant funerals and burials, sans all the dramatic weeping and overpriced caskets.

Even as that rumbling cacophony continued, two more rods punched with sudden flashes into the hangars, and once more the buildings rose as though carried on typhoon seas, colliding with one another as massive puzzle pieces of asphalt hurtled into the air, trailing swirling dust clouds that whipped over the MiGs whose pilots were still trying to lift off. Several planes were just leaving the runways, others lining up, idling, while still more were kicked onto their backs by the rods' initial impact—until a third and fourth rod struck, blanketing the area in so much flying debris that Lex couldn't see anything.

Off to the south, where hundreds of troops were just evacuating the barracks and attempting to cross the field toward their waiting APCs, came the next two rods. Lex gasped. The double impact catapulted those men into the air like confetti, a fountain of tiny bodies blasting skyward and quickly joined by their vehicles, tossed around like toys.

The next six rods struck in quick succession, obliterating the big TELs with their S-300 missile tubes erected, the earth cracking all around them and literally swallowing several of the launchers.

Lex wasn't sure how many of the artillery pieces had been destroyed, since a wall of sand and rock had suddenly been formed, the rods digging a massive trench along the base's west side.

That several of the guard towers had remained intact was a small miracle; however, the troops manning them were already abandoning their posts and climbing down with reckless urgency while below them, the convoy of Cockroaches that had been assembling before the strike vanished into yet another deep fissure cutting a jagged line from the runways all the way out to the southern perimeter.

With the ground still shaking hard beneath his boots, Lex stowed the tablet and got to his feet. He signaled to Slava, and together, they rigged up.

"Raider Team, this is Actual. Radio check, over," Lex called.

Each man sounded off.

"All right, we got the ultimate diversion down below. And it looks like the evacuation from the HQ is already in progress. We're going down."

"We got you covered up top here, boss," said Borya as the first wave of dust came in, followed by a much denser wave, and suddenly they were standing not in a snowstorm but a billowing dust storm with visibility down to a meter.

Over the side they went, with Lex stealing looks at the mountain road below and the blast doors that had slid open to allow those on foot to come charging outside, some of them collapsing to their knees and passing out, while a few wearing masks attempted to wave the others onward.

They didn't have much time. He and Slava needed to get down to the motor pool and cut off all those vehicles there to prevent Ragland from being smuggled out that way. He'd memorized the facility's layout, had selected the correct charges, and would be pleased to get in touch with his inner pyro within the next two minutes.

Slava was a beast on his ropes, rappelling down the mountainside nearly twice as fast as Lex, who planned to later remark that the man's considerable weight was what allowed him to drop like a rock.

They'd picked a location along the mountain that would help conceal them as they drew up near the blast doors, descending along at an angle that put them off to the west, about a hundred meters away, with a broad lip of stone standing between them and the entrance.

But now, with all the dust—much more than Lex had ever considered—that didn't matter. Anyone without a mask was now choking or rushing back inside. The roiling clouds reminded Lex of some of the artillery barrages he'd survived, the smoke and fires so dense back then that all you had were your buddy's shoulders for reference.

It dawned on him as he booted off the rock and zipped down the line that their plan to flush out the Spetsnaz might be backfiring on them. The storm had shifted the wind's direction and the debris was now blowing up toward the mountain. The Russians would know this and want more than ever to evacuate the Cockroaches and APCs lying in wait in that motor pool.

His breath shortening, Lex pushed off and made a tremendous drop, one so aggressive that he nearly lost his footing, but saw he was quickly gaining on Slava.

Barely fifty meters now to the road, which vanished once more in the next wave of dust.

Just then, as he took in a deep breath to prepare for the next push, the trembling ceased, the mountain growing still.

"Slava, we need to cut off that motor pool. Let's haul some ass, bro! Come on!"

"Waiting on you, boss. Just hit the ground!"

"Here I come."

Lex slammed hard onto the road, his knees buckling for a second, but then he leaned back on the cliff, caught his balance, and began to unclip his rope.

They tucked in close to the mountain, readied their rifles, and double-checked their web gear. Lex gave Slava the hand signal to go.

Four guards were hunkered down beside the open blast doors, the checkpoint abandoned, the secondary pedestrian entrance also unguarded.

He and Slava rushed toward those men.

THIRTY-ONE

Spetsnaz Headquarters
Fort Levski
Bulgaria

The Snow Maiden couldn't recall if this region of Bulgaria was prone to earthquakes. It was certainly prone to attack, and whatever they were hammering the base with—bunker-buster bombs, a kinetic strike, something—they were doing one hell of a job, the floor rolling beneath them, the concrete walls cracking and groaning like the hull of some ancient ship.

She'd felt her legs come free just as the first impact reached them, and in those next few seconds, she'd found her opening and taken it:

She slid her legs up and around Osin's shoulders, locked those legs around his neck, and drove her knee into the back of his head, effectively cutting off his air. She called on everything she had left—

Squeezing. Squeezing. The floor shaking. Osin gasping

behind his gas mask, his fingers digging into her legs as he writhed, his entire body shaking for a moment as she shifted position, trying to force off his mask with her other knee.

When she'd been recruited by the GRU, they'd told her you never forget the first man you kill. There might be dozens after him, but you never forget the first.

What they didn't know, what they couldn't possibly know, was that she had already killed years prior. She'd been seventeen, and her victim was a woman at least ten years her senior.

It came back to her in flashes now, the memories disjointed by time, guilt, denial. A walk home from her part-time bakery job late at night in Vladivostok. Piles of dirty snow lying along Fokina Street. Power lines drooping with icicles spanning the street between the old buildings. And then shouts. A woman being assaulted by another. The Snow Maiden intervening, telling the younger woman to run away, she taking on the assailant, a foreign woman waving a small knife. She might've been Chinese, Mongolian, the Snow Maiden wasn't sure.

A feeling had overcome her, one she couldn't control. A hand to the wrist, stopping the knife, freeing it.

Then fingers around the woman's throat, some crazed desire to kill her, as though this woman represented everything she hated in her life. Why did she feel this way? Explanations were meaningless.

There was only the rage, and the rage had frightened her because deep down it felt terribly good. And when she'd run off, leaving the dead woman lying there with that cold, vacant look in her eyes, she knew her life would never be the same. She was a killer. All the GRU had done was teach her how to do it more efficiently. The resolve had always been there.

Maybe this guy, this Lieutenant Colonel Osin, really was trying to save her. His mistake. His body went limp between her legs—

But she wasn't foolish enough to release him. Not yet. She knew that old gambit. She held her grip and ticked off another sixty seconds as the reverberations grew more intense.

The lights flickered and went out.

In the dark now, she booted herself around, fumbling blindly for the keys. She found them beside Osin's leg and began the excruciatingly slow process of inserting one after another until the shackles finally clicked open and she slipped free her hands, reflexes causing her to rub her sore and swollen wrists.

Red emergency lights flickered near the ceiling as she shot to her feet, grabbed Osin's pistol, searched him, found his mini tablet and smartphone. If she could crack them, they might reveal his true intentions for trying to rescue her.

She remembered her prisoner's uniform, bright orange with a smiley-face sticker on the breast that said *Hello, I'm the World's Most Wanted Terrorist*—or it might as well have. Off came Osin's pants and shirt, slightly too large for her, but she rolled back the sleeves, tightened the belt to the very last hole. She'd fool them only from afar, so she'd avoid any close encounters. She went back to the guards and took their sidearms, tucking one in her pocket, the other in the waistband at her back. She grabbed a fourth pistol, then used the heel of her hand to shove the gas mask a bit tighter around her face.

Then, for just a few seconds she reflected on the moment. Earlier she'd been sitting in that shower, trying to reconcile with the last chapter of her life. She laughed incredulously, then shivered back to the moment. She might have a chance.

With that, she bounded up the hallway, toward the elevators and stairwells, leaving—as always—death in her wake.

Spending a few seconds telling the guards a story of why they needed to get into the base was an option that Lex could have employed. He felt confident that he and Slava would be as convincing as ever.

Donning their active camouflage and moving in short bursts was another possibility—but it would slow them down.

Bullets were the most expeditious way of gaining entry, and the drone's first scan had indicated that these were the only guards outside at the moment.

Lex and Slava ran up, waving their arms to get the guards' attention through all the swirling dust.

The men got to their feet, presenting larger targets. Lex clutched his suppressed pistol with both hands, the clicks like those produced by air guns, the results, of course, much more deadly. The troops fell in succession. That this encounter had been captured by security cameras at the entrance didn't matter; those troops were assumedly busy with the evacuation and had long since left their stations.

Slava moved up as they raced past the bodies and inside, beyond the blast doors, then hunkered down near the four-meter-tall hydraulic and motor assemblies just behind.

Lined up along the wall were several battery-powered transports, the military version of a golf cart used by officers and dignitaries too damned lazy to walk around the base. Lex and Slava climbed into one, and Lex took the wheel and tapped the touch-screen controls. No security locks or passwords here because those same officers didn't want to remember a pass code or even be inconvenienced by waving a security ID before a scanner. They raced off down the two-lane passage, Slava's tablet indicating they had a half-kilometer trek into the mountainside.

Along the route they passed at least ten overloaded carts heading in the opposite direction, a few of the masked passengers waving at them to turn around.

"Borya, we got some coming out," Lex reported over their team channel.

"Don't worry, boss, I'm on it."

"Roger that. Might lose comm soon."

"Okay, still good for now, though," answered Borya.

Abruptly, Lex and Slava reached level one: the motor pool.

Holy shit, Lex thought as he jerked the wheel and pulled the cart off the road and into a service lane. He and Slava hopped out and hunkered down.

They'd entered an absolutely mammoth-sized cave, much larger than the schematics suggested, with rows of vehicles stretching off into the distance. A few squads of masked troops were running toward the idling APCs—eight-wheeled BTR-82s, and all around the perimeter more troops lay supine or prone, victims of the gas before they could find protection. There had been no way to tell exactly how many gas masks the Spetsnaz troops might have available to them, but the assumption of "not enough" was panning out.

The backup generators lights were burning, and it took a moment for Lex's vision to adjust as he and Slava reached into their packs and produced their CQ9 tactical charge launchers, better known by Marine Corps engineers as "breach barrels."

Each short-barreled rifle was fitted with a magazine containing a half dozen L45C4 dome-shaped "sticky" charges composed of C4 and a special adhesive polymer containing a wirelessly triggered Class B-W blasting cap no larger than a thumbnail.

The primary electronic detonator was located within the rifle itself, and all Lex needed to do was throw a switch to shift from firing the charges to triggering them via a wireless signal. Point, shoot, thump, charge in place, wait for the green light. Boom!

The only snafu was bad aim—then you were stuck blowing up the wrong object or location or abandoning the charge, which in turn compromised operational security.

No, that wouldn't happen now. They opened fire on the ceiling above the tunnel, carefully positioning all twelve of their charges. The engineers had analyzed this section of the headquarters and had issued their report for what they quipped was the proper, decent, and correct application of high explosives (always a good thing) for maximum demolition based on the design and integrity of the support structure. Lex's math was much simpler: $X + Y =$ blow shit up!

Once the charges were set, Lex and Slava rushed toward the elevator column erected like a gleaming black megalith in the center of the circular motor pool.

Over the team channel, Lex gasped, "And three, two—"

They squeezed their triggers, and the towering cupola of rock above the tunnel entrance, along with the tracks for the secondary set of blast doors, exploded in thundering strings that boomed in an arc before bringing down enormous pieces of stone right into the tunnel, the rubble piling up fast to cut off the IFVs, BTRs, and any other smaller vehicles like the carts whose crews and drivers would try to escape.

Like the exterior entrance outside the mountain, this tunnel also had a pedestrian exit that as planned would remain untouched. They'd discussed how Ragland might be smuggled out aboard a vehicle during the attack. They needed to flush out the base but force personnel to do so on foot. A tricky gambit to be sure, but the engineers had come up with a decidedly effective solution.

Now it was time to put their Metal Storm ordnance to work, creating a secondary diversion within the motor pool. Each of their Izhmash assault rifles had been fitted with a 3GL forty-millimeter semiautomatic underslung grenade launcher. Unlike single-shot weapons, these clip-on launchers tripled their effective firepower and eliminated the hassle of carrying a separate weapon. Each of the grenades was preloaded and fired via an electronic signal; thus the only moving parts on the unit were the grenades themselves.

They cut loose on the APCs and IFVs, sending grenades flying and exploding across the vehicles, troops ducking before being swept up in the clouds of dust now swelling from the collapsed ceiling.

Beaming at each other, they tossed away their barrels and clipped in new ones. Six more grenades flew across the motor pool and exploded in blinding flashes, the subsequent fires and burning shrapnel rising in veiled columns of orange light that seemed to undulate and quiver with a life of their own.

There was so much chaos and confusion spreading like a virus through the level that most of the troops were leaping for cover instead of pinpointing the source of fire, and Lex and Slava were already charging around the lifts before they ever emerged from their positions.

That, Lex thought, *is what Marine Corps combat medicine looks like.* He caught his breath, cleared his throat, and spoke loudly through his mask. "All right, I want two Seekers up here."

Slava nodded and fished out the pair of micro UAVs shaped like weird cyborg insects with pairs of rotating rotors and equipped with large camera eyes to gather imagery processed through facial recognition software. Each drone was no larger than Slava's hand and programmed to automatically seek out and scan personnel, checking them against photographs and video of Dr. Helena Ragland. Tests conducted with soldiers wearing gas masks proved that the drones could still identify individuals based on their eye colors and shapes, along with their brow lines, with up to ninety-two percent accuracy. Should one of the Seekers spot Ragland, an alarm would flash in Lex's HUD, along with the current GPS location and map overlay. The Seeker would lock on and not lose her. The plan was to release two drones on every level while en route to the basement.

"Okay, launching," Slava reported, hurtling the devices into the air, where they automatically activated and flitted off. Between the Hummingbirds (now assuming overwatch positions atop the mountain), the Seekers here, and the larger UAV along with more Seekers controlled by Borya just outside, they had sizable backup of electronic eyes to feed them real-time data in one hell of a rapidly evolving battle space.

"Let's go," Lex ordered. He turned back for the stairwell door, noting that the biometric security system had been manually bypassed via emergency protocols as expected, hallelujah. He chanced a look back at the motor pool. It'd take the Spetsnaz Cockroaches and BTRs thirty minutes or more to punch a hole in that wall of debris. That was all the time he and Slava needed.

In fact, their handiwork might've just bought him a few extra minutes for a secondary mission, one he had not discussed with his men. He'd promised to abort that mission if it jeopardized their primary objective; however, the odds were now leaning in his favor.

"Hey, boss, the drone's still on the pedestrian exit," Borya told him. "I used the Seekers to scan every troop coming out on those carts. No matches so far."

"Good man. I still think she'll be dressed like them and wearing a mask. You spot anything suspicious or something the drone might've missed, you track 'em and don't lose 'em."

"Roger that."

"Okay, we're going down now and will definitely lose comm. I'll be in touch when we get back up. Actual, out."

THIRTY-TWO

Spetsnaz Headquarters
Fort Levski
Bulgaria

Either the elevators were not operating on reserve power or someone had manually shut them down, drawing a string of epithets from the Snow Maiden before she found one of two stairwell doors and practically threw herself inside.

She stood there for a second, wondering why the hell the door had opened so easily. She opened it again, peeked out, and saw that the security panel was shut down, suggesting that every security door had been opened inside as part of the HQ's evacuation plan. She ducked back. Took a few breaths. Composed herself. *Okay, move . . .*

She glanced up at a stairwell that seemed to rise for kilometers, with several of the backup lights flashing on the landings, their electronics rattled by the quakes. She pounded her way up the macabre conduit, her boots echoing, heart racing, breath heavy through her mask. She hated wearing the thing and how it cut off her peripheral vision, but she wouldn't dare sample the air. It might take hours for the contaminant to clear.

Movement above. Heavy footfalls. She froze, hit the wall, and just listened. Shouts, something about locking down and securing the ordnance, an evacuation plan not coming together, and then the pounding on steps. Silence. She remembered to breathe and kept on, arriving at a door marked in Cyrillic as LEVEL 6 ARMORY AND REPAIR.

Before she could mount the next step, the door slammed open behind her, and she came face-to-face, or, rather, mask-to-mask, with a bald, bug-eyed lieutenant leveling his pistol on her chest. He noted the uniform and frowned.

"Hey, what're you doing here?" he asked.

Reflexively, she ducked, leaned forward, and shot him in the groin. As he reared back, she drove back his gun and put a bullet in his head. She was back on the stairs before he hit the ground.

What am I doing here? she thought. *Well, that's an interesting question. I was going to have dinner with the president, but he'll have to take a rain check.*

Another shuffling of feet sent her ducking to the wall. Shit, she'd never escape at this rate. She leaned out and stared up, spotting a few of the lab techs and doctors in blue scrubs rushing up the stairs. She charged after them, using their commotion to disguise her own ascent, and when she arrived on that landing, LEVEL 5 HOUSING AND HOSPITAL, she stared slack-jawed at the piles of men and women lying there, perhaps twenty in all. She leaned over and checked for one man's pulse. Weak, thready, but still there. Clever bastards, this attacking force. They were using a gas like Kolokol-7. She'd seen that agent's effects.

Literally stepping on the unconscious personnel, she reached the stairs, and with a renewed shudder of urgency, she kept on. Just climbing, climbing, the stairwell endless now, her thoughts drifting to the Euros, the Americans, the Forgotten Army, wondering if any of them were responsible for the attack. Were the *Ganjin* involved? Hell, she'd worry about that later. The point was, everyone wanted out, and she'd ride the wave.

But damn, knowing whom she might find outside was important, as in *lifesaving* important. This attack seemed expertly timed, and maybe Osin *was* working for someone else, the Americans or even the *Ganjin*.

Or maybe that miracle she'd been asking for had simply come through, and this attack had absolutely nothing to do with her and was part of a strategic plan put forward by the motherland's enemies—

And the motherland was not short on enemies. Osin had simply been acting on the president's behalf to rescue her so that she could be interrogated, tortured, and murdered at a later and more convenient date.

Ah, it was all supposition. All bullshit. She shook her head in frustration and fought for more breath. What was the next level? Research and development. Geek central, they called it, where the Russian special ops nerds perfected their gadgets, gizmos, poisons, and explosives. She gasped and climbed harder, her quads warming in protest. As she pounded across the next landing, the booming of at least two pairs of boots on the stairs overhead stole the rest of her breath and sent her to the door, tugging it open, and rushing inside.

She willed herself into a statue, her breath turning shallow. The hall ahead was cast in a crimson glow and spilled out toward the laboratory stations positioned along the curving back wall. She'd visited this level only once or twice before, but she remembered marveling over the length, breadth, and numbers of experiments and complexity of the research being conducted here—everything from nanotechnology across a number of disciplines to limb replacements to the more traditional forms of weapons development best suited for the special forces operator. Chairs lay askew from their stations, terminal screens flashing in their locked-out modes, suggesting the teams had time to escape before the gas reached this level.

She tensed as movement came from just outside the door—and then, abruptly, the door swung open, she remaining just behind it as a burly Spetsnaz officer wearing a gas mask hung his head inside, then pulled from his pocket something that flashed as he tossed it into the air. Two flashes.

He shut the door and left.

She took her breath, waiting.

Something hummed nearby, and then, in the next breath, a micro UAV hovered not a meter from her face, a tiny red light flashing below its twin cameras.

She frowned and whispered, "Hello." Then she reached up and tried to swat it, but the drone buzzed away.

* * *

Instead of engaging the doctor and techs coming up the stairwell toward them, Lex and Slava had managed to duck inside the entranceway to the intelligence and signals division, waiting near the door as those men passed. Unsurprisingly, the stations behind them were empty, probably the first ones to be vacated at the sound of an alarm. Most intel and signals personnel had no taste for things that went boom and disrupted their trancelike stares as they reviewed data streams piped in from around the world. Didn't matter what country they came from or whose side they were on.

Lex and Slava deployed the next pair of Seekers, then moved out, reaching level five, and repeated the process. Slava reported no movement from inside the R & D level, although one of the Seekers did pick up a target that failed to match Ragland; that officer's ID was still being processed.

With an ironic grin, Lex mused that the rescue could become far easier than they had anticipated. When the evacuation orders were given here, there was the outside chance that the prisoner would be left in her cell to succumb to the gas, only to be accounted for later. That was the path of least resistance for administrators—an unlikely one to be sure, but stranger things had happened to Lex in his long and turbulent career. Bottom line: He and Slava needed to clear the entire interrogation level. Ragland was either still there or being moved to the surface, where Lex's teammates would be waiting for her.

Even more determined now, they double-timed their way down the stairs, releasing drones on levels five and six, then gasping as they reached the confinement and interrogation level. They slammed through the door, rifles at the ready—

"Wow, boss, look at this guy," Slava cried, rushing up to a white-haired man who could have been mistaken for an albino. He was lying supine in his skivvies. "Someone had a bad night."

Lex crouched down and checked the officer for a carotid pulse, noticing the red marks across the man's neck. "You're right, he's dead. Looks like he was strangled, shit."

"Check these guys. Weapons gone. Somebody shot 'em up."

His mouth falling open, Lex gaped at the wounds on each of the guards.

"And what're these?" asked Slava, holding up a set of steel shackles, real old-school Russian restraints that were far more cumbersome than the more modern zipper cuffs they employed. The keys were still hanging from the heavy wrist cuffs. "Whoa, look at that," Slava added, pointing to the orange prisoner's uniform lying in a pile beside the desk.

A sharp pang struck Lex's gut. Intel had indicated that Ragland was, at the moment, the only prisoner being held at the HQ. "I don't believe this," he gasped. "It's like somebody else broke her out."

Slava's eyes seemed magnified behind his mask. "Boss, are you serious? Who'd want her?"

"I don't know, maybe this *Ganjin* group. Who the hell knows!" Lex's pulse leapt forward as he rose. "Put those chains in your pack. They might be good for DNA later if this all goes south. Drones up! We've still got ten cells and four chambers to clear, and we ain't leaving till we're sure."

Lex stuffed the prison uniform in his own pack, and then they split up and shifted down the curving hall, continuing their sweep, clearing each cell, one by one, right and left, the drones flitting off behind them. Every time Slava called, "Clear," Lex's heart sank a little further.

His aim grew shaky as the enormity of the mission and the thought of failure took hold. He cleared the next few rooms. Empty, empty, empty.

"Hey, check it out!" Slava cried, bounding ahead, skipping the next two doors and steering his big frame straight for two more bodies lying just outside the farthest cell door.

As Lex jogged up behind Slava, the blood puddles and gaping wounds were unmistakable.

"This had to be her cell," said Slava, pushing open the door. "Right here."

Lex stiffened and spoke through his teeth. "Bad timing . . . bad intel . . . just what the hell is this?" His mind leapt forward in a panic, and he got on the radio, forgetting that the signal wouldn't get through. "Borya, it's me. We're finishing up down here. Looks like someone else got to her first. I need your eyes now, buddy."

"Can't . . . hear . . . you, boss. Signal breaking . . ."

Lex cursed. "I'll try again when we get up top!"

"Say again?"

"Just stay sharp!"

"All this for nothing?" Slava asked.

Lex fought against the nerves. This wasn't him. He was a seasoned operator, for God's sake. Marine Corps Raider. When they needed a hunter, they called him because he never let a situation overwhelm him. No fog of war. Only clarity, looking at it . . . seeing what must be done. He took a deep breath and spoke evenly:

"Sergeant, you think we'd launch an attack like this without a secondary objective? We're using Ragland's kidnapping as an excuse to our allies to blow the shit out of this place. We've known about this HQ for the past year, and the general's been arguing about taking it out, along with the rest of Fort Levski. The politicians have been dancing around it because they feared the reprisal."

"So we're still cool?"

"No, we're *not* cool. And we're *not* leaving here without our package. She's gotta be on her way up top right now. Let's go get her."

The Snow Maiden stood near the door leading out into the motor pool. Her face was covered in sweat, the mask beginning to fog up as she slowly peered outside.

She did a double take.

Two Cockroach drivers were trying to blow through a mountain of rubble rising nearly five meters, while behind them a dozen or more vehicles were on fire and waves of black smoke hung like smog over the entire cave.

She spotted the pedestrian door to the left of those big IFVs. Ten or twelve more troops were rushing though it. She picked her path behind a row of BTRs, a few of them with smoke pouring from their gunners' stations, then darted off, unsure if anyone had seen her.

Grimacing, she reached the rear of the nearest carrier and stooped behind the heavy metal plating.

A shadow passed over her.

She glanced back at a troop holding his rifle on her. His gaze narrowed behind his mask. "Wait, you're not . . . wait . . ."

She put a finger to her lips.

"I have one here!" he cried. "Here!"

His gaze had left her for just a second, searching for his comrades.

She went for his mask and rifle at the same time, knocking the gun up with her right forearm, while driving the barrel of her left pistol beneath his chinstrap. The mask came free at the same time she fired.

The gunshot was like the starting pistol of an Olympic sprint, and she stole only a few seconds to seize the troop's rifle, abandon one of her pistols, stow the other, then rocket along the back of the APCs. Sometime during all of that, the troop fell back and died.

Now, two more troops were rounding the corner of the last carrier in the row, having responded to the first man's cries—

And the Snow Maiden used her forward momentum to leap nearly a meter into the air, leaving them all of a second to react.

They were lifting their rifles toward her, but she'd already opened fire, leveling both men as she hit the ground, slipped, and fell flat on her chest, the rifle sliding sideways, the wind blasting from her lungs.

A fire woke in her knee.

She lay there, not believing that she'd actually fallen. Her internal voice screamed for her to get up. With aching eyes she slowly rose, tugged up the rifle, and started off once more, limping over the spiking pain. Damn it, she'd jumped like that a thousand times. So much for the acrobatics of youth. She'd best rely on age and treachery now.

Gunfire ricocheted off the next row of Cockroaches as she darted from one to the next, closing in on the exit. If she fell again, they'd have her.

One troop barked for his comrade to close the door, and the Snow Maiden stopped, rolled back, and shot him three times in the chest for his efforts. She lowered her rifle and shivered, and the mask suddenly felt as though it were slipping off. Growing paranoid, she shoved it much harder into her face.

Don't stop now, she reminded herself. With a groan, she was back on the move, weaving between the parked Cockroaches, an apparition as immaterial as the shadows between the towering 7.62-millimeter machine guns, shoulders rubbing along the armor plates, closer now, the door only fifty meters away.

Two troops charged toward that door, more like a hatch with big horizontal and perpendicular handles, just as the last of another group filed through. They shut the door and rolled back, bringing their rifles to bear, shifting their aim across the motor pool to scan the area in her direction.

Something buzzed past her shoulder and she stopped, craned her neck, spotted another of those micro UAVs flying by. The drone streaked past her and toward the guards, zeroing in on them, as though getting a bead on their faces.

She frowned. No, those little buggers didn't belong to the Spetsnaz, as evidenced by their reaction:

Both troops opened fire on the UAV, and the Snow Maiden tore free from the shadows and raced straight for them, exploiting the diversion to strike one in the upper shoulder, the other in the neck, pounding them into the ground. They were stunned, still moving, so as she neared them, she finished the job as one tried to roll over, while the other struggled to raise his rifle.

More shouts lifted behind her. Entirely out of breath, she swung open the heavy industrial hatch—

Just as dozens of superheated rounds pinged and sparked and ricocheted off its surface. She screamed against the fire and slammed shut the hatch behind her.

No way to lock it. The security system bypassed. Nothing else to do but run—

Half a kilometer in the dim red light.

The long tunnel seemed even more vast, the strings of lights swirling into a kaleidoscope on her periphery as she picked up the pace.

Her knee hurt like a bitch now. The limp came and went and she fought against it, gritting her teeth in agony.

And then came the dreaded waves of gunfire stitching along the pipes, the walls, the asphalt, not a meter from her boots. She'd come so far. She was almost there. She couldn't quit now—

But her body had had enough. She'd endured more physical pain and suffering in the last few days than she'd probably had during her entire career. The jumps, the falls, the ice, the shackles, the physical and mental horrors . . .

How could she go on when she felt like this? How could she reach deeper?

She needed to embrace the pain, even welcome it. Only through her suffering would she manage to escape. How much could she suffer?

Just a little more.

She told her body to suck it up. Run harder. Faster. She shifted closer to the pipes attached to the tunnel on her right side, gaining what little cover she could. Another round bit into a cable at her shoulder. She swore aloud and broke from the limp into a full-on sprint.

Embrace the pain.

The knee grew wobbly. She wouldn't stop.

There'd be no light at the end of this tunnel. Good. She and the darkness got along just fine.

THIRTY-THREE

Spetsnaz Headquarters
Fort Levski
Bulgaria

Lex and Slava recalled the drones from each level as they ascended. Once they reached the command-and-control center, just below the motor pool, Lex couldn't help himself. He only needed a minute. He just had to take it, otherwise he might regret this for the rest of his life.

He ordered Slava to wait outside the main door.

"What's up, boss?"

"I'll be right back." He took off running, turned down a short hallway, pushed past the open door, and reached a series of intel stations lining the bowed wall, each one painted in the multicolored glimmer of holographic and standard displays, all of the computers locked out as expected, screen savers and standby messages flashing.

Lex dropped into the nearest chair and tugged free

298 TOM CLANCY'S ENDWAR

the wafer-thin card from his breast pocket. He touched a small metal square on the card's corner, and a tiny green light switched on.

He took a deep breath and waited.

This was the deal he'd cut with General Mitchell. *"You want to send me into hell, then you let me tap into the devil's database while I'm there. You get me the most sophisticated wireless hacking system on the planet, and you get me into those files. All I need is a name and a location. The rest is yours."*

The computer and holographic screens all around Lex blossomed to life. It was an electronic carnival with enough displays scrolling and flickering to make Lex dizzy. The green light on the card flashed. Download in progress. Those intel nerds and their associates at the NSA had made it easy for an ape like Lex.

A touch screen to Lex's right flashed, and suddenly it was there:

Her dossier. In Cyrillic.

Captain Oksana Alexandrov.

Pictures, full military record.

While the download continued, Lex scrolled via the motion sensor through the record and found another link:

FEDERATION DETENTION CAMP 106, IRKUTSK OBLAST.

He made a tapping motion in the air, scrolled through another list, found it: current prisoner-of-war roll. He clicked, held his breath, scrolled again.

Her name was near the top of the list, right beneath a man whose current status read *DECEASED*. Hers read *POW*.

Fourteen months of searching was over. He'd located his sister at a POW camp in Siberia, one he'd never heard of before, one he was certain the JSF did not know existed because he'd already searched all of the known ones. He couldn't hold back the tears, and at the sound of Slava's approach, he shot up, tried to compose himself, and screamed, "Sergeant, I told you to watch that door!"

But the man wearing the gas mask and pointing the assault rifle at Lex wasn't Slava—

He was a Spetsnaz captain, according to the triangular four-star insignia on his uniform, and in broken English he said, "Your friend is dead."

The Snow Maiden was on the brink of total collapse when she spotted the twin silhouettes of the open blast doors. A group of about twenty or so troops, along with the medical personnel and administrative and support staff (probably thirty in all) were being loaded into a pair of Ural-4320 6×6 trucks like the one that had delivered her here. The trucks had been backed up into the entrance, which was now being devoured by a thick haze pouring in from the darkness outside. By the time she blinked again, she could no longer see either truck—but they were there, and that gave her hope.

She stole a look back at the four guards who'd been following her down the tunnel. They'd stopped firing but were still on her heels, vanishing themselves into the dust as she neared the exit. She came through the clouds and found herself between both trucks, someone shouting from behind for her to get inside.

"Okay, no problem," she answered, racing around the front of the vehicle to the driver's-side door, which she ripped open as the man at the wheel looked at her.

She tapped the insignia on her shoulder: lieutenant colonel. "Get out!"

As the driver rushed from his seat and hopped down, the guards following her from the motor pool started hollering, and the troops loading people into the back of the truck broke off and came around to stop her.

Too late for them. She threw the truck in gear and floored it, gears grinding as she shifted and turned hard, her body thrown against the door as she barreled onto the mountain road.

The truck's headlights shone thickly through the dust, and she could barely see much more. To her right, flashes like heat lightning shone across the valley. An amorphous cloud of dust backlit by fires far below and by more of those bluish-white explosions suggested something huge had struck the fort, bunker-buster bombs or even a kinetic strike. The windows were open, and she began to hear the thumping of choppers and the higher-pitched roaring of jet engines.

She cut the wheel, avoiding the cliff by less than a meter, and then, from the corner of her eye, she caught movement.

A brave troop had scaled his way across the side of the

truck and wanted to gain entrance to the passenger side of the cab. He clutched the door with one hand and tried to raise his pistol with the other.

The Snow Maiden sighed over his futile effort and summarily shot him. He fell away.

Her gaze flicked back to the road, and she drew her head back in surprise. A much larger UAV than the ones she'd encountered inside now hovered over the truck's hood, scanning her once again then flying off behind the truck.

All right, they'd taken a very good look at her, who-ever they were. She jammed her boot harder onto the accelerator as the truck jostled over two potholes that tossed her violently into the steering wheel.

As the road leveled out, the dust cleared enough to expose a hairpin turn festooned by low-hanging limbs. If she didn't slow down, she'd roll the truck. She saw how dense the forest was on either side of the turn, how the slopes weren't too steep and unfurled into the valley. This was as good a place as any.

She put the pedal to the metal and waited until the last possible second.

Three, two, one . . . she shoved open the door and threw herself out, crashing into a pile of snow on the side of the road and tumbling through it as the truck lum-bered on, leaving the road and careening down the hill, sideswiping trees with sharp cracks before disappearing.

The Snow Maiden rose, and the din overhead had her staring up through a pocket in the dust. A V-25 Gos-hawk tilt-rotor troop transport used by the Joint Strike

Force streaked by, trailing a pair of smaller HH-60H Seahawk helicopters whose door gunners were opening up on targets well ahead and out of view, the streams of brass casings tumbling like chaff through the canopy.

She had her answer: The Americans were here, and this was their attack. All she needed to do was reach them and defect, just like she'd planned back on Sakhalin Island. They'd keep her alive. She was valuable to them. Kapalkin only wanted his revenge.

Then again, she was in Bulgaria. She could try to make a run for it. Whom did she know here? Were there any contacts left she could trust? The price on her head was very high, indeed. Greed trumped friendship. Even if she found a contact and escaped, she'd be back to running. From everyone.

No, she couldn't do this anymore. She'd go to them. She would, as her father had instructed, do the right thing, warn them about Dennison and Izotov. Help them. The enemies of the motherland would become her friends.

She bit her lip and pulled herself up out of the snow, and at the sound of the second truck coming down the road, she started through the twisted limbs sparkling in the truck's headlights, pausing a moment to observe the truck, whose driver rolled right past her—

Leaving three Spetsnaz troops in his wake, the men having been standing on the tailgate only to hop off. One pointed in her direction, and all three came running toward her.

The Snow Maiden ripped off the gas mask and took a

quick breath. The air reeked of jet fuel and fires, but it was still breathable, despite all the dust. It was good to be out of that damned thing.

She eased back deeper into the underbrush, finding a crevice between two thick roots, where she got down on all fours and waited for the troops to get closer.

Only then did she notice it was snowing, the cold hiss permeating the forest and working into her bones, calming her as the troops trudged down on their heels, clicking on flashlights, the beams cutting at sharp angles against the warren of bark and pinecones and snow.

A twig snapped beneath one man's boot.

The others shushed him.

The Snow Maiden took a deep breath, calculating each man's position before she rose from the roots and fired three shots, one after the other, and it was as though the troops were magnetized and there was no way she could miss them. Her senses were raw now, fully exposed, everything heightened despite the lack of sleep and extreme duress.

She was running as they fell like scarecrows behind her, running in the direction of those American helicopters. They would land and drop off troops. She could only hope they were taking prisoners.

Lex rose slowly from the computer station and raised his palms. He glanced at both the data card and his rifle lying beside it. The card had not finished its download, and he'd promised the general he'd return with it.

"American spies who dress like us, talk like us. I bet you were born in Russia, huh? You fucking traitor," said the captain, shoving his rifle at Lex as though wanting to open fire but restrained by orders.

If this son of a bitch had killed Slava, then why hadn't Lex heard the fight or been warned over the team channel by his teammate? And sure as shit, Slava would not have given up without a fight. Not him.

"You're lying, asshole."

"You want to come with me and see for yourself?"

Lex gave the captain a once-over, noting the size and shape of the pistol strapped to the man's right thigh. It had a yellow stripe on its handle, IDing it as a Less Than Lethal sidearm that fired darts.

"You're going to take me prisoner and be a hero tonight, is that it?" Lex asked. "And you're going to do this while the fort burns outside?"

"We'll stay here until reinforcements arrive. They're already on their way. I'm taking you down to a cell." The Spetsnaz captain shifted over to Lex, trying to get in close enough so he could snatch the data card from the desk.

Over the captain's shoulder, at the far end of the hall, came Slava, limping forward. His gas mask was gone and two darts jutted from the side of his neck. He was clutching his waist, where he must've been shot or stabbed, and one boot left a blood trail across the floor.

Yes, he'd been left for dead, but the Spetsnaz captain had not removed the reserve pistol Slava kept tucked in the ankle holster of his left leg. The captain's search had been too hasty, and Slava fought his way closer, raising his arm, the pistol clutched in his gloved hand.

"I'm not done with you," he cried.

The captain swung around—

And at the same time Lex dove for his rifle while the two men opened fire.

By the time Lex got his hands on the Izhmash, both Slava and the captain were falling back toward the floor, the captain still squeezing his trigger and driving rounds into the ceiling panels, Slava emptying the rest of his magazine before he landed on his back.

Screaming with rage, Lex opened up on the captain, riddling his chest and head with at least a dozen rounds before ceasing fire.

Panting, he charged across the hall, dropping to his knees before Slava.

The bear of a man, the secret weapon on Lex's team, lay there, bleeding from his neck and thighs, his chest saved from the more serious rounds by his Kevlar plates, but he was still bleeding terribly, gasping, eyelids fluttering.

"My fault," he said, coughing and spitting up blood.

Lex could barely face him. "Not yours." He fumbled through his medical kit, producing the QuikClot bandages, the scissors. He cut open the uniform around the gunshot wounds and slapped the 4×4s home, but they were already darkening with blood.

He looked back to the desk, then at Slava.

What had he done? An imaginary fist clamped around his heart. He stopped breathing.

Slava cleared his throat. "Let's go, boss."

"Okay, hang on." Shuddering, he went back for the data card, tucking it into his hip pocket. He hated his decision to pause here, hated the card, hated what he'd done to his teammate.

You don't leave your buddy—

But the temptation to find Oksana had been too great.

He sprinted back to his friend, took a deep breath, steeled himself, then lifted Slava in a fireman's carry. With burning eyes and a mouth hanging open in fury, he carried his fellow Marine into the stairwell and all the way up to the motor pool level, his quads firing on pure adrenaline as he mounted each step, the effort herculean, but he deserved the pain, deserved every second of it. This was punishment for putting his friend and teammate in danger, and he deserved much more.

Just inside the door leading outside, Lex lowered Slava to the floor and checked the man for a pulse. Very weak but still there.

Out of breath and dizzy, he keyed his mike. "Borya, this is Actual. You read me, over?"

"Just barely, Actual."

"I'm in the motor pool stairwell. Slava's been hit. I need evac. Send down Vlad. Tell him to commandeer one of those carts and get his ass to my location."

"Roger that. I'll send him now."

"You spot our package?"

"Negative. But, sir, the ID came in on an officer we picked up on the R & D level, then we got her up again driving one of the trucks out of the tunnel. You're not gonna believe this. It's the Snow Maiden."

"Say again?"

"I'm saying that Colonel Viktoria Antsyforov, the Snow Maiden, was inside. She was wearing someone else's uniform, but she was definitely there—and I bet she was the prisoner we saw being transferred."

Lex took a few seconds as the news sank in. Every Special Forces operator worth his salt not only knew who the Snow Maiden was but had studied every classified and declassified doc the JSF had on her. She was for many the ultimate prize, the Osama bin Laden of their decade.

And she was here?

His mouth finally worked. "Borya, tell me you've locked on to her."

"Negative, we lost her when the drone had to scan the rest of the passengers in the back of the truck. Best I can tell, though, she sent the truck off the road and got out of there on foot."

"Okay. And hey, one more thing: Tell Vlad to contact me when he's close. I'll put up smoke."

"Sir, it's me, sir," said Vlad. "On the channel now. Roping down to your location. ETA two minutes."

"Gotcha. Hurry up."

"Trust me, boss, I'm moving!"

"Good. Actual, out."

Lex leaned back on the wall and tried to clear his head.

Ragland wasn't the prisoner here. She never had been. The Snow Maiden was.

That was it. The Snow Maiden, a traitor to the motherland, had finally been captured, but the Russians had not announced it. They'd brought her here for interrogation.

And someone else wanted her busted out. Her allies? If so, had they known about the attack?

Or had they helped orchestrate it?

Were they the ones responsible for feeding false intel to the JSF? Because this sure as hell had been false intel.

Lex's eyes widened, and his pulse rose with the desire to contact General Mitchell. The JSF attack had provided the means and opportunity for the Snow Maiden to escape. Lex, his men, and the rest of the JSF forces were only pawns in something else. Meanwhile, Dr. Helena Ragland might still be out there, somewhere.

Lex crouched beside Slava and checked the man's pulse again. Weak. Very weak. The sergeant was unconscious now, and while waiting for Vlad, Lex rolled the man on his side to inspect that wound. The bandages were soaked.

He couldn't bear the moment any longer. He stood and got to work, removing his web gear, setting it down beside the door. He had six L12-7 heat-seeking grenades, as did Slava. Lex armed all twelve, set them down in neat rows at his feet, then lined up all four of the smoke grenades.

He slowly opened the door and chanced a look into the motor pool, where the Cockroaches had just finished breaching the rock pile wall, and two of them rumbled on through and into the tunnel.

"Hey, Vlad, this is Actual. You got vehicles heading your way. Just stay close to the wall and ignore them."

"Gotcha. I'll keep my head low."

Lex ducked back inside, then jerked at the sound of heavy boots trudging up the stairs.

He shifted silently across the landing and peered down to spy three troops mounting the stairs, two at a time. Where had they come from? Hell, did it matter?

There was no need to get into a protracted gunfight. He scooped up one of the heat seekers, reared back, and let it fly down into the stairwell. In the next heartbeat he bounded away and threw himself over Slava, bracing himself as the blast cracked and boomed, the landing quaking as a mushroom cloud of black smoke filled the well and had Lex shielding Slava's mouth and nose. He rose to wedge open the door as Vlad's voice crackled in his ear: "Boss, I'm in a cart. ETA just thirty seconds. Little help."

"Roger that, you just hold a course straight through to the lifts. Do not veer off. Here we go!"

Lex slammed open the door, and while still on his knees he began hurling the tiny missiles right and left, the motors instantly igniting, miniature guidance systems homing in on the strongest heat sources, which in this case were the engines of the armored vehicles as they fired up and turned toward the exit.

While he didn't expect to disable the vehicles with a single grenade (although that might be possible via a lucky shot that might cause internal systems to overload), the explosions would force any of the troops still dismounted in the motor pool to seek cover, as they had during the first round of explosions.

Once he set free the last grenade, Lex lobbed off the smoke canisters that in short order created a thick screen all the way out to the blast doors.

Through those diaphanous walls of smoke came Vlad, one hand on the cart's wheel, the other gripping his pistol, his entrance heralded by a chorus of explosions that echoed so loudly that they drowned out the APCs' rumbling engines. Vlad rolled up to the stairwell door and hopped out, holstering his pistol.

"How is he?" asked Vlad.

"Bad."

"We got time to get a line in? Got some Ringer's and morphine on board?"

"Do it."

"Yes, sir." Vlad's tone had gone all business. He rifled through his med kit, got an IV in place on his first try, and hung the liter bag of lactated Ringer's around Slava's neck. Then he prepared the syringe of morphine and injected it into Slava's line. He faced Lex and said, "Good to go."

"I'm glad we saved your meds," Lex told him. "It was a good call."

Vlad pursed his lips and nodded. They stood and carried Slava to the back of the cart, where they propped him in a seat and Lex held him upright. He checked again for a pulse. Nothing. He began to lose his breath as he tried a second time. There it was, barely perceptible . . . but there. The son of a bitch was a fighter, all right.

"Long-range comm back up in a minute," said Vlad, steering them into the smoke, leaning forward into the wheel as he drove blindly between the piles of rubble.

Suddenly, he blasted straight into a troop who was crossing their path. The guy rolled across the front of the cart and splayed across the floor. The impact sent them caroming off some rocks and back into the gap.

"I got it, I got it," cried Vlad, cutting the wheel as Lex glanced over his shoulder and directed his own pistol toward the back of the cart, where a few more troops materialized from the smoke.

"Go right," Lex shouted, then fired—just as a few of their rounds cut into the wall to their left.

"Deep Raider Actual, this is Guardian, over."

Lex blinked hard and swore. Commanding officers always had perfect timing, didn't they? "Guardian, this is Deep Raider Actual. We've completed our sweep. No package. Repeat. No package. I have a man down and need immediate evac, over."

This was hardly the report Lex wanted to issue, and he wished he could take it back, but his was a life of intel and of cold hard facts.

"Roger that, Actual. QRF and second strike team are there now. I'll coordinate, but you'll still need to get to your rally point because we have inbound enemy aircraft and IFVs along the mountain."

"We'll get there. Sir, I don't think the package was ever here."

"We'll follow up on the intel and see what happened. Make no mistake, heads will roll."

"Roger that, sir. Seems like another group might've used us as a diversion to break out the Snow Maiden. We confirmed she was here."

"We've been monitoring your drone feeds and sent back the ID. We've got everyone looking for her now. Anyway, get out of there, Captain. You've done what you could."

"On our way, sir. Deep Raider Actual, out."

After a second of just shaking his head in frustration, Lex switched to the team channel and told Borya to be ready for them. The exit was coming up fast.

His gaze lowered to the cart's floor, and he shuddered over the swelling puddle of blood. The bandages could no longer hold back the torrent. Dreading it, Lex reached up and checked Slava's neck for a pulse.

The man was growing cold.

THIRTY-FOUR

Spetsnaz Headquarters
Fort Levski
Bulgaria

Major Stephanie Halverson was exactly where she belonged: behind the stick of an F-35B Joint Strike Fighter and studying an incoming force of MiG-29 fighters lighting up her display.

She wasn't concerned about the MiGs. She and the rest of the twenty-four strike fighters from Carrier Air Wing Eight (CVW-8) attached to the USS *George H. W. Bush* would dispatch them quickly and efficiently before they were ever picked up by enemy radar. The Joint Strike Fighters were far more stealthy than the federation's old fleet. Moreover, the MiGs would still need to be cued in via an airborne radar plane or ground station, and even then, they'd still have trouble picking up the F-35s. Halverson's colleagues were already targeting the radar planes, and the nearest ground stations had already been obliterated.

However—and this was a big *however*—the MiGs weren't the only aircraft in this arena. The Federation had scrambled at least twenty Sukhoi PAK FA T-50 stealth fighters from Sevastopol International Airport (now primarily used as a military fighter base). With their pairs of thirty-millimeter cannons; state-of-the-art avionics packages including X-band AESA (active electronically scanned array) and L-band radars for picking up stealth-specific aircraft; and Kayak, Kilter, and Archer missiles, the T-50s were Russia's most formidable, maneuverable, and hard-to-detect fighters. They had gone head-to-head against the F-35s several times, mostly during standoff missions with air-to-air missiles exchanged at extreme distances.

This battle was different. All the dust in the zone would diffuse their radar signals through absorption, reflection, and scattering, creating much smaller echoes and making it much harder to acquire targets. That handicap might cause pilots to get in close for those rare but certainly not unprecedented dogfights, along with descending much lower than usual to visually acquire their ground targets before unloading their ordnance.

Halverson's own ground targets were strung out below. She confirmed that some of Fort Levski's Cockroaches and BTRs had been spared from the kinetic strike since they'd been parked inside the mountain, and those vehicles were now taking up positions along the mountain road and targeting JSF air elements, most notably the slower-moving Seahawks, the enemy guns flashing like a short-circuiting string of casino lights.

The irony was that neither she nor any other pilot from CVW-8 had permission for a missile strike against those guns, since a Marine Raider team was still in the process of exfiltrating from the base.

Halverson, of course, wasn't one to blindly follow orders, and she dove toward the mountain, evading the AA fire outlined in her helmet-mounted display system to get a good look at each of those Cockroaches, six in all now, positions marked along the snaking road.

As she pulled up and away, she concluded that their ground team would have a hell of a time getting past those vehicles and those crews, along with the dismounts that had flooded out of the mountain. In fact, you didn't want to be near an AA gun while it was lobbing shells. Between the ear-shattering racket, the danger of a misfire, and the threat of incoming missile fire from your own forces, getting close to one of those IFVs was putting one boot in the grave.

She called back to the tactical air commander with an urgent message for General Mitchell.

After a ten-second pause, she was put through: "Guardian, this is Siren. I'm ready to provide Close Air Support for our Raider team. Request permission for a direct link with that team leader on the ground, over."

"Roger that, Siren. I know what you have in mind. Standby for Deep Raider Actual."

"Standing by."

*   *   *

The booming from the anti-aircraft guns outside the main entrance unnerved Lex. He ordered Vlad to head for the service road just inside the blast doors. They pulled to a stop and sought cover behind a haphazardly parked collection of more carts. Lex hopped out, ripped off his gas mask, and looked at Vlad. "Slava's dead."

Vlad tugged off his mask, cursed, then turned and hurled it toward the wall. He crossed back to Slava and put his hand on the man's shoulder. "God damn it."

"Deep Raider Actual, this is Siren, over."

"Siren, standby." Lex frantically slipped off his pack and dug out his situational awareness visor, this one a backup that resembled a pair of wide skier's sunglasses. He booted up the SAV via a button by his ear. A databar opened and floated at arm's length to show the cockpit view of the incoming caller, along with full ID: F-35B Joint Strike Fighter pilot Major Stephanie Halverson, call sign "Siren."

"Okay, Major, I'm here."

"I'm looking at your blue force beacon and see you're just inside the main exit. You got six Cockroaches on the road to get past."

"Only six? Got more coming out now."

"Roger that. I'm seeing you got one observer up top. He needs to find cover."

"I'm on it."

"Good. I'm taking out the farthest guns from the entrance with missiles. The ones closest to you get the cannon. After my second pass on them, be ready to haul ass, over?"

"Shit, lady, you don't have to ask me twice. Waiting on you. Go for it!"

"Okay, I'm coming around. One last question. Do you have the package?"

"Negative. No package."

Halverson's tone shifted dramatically. "Uh, can you say again?"

"No package."

"Oh, all right. Stand by."

Lex switched to the team channel. "Borya, this is Actual, you read me?"

"I'm here, boss."

"Get down here, right now! Air strike coming in."

"Can't do it, I'm cut off. Lots of dismounts on the road right now, right under the lines. I'll be too slow if I go with the camouflage."

Lex nodded, already visualizing Borya's secondary escape plan. "I hear that, Sergeant. You fall back to the air shafts. We'll link up with you after the strike. Stay down!"

"No worries about that, boss. How's Slava?"

Lex hesitated. "He's gone. Now get out of there."

In the airspace above Bulgaria, President Kapalkin had been watching the attack on Fort Levski from his private jet, the distorted and static-filled security camera images sent to him via Moscow from the minister of defense, while his own pilots, along with his T-50 fighter escort, reported the devastation in the distance. Kapalkin's outrage over what was happening had already resulted in two destroyed tablet computers and a broken bottle of Leon Verres vodka, the bottle itself covered in fur and diamonds and one of the priciest in the world.

While his pilot had just made a hasty course correction, guiding them far away from the danger zone and taking them back toward Moscow, Kapalkin called the American president and demanded answers.

"President Kapalkin, I was expecting your call."

"I'm sure you were."

"I'll get right to the point, then."

Becerra tried to sell Kapalkin a story about the Spetsnaz abducting one of their engineers and that the Russian Federation had instigated the entire attack.

"A pathetic excuse for your allies? Is that what this is?" Kapalkin asked him.

If that weren't enough, Kapalkin's people on the ground had informed him that Lieutenant Colonel Osin was dead and that the Snow Maiden was missing. It appeared someone had helped her escape.

"We don't have your engineer," Kapalkin repeated. "We didn't abduct her. And if I may say so, I believe we're both being played for fools."

"Who's playing us?"

"Who isn't? The Euros? The Forgotten Army?"

Becerra's expression grew harder, his gaze penetrating. "You left out the *Ganjin*. What do you know about them?"

Kapalkin snorted. "What do *you* know?"

"You came to us when the terrorists had nukes in Canada. We helped you save both of our economies. Now it's time for you to help me. I'm asking you one more time: What do you know about the *Ganjin*?"

"I'll admit we've heard the name. Only the name. To me they're a myth. Where is their headquarters? Where is their army? Who are their generals? What do you know?"

"We're not sure, but the Forgotten Army works for them—as does your rogue colonel, the Snow Maiden. That's right, we know she was there and escaped."

"Do you know where she is now?"

"I'm willing to work with you to find her and asking you to help us find our missing engineer. This *Ganjin* group might be the key to everything."

Kapalkin settled back deeper into his seat. "That's an interesting proposal, Mr. President. But speaking bluntly, this attack in Bulgaria is a strange way to ask for help. A simple request to our ambassador in Washington would have sufficed."

Becerra shook his head. "We're not sure that your ambassador still reports to you, and we believed that our engineer was being held at Fort Levski. Sir, we can drag out this verbal sparring for years but, eventually, both of us will have to answer to the world and our own people for our actions. We worked together in Canada. Why can't we do it again?"

"I'm forced to question your veracity, Mr. President, in the face of the satellite images I've seen showing you training ground drones in military maneuvers in your Mojave Desert."

"I'll be frank. Those aren't military maneuvers. Since the war between us broke out, we've been watching you pour your petrodollars back into your economy, but now my geologists tell me you're fast approaching peak oil. The rest of your reserve is now much more difficult to extract, requiring extensive processing. As your output diminishes, you'll be forced to cut back on exports just to satisfy your own needs. When you do that, you'll upset some of your allies. You've got yourself a Siberian tiger by the balls and you can't let go. Energywise it'll eventually cost you a barrel of oil to extract a barrel of oil from the ground. That's a game changer, Mr. President. You know it, and we know it."

"So what are you doing out there in your desert?"

"I'm told that even though the Middle East is too radioactive and untenable for humans to work on the desert surface, the oil *beneath* the surface is *not* contaminated. When you see my drones in a huddle, they're training to build pumping stations, and when you see them in a long line, they're learning how to lay pipeline— all the way out to the coast."

"So you plan to go back in there."

"We don't have to do it alone. We could turn this into a joint effort, let it become a symbol of renewed trust, and finally, let it help put an end to this conflict. This doesn't have to be complicated. We can make it so simple."

Kapalkin furrowed his brows. "I don't trust you, Mr.

President, but I'm willing to hear more. When I land in Moscow, I'll form a negotiating committee. They'll meet secretly with your people in Geneva, seven days from now. We'll be in contact to firm up the time and place. Good-bye, Mr. President."

"My people will be there, sir."

Kapalkin immediately made another call to General Izotov, who had successfully passed his polygraph exam and whose loyalty was, according to Kapalkin's experts, unquestionable. Kapalkin gave the general a summary of his call with Becerra, after which Izotov asked, "So how would you like to punish them?"

"I'm not sure yet."

"May I suggest cutting off their oil?"

"How much?"

"All of it."

"Are you serious? Do you understand the implications that will have on our own economy? It'll create a surplus and lower the price for our other customers, which in turn will lower our profits, decrease revenues, and strangle our defense budget during a time of war."

"It's only a temporary measure," explained Izotov. "To let them know we're serious, and believe me when I say there is nothing more serious than their thirst for oil."

Kapalkin balled his hands into fists. "All right, but only I give the order, and I won't be doing so for at least seven days."

"Why the delay?"

"That'll become clear to you, General. Good-bye."

THIRTY-FIVE

Spetsnaz Headquarters
Fort Levski
Bulgaria

Lex and Vlad had crouched behind the cart, with Slava's body still slumped in the seat above them.

Two more Cockroaches roared by, along with three more BTRs. The combination of all those screeching engines and the booming outside left their ears ringing.

Vlad was rubbing his eyes, trying to hide his grief from Lex. Ironically, Slava and Vlad had not been that close. They were professionals to be sure, but they never spent any time together outside the Corps. When the team went to a bar, Slava took off by himself. Maybe Vlad was feeling guilty over never getting to know the guy or that Slava was always chiding him about his constant doom-and-gloom reports.

Lex and his three men had been an outstanding team. There was no denying that. It was the end of an era, and

Lex found himself rubbing his own eyes as a breath-robbing explosion struck outside, followed by a second, then a third as part of the ceiling on the far end of the cave began to collapse. He stared up, wondering how long they had until this part of the tunnel gave way . . .

He tucked himself in beside Vlad and said, "Hang tight, Sergeant. We'll get out of here in a minute."

Vlad nodded. "Goddamn Slava had to go and die on us, you know? Son of a bitch . . ."

"I know."

"He was so hard-core he couldn't admit he was just a guy who could bleed out like anyone else. And now he bought it. The toughest mother I ever met. So where does that leave us?"

Lex hardened his tone. "That leaves us here . . . to bring him home."

Halverson should have grinned over the awe-inspiring AIM-9X missile strikes delivered from her wingtips with deadly precision.

The Cockroaches were exploding one after another as though they'd been rigged from the ground. Infrared emissions were detected and armor was penetrated in an unstoppable death blow. Any pyro junkie would've received her fix and then some as half the mountainside grew alive with dancing flames fighting to shine up through all the dust.

However, news that the team had failed to recover Dr. Ragland was just . . . devastating. She wanted more answers—was her friend Ragland still missing? Was she dead? Had the Spetsnaz managed to smuggle her out before the attack?

Wincing in frustration, she banked hard right, coming around for the next pass, this time taking advantage of the jet's VTOL capability to hover in midair like a helicopter. The big flip-top lid covering the vertical thrust fan behind the cockpit rose like a wing flap. She neared the Cockroaches, slowed, then hovered as their shocked crews maneuvered guns toward the insane pilot who'd presented her aircraft on a silver platter.

But that was hardly the case. She opened up with her GAU-12 twenty-five-millimeter cannon mounted in its external pod, targeting the driver's cupola along with the housing around each fifty-seven-millimeter gun, knowing those areas were the weakest parts of the IFVs. She put 50 of the 220 rounds she carried on the first Cockroach and then broke from the hover and thundered off, targeting the next one, noting that the first one's guns had gone silent.

This, as she'd told the ground team leader, was a surgical strike on the vehicles nearest the HQ entrance, keeping the Marine Raider team safe from blue-on-blue fire. The risk was all hers now, of course, and while she'd been firing at the first Cockroach, the second one had been homing in on her, radar alarms blaring, fifty-seven-millimeter rounds stitching only a few meters off her port side.

She cut loose with a barrage of cannon fire now, even as she got on the radio: "Deep Raider Actual? Ten seconds to go!"

"Roger that, Siren."

"All right," she said breathlessly, jerking the stick and throttling up. "Get out of there!"

Ignoring the new IFVs and BTRs that were racing past the burning and disabled vehicles, Halverson came back around once more, zooming in with her cameras to see if she could spot the Marines.

There they were in a small cart, dressed like Spetsnaz troops, one at the wheel, two in the back, their IDs floating over the image as blue triangles. They might very well go unnoticed among all those other dismounts. It was pucker-up time for them. And her.

A report came in from their E-2 Hawkeye airborne early-warning command-and-control aircraft. They were out of time. The T-50s were already engaging the squadrons from long range, the sky now alive with so much missile fire that Halverson throttled up and dove straight down, into the smoke, coming within fifty meters of the ground, roaring across the massive craters and sections of upheaved earth lying across the tattered comm ditches and guard towers smashed apart as though constructed of coat hangers and duct tape. It was a surreal graveyard, all right, excavated by titanium and tenacity, and she was about to become its next resident if she couldn't shake the two missiles that had just locked on.

Of course, her Russian foes had sent only the best:

The AA-11 Archer R-73 was the premiere short-range air-to-air missile in the Federation's arsenal and could engage targets maneuvering with g-forces up to 12. It could intercept a target from any direction, under any weather conditions, day or night, in the presence of natural interference and deliberate jamming. She'd thought the dust would give those T-50 pilots more trouble than it had. *Shit.*

Well, the crews aboard the carrier hadn't loaded up her aft canisters with flares and chaff for nothing. She released the white-hot countermeasures, then dove toward the burning barracks and violently hit the brakes, slowing into a hover and rapid descent—just as the missiles took the bait and detonated behind her.

She gasped—*Jesus, too close*—just as the next alarm beeped. They'd locked on again.

Throttling up, she set free another burst of chaff and flares, then ascended, wheeling around the fort as an unexpected surprise lit her screens:

She now had two Russian fighters on her own radar, range only three kilometers. Missiles locked. Even as she leveled off, her thumb flicked across the joystick.

The AIM-120s ignited from the jet's inner pylons and leapt away, leaving fire-lit contrails in their wake. They closed to self-homing distance, turned on their active radar seekers, and found their targets, a one-two punch whose explosions flashed across her canopy on either side.

Adios, bitches.

Lex was barking orders in Russian at the men trying to put out the fires around the nearest Cockroach, waving a hand as though he were in charge: "Fall back inside the motor pool! More air strikes coming in! Evacuate the wounded back inside. The gas has cleared."

Meanwhile, he and Vlad did just the opposite. Lex steered the cart through the scattering personnel and across the burning fields of debris, following the road as it curved down the mountainside. Twice he nearly lost control of the cart as they rumbled down and up a depression created by the missile strikes.

The rally point stood in a clearing about a click southwest of the entrance, a heliport with four pads used for dropping off supplies for the headquarters. The pallets were loaded aboard 6×6s and ferried up to the base. Two Seahawks were already en route there, and the Marines aboard would take out any troops manning the checkpoint and lone guard tower. They'd secure the heliport before Lex and his men arrived.

He needed to believe that.

There was no Plan B at this point, save for evacuating back into the mountains, where they could become a midnight snack for the wolves.

"Deep Raider Actual, this is Siren. Looks like you are clear to the rally point. I'll check back on you momentarily, over."

"Roger that, Siren. Outstanding job back there!"

"Just get home safe. Siren, out."

Lex tightened his grip on the wheel and glanced over his shoulder, where Slava was lying across the backseat. They'd used the big man's belt to batten him down.

The road grew much darker, but the cart was equipped with a pair of headlights that did a fair job of lighting the dirt road and exposing the ruts, now being draped in snow. They could already hear the idling choppers in the distance, and Lex lifted his voice and told Vlad, "Almost there!"

At the moment, Borya had left his cover point near the air shafts and had found an alternate route down the mountain, coming in to the rally point from the northeast side. He could descend without the need for a rope, but his evac would be slower and more arduous. He'd called back the drone and was using it to scout his own path. They would link up at a grid point about halfway to the helipads.

A flash in the sky—like a falling star—shone ahead, followed by a massive explosion of multiple fireballs rising from the trees in the distance.

"What the hell was that?" Vlad cried.

Lex checked the map floating on his head-up display. "Holy shit. That was the rally point."

THIRTY-SIX

Raider Team Rally Point
Helipads
Fort Levski, Bulgaria

The Snow Maiden had been running toward the helipads. She'd widened her eyes at the two Seahawks idling there, with the Goshawk just setting down to the rear when a brilliant flash enveloped the entire clearing.

Squinting and feeling as though someone or some-*thing* had just sucked all the air from the forest, she lifted a palm against the glare. The nearest chopper exploded in a fire-ringed blast just as the JSF Marines were storming out.

The concussion struck her like a main battle tank, booting her several meters backward, into the air, the pressure across her chest feeling as though it might crush her ribs.

She came crashing down just behind a tree as shredded parts of the chopper's fuselage came cartwheeling into the forest, striking the tree directly in front of her, followed by the rotor blades, blown off and still slicing through the air. One of the blades thumped into the snow just a few meters to her right, while burning men were flung up into the branches to remain there, some dead, some screaming and writhing like grotesque Christmas tree ornaments.

She rolled over and watched as the crew of the second Seahawk began evacuating the aircraft, its side windows and doors punctured by debris, the pilot and co-pilot falling to their knees, then collapsing right there in the snow.

At the same time, the Goshawk lifted off, its tilt rotors delivering hurricane-force winds across the flaming devastation, with debris blowing wildly and the stench of fuel and burning electronics and flesh permeating the clearing as more Marines sought cover.

Fighter jet engines resounded to the west—

And then, just at the aircraft pitched up, it was struck by a missile and burst apart so loudly, the wave so powerful, that the Snow Maiden knew if she didn't get down the debris field would tear her apart.

She screamed through a curse and dove forward, burying her head against the tree and shielding her eyes.

Then it came, a whoosh and hiss as though a thousand giant knives had been thrown simultaneously through the forest, slicing through leaves, branches, entire tree trunks, accompanied by the sounds of limbs being snapped off or crushed or creaking as they were bent back under the weight of flying wreckage.

The detonation continued, like thunderheads before a rainstorm, the ground reverberating, the stench of jet fuel choking as more pieces of the aircraft sounded as though they were jackhammering across the helipad, hacking apart the asphalt.

By the time the Snow Maiden lifted her head and stole a glimpse forward, the Goshawk was all but obscured by a skyscraper of blue-black smoke encompassed by bodies and jagged sections of wings and rotors rising like a postapocalyptic skyline.

More jets streaked overhead, just as the deeper booming of AA guns came from the mountain and sharper cracks echoed down from above.

She couldn't wrap her thoughts around the moment. Could fate be this cruel? Had the universe been dangling her from a string all this time, only to dip her now into the eternal fires?

This was the end of the line. These were the people who were supposed to save her. Yes, these Marines, lying here, bleeding and dying in the snow. These Marines burning up in the trees. She lost her breath and just sat there, turning her gaze to the sky and listening, searching for an angel shaped like a helicopter and whomping toward them. Nothing.

And then, from behind, came the thin, high-pitched hum of a cart used back at the headquarters. She crawled toward the dirt road, got to her feet, then spotted the dim headlights approaching.

As they drew closer, the knot in her gut tightened. They were Spetsnaz.

* * *

Lex called Borya and told him to head directly to the rally point. No midpoint rendezvous. He and Vlad needed to find out what the hell was happening down at the helipads and were high-tailing it there right now. At least two major explosions had come from that area, and he could only hope against terrible odds that their exfiltration team was okay. Moreover, that clearing represented the only good spot to land rotary aircraft, save for what was left of Fort Levski: the airfields unstable, the ground between the barracks tilled like farmers' fields. Lex wasn't sure they'd ever reach a secondary rally point in the cart. The thing would either run out of battery power or get stuck in the ice and snow. He was barely making it across the dirt and thinner sections of snow as it was.

"Hold up, boss!" cried Vlad.

The sergeant was wearing his own visor and scanning the woods to their right, his rifle coming up to his shoulder, his breath rising above him in the frigid air. "I got movement out there."

"I see it, too," said Lex, climbing out of the cart and starting toward the edge of the road.

Vlad arrived beside him, and they kept tight to the cart for cover.

For a moment, they just narrowed their gazes and remained there, probing the darkness.

Shouts in the distance, two smaller secondary explosions. More jets rushing unseen through the dust.

"Anything?" he whispered to Vlad.

The gunshot struck Vlad in the chest and knocked him away from the cart and flat onto his back.

Lex had already jerked from the sound and was dropping to his knees.

"Hit the plate, I'm okay," Vlad cried. "Get the bastard!"

Lex bolted away.

It was an insane move, running toward a sniper, and his common sense finally caught up with his legs, so as he headed for the nearest tree to gain cover, he reached into his pocket and let fly one of the Seekers.

The Snow Maiden had no intention of allowing these Spetsnaz troops anywhere near the helipads and her possible escape route. She'd kill them first, but her shot had dropped, striking the first troop in the chest instead of the head, and the other one ducked and broke away before she could fire again.

He was coming up fast behind her now, and she worried that with her battered knee she couldn't outrun him or try to lose him in the forest before she confronted the Americans. She rushed toward the clearing and the fires blazing farther out like tribal torches beneath the thickening snow.

She stole a look back and wished she hadn't. He was gaining on her. One hell of a big troop wearing an odd pair of glasses.

Willing herself into a calm, she came around the next

tree and thought, *All right. One last man to kill. Not a problem.* It was just them being them. They wouldn't leave her alone, right up to the last second when she surrendered to the Americans. This fool was just another of Kapalkin's automatons. He wouldn't stop her. He couldn't. He'd lose his life because he'd bought into a lie about serving his country and living a better life.

She almost lost her footing as something flashed in her face. She cursed. It was another of those micro UAVs come to harass her again. She swung futilely at the thing and steered herself between two more trees, just as the fuel tanks of the choppers caught fire and whooshed loudly across the circular tarmac. She was about to leap down to the asphalt from a ridge above but spun back at the sound of boots mashing into snow and pine needles, crunching across pinecones.

She never saw his face, only the black uniform as he slammed on top of her, driving her into the ground with a terrible and unstoppable force, one hand already locking around her pistol, her head barely escaping impact with the ice.

"ID confirmed, boss," cried Borya. "It's her!"

That voice in Lex's ear sent a wave of adrenaline coiling up his spine.

It was her. The Snow Maiden.

Blinking hard, he straddled the woman, growling in Russian as he drove her wrists back toward the ground. "Just stand down, and I won't kill you."

She fought against his grip, knocking away his SAV glasses. He was, however, much heavier, using his weight to gain the advantage and pin her all the way down, knees on the outside of her legs, ankles on the inside.

Her face creased in exertion, and he couldn't help but admire how aggressively she fought back, no fear or anxiety or anything else—just animal instincts, it seemed.

He got closer, studied her face, the deep lines, the short hair, and something much more interesting in her eyes, an image of a younger woman that took him aback and made her seem more human, unlike the horror stories he'd read.

Suddenly, he found himself wanting to rescue her. He imagined that she needed him, that all the lies and the killing had caught up with her, and she needed more than just a troop. She needed a shoulder on which to rest her head, someone to listen to her, to understand her—

And that made her achingly attractive.

But this was how she operated, wasn't it? She got you close. Made you want her. And then she slashed apart your arteries with her talons.

With a half-strangled cry, she kneed him in the back, tugged one arm free, and launched him forward, over her head. He kept his grip on her weapon and ripped it from her hand. By the time he came around to face her, she already had another pistol trained on him.

Standoff.

"You want me alive," she said. "They always do."

He snorted. "I wouldn't assume anything."

She smirked, and then her gaze flicked to his SAV

lying in the snow. She frowned and asked, "Who are you?"

"The Spetsnaz don't use those, do they?"

She shook her head. "Are you an American?"

He answered her in English. "I'm a JSF Marine undercover, and if you come with us—"

"Okay," she said in English.

"What?"

"I surrender." She rolled her pistol in her grip and proffered it to him.

Just like that. He was stunned. And she went on:

"I seek asylum in the United States. I need to speak to your president right now."

Four Marines came running up behind them, the young lieutenant shouting, "Don't move! Both of you, hands behind your head!"

"Check your visor, son," Lex said. "I'm your package. And so is she."

The Marine flipped down the visor on his helmet, studied it for a second, then said, "Sorry, sir. But who exactly is this woman?"

"This is Colonel Viktoria Antsyforov, formerly of the GRU. She's my prisoner. I'll be escorting her myself. I've got a man hurt back on the road, another KIA in the golf cart. And I need them brought here."

"Roger that, sir. Just one problem. The chopper pilots are hurt bad. Bird looks okay, but we got no one here qualified to fly us out. Higher says they can't get another helo out to us for more than fifty minutes."

Lex glanced to the Snow Maiden. "Cuff her. She

doesn't leave my sight." Lex retrieved his SAV glasses, slid them on, then got on the team channel. "Borya, you close yet?"

"Maybe ten minutes, boss. I feel like I missed the whole party."

"Are you kidding? The smartest guy always takes the high ground. Hey, I know you got your private pilot's license, but you wouldn't by chance know how to fly a Seahawk, would you?"

"Sorry, sir. Fixed-wing only, sir."

"No worries, just make it back. That's an order." Lex switched channels again. "Siren, this is Deep Raider Actual, you still up there?"

"Roger that, Deep Raider," she responded, sounding distracted. "Just . . . a little busy . . . right now . . . Okay, okay, I'm here!"

"Can you fly a Seahawk?"

"I can fly anything."

"Nice. We lost two transports. Still got the one chopper. Crew's hurt. We need you to get us out."

"You're sure the chopper's not damaged? I saw those first two go up."

"They tell me it works."

She laughed incredulously. "Check to make sure none of the fuel lines are damaged and that she's not leaking anything else. I'll get back to you."

There were no average fighter pilots in this war.

You were either an ace or a target.

When Halverson was behind the stick of an F-35B, she sure as hell was an ace (her most recent mission notwithstanding), but now this jarhead was asking her to paint a much more sizable target on her back. The HH-60H Seahawk, aka "Rescue Hawk," was, arguably, one of the most survivable choppers in the world, with its FLIR turret, infrared jammers, laser and radar detectors, missile launch detectors, and chaff/flare dispensers. Even its exhaust had been rigged with deflectors to reduce heat and provide a bit more protection from heat-seeking missiles. But at a top speed of 224 miles per hour as compared to the F-35B's 1,199 miles per hour, you didn't need a course in advanced calculus to realize that the difference here was crawling versus running, and in this theater, speed was everything.

Of course, that didn't mean she'd pass on the challenge. In truth, she was down to sixty rounds in her cannon, and her under-wing pylons were empty. At the moment she was assisting the rest of the carrier wing with IDing the remaining T-50s who were giving her colleagues a terrible time, with three aircraft already lost, their pilots ejecting safely over the fort. They needed her, but so too did that ground crew. She posed the question and request to General Mitchell, who, as expected, asked the most obvious question. "If you put down, who returns your aircraft to the carrier?"

At first, she couldn't answer, but then she blurted out, "I guess those Marines on the ground aren't worth more than this jet? Is that what you're saying, General?"

His reply came in a rasp, hard and quick: "You get to

those men. You get them out of there. But before you leave, you have those Marines destroy your aircraft. I'm not handing it over to the enemy. Do you understand, Major?"

"Hell, yeah, sir. I read you loud and absolutely clear."

"And that's two aircraft you owe us," he added quickly.

"Unless you're counting Canada. Then it's three. Not sure I can pay my tab."

"You get back, and we'll call it even. Guardian, out."

Finally, she had something to grin about. "Deep Raider Actual, this is Siren. Standby, I'm on my way. ETA sixty seconds."

The Snow Maiden was taken to the forest on the perimeter of the helipads, where she sat cross-legged beneath the snow-covered trees with the remaining Marines, eleven men in all, including those dressed like Spetsnaz troops. The big blond who resembled a Russian ironworker with his broad shoulders and thick neck, the same one who had captured her, came over with a tablet computer tucked under his arm.

"Were you the only prisoner up there?" he asked.

"They want *you* to interrogate me?"

"Actually, I'm doing this for me."

"Why?"

"Answer the question."

She made a face. "Yes, it was just me."

"How'd you escape?"

She grinned crookedly. "That tablet and phone you confiscated from me? Those belonged to the late Colonel Osin, Spetsnaz intel officer. He was supposed to keep me safe."

"And that's his uniform you're wearing?"

"Very good."

"So he went down there to get you out, and you had other plans."

"I'm a socialite."

Now he made a face. "Once we're under way, I'll see if I can put you in contact with the president. I can't make any promises, but I'll try."

"Thank you. Now why don't you talk to me in Russian? I like the sound of your voice better in our native tongue."

"Okay," he said, realizing he hadn't told her his name yet. "Uh, yeah, I'm Captain Mikhail Alexandrov. Most people just call me Lex."

"Well, Lex, maybe you're going to be famous for capturing me. Can you handle the fame?"

"That'll never happen. This is all classified. And I wish I could say capturing you makes me feel something, but this is a bad night. I lost a good man." He lifted his head to the body bag lying near the group.

She bowed her head. "I lost . . . everyone."

He looked at her. "How many of them did you kill yourself?"

She glared at him.

"Yeah, well, I guess it's a safe bet you didn't kill them with kindness."

She opened her mouth, ready to fire back, but he was already on his feet at the quavering roar of jet engines.

The strike fighter hovered over the helipad, then settled down, just like a helicopter. The Snow Maiden had watched videos of these VTOL aircraft, but she'd never seen one in person. The canopy opened, and the pilot, who resembled an alien with a bizarre helmet, began to climb out. This pilot was here now to fly the helicopter, if the Snow Maiden had understood things correctly. She frowned as she watched some of the Marines planting C-4 charges on the expensive aircraft.

Ah, they wouldn't let it fall into enemy hands. She had to grin, though. The GRU probably knew all about this jet, knew every inch of its cockpit and had already acquired the schematics of its avionics and weapons systems. Perhaps she was being too cynical, but every man or woman she'd ever met had a price.

She caught a couple of the Marines staring at her and cocked her brows. "Do you want an autograph? Set me free, and I sign one—in your own blood." She smiled evilly, and they quickly turned away.

THIRTY-SEVEN

Raider Team Rally Point
Helipads
Fort Levski, Bulgaria

"Are you Captain Alexandrov?"

Lex nodded and took the woman's gloved hand, shaking it vigorously. "Major Halverson, glad to meet you."

"Glad I could help." They began walking quickly toward the Seahawk. "So you didn't see Ragland up there?"

"I wish I could answer that."

"Any indication she was actually there, then moved?"

"Again, I can't discuss any part of my mission."

"Captain, let's cut through the bullshit. I was working on the same project with her. She's my friend."

"I didn't know that."

"So how about you let slip a little for me, the skinny little girl who saved your ass back there?"

Lex winced through the guilt. "Look, you didn't

hear this from me, but I don't think she was ever up there."

"Shit."

"Yeah, I know. It's all about the intel, right? When it's bad or been altered, we got nothing. And men die. Everything we got out of Moscow was a joke. Our people there are either moles or double agents, or they didn't verify their sources."

"Damn. But hey, I'm glad you tried. Any scuttlebutt on where she might be?"

"Nothing yet. They'll pull me out of here, and it's on to the next one. If I were you, I wouldn't hold my breath. The longer she's gone, the greater the chance that they'll get what they want out of her, and then . . ."

She sighed deeply. "Yeah, I know."

"But hey, it's not all bad. Coming here wasn't a total loss."

"Why do you say that?"

"You'll see."

The smoke was still swirling around them, making Halverson cough as they neared the chopper and the Marines escorting the Snow Maiden toward the open bay door. Lex gestured for them to hold.

"Major Halverson? This is Colonel Victoria Antsyforov, but you might know her as the Snow Maiden. She's sorry she can't shake hands right now."

The Snow Maiden eyed Halverson like a viper sizing up its prey.

Halverson gaped and faced Lex. "Jesus Christ. Are you serious?"

"Hell, yeah. And you contributed to her capture."

"Does Guardian know?"

"He does now. He's given us orders not to get shot down, since we now have a high-value target on board." Lex gestured for the Marines to finish loading the Snow Maiden, who flashed them an ugly grin before being shoved onboard.

Halverson looked after her and said, "Yeah, she's the only one who isn't expendable."

Lex snickered, flicked his glance at the rush of more fighter jets, and then, in an exaggerated gesture for her to see, he blessed himself as they climbed into the bay.

Just as he plopped into his seat, surrounded by the rest of the Marines, the medics treating the wounded, the chopper overloaded by at least three or four, according to Halverson, Borya charged up and threw himself inside. Behind him came the drone, deactivating and plopping into his lap.

He took a seat next to Lex and began buckling himself in. "Almost missed the bus," he shouted.

Lex motioned that he don the headset and microphone so they could talk over the Seahawk's bellowing engines.

"What's up?" asked Borya.

"They're gonna blow that jet."

"Seriously?"

"Check it out."

Lex switched to the command channel, listening to Halverson in midsentence speaking with General Mitchell:

"—because he's only about two clicks from here. I can get him and bring him back. It'll save the S & R team some trouble, too."

"Roger that, Siren. Permission granted. Just get moving and do not endanger our package."

"Roger, Siren, out."

Lex switched to the intercom. "Hey, Major, what's up? Any problem?"

"We're making a little detour. I found a pilot who can fly my jet. He was shot down over the fort and ejected."

"So we're not blowing up your ride?"

"She was a loaner in the first place. Anyway, the taxpayers will be happy."

Lex looked at Borya and sighed. So much for going out with a bang.

They found the pilot in the middle of Fort Levski, standing on a huge section of broken comm dish forming one of the few sections of unbroken ground. Dust peeled off the dish like layers of shedding skin as they hovered over the pilot. His chute was hooked over some more debris and rattled loudly behind him. Lex watched as Halverson got the chopper in close enough for the Marines to haul the pilot into the bay without ever setting down her wheels.

They handed him a set of headphones, and Halverson spoke rapidly with him over the intercom, his praying mantis flight helmet balanced on his lap.

She wheeled them around and raced back toward the

clearing, once more hovering over the tarmac from where they'd taken off, the pilot hopping out and jogging over to the fighter.

Noteworthy flight he'd have, delivering a fighter plane rigged with C-4 all the way back to the carrier. He wasn't wasting a second to remove all the charges . . .

His takeoff, it seemed, would be equally interesting, since the moment he lowered the canopy, dismounts from the mountainside began swarming down toward the helipads, small arms firing already popping off his wings and the Seahawk's fuselage as they pitched forward and Lex's stomach dropped. Halverson cut the stick, throttled up, and they were soaring up, through the dust, and higher into the swirling snow.

Soon, they cleared the dust clouds and Lex caught a glimpse of the snow blasting against the cracked canopy. He looked over at the Snow Maiden, who was buckled in, eyes shut, her face ashen and drained.

The general had said he'd call Lex once he spoke to the president, but when he did, the Snow Maiden was still asleep, and Lex told him they'd push back the call until they were onboard the carrier. He'd already shared her request for asylum and told Mitchell that he'd confiscated a tablet and smartphone belonging to an intelligence officer she'd killed. Mitchell said they were still working on leads regarding Ragland's whereabouts, but perhaps the tablet and phone would provide more clues, as might the Snow Maiden herself.

Lex had to thank the woman for one thing: She'd provided a glorious diversion; otherwise his thoughts remained on Slava, dead because Lex had placed him alone outside while he retrieved information about his sister. Oh, sure, he could justify the whole incident by saying the general had granted him permission and that he was also gaining secondary intel for higher in the process.

But God damn it, he should have told his men. He should not have left Slava alone. The men would have understood. They knew all about his sister. And if he didn't rescue her, then had Slava died for nothing? He was a Marine, performing his duties, serving his country, knowing the risks. Did it matter that Lex had put him in harm's way for a personal reason?

Maybe the Corps would look the other way, but Lex couldn't. He wouldn't.

THIRTY-EIGHT

Christopher Theron leaned back in his leather chair custom made by Italian car designer Pininfarina. He closed his eyes and listened to the news from his operative in Moscow.

He concentrated on his breathing, on his pulse, not allowing anything the man said to disturb him.

The Wraith pilot, Major Stephanie Halverson, had escaped from the Caucasus Mountains. Lieutenant Colonel Osin was dead. The Snow Maiden had been captured by the Americans.

Multiple failures and terrible timing.

He breathed. And breathed again. He would not smash the phone against the hull. He would not grab his Vektor SP1 from the desk and empty all fifteen rounds into a window. He would not hurl one of his flat screens across the salon. He'd promised the crew he would never do any of those things again.

And so Theron sat there, eyes wandering as he tried to let the room calm him. He'd converted his yacht's upper-deck salon into a lavishly appointed business study with lots of greenery, artwork from France, and pieces of pottery collected from all over the world. Satellite communications and multiple computer terminals allowed him to monitor the markets and place video calls to anywhere on the planet.

When the salon's door was closed, the crew knew better than to interrupt him. So when that door did yawn inward, he guessed right that it was Dennison peering inside, her silk robe barely tied at the waist. She grinned and padded into the room, clutching her drink. "Are you ever coming to bed?"

He waved her off and issued orders to his man on the phone. "Tell General Izotov I'll be contacting him shortly. We'll need to move tonight." As he set down the phone, he faced Dennison and said, "Trouble."

"Nothing you can't handle."

"We've lost the pilot. And Osin. And the Snow Maiden."

"What about Ragland?"

"Still secure."

"Then we've lost nothing, really. You can always get another pilot. And with your chip technology, spies are a dime a dozen, aren't they?"

She was right. In point of fact, the abduction of Ragland was only the initial step in Theron's goal to create a

South African hypersonic air force that would assure air supremacy over the entire Indian Ocean theater of operations. The Bilderberg Group would deploy this force to intimidate the countries along the Indian Ocean rim and the governments controlling the strategic straits so vital to world commerce. To dominate by air would effectively neutralize the formidable American sea presence without a face-to-face confrontation.

An undertaking this clandestine and this complicated could not be executed by Theron alone. His partners from the group had procured him shadows from India who would provide the aeronautical engineering team to South Africa and help build the plane and scramjet engines for the Wraith clones. While these teams operated independently from the Indian government, Theron had promised that their country would be a favored nation and had much to gain from this arrangement.

Gathering what his people could from Ragland and Dennison and stealing intel from the Russian Federation regarding their own Ayaks hypersonic program (still in disarray, though, because of budget cuts and the war) were the first crucial steps toward asserting control over the world's oil reserves and preventing a truce between the Euros, JSF, and Russian governments. War was, at the moment, good business, and the tug-of-war over territory, shipping lanes, and the overall "fight to restore democracy" through conventional weapons kept the Bilderberg Group content.

The second step of Theron's plan involved Izotov and Dennison. They would help him create the political

and military instability that would allow his partners and allies to move in and take advantage of both
governments, using battles to make assassinations appear
as accidents and destroying careers by framing individuals for security leaks. That was only the beginning—

But he hadn't planned to cut them loose so soon.
He'd wanted to fully secure Ragland and get the Wraith
clone project under way first.

Questions born of anger gripped his thoughts. How
much did the Snow Maiden really know about him?
He'd shielded himself from her former employers, Dr.
Merpati Sukarnoputri and Igany Fedorovich, as much as
he could, but she was a clever bitch, that one. Had she
tapped into their communications with the Bilderberg
Group? And what of Osin, the intelligence expert? Were
his communications as secure as he'd boasted?

And then there were other possible leaks: Nestes
down in Ecuador . . . and his woman Brandenburg up in
the Caucasus Mountains . . . She was dead according to
her second, but another in their ranks, a man named
Aslan, had escaped. How much did he know about Theron's operations? You could compartmentalize information as much as you wanted, but when you were dealing
with human beings, security was too often compromised
by simple greed.

Theron pulled away from Dennison, took a seat
before one of his flat screens, and brought up the GPS
location of the submarine carrying Ragland.

"Is that where she is now?" Dennison asked, pointing
to the blip on the map.

"It's not the route I would have preferred, but the skipper told me sailing under the Arctic ice via the Northwest Passage was too risky for a diesel submarine, which is why he's chosen the Panama Canal route to Vargas, Venezuela, then all the way up. He's got about eighteen days till he gets there. The delay is maddening, but I wouldn't risk this anyplace else. I want Izotov and his assets close to us."

"So where exactly are they taking her?"

"Don't trouble yourself with the details. Suffice it to say we can't perform the delicate chip operation onboard the submarine, and this is another of my remote and secure locations."

She pouted. "Still keeping secrets? Just for that I'm going to . . . do something to you . . ." She sat on his lap and draped her arms over his shoulders.

"You can punish me," he said.

"First, can I tell you something?"

He nodded.

"I had a dream about her last night."

"Who?"

"The Snow Maiden. She was coming for us. Is that weird?"

Theron snickered, and then he leaned forward, snatched up his phone, and speed-dialed the bridge. "Get us out of here."

"Where to then, sir?" asked the captain.

"I don't care. South. Just get us moving."

THIRTY-NINE

USS *George H. W. Bush* CVN-77
***Nimitz*-class Supercarrier**
Mediterranean Sea

Lex appreciated many of the finer things in life: the deli-cious ales of the Terrapin Beer Company of Athens, Georgia; his vinyl record collection of AC/DC and Aerosmith albums; and, of course, bacon. Any kind. Any place. Any time.

He'd never had any particular gratitude toward a pilot's skills, so long as he or she got him there in one piece and on time. However, he would now add to his list of life's pleasures the piloting skills of one Major Stephanie Halverson.

Despite the snowstorm and the Seahawk being over-loaded, she returned them to the carrier in one piece. The flight included both a midair refueling and a detour allowing their fighter escort enough time to take out more T-50s in pursuit. Her voice never once quavered as those enemy fighters had locked on to the chopper, nor did she break into any maneuvers that might leave them retching.

Meanwhile, the pilot who'd gone after Halverson's ride had also returned, landing the rigged-to-explode F-35B without incident and to curious looks from the flight deck.

Before leaving the chopper, Lex thanked Halverson and once more expressed his regrets for not rescuing her friend. They awkwardly shook hands in case they didn't see each other again, and then he and Vlad silently carried Slava's body out of the chopper, while Borya grabbed their packs.

The next few hours were a whirlwind of video debriefings with Lieutenant Colonel Pat Rugg, commanding officer of the Special Raid Teams Group, then with General Mitchell and President Becerra. He went over the team's every move in excruciating detail, from the drop in, to the trek through the woods, to evading the wolves and infiltrating the base. They grilled him repeatedly. The tablet and smartphone he'd confiscated were being flown back to Langley to be dissected by computer forensics engineers at the CIA's Directorate of Science and Technology.

Once the president had left the conference call, Lex spoke privately with Mitchell and said, "I have the data card, sir."

"Excellent. I'll collect it from you personally, Captain. Your CO and the president do know about it, but I still appreciate the security."

"Thank you. And, sir, I found my sister. They've got

her in a *sharashka*. I know where it is, sir. You could talk to Colonel Rugg and recommend I lead the team for the S & R."

"We'll send a team. Just not yours. You guys are exhausted. We'll get her for you."

"Sir, you understand that getting that information . . . well . . . it cost me a lot."

"I know, Captain."

"I can't reconcile with that unless I know it wasn't for nothing. They need to get my sister."

"And they will. Two weeks R & R for you and your men. You sure as hell earned it."

"For accidentally bringing in the Snow Maiden?"

"You're too hard on yourself, Captain. Go home and get some rest."

Lex opened his mouth, but Mitchell's expression said he wasn't budging. "Thank you, sir."

After tapping out of the link, Lex pillowed his head in his hands and stared at the blank screen.

Maybe he shouldn't have asked. Maybe he should have gone AWOL, gone after her himself.

But hadn't he bent the rules enough already? He needed time to clear his head—so he could write that letter to Slava's parents. Ironic, yes, that he'd just captured one of the world's most wanted terrorists, but all he wanted to do now was sleep.

The chief master-at-arms had placed the Snow Maiden in a "special quarters" padded cell within the carrier's brig.

She was allowed to roam without cuffs but was being observed via security cameras. She'd assured the chief that she'd make no trouble and asked again that she speak to the president. He'd politely indicated that he had no power to grant such a request but that he'd pass along her wishes. She wondered if Lex and the chief were just paying her lip service.

After making her request to use the bathroom and being escorted while she did her business, she was taken back to the cell to find a tablet computer lying on her bunk. The chief told her the president was now on the line, waiting for her.

She rushed to the bunk, seized the tablet, and touched the open comm button.

President Becerra was seated in a small conference room with towering bookcases behind him, probably part of the White House Situation Room. His eyes were gray, his face more gaunt than she'd seen in the media. He wore a collared shirt but no tie, and his hair was slipping down into one eye.

"Hello, Colonel." There was no warmth in his tone, just a hint of warning and, maybe, trepidation.

"Mr. President. I seek asylum in the United States, and I'm willing to earn it."

"You're a war criminal and a terrorist. You're a traitor to your country, and you'd like our endorsement."

"I have information that'll help protect your government. This concerns Major Alice Dennison and General Sergei Izotov. It also concerns an organization that used to employ me. They're called the *Ganjin* . . ."

The president leaned forward and widened his eyes. "All right, Colonel. You have my full attention."

Just then another man appeared beside Becerra and whispered something in his ear, and the president's expression soured. He faced her and said, "I'm sorry, Colonel, we'll pick this up later. I need to go now . . ."

The link suddenly broke.

She burst from the bed and stormed across the room, then began pacing along the wall.

Was it too late? Had Dennison and Izotov already opened the gates of hell?

FORTY

Ivanovskaya Square
Near the Kremlin Armory
Moscow

General Sergei Izotov stared up at the Tsar Cannon, barely visible in the cold morning fog. He was waiting for his contact to meet him. He checked his watch: 0640. He was right on time. Where was the man?

A silhouette appeared in the fog and materialized into a gray-bearded figure wearing a black woolen coat and manipulating a gnarled wooden cane. He looked like an old wizard who'd wandered out of a medieval fantasy novel. The man nodded and grunted, "Confirmation?"

"Yes," said Izotov.

The old man continued on, driving the end of his cane into the stone.

Izotov stared after him, growing warm despite the bitter morning breeze. Dennison had been right. The chip had changed his life. He finally felt good about himself, no longer torn between hubris and self-loathing, between envy and thoughts of quitting the government. He loved his wife again. His children. He wanted to be a good man. Obedient. When he complied with an order, he felt such extreme pleasure that he couldn't help himself but smile. He was a boy, fishing in the mountains, playing catch with his father.

The previous evening, Theron had asked him to commence with the operation of sharing some specific information with the Americans. He'd explained that secrets on both sides would be divulged to each other, disrupting intelligence communities and sending a bolt of panic through both governments.

Along with a list of the names and current whereabouts of Russian Federation operatives within the United States and abroad, and a map of every thermobaric mobile missile launcher within Russian territory, Izotov had just supplied the JSF with the communication signal sequence to permanently disable the Kobalt-M satellite film reentry pods that ejected surveillance film back to Earth.

Unlike U.S. satellites with digital processing, Russia's eight 6.7-ton Kobalt-M satellites still used film that in many situations (and contrary to popular belief) provided superior resolutions to any digital images they could capture. The film was routinely returned to Earth via one of three reentry pods on each satellite for developing and processing.

The consequences of a security breach like this were dire. Preventing access to timely tactical and strategic updates would leave the Federation blind and allow the JSF and Euros to exploit this window and move their weapons and personnel with impunity until such time that the Federation could reroute cameras to secondary satellites and get more birds in the air.

Stage two of Izotov's plan, and the part he'd spent hours preparing, was to provide the minister of defense with intelligence indicating that a Spetsnaz strike team was in place to bring down the European missile defense shield (aka the SLAMS—Space-Land-Air-Missile-Shield network) at the Rovaniemi air base in Finland. This was a difficult scenario to present because the network had been brought down once before by Spetsnaz posing as terrorists in order to escalate tension between the Euros and Americans. Security at the air base had been increased, their computer firewalls and other network protection software updated and strengthened. Taking out the SLAMS needed to be an inside job with the assistance of senior officers issued the highest security clearances.

This time, however, the gambit was much different. There were no Spetsnaz. The missile shield would not be brought down. He only needed the minister of defense to *believe* those operations were in place, so the full-scale invasion of London could commence—at the order of the president himself, an order manufactured of course by Izotov. The Brits had remained neutral in the war thus far, but they were flirting with the idea of joining the European Federation, a move that would allow them to draw some of their oil from the Euros and weaken the

Federation's grip on them. The Russians had attacked them several times before, skirmishes that still left their government in place, but the time was now to seize full control, along with destroying their mining operations off the coast of Scotland.

Once the Russians invaded, the Euros and Americans would pounce on them, perhaps even launch their missiles at the motherland.

Of course, Kapalkin would never go along with any of this. Thus removing him from power was stage three of Izotov's plan. The key was getting to the vice president first. There was no time now to have him fitted with a chip like Izotov, so an enormous bribe had been presented, along with a formidable threat against his family. He'd remained undecided—

Until he'd watched the news coverage of President Kapalkin's Russian-built ZiL limousine exploding from the inside out as he arrived in Moscow.

He and Izotov had shaken hands, as behind him, the limo burned violently on the TV screen.

Yes, everything was in place. Izotov raised his gaze to the Tsar and smiled.

The cannon had been fired.

FORTY-ONE

MacDill Air Force Base
U.S. Special Operations Command
Joint Strike Force Command Headquarters

General Scott Mitchell was seated at his computer command suite, surrounded by his staff as he sifted through the incoming intelligence with virtual-reality gloves and VR glasses, his fingers flicking as he zoomed in on satellite imagery of Russian T-50 stealth fighters, Tu-160 bombers, and dozens of choppers, including Ka-50s and Mi-8s, all bound for London.

The Snow Maiden did know something. The world was turning upside down before his eyes: the Russian president murdered, a full-scale invasion of London in progress, Russian missile launchers and satellite reentry pod codes compromised, names and locations of their spies handed over.

It was as though several senior officers of the Federation's military had gotten together for coffee, written all of their secrets down on napkins, then had them delivered via waiter to an American spy sitting behind them. A breach like this was unprecedented . . . and unnerving . . . because if Izotov was responsible for this, then what were Dennison's plans?

Mitchell groaned in disgust and longed for his youth, for his days as a Ghost Lead, taking his team all over the world, putting boots on the ground and getting muddy, worrying only about the tactical situation, about achieving the objective and getting back home. He was just a kid from Youngstown who liked to make projects out of wood, not a complicated old man wrestling with monumental decisions involving the most powerful military on the face of the planet.

Major Charles Baxter, the officer who'd replaced Alice Dennison, lifted his voice: "Sir, we've just maneuvered the X9-C to evade a missile attack."

"Say again, Major?"

"The Russians just tried to take out our Argus orbital recon drone."

A three-dimensional image of the ORD, which resembled one of NASA's old space shuttles sans windows and with a prominent V-tail, appeared in one of Mitchell's displays.

"That's a first. It's got to be Dennison."

"Concur, sir."

Six months prior the unmanned Argus X9-C was launched from Cape Canaveral aboard an Atlas rocket to become the ultimate USAF reconnaissance asset with its three-kilometers-per-second delta-V potential—meaning the shuttlelike craft could change its orbital inclination to cross-range twelve thousand miles in ninety minutes. Simply put, it could put its camera payload over any point on the Earth in sixty to ninety minutes without being enslaved to the predictable orbit of a traditional spy satellite. One of two limitations to the earlier twenty-nine-foot X9-B was its restricted fuel storage capacity so vital to the maneuvering thrusters. Only a select group of people were aware of the existence of the now-orbiting, second-generation X9-C, a nuclear-powered solution to that fuel problem.

"Get me Colorado. And stay alert for repeat attacks," Mitchell grunted.

"Yes, sir."

Dennison could have divulged many secrets about orders of battle and numbers and composition of forces around the globe. There were many pieces of classified information she could share regarding weapons systems capabilities and friendly nations who possessed such ordnance unbeknownst to the Russians.

But telling the Russians about the Argus . . . that was just unimaginable. And if she had given up the drone, then Mitchell had to assume she'd included what limited information she had on the X-2A Wraith—because those projects were related to each other with the ultimate goal of creating the JSF's most far-reaching and swift Quick Reaction Force. This force would be used, in part, to defend the country's oil-mining drones (now being tested in the Mojave Desert) and soon to be placed in the Middle East. Armed X-9Cs on the front line would buy the JSF the first sixty minutes of battle, backed up by Wraith strike forces that could be on the scene from anywhere in the world at the conclusion of those priceless sixty minutes.

"Another report from Third Echelon, sir," Baxter said, his gaze riveted on a tablet computer. "So far they've lost contact with eleven Splinter Cells operating in Europe and four more in Moscow. They confirm now that Major Dennison had put in a request for their records and current operations before she left. The request was based on the president's order to capture the Snow Maiden and that she was coordinating a new search after our Ghost team failed to bring her in during that mission in Dubai."

"So she's giving up our spies, just like Izotov did. Get me the president."

"I'll have to reroute," Baxter told him. "Primary network just froze. It's being rebooted now. Again, what's happening seems more a nuisance, meant to make us believe a more complicated cyberattack will occur. All right, we're on the secondary. I'll have the president for you momentarily."

Mitchell squeezed his hand into a fist.

Wasn't this terrorism in its most pure form? You didn't need weapons of mass destruction.

All you needed was fear.

FORTY-TWO

USS *George H. W. Bush* **CVN-77**
***Nimitz*-class Supercarrier**
Mediterranean Sea
Two Days Later . . .

Lex had never seen anything like it.

In just forty-eight hours the world had changed, with announcements flooding the media about massive security breaches within both the American and Russian governments, as if each side had decided to hand to the other its major secrets.

Those breaches caused both militaries to engage in massive troop movements and maneuvers of naval vessels. Lex guessed that several of the more dramatic media pundits had already keeled over from heart attacks . . .

The flurry of panic and activity notwithstanding, it seemed Halverson and Lex were literally and figuratively in the same boat: Both of their requests to be sent to London to join the fray had been denied. Halverson was being shipped back to California, where she'd return to her duties as a test pilot, working directly with Dr. Ragland's associates to investigate the failure of the new radar system. Lex and his men would remain on the carrier until they could secure a series of plane rides home to CONUS.

As Halverson had joked, "No fish and chips for us."

"At least we get to thank you again for the ride," Lex had told her. "One hell of a ride."

According to General Mitchell, the Snow Maiden was being flown directly to Langley, to CIA headquarters, where she'd meet with the president himself. She'd already handed over a plethora of information regarding the GRU's assets and activities, along with everything she knew about the *Ganjin*.

Osin's phone and tablet computer, along with the chip that was in Nestes's arm, uncovered cable links to the group called the *Ganjin*; however, some of the *Ganjin* leaders the Snow Maiden had named (Sukarnoputri and Fedorovich) were reported missing, as was escaped prisoner Colonel Pavel Doletskaya. A search by Russian police of the SinoRus refinery and headquarters on Sakhalin Island had been conducted, but their findings were not yet released.

For his part, Osin had been communicating directly to someone onboard a yacht off the coast of Africa, a vessel owned by Dominion Group, a major South African financial institution. Third Echelon had already sent a man to investigate that lead.

More intel indicated that forty-eight hours after Ragland's abduction, the Defense Intelligence Agency (DIA) had received a routine report of a foreign combatant vessel transiting the Panama Canal—part of the U.S./Panama agreement when the canal was turned over to Panama. The report listed SAS *Kapstaad*, a South African diesel submarine, transiting the canal from Pacific to Atlantic. In follow-up interviews, the mandatory Panamanian pilot on board during the transit overheard the crew discussing a female "passenger" on board. There was no earlier report of the sub transiting from east to west. An Atlantic transit from South Africa to the canal was a lot shorter than a Pacific transit. An extended diesel submarine deployment required replenishment at sea. The west-to-east canal course suggested expediency over stealth.

"You think they've got her on a sub?" Lex asked.

"We have a few links to South Africa already, and that sub sent up a red flag. You've got a valuable POW you don't want to be found, and you've got a sub at your disposal, then why not?"

"Because our subs are very good at finding other subs."

"You're correct. This one's out there, somewhere in the North Atlantic, and we've got a lot of ears listening for her."

"I appreciate you sharing this with me, sir."

"Well then, I'll make my intentions clear. If we do locate that boat, I'll be sending you and your men after her. Your CO already approves."

"You'll let me finish what I started."

"Exactly. If you're like me, you hate loose ends."

"Yes, sir. I hate 'em. And my sister?"

"I knew you'd ask. Bad news there, I'm afraid. When we accessed the records, the Russians must've been tipped off. The team I sent just reported the place is empty. They've moved all the POWs . . . not sure where, but that team had to pull out."

"Damn, that's . . . I guess I would've wasted my time going up there."

"I'm sorry, Captain."

Lex tried to contain himself. There'd be another time, another place. "I appreciate the effort, sir."

"Captain, for what it's worth, you've built a sound reputation in the Corps. You're a guy whose head's always been in the game. Just keep it that way."

"Yes, sir. We'll be ready. And please keep me updated about my sister if anything else comes up."

After the call, Lex headed to Ward Room #3 for some breakfast. The room was reserved for officers only, but Lex received permission for Sergeants Borya and Vlad to join him there. They gorged themselves on scrambled eggs, toast, and coffee, and afterward, Lex lowered his voice and met their gazes. "You guys doing all right?"

"I'm okay, sir," said Borya.

"Yeah," added Vlad. "It is kinda weird without him, though. I keep thinking he's going to rag on me, then I turn and he's not there."

Lex nodded. "I'm sorry."

Vlad shrugged. "I'm not sure what to say."

"Slava was a real asshole sometimes," Borya said. "He really pissed me off. Even the way he died was aggravating, no big blaze of glory the way he talked about."

"Yeah, but he did help me get in there and get some data," Lex confessed. "I found out where they're holding my sister. The general also told me they got some good stuff about Spetsnaz ops in the Middle East."

"That's cool," said Vlad. "Sucks being on a need-to-know all the time."

"Well, now you know," Lex said. "I never thought it'd come to this."

"It's okay," said Borya. "Time to chill for a while, then we'll get back out there, and get rocking. Slava would have some choice words for us if we didn't."

"Oh, yeah, he would," said Vlad. "And he's probably looking down on us right now, and he's totally pissed that he didn't get a chance to capture the Snow Maiden."

Lex grinned. "He probably would've hit on her."

"She was definitely hotter in person," said Borya. "For a slightly older woman."

"Hey, you watch that," said Lex. "But you're right about her . . ." He got to his feet. "Let's see if we can find a way to get shot off this floating runway."

FORTY-THREE

They'd been carting her all around Washington and Langley for more than two weeks now, submitting her to polygraph exams and enough interrogations to have her mimicking the questions even as they asked them. She repeated the same answers, told them anything and everything she knew, assured them she was being absolutely honest. She held back nothing.

Snegurochka, the Snow Maiden, was dead, she'd told them.

She was just Viktoria now.

The house was appointed with Colonial-style furniture, and the oak floors squeaked under the pair of running shoes they'd given her. She was impressed that they hadn't thrown her in some maximum-security cell and forced her to undergo "creative" interrogation techniques the way the Federation would have. That she was readily cooperating and that her information turned out to be correct had obviously earned her better quarters.

They even allowed her to watch the morning news, with CNN reporting that the last of the Russian troops, a few stubborn snipers, had been driven out of London, the city once more secure, the damage estimated in the billions.

The Russian Federation had resumed supplying oil to the United States, but only in very limited quantities. Gas prices had already doubled, with nationwide rationing measures taking effect. Odd and even days at the pumps, with citizens waiting upward of eight hours to fill their tanks.

The vice president of Russia, now acting president, was making speeches about American aggression and how this conflict might continue to escalate into the "war to end all wars," borrowing a phrase used to describe the First World War and hinting that the Federation might have some means of bringing down the European missile shield.

All she could do was mutter under her breath and swear over the lies and deception. She glanced up from her breakfast cereal at a commotion coming from the front door, and by the time she pushed back her chair, President Becerra was already gesturing for her to remain seated and that the two agents who never left her side should leave the room.

He took a seat opposite her. "Sorry to interrupt your breakfast."

"It's fine. And it's good to see you again. I appreciate the way you're treating me."

"You gave up those double agents for us in Moscow and it took a while, but we were just able to plug those leaks."

"They provided the intel about Ragland."

"Yes, they did. False intel."

"Have they confessed who their employer is?"

"No. They claim they've never heard of the *Ganjin*. They reported to Osin."

"And who did he report to?"

"We're very close, but we're not certain yet. I'll ask you this again, and you need to think harder about it: Did the *Ganjin* have any connections to South Africa?"

"Like I said, I never heard them talk about the country. I've been trying to remember every conversation I had with Patti, and I don't remember her ever mentioning South Africa . . ."

"Okay, here's a new one for you. What about a man named Christopher Theron?"

She let the name roll off her tongue, then asked, "Who is he?"

"One of the richest men in South Africa."

"I wish I could comment, but I don't know him or how he might be involved."

Becerra raked fingers through his hair and nodded. "I'm actually here for another reason."

"The Raisin Bran?"

He smiled weakly. "I'd like some advice. I'm having,

shall we say, a difficult time negotiating with the acting president right now."

"I told you. You're not negotiating with him. Izotov is running the country—or should I say the people controlling Izotov. Maybe the *Ganjin*. Everything he does is on their behalf. They created this situation because it benefits them."

"They'll destroy both countries."

"To be honest, I've always wanted to see the motherland burn."

"I know. I watched your polygraph exams."

"Then you know why I hate them so much."

"Yes, but this is a global economy. They burn, we burn."

"He's bluffing, you know. They can't bring down the shield."

"They won't have to at this rate. We're slipping into a depression far greater than any this nation has ever experienced."

"You said you wanted advice; well, here it is. General Izotov needs to die. At the very least, somebody needs to capture him and rip that chip out of his eye. Let me check my calendar." She lifted her palm as though clutching a phone. "No, I'm not doing anything today. I'll go kill him for you."

"I appreciate your sense of humor, but I—"

"What is it?"

His expression had gone long. "I can't believe I'm saying this, but we could try to abduct him."

"Good luck with that."

He glanced over at the TV, at footage of a riot outside a gas station in Detroit. "This is crazy."

She leaned forward and lowered her voice. "Put a tracker on me. Send me to Moscow with an escort, I don't care. I won't run. I'm the only one who can get in there and get the job done. Your other agents don't stand a chance. Think about it. The vice president's got a gun to his head right now. The State Duma's in a shambles. We free him up, and you'll be able to talk to him. Rationally. He'll listen. I know it."

"Why would you do this for us?"

"The enemy of my enemy is my friend."

"But you're Russian."

"I don't hate the people, only the government. Kapalkin is gone. Only Izotov is left, and when he's gone, I'll be a proud Russian again."

"I can't cut you loose. My career would be over."

She put a finger to her lips. "Only tell a few . . ."

One of the president's Secret Service agents appeared in the doorway. "Sir, I'm sorry, sir. An urgent call."

Becerra rose and said, "I'll be in touch."

She nodded. "I hope so."

FORTY-FOUR

HH-60H Seahawk
Norwegian Sea
1710 Hours Local Time

Lex was dozing on his parents' sofa in their Eastport, New York, home when he got the call and the bottle of vodka fell out of his hand.

He'd been okay the first few days after coming home, helping his aging parents with some home improvements and visiting with two old buddies, but then the boredom had set in, followed by the depression and the nightmares of watching Slava die. However, to his credit he hadn't turned to the vodka until one afternoon, a few days before the call, when he'd been watching an old war film called *Kelly's Heroes* and realizing he hadn't slept for more than two hours at any clip. He reasoned he was using the alcohol for medicinal purposes and began drinking himself into a stupor, followed by a sound sleep.

Maybe that call from General Mitchell had saved his life, he mused now while seated aboard the Seahawk, dressed in full Arctic camouflage combat gear, armed to the teeth, ready to deliver a lecture of death and destruction to all those who would dare abduct a citizen of the United States.

Across from him sat Vlad, Borya, and Slava's replacement, a veteran operator and newly promoted master sergeant named Raymond McAllen, who by no small coincidence, was responsible for rescuing Major Halverson when she'd been shot down over Canada. McAllen had just transferred to the Special Raid Teams Group, and Lex had enthusiastically welcomed him aboard when they'd left Royal Air Force Station Alconbury earlier in the evening. McAllen's first mission with the SRT promised to be challenging, but he sounded secure and confident. "When we get back, I'll tell you all about my S & R up in Canada. That was some serious shit!"

General Mitchell, Lieutenant Colonel Rugg, and the rest of SRT brass had attended the hasty video briefing. Once learning that Ragland might be on that South African sub, the JSF had made multiple attempts to localize it and were baffled by their inability to pick it up, eventually relying upon a defunct former Norwegian Sound Surveillance Station (SOSUS), now a scientific facility for the study of ocean acoustic biologics and sea temperature studies.

Two days prior, the facility began to report interference with its whale verbalization studies to NOAA due to the periodic acoustic signature from a snorkeling diesel submarine. NOAA queried the JSF Navy about the operation of a diesel submarine in a restricted OPAREA.

From a covert drone base in northeast Iceland, the JSF Air Force launched an MQ-9 Reaper UAV to begin photographing that OPAREA, identifying a UT 776 platform supply ship whose port of registry was Bergen, Norway. Oddly enough, she was loitering off the coast of Jan Mayen Island, and there was a good chance she was waiting to rendezvous with the submarine since she normally did likewise for oil platforms.

Jan Mayen, Lex quickly learned, was a volcanic, mountainous island in the Arctic Ocean and part of Norway. It was situated about 370 miles northeast of Iceland and 310 miles east of Greenland. It was small, only thirty-four miles long, partly covered by glaciers, and divided into two parts: the larger northeast portion, Nord-Jan, and the smaller Sør-Jan. They were linked by an isthmus two and a half kilometers wide. There was an abandoned LORAN-C facility in southern Sør-Jan, along with a small meteorological station just northeast of there, but the place was mostly uninhabited.

Either Ragland's captors planned to resupply the sub and keep her aboard it indefinitely, or they were transferring her to the island, which, given its remote location and lack of population, made it a rather attractive place to hold a prisoner. Either way, Lex and his men would crash their party, ruin their evening, drink their booze, get their lady, and go home. In exactly that order.

Alas, the proverbial clock was ticking. Once the sub

surfaced, she wouldn't remain there long, an hour or two at the most to resupply and/or transfer crew members.

Lex was wearing his SAV, and a window opened to show Mitchell back at his station in Tampa. "Actual, Guardian here. With your refueling completed, we now have your ETA to the island at about twenty-five minutes. Good news now. The Reaper just picked up the sub. She's surfaced. Just as we thought: resupply."

"Roger that."

"Well, that's the good news."

"Maybe I should stop you there, sir."

"I wish you would. We count four Mi-8s carrying Spetsnaz, along with another four Howler gunships heading to intercept. They launched from Kilpyavr Air Base in Murmansk. We're seeing some MiGs take off as well."

"If they picked us up, they would've just scrambled MiGs, right?"

"Exactly. Which means something's up. Possible transfer of our package to the island if they're towing a ground force."

Although he wanted to curse, Lex kept his cool and said, "That's interesting. ETA?"

"They're about fifty minutes out."

"That doesn't give us much time," Lex said.

His own strike force was composed of five Seahawks carrying four Raider teams and a ten-man unit from the Forsvarets Spesialkommando (FSK), a special-forces group from the Norwegian Ministry of Defense, since they owned the island and wanted to oversee the raid.

Also on board was a full medical team who would immediately evaluate and treat their rescued engineer. In truth, they hadn't planned on strong resistance from the sub crew, let alone a Russian assault force, so the general's update sent a tremor up Lex's spine.

"I'll get you some drone support," said Mitchell.

"What about Siren? What's her ETA?"

FORTY-FIVE

X-2A Wraith Prototype
Speed: Mach 6
Height: 70,000 Feet
En Route to Jan Mayen Island

The distance from Edwards Air Force Base to Jan Mayen Island was 4,506 miles.

At Mach 6 (4,567 miles per hour at sea level on a standard day), Halverson could be over the top of the island and on target in a hair under an hour.

Assuming the sub needed to take on fresh provisions, the entire replenishing operation could run sixty to ninety minutes, possibly a bit more, she estimated. It'd be close. Without a chopper, the food stuffs and personnel would be transferred over by small boat in choppy seas—doable but time-consuming, which worked in her favor.

With the pressure suit adjusting slightly around her hips, and her instrumentation brilliantly displayed in her three-dimensional HUD, she once more studied the map.

The exact positions of the submarine and supply ship were marked by glowing red triangles over a wireframe representation of the Norwegian Sea, the blips slowly materializing into 3-D outlines of the actual craft themselves.

ETA to target: nineteen minutes, thirty seconds.

Chills of awe fanned across her shoulders. This was the most incredible aircraft she'd ever flown, its manta-like "all-body" design an engineering necessity in order to spread air over the entire length of the body. In a hypersonic scramjet craft like the Wraith, the underside of the forward body acted as a ramp that compressed the air, while the underside of the tail served as an exhaust nozzle. The engines required an enormous inlet area to kick out high thrust and consequently occupied most of the space beneath the vehicle. They also required huge amounts of fuel; thus an all-body design was most feasible.

While this was just a prototype, Halverson had talked Ragland into arming the bird with twenty-five-millimeter cannons and a modified advanced tactical laser that took Boeing's old design housed in an AC-130 and reduced its size and weight by seventy percent. The laser was so accurate that Halverson could hit a moving target just a few inches wide and limit the strike zone to that space, reducing collateral damage to zero in most cases, which was why the president had called and had asked her to disable that submarine. She would be on time, on target.

Moreover, he wanted the Russians to get a glimpse—just a glimpse—of the Wraith in order to give them pause in this month of crisis.

He didn't have to ask twice.

While the Wraith was fitted with sensor and communications packages similar to the F-35B's, speed was king, and it didn't matter if an enemy picked up her tiny signature. She could outrun pretty much anything they threw at her. Even the Federation's most lethal Archer missiles had a max speed of just Mach 2.5.

The trick was getting her own ride up to speed in time—

And having enough fuel.

In fact, she'd have just enough JP-10 to get in there, get the job done, then rendezvous with the tanker so she could get back home. Any deviation would turn her 691-million-dollar aircraft into a balsa wood glider you could buy off the impulse rack at 7-Eleven. That the scramjet relied on conventional fuel was thanks to a modified design first introduced by Johns Hopkins University's Applied Physics Lab, where Ragland herself had done some research.

For a little reassurance, Halverson checked in once more with the KC-135 Stratotanker's captain, who assured her he'd be on time and meet her over Greenland. According to the radar, he was right on course.

After another time check, she began her slow descent, praying that her boss and friend was there and that those Marines would bring her to safety.

FORTY-SIX

SAS *Kapstaad*
Jan Mayen Island
Near LORAN-C Station

Dr. Helena Ragland had spent nearly three weeks on board the submarine, confined to her quarters. Her only contact with the outside world was through Werner. He arrived three times daily to bring her meals and continually refused to answer her questions. Some days he'd come inside, sit with her, and read questions from his tablet, stumbling through them as though he had not written them himself, questions about the Wraith project. He wanted to know details regarding the scramjet engines and fuel, the body design, anything she'd be willing to share. He asked her evenly, without emotion, without threat.

She told him time and again that the project was classified and that she would not betray her country.

He'd said okay.

Werner's interrogation techniques were chillingly odd, as though the questions weren't meant to be answered but remembered by her. When she'd confronted him with that theory, he'd just smiled and told her yes, she should remember them.

When asked why they weren't drugging and torturing her, he'd smile and say, "We're not here to hurt you. There's no need for anything so barbaric. This is just a process, and when we're finished, you'll be fine."

About ten days into it, she broke down, drummed fists on her hatch, told them she'd talk, tell them anything they wanted to know.

Werner had looked at her sadly and said, "You'll make it. We're almost there."

"But don't you want to know? I'll answer all your questions now. Can you tell me about my daughter? Can you tell me anything?"

"Yes. Everything will be all right."

"Do you have any children?"

"No."

"Then you don't understand."

"Really? You don't think I know about love? About losing someone close to me?" With that, he'd slammed the hatch in her face.

That was eight days ago. Another man she didn't recognize brought her the rest of her meals. He never said a word.

Now they had her blindfolded and cuffed, dressed in a heavy winter parka, and they guided her out of the submarine, through the hatch, and outside. The waves crashed against the hull, the salty, ice-cold spray cutting across her cheek. The sub bobbed like a piece of flotsam, and the sea now washed across the deck, threatening to sweep them off.

They were shouting, speaking in English and another language that sounded like Dutch or Norwegian, she wasn't sure.

"Werner?" she cried. "Werner, are you there?"

"Right behind you. We're going to a small boat now. I'll guide you with the other men."

"Where are we? It's so cold here."

"We're up north, a place where you'll be safe."

Hands clutched her forearms and shoulders, more hands seized her ankles, and suddenly she was lowered into the boat and onto a firm but wet seat. An outboard motor buzzed behind her, and the waves rose so sharply she shuddered as she imagined them capsizing.

A shout in English for them to leave came from the submarine, and her head jerked back as the outboard wailed and they pulled away, riding up and over the waves on a nauseating course. She shivered again and again, found herself shaking steadily as an arm draped around her shoulder and pulled her in close.

"Almost there," Werner said.

She imagined driving her elbow into his face then leaping off and into the icy waves.

But then she was at her own funeral and watching Lacey cry as her daughter leaned over the casket and said, "Mom, I'm only sixteen. It was too soon to leave me."

So Ragland sat there, clutching her captor, hating every moment of it, fear rising like bile at the back of her throat, threatening to burst. Where were they taking her? What would they do?

And then she heard it, a sound so achingly familiar that she thought she was hallucinating.

But she wasn't. She heard them. The unmistakable roar of scramjet engines.

The Wraith.

FORTY-SEVEN

X-2A Wraith Prototype
Norwegian Sea
Approaching Jan Mayen Island

The submarine and the supply ship appeared in multiple displays in Halverson's HUD. She saw them as radar contacts and as glowing white heat sources via her forward-looking infrared radar (FLIR), which also picked up three smaller craft—Zodiacs, she assumed. With her helmet's integrated day/night-vision camera, she zoomed in on one Zodiac leaving the sub. The camera's resolution was powerful enough to reveal a blindfolded person tucked into a seat ahead of the coxswain.

She gasped. That had to be Ragland.

And now they'd rescue her with help from the very plane she'd designed.

The Wraith's sensor fusion kept Halverson on target no matter how she maneuvered, combining both radio frequencies and IR tracking. The synergy between systems linked to the main processors allowed everything she did to support the main mission of incapacitating that submarine, with her multimode radar communicating directly with the tactical laser's targeting control system.

"Guardian, this is Siren, I have the target in site, TCS locked on. I believe the package is being moved via Zodiac, over."

"Roger that, Siren, we're looking at your video now and we concur," said Mitchell.

"Roger, package is clear of the target. Permission to fire?"

"Keep that weapon tight, submarine only, over."

"Roger that, I have the target in sight. Locked. Ready to fire. And firing . . ."

Halverson flicked her thumb across the button on her joystick and the entire Wraith seemed to hum for a moment.

The laser's targeting display popped up in her HUD, showing a preprogrammed wireframe model of SAS *Kapstaad* and all of her internal targets glowing a phosphorescent green.

Halverson's laser beam, represented by a shimmering crimson line, cut across the display as she fired, the reticle moving in precise increments along her HUD.

Her first shot penetrated the hull near the aft section, cutting on through the propeller shaft thrust block and bearing . . .

The next beam burrowed through the hull once again, bound for the rudder and hydroplane hydraulic actuators.

Two more laser rounds tore through the turbo generators, port and starboard.

She wheeled around for the next pass, descended, and fired six more shots across the waterline, targeting the sub indiscriminately now, simply burning holes in the hull as a few crew members sent small-arms fire into the air, their muzzles flashing, their shots far afield in the rolling sea and high wind.

While it was true that just a single hole anywhere on the sub's pressure hull would prevent her from submerging and thus render her vulnerable, Halverson wasn't taking any chances, and the word *overkill* was not in her vocabulary. She'd exploit this opportunity to field-test the laser/Wraith combination in a true combat environment, making sure that the boat could neither submerge nor navigate.

In a matter of minutes the sub would lose buoyancy and go down by the stern, her crew abandoning her before she took on enough water to vanish beneath the waves.

Halverson was about to call in her report when missile lock tones resounded in her ears, the current HUD configuration vanishing, replaced by radar images of incoming missiles being IDed even as they streaked toward her.

"Missile lock warning," came the computer's voice. "Missile lock warning."

The Wraith's electro-optical distributed aperture system created a protective sphere around the aircraft, its sensors alerting her of threats from any angle. The system had done its job. Now she needed to do hers with only seconds to go through the OODA loop: observe, orient, decide, and act.

She saw the threat via the aircraft's sensors. Automated target tracking kept those missiles in sight so she could orient herself to them. The fusion of all those sensors made the decision of how and when to evade far easier.

Vympels inbound, R 27Rs to be precise, with semi-active radar homing. Speed and range data scrolled beside the red triangles, now outlined by white boxes. Even as she studied them on her HUD, the computer spoke to her, ticking off the data in its cool, feminine voice.

She knew that the Russian strike team was out there, but they had come within range much faster than she'd anticipated. The Archers were in the lead, and she juked right, releasing flares and chaff, then throttling back up to Mach 2, 3, 4, sweeping over Iceland, twin fireballs erupting like tiny supernovae behind her, shimmering across the blue-black sky. She immediately throttled down to conserve fuel.

The third Vympel targeted the explosions, homing in to detonate, while the fourth one continued to dog her, its seeker capable of "seeing" the Wraith up to sixty degrees off the missile's centerline. Additionally, the Vympel's simple but effective system for thrust-vectoring forced Halverson to hold speed at Mach 3.1 as she released another cloud of chaff and flares.

She checked her map and tensed. She'd pulled far off course from the rendezvous point with the Stratotanker and now wheeled back toward those coordinates over Greenland.

Just as she came out of her turn, the last Vympel took the bait and tore apart nearly a thousand feet below.

She rapped a fist on the canopy, as if to thank the Wraith.

Hell of an aircraft. Hell of an escape.

But her relief was short-lived as an urgent voice broke over the radio: "Siren, this is Big Ben. I'm taking fire. My escort has pulled off to engage. Might have to bug out if you can't get here in the next few minutes."

Before the Stratotanker's pilot finished with his SITREP, Halverson's fuel warning lights were flashing, the computer telling her she was down to fumes.

She looked at the tanker's current position and began to shake her head. Unless he could turn and scream toward her at 800 miles per hour, she wouldn't reach him in time. The tanker's max speed was, of course, only 580 miles per hour.

Decision time: Either gain more elevation, which would buy her time to better select a landing zone, or simply head to one of Greenland's dozen or more airports and airfields.

Without warning, the Stratotanker disappeared from her radar, and a breath later, General Mitchell's voice crackled over the radio: "Siren, they've taken out your tanker. You have MiGs closing on you now. Get out of there. Save that aircraft."

"Roger that. Searching for a place to put down."

"We'll launch another tanker to rendezvous with you on the ground. Can you reach Nuuk Airport?"

She checked her map. Nuuk was the capital of Greenland, with the airport located on the country's southwest coast. "Don't think I can do it, sir. Runway's not big enough anyway. I may have to land on the glacier."

"It's your call. We'll get the QRF to your location with fuel."

"Thank you, sir."

Halverson flicked her glance to the radar display in her HUD. Two MiGs were narrowing the gap, about ten kilometers out now. They'd probably fired all of their air-to-air missiles and were hoping to put thirty-millimeter cannons mounted in their port-wing roots on her.

"Warning: low fuel level. At current speed, estimate zero fuel level in two minutes, thirty-one seconds," said the computer. "Low fuel level clock displayed."

If she was going to put down on the glacier, she had to lose these bastards first.

"Oh, what the hell," she grunted, shivering through her words. She cut the stick, banking high and away then rolling over and heading straight back for the MiGs.

FORTY-EIGHT

Marine Raider Team
Jan Mayen Island
Near LORAN-C Station

Lex was already watching the situation on the ground
unfold via the SAV attached to his helmet. The images
came in from both a Joint Strike Force keyhole satellite
and Halverson's cameras aboard the Wraith and were
automatically forwarded to both his Raider team, the
other teams, and Strommen, the captain with the chin
curtain beard who was in charge of the Norwegian FSK
group.

"Everyone, listen up," Lex began. "This is Alpha
Team Leader. Go through checklists. It'll get hot very
soon. Gray Wolf, are your boys ready?"

"No problems with Gray Wolf Team, Captain,"
Strommen answered, his accent thick but not an issue.
"And like I said, I hope you didn't shave for this
mission."

That admonishment was an old joke among the FSK guys and part of Arctic survival. Shaving in the morning, then heading out in the Arctic air, hastened frostbite, but too many rookies or foreign operators in the region succumbed to that simple mistake. Shave at night, let your pores close up for eight or so hours, and then you were good to go.

Lex scratched at the stubble on his cheeks. He hadn't shaved at all. There, done.

Now he monitored the command net as the five Seahawk pilots spoke to one another and with the pilot of an RAF Boeing E-3D Sentry AEW1 accompanied by two fighters, Panavia Tornado F3s. The British pilot in the radar plane was confirming the positions of the four Howler gunships as the Seahawks fanned out to engage them before coming around to land on the island.

The chopper rocked hard as the four AGM-114 Hell-fire missiles mounted to its extended wings began to launch, one after another, the sky outside the window flickering as the other Seahawks cut loose their missiles.

Next came the terse reports as enemy S-8 rockets splayed across radar screens, and all five pilots broke away to evade, the muffled thumping of chaff and flare pods coming from the aft section, the chopper pitching forward in a steep dive that had Lex clutching the shoulder harness attached to his seat.

"I won't say it," Vlad began over the intercom.

"Good," answered Lex.

"What was he going to say?" asked McAllen.

"The usual," said Borya.

"Sergeant McAllen, I'll put it this way," said Lex, groaning as the g-forces pressed harder on their chests. "He likes to rattle our nerves."

"Well, we don't need him," answered McAllen with an uneasy laugh. "We got this pilot about to kill us now . . ."

Just then the pilot leveled off but Lex's stomach remained somewhere near Iceland.

Something flashed brilliantly near the window, followed by an echoing boom and sudden gust that buffeted the chopper.

"What the hell was that?" cried Borya.

Lex heard it over the command net: They'd lost one of the Seahawks, the one carrying Charlie Team and the medical personnel.

He shared the news with his men, then closed his eyes, bit back the loss, and sat there. He would remain calm. He would keep his head clear. He would get the job done. No matter what. There would be plenty of time—too much time—to grieve later.

After a deep breath, he opened his eyes and leaned out from his seat to stare through the canopy, spotting the dark outline of the once-deserted LORAN-C station. "All right, guys," he began, hardening his tone. "We're still on mission and still in this fight. Almost there. Review your maps."

Lex tapped a button on the side of his helmet, and the HUD switched to a three-dimensional, rotating image of the entire station with cutaway walls. The base was an M-shaped collection of prefabricated buildings with sloped tin roofs and aluminum-siding walls, along with a couple of water tanks and radio towers with attached dishes. A steep mountain range wound to the west, rising up behind the station like a white collar of stone, with an ice-covered dirt airfield lying to the north.

In the past, an eighteen-man crew had staffed the station when LORAN-C was used to help with ship navigation. GPS technology had long since made terrestrial radio navigation systems obsolete; thus the station had been abandoned for nearly two decades—

Which raised the question of why many of the buildings were lit up from outside and within, the generators obviously repaired and/or replaced, even the radio tower's light flashing, as Lex accessed the chopper's night-vision cameras from his HUD.

"Two Zodiacs on the beach with a third coming," reported the pilot. "Count eight armed men in the third. Estimate same numbers from the first two, meaning sixteen or more inside."

"Roger that," said Lex. "Same LZs, no deviation."

"You got it," said the pilot.

The crew chief threw off his harness and clambered to his feet, barking sternly into the intercom. "All right, gentlemen, show time. We'll be on the ground in thirty seconds. Mi-8s carrying that Russian greeting party will be here in less than ten minutes, along with two of the four Howlers. That's all the time you got. I'll expect every one of you knuckle-draggers back here in less than ten. Can you count that high?"

All of them barked in unison, "Yes, Crew Chief!"

"Thank you, Chief," Lex said, unbuckling his own harness and springing to his feet. "Listen up, people. By the numbers. We clear from the outside in. Alpha is still point, along with Gray Wolf. Bravo, you're now on over-watch up in the mountains. Switch out to the MKs. Keep a good eye on that beach. Delta Team, you work the south side inward. Team leads sound off."

One after another the Raiders reported back, and then Strommen spoke to Lex on the command net: "Captain, I hope for all of our sakes this goes quickly. If not, the Russians will have over one hundred men on the ground before we leave."

"No worries, Captain. I carry at least a hundred rounds. What about you?"

While the man didn't say it, Lex knew he was think-ing it: *Wiseass.* Instead, Strommen replied, "We have a lot of ammo. I'll see you outside."

The Seahawk's wheels thumped on the hard snow, sending a shudder up through the fuselage, the whole bird rocking up and down for a moment. Then the crew chief wrenched open the side cargo door, hollering, "Go, go, go!"

Lex ducked, then leapt down from the chopper, hit-ting the snow and taking in a cold breath of −5°F air. Nice. His nose already stung. Borya, Vlad, and McAllen charged up behind as he headed straight for the nearest building, a boxy structure with heavy electrical cables snaking out from its walls, IDed as one of three genera-tor stations. Exhaust rose from pipes jutting from the roof, and the hum of diesel engines emanated from within.

Behind them, the rest of the choppers touched down, and Strommen's men—dressed in a modified Arctic white pattern camouflage whose darker sleeves made them more easily distinguishable from Lex's Marines—came charging up toward the team. The other Marines hit the snow and moved out, as, one by one, the Seahawks dusted off and were supposed to head to a waiting area about two clicks north on the beach, not far from the meteorological station.

However, since two of the four Howlers had survived their first engagement, Lex knew those pilots would go to Plan B: with two choppers engaging the Russian gunships while two held back to evac the package and ground troops.

Sixteen Marine Raiders and ten FSK special forces troops were now moving up on the station. While the landing zone was a quarter click north of the buildings, the sub crew would already be digging in and waiting for them.

Along with providing night vision through the now-swirling snow, Lex's SAV placed a holographic map to his left, showing the blue-colored silhouettes of his men, the green silhouettes of the FSK troops, and the flashing blue dots of the drones as each Raider team sent four Seekers and their larger quadcopter UAV out ahead to scout the exterior and take a peek through the windows.

As Lex and his men reached the generator building,

the first crack of automatic weapons fire broke though the wind.

"Everyone hold fire," Lex ordered.

His HUD flashed. Two men outside one of the main terminal buildings in the center of the station must've spotted one of the drones.

Lex gave Borya the hand signal to get inside the generator and cut the power. The sergeant used his laser, and in five seconds he'd burned the lock off the door. He vanished inside for just another ten seconds before the big diesel engines fell silent.

"That brought down station power. The other two generators are for the tower and are switched off anyway," Borya reported.

"Good."

"Boss, one of the Seekers picked up something inside the main transmitter station," said Vlad.

Lex's HUD showed the Seeker's camera zooming in through a window to spot a blindfolded figure being shoved down a hallway. Lex recognized the hair and body type from the many photos of Ragland he'd studied, and while the Seeker had not picked up a clear image of her face, Lex felt certain that after everything they'd been through, after losing a good man, they'd finally— *finally*—found her. "Everyone move out!"

By the time they shoved Ragland into the chair, her face was burning from the wind and the cuffs were digging painfully into her wrists. She kept calling for Werner, but he wasn't answering, and the man next to her now, whose voice was unfamiliar, kept telling her not to move. Hearing those scramjet engines and believing against the impossible that the Wraith was up there sent Ragland's pulse pounding, her chest growing warm, and now the gunshots meant so much more: They'd found her. Rescuers were on the ground and Halverson was up there in the Wraith, on the attack.

But how many stories had she read about failed rescue attempts, doctors and other humanitarians seized in hostile nations, then executed out of spite when their abductors were cornered?

Suddenly, it was hard to breathe. This might be it. These could be the last moments of her life.

She couldn't die in darkness. "Please, take off the blindfold."

"No."

"If we have to move, I can go faster without it."

"That's true." Abruptly, hands fumbled behind her head, and the cotton cloth was peeled away. She flicked open her eyes, the beams of two flashlights causing her to squint.

The room was small, perhaps twelve square feet, the walls hidden behind towering metal cabinets for instrumentation manufactured in the 1970s or 1980s but seeming even older, like props from a set of an Irwin Allen TV show from the 1960s. She spotted microphones, radio gear, communications equipment. Maybe even LORAN, with clocks and circular scopes, big toggle switches, and bulbous status displays.

She was north. Some place excruciatingly cold. The Arctic perhaps? The sea. An island. A comm station of some kind . . .

Dusty old pendant lights hung from the tin-roofed rafters, and she lowered her squint to the left, where a short man holding a military-style rifle and wearing a woolen cap pulled tightly around his head stood, facing the door opposite them. To her right, she spotted Werner, his face ruddy, eyes narrowed on the door. He, too, clutched a rifle. Their flashlights sat on a desk, aimed at the door.

"They're coming for me, aren't they?" she said.

"Shut up now," Werner snapped. "Everything will be okay."

"No, it won't, you asshole."

He looked at her, then shoved his rifle's muzzle in her face. "I said, shut . . . up . . ."

Gunfire popped from somewhere outside, and both men dropped to their knees, rifles once more trained on the door. Ragland glanced up at a window, where something metallic shimmered in the darkness. She widened her eyes on the object, blinked hard, and then it was gone.

Lex gave Borya a hand signal, and the sergeant immediately scaled a service ladder on the rear of the barracks beside the transmitter main station room where Ragland had just been identified. Their Seeker was in place outside the window, and Lex thought Borya could get a clean shot inside.

"Hey, boss," McAllen called. "Vlad and I in place to breach the back door."

"Roger that. Stand by." Lex switched to the command net. "Guardian, we're in position."

"Roger. Move in and extract the package."

"Here we go . . ."

Six enemy guards remained outside, armed with R4 South African–made assault rifles with thirty-five round banana clips. Eight more of their buddies were en route, jogging up from the beach where they'd left their Zodiac.

"Delta Team, you cut off those guys who just landed. Bravo, I want your snipers on the guards outside the terminal building."

Lex checked his HUD again. ETA of Russian Mi-8s: three minutes. Damn, they'd wasted too much time already.

Captain Strommen's men were positioned throughout the complex, at corners and on rooftops, all focusing on the terminal building. Lex called the captain, reminded him to hold fire until he gave the word.

"It's your engineer, Captain, but my island," said Strommen, an allusion to the tension they'd had over who'd be in charge of the search and rescue. The Norwegian had begrudgingly allowed his American counterparts to take lead of the actual mission, but he'd wanted to oversee any prisoners captured and ensure that "the Americans cleaned up their mess before leaving."

"We have authority from Guardian," Lex told the man. "Would you like to give the order?"

Strommen hesitated. "No, as we planned. We're ready."

"Excellent. Stand by."

FORTY-NINE

X-2A Wraith Prototype
Over Jan Mayen Island
18,500 Feet

Halverson raced past the two MiGs as they tried to strafe her with cannons. She struck the cockpit of one aircraft with her tactical laser but missed the second because her engines cut out at that precise moment and the targeting computer couldn't catch up with the sudden drop in airspeed.

While the first MiG broke into a flat spin and vanished in her wash, the second raced on, and Halverson realized this was it: Either she'd be a sitting duck as she tried to land, or she had one last attempt to get him and probably no time to pick a safe landing zone. Whatever part of the glacier she could reach via gliding would have to do.

She turned into the wind, trying to gain a bit more altitude, the Wraith strangely silent, the instruments glowing like candles. She hung there, a metallic manta crucified across the sky and utterly vulnerable.

The radar told the story now:

He came around, five thousand feet below and ascending fast, already opening up with his cannon, just as she jammed the stick forward and dove straight at him.

Either way this maneuver would cost her dearly, but there was too much fight in her to give up now. She grimaced as the aircraft shuddered and gained more speed.

"Target locked," said the computer.

Her thumb had already settled on the laser's trigger, the HUD showing one, two, three beams cutting into his canopy and slashing through his control systems.

The flashes coming from his cannon went dark, and the MiG dropped back and away like a falling leaf, tumbling end over end, a silent death delivered by an equally silent weapon.

She pulled up, leveled off, and allowed herself a sigh. Warning lights flashed in the HUD, damage control sensors indicating breaches to the wings—cannon fire to be sure, but she was still in one piece. Getting that piece onto the ground was another story—

Hopefully one with a happy ending.

As she scanned the map, she brought up the command and team nets, eavesdropping on the Marine Raiders calling out shots and positions of enemy troops, the Norwegian captain talking to Lex, the much steelier voice of General Mitchell announcing that the Mi-8s were now only two minutes away.

Two minutes?

There was no way in hell Lex could get in there, snatch Ragland, and exfiltrate aboard the choppers before those Russians arrived.

No way in hell.

Halverson stared hard at those choppers on her radar screen, did the calculations once more, and her blood turned cold.

FIFTY

Marine Raider Team
Jan Mayen Island
LORAN-C Station

The Marine Raiders of Bravo Team posted in the mountains were well-trained and proficient snipers, armed with MK 11 Mod 0s, and were ready to carry out Lex's orders to the letter.

And so he gave them. Bravo's first four shots dropped four of the guards outside the terminal building, while two more rounds from Strommen's men dropped the guards out front.

At the same time, Strommen's men moved up, McAllen and Vlad blew the back door on the building, and Lex met up with Strommen at the front door.

A rusting aluminum sign painted in bright blue read: FTD STASJON JAN MAYEN. Below that, written in Norwegian and translated by Strommen at their video briefing, was the old station's motto: *"Theory is when you understand everything, but nothing works. Practice is when everything works, but nobody knows why. On this station we unite theory and practice, so nothing works and none understands why."*

The geeks here had had a sense of humor—but Lex had little time to appreciate that now as Strommen kicked in the door and Lex tossed in a flash-bang grenade that detonated with its signature flash and cloud of gray smoke. At the same time, two Seekers flew forward and inside, immediately mapping the interior, noting the positions of the hostiles inside and sending that data back to the team's HUDs.

The interior was split into a central hallway with rooms on either side and a main entrance foyer. The furniture and paneling on the walls were decades old, along with dust-covered framed photographs of the station under construction. Lex took this all in at once, but he paid most attention to his HUD, where a blue flashing symbol generated by the Seeker showed Ragland in the last room on the right side of the hall.

As he hustled forward, he came face-to-face with two men rounding the corner. They wore gray parkas with fur-trimmed hoods pulled tightly around their faces. Lex's HK416 assault rifle flashed, and the men fell back toward the wall, firing wildly and driving Lex and Strommen to the deck.

The foyer met the main hall in a T-shaped intersection, and now Lex and the Norwegian were on all fours and taking gunfire from the right and the left, effectively cut off.

Lex crawled back against the wall and gestured for Strommen to take the guys on the left. The big captain tugged free two grenades from his web gear, ducked out into the hallway, and let them fly.

Not two seconds after the explosions rattled the building and smoke clouds rushed through the hallway, Lex raced at full tilt down the hall on the right, firing at two more men who dared peek out from a doorway. He caught one in the leg, the other in the shoulder, and they retreated back into the room before he could finish them. They wailed as he jogged by—

But then he stopped, did a double take.

Beyond the bleeding men was a pair of surgical tables draped in sterile sheets, with a collection of medical equipment forming a semicircle around them. He couldn't believe it, but this was a modern and fully equipped operating room lying beneath a trio of powerful lights attached to a boom positioned over the beds. Smaller carts near the beds contained rectangular sealed packages that Lex guessed were sterile surgical tools. The sub crew hadn't brought this here; the room had been waiting for them. Was the room meant for Ragland or someone else?

The wounded men looked at him, and one said in an accent that sounded British or Australian, "We're just sailors and hired guns, mate."

Lex smirked. "POWs now—*mate*. So long as you keep your hands in the air."

At the sound of more gunfire from outside, Lex broke away and sprinted for the last door.

His hackles rose. Instincts told him to twist and fire.

A heavyset oaf who'd thought he'd ambush Lex stumbled back as his parka dented with bullets.

At the far end of the hall, beyond the big guy, came two more, and Lex pitched an L12-7 heat-seeking grenade at them, the rocket whooshing up the hall to detonate in one man's face. The flash and boom sent Lex to the wall for cover—

Just as the door beside Ragland's swung open. A hand appeared. A grenade hit the floor and rolled toward Lex.

He spun back toward Ragland's door, screaming into his mike, "Borya, fire now!"

Ragland jerked back as the old wooden door smashed open, with pieces of doorjamb flying.

A soldier in Arctic white camouflage appeared like an angel haloed in smoke, his eyes covered by a tinted visor.

At the same time, the window shattered and Werner's head exploded, showering her in blood.

The other guard was about to fire at the soldier when Ragland shoved herself in the chair, knocking his aim wide. As his gun went off, a second crack from outside echoed, and the man fell across Ragland, slumping to the floor. The back of his head was gone.

Meanwhile, the soldier who'd burst inside threw himself on top of her—just as an explosion tore through the wall behind. The floor shook, the smoke and dust were suffocating, and now the icy wind was roaring inside.

The smell of something terrible blew over as pieces of Sheetrock and two-by-fours slammed into them, the soldier shielding her from the debris.

She couldn't hear a thing, save for the ringing repetition of the explosion, her face dripping with more blood, the soldier drawing himself up and mouthing something. She couldn't understand him, but her gaze lowered to the American flag patch Velcroed on his shoulder. Through the dust and blood and utter shock, she nodded.

Lex's earpiece had protected his left ear from the blast, but his right ear buzzed like a bitch. He realized Ragland couldn't hear him, but she understood enough. No time to get her out of the cuffs. He rose and helped her to her feet.

Strommen arrived in the shattered doorway, looking stunned as he took one of Ragland's arms and they steered her forward over the tattered wires and boards and beams while from another part of the building more automatic fire cracked hard and fast.

"Guys from the third Zodiac are trying to move up, boss," said McAllen. "Delta's got them pinned down, but you'd better use the back door, over."

"Borya, can you target some of those men on the beach?"

"Uh, boss, I can but you'd better get out here—quick."

Video captured by Borya's helmet camera appeared in Lex's HUD:

The four Mi-8s were on final approach to the airfield, their noses pitched up as they prepared to land exactly where the Seahawks had dropped off Lex's team. Thundering down behind them like starving vultures were the two Ka-65 Howler gunships whose pilots unleashed streams of tracer-lit, thirty-millimeter suppressing fire on the Marines in the mountains.

"Okay, okay, we're bringing her out now," Lex responded, beginning to lose his breath. "Call Guardian. We need the choppers to pick us up on the south side of the station, right on that ridge back there near that giant tree stump. Pull up those coordinates and send a drone for combat control."

"I'm on it."

One of their UAVs would now fly over to the new landing zone and laser-designate it for the Seahawk pilots, performing the task of an air force combat controller.

Moving more slowly than they would've preferred, Lex and Strommen guided Ragland through what was once the back door, now a gaping and tattered maw that had *Marine Corps Was Here* written all over it. They kept tight to the building, with Ragland shaking hard against the cold. They paused at the corner, where Lex tore off his gloves and told her to put them on. As she did, something odd flashed from the corner of Lex's eye, and he craned his neck skyward.

Up there, through all the swirling smoke and snow, came an improbable sight: a manta-shaped aircraft diving silently toward the Russian choppers.

"Is that what I think it is?" asked Strommen.

Lex swore unconsciously and got on the radio: "Siren, this is Alpha Team Actual, what the hell are you doing?"

"Actual, this is Siren, get to your rally point."

The Wraith banked hard, its belly passing directly overhead as Halverson leveled off, then dove again—heading straight for the Mi-8s as they touched down.

"Come on, Major, don't do it," cried Lex.

"Get out of there," Halverson shouted. "Just go, go, go!"

Halverson had been able to evade those Howler pilots and their high-frequency radars via the Wraith's contouring design and radar-absorbent coatings, as well as by maintaining a consistent angle of approach until the very last second. While she was certain they were receiving faint or fleeting radar contacts and were aware that a stealth aircraft was present, interception couldn't be reliably vectored to attack her, which of course was pilot-speak for sneaking up behind them with cold engines.

By now General Mitchell knew what she was doing, and he'd tried repeatedly to reach her over the command net. She turned off the radio and triggered the laser, opening fire on the gunships simultaneously, striking both choppers head-on.

One Howler banked suddenly to the left as explosions lit beneath the twin main rotors. This was part of the Howler's complicated ejection system. The rotors flung away like boomerangs, and a second later, the chopper's canopy blew off and the pilot ejected as though he were flying a fixed-wing aircraft. The system was rare in gunships, and Halverson found herself observing the pilot's escape in awe.

The second gunship pilot lost control of his bird, tried to eject, but the rotors failed to release. When his canopy blew off, it struck the rotors and was shredded, sending a hailstorm of pieces into him, even as his seat blew and he was catapulted into the slicing blades. The impact sent the gunship rolling onto its back and plunging into the sea. A shimmering white fountain veiled the helo before the rotors snapped.

Now she'd finish the job. The Mi-8s were on the ground, the troops spreading out as she jerked the stick once more and checked her altitude: 200 meters, 190, the Wraith gliding to glory in a magnificent kamikaze run, as Lex began hollering again: "Get out, Siren! Come on!"

More Spetsnaz troops hopped down from their choppers and stopped, fingers lifting in her direction as she opened fire with her cannon, intent on emptying the gun.

She was their angel of death—

With just five seconds until impact.

FIFTY-ONE

Lex's eyes burned.

Halverson was going to sacrifice herself and her aircraft to take out that Russian ground force. She wouldn't kill them all, but she'd buy them time enough to escape.

She was the bravest son of a bitch he'd ever seen.

He stared at the Wraith, rapt, as Strommen hollered for them to go. They had to go.

She was just a breath away from impact now.

And then he saw it.

He had to blink to be sure. Yes, it was there—a bright orange glow rising in the sky. An ejection seat. Drogue chute. Three, two, one—

A parachute.

Good opening. It was her. She'd made it!

A rumbling thunder followed, along with a nails-onchalkboard screeching as the Wraith collided with the choppers and fleeing troops.

A series of discordant explosions—like a munitions factory going up in flames—brought them to their knees. Multiple whooshes of air and fireballs of varying size and shape mushroomed into the night and cast an eerie glow over the station. While the beating of rotors died, it was replaced by a sudden hammering, and then, in the next breath, rotor blades cut through the sky in all directions like thrown machetes, their surfaces gleaming with reflected fire.

As the detonations continued, Lex told Strommen to wait as he raced back to the edge of the building. From there he could see the entire airfield.

Three of the Mi-8s lay in twisted, burning heaps cordoned off by still-rising flames that swelled toward the only undamaged chopper. That pilot began to take off—just as another explosion from the nearest chopper tore into his canopy. The helo pitched forward, the rotors chewing into the snow before snapping off in what seemed like a thousand pieces, the bird hitting nose first and then flipping onto its back, tossing up a cloud of snow and pieces of fuselage, the air thick with the stench of spilling fuel.

And somewhere within all that twisted glass, rubber, metal, and plastic, was the Wraith, jagged black sections of the wings appearing now, jutting up like dorsal fins between flaming corpses—

While above it all Halverson floated soundlessly on the wind, heading toward the mountains behind the base.

The remaining Spetsnaz—twenty or thirty, Lex estimated—saw the chute as well. Six troops broke off in pursuit.

Despite the dizziness and nausea from the ejection, Halverson smiled so hard that it hurt. She fully appreciated the irony here. Another aircraft had bit the dust. Crash and burn. Maybe Becerra was right. She should become a politician. The government couldn't afford her piloting skills anymore. She actually laughed aloud as she steered herself toward the snow-covered peaks that formed a bulwark around the base, trying to aim for the pickup zone but finding herself forced back by the crosswind.

Her smile faded as she spotted the troops below running in her direction. At the station, the Marines were breaking off and heading away, taking a few prisoners with them. It'd probably be a good idea for her to contact Lex and see if she could bum a ride. Yeah, a good idea.

"Alpha Team Actual, this is Siren, over."

He sounded out of breath, "Jesus God, Siren, really? How 'bout a heads-up next time!"

"Sorry, it was a spur-of-the-moment thing. I owe the government a lot of money."

"I think your credit's still good."

"Need you to return a favor."

"I figured. By the way, in case you didn't hear, we have the package. We're getting her back to the rally point now. My team's breaking off to get you. Just hang on."

She clutched her steering lines a little tighter. "No pun intended, right?"

"Hell, yeah. We'll be right up. Actual, out."

Bravo and Delta teams linked up with Strommen's men, and together they escorted Ragland to the southern part of the base where the Seahawks were now landing.

Lex got word a few minutes later that Ragland was safely on board one of the choppers and was being flown off to the refueling point in Iceland.

At the same time, the remaining Spetsnaz were charging into the station and Lex's men were watching them from the mountain above, scaling their way along the ridge toward the cliff where Halverson had just set down.

"I can see your chute on the side of the mountain," Lex told her.

"I'm just above. You better hurry. That squad's coming up fast."

Halverson pushed up on her elbows and chambered a round in her Beretta. She placed the extra fifteen-round clip on the snow near her chin. She got back down on her stomach, listening as the Russians approached. She couldn't see them from her angle, the cliff too steep. If she broke and ran along the ridge, she'd be in plain sight from below, and they'd easily cut her down.

She kept reminding herself that she had the high ground, the advantage, but if they came up at her from the left, they'd spot her. There was no cover, not one stinking rock.

The wind began to howl, the snow falling much heavier and blowing sideways. That would help a little. Above that din, like faint static from an old TV, she heard the ice crunching beneath the Russians' boots.

Oh my God. Here they come.

"Actual, where are you?" she whispered.

"A minute out."

"Hurry."

"When I tell you, you get up and run," Lex said.

She didn't answer because the first troop emerged at the far end of the ridge, picking his way up onto the cliff, his Arctic camouflage flashing like disembodied spots against the mountain.

Halverson resisted the urge to fire and whispered into the boom mike, "They're right here."

"Wait for the chopper," he said.

The helicopters were lifting off from the rally point, but their engines had been growing distant. Now, suddenly, one helo was much closer, rising over the top of the mountain, spotlights wiping across the snow, door gunners already opening fire with their M240s, rounds creating a wall between the Spetsnaz troops and Halverson.

"Go!" Lex cried.

She took a deep breath—

Then sprang up, turned back, and sprinted along the

ridge, her boots sliding over the ice beneath the snow, her balance nearly lost as she spotted the four-man Raider Team just twenty meters ahead, jogging toward her.

The helicopter's engines changed pitch, the gunners broke off, and for a second, Halverson stole a look back.

One Spetsnaz troop had broken off from the group and was storming toward her, his rifle tucked into his chest.

She was torn between stopping and firing and just racing on, the Marines shouting for her to go.

Pouring everything she had into her legs, she faced forward and lunged away.

The troop's gun went off, sending a bolt of panic up her spine, followed by needling pains in her back, at least two. The pain vanished—then returned with a vengeance as her torso began to feel damp.

She kept running, but the effort doubled, as though she were pushing through water, and when she took her next breath, nothing came. She coughed and tasted blood.

The Marines ahead opened up on targets behind her, their rifles rattling and winking in the darkness.

She hit the snow before ever realizing she'd tripped, and the pistol was gone from her hand.

More gunfire. Shouts of "Down!" and "Secure!"

They were on her, rolling her over, a flashlight in her face, a familiar and oh-so-comforting voice, "Stephie, baby, I'm here. I'm here. We got you."

It was Ray, her Ray, Sergeant Raymond McAllen, and all she could do was lift her arms and whisper, "Hold me."

* * *

Lex was unaware of McAllen's relationship with Halverson, and while it wouldn't have changed his opinion of them, some prior notice would've been nice. Obviously, Halverson had a problem with that. Yes, Lex thought he might've had a chance with her. A lot of guys probably thought the same. Well, that idea was summarily nixed. He shuddered off the petty thoughts and ripped off his pack to retrieve his medical supplies.

Borya hunkered down and did likewise. They rolled Halverson onto her side and began cutting off the back of her flight suit to inspect the gunshot wounds.

There were two: one near her left shoulder with a clean exit wound, and one at her waist on the right side. That round had no exit and might've lodged in her kidney. Thankfully, they'd missed her spine, but she was already losing a lot of blood, though, and that shot to her shoulder might've already punctured her lung and caused it to collapse.

Borya got a line started so they could administer fluids while the chopper landed on a broader ridge just below them. Lex placed QuikClot 4×4s on her wounds to control her bleeding, and McAllen joined him in applying pressure to the bandages.

Vlad ran off to fetch a long backboard they kept stowed on the Seahawk. McAllen held Halverson's hand and continued to reassure her that she'd be all right, but by the time they transferred her to the backboard and had immobilized her head, her pulse was weak and thready, the 4×4s soaked with blood.

They got down to the helo and took off, leaving the remaining Spetsnaz stranded on the island while just off the coast, the submarine was beginning to sink.

Lex looked at Halverson lying on her backboard. McAllen was holding her hand and looking grim. Vlad and Borya had changed her bandages and were holding them tightly, but the bleeding wouldn't stop. They faced Lex, and Vlad shook his head.

Lex shifted in beside them and lowered his head toward Halverson's, speaking directly into her ear. "Major, Dr. Ragland is safe and we're on our way back."

Her eyes flicked open. He put his ear to her mouth. "Good," she managed.

"You saved us all."

She nodded. "But I broke my plane."

He almost smiled. "That's okay. I just want to say thank you. I mean it."

"You're welcome."

She shut her eyes, and Lex faced McAllen, about to give the man a reassuring nod, but the sergeant's tear-stained face and trembling hands were too much to bear. Lex glanced away and returned to his seat, buckling himself in. He lowered his head and buried his face in his palms.

FIFTY-TWO

Mamaison All-Suites Spa
Hotel Pokrovka
Moscow

General Sergei Izotov saw his massage therapist, Polina, every Friday evening at six P.M. at the Algotherm Spa Center within the hotel. He'd been a loyal patron for more than twenty years, and the staff knew him well and often expressed their honor to serve him. He much preferred the spa setting to having his therapist come home, where his wife caused constant interruptions.

Recently, he'd been asking Polina for the "Deep Blue Massage Bora Bora," which was performed with Polynesian massage stamps and seaweed and aimed at detoxifying his body, improving his circulation, and toning his muscles.

His two bodyguards always accompanied him and waited dutifully outside his treatment room. Presently, he lay on the massage table, facedown, his cheeks and the sides of his head balanced between the cushion, his mouth, nose, and eyes exposed to the white marble floor. Polina had already begun burning the frankincense to promote calming and peace, and the music was, of course, Tchaikovsky, his "Serenade for Strings in C Major." Izotov had already had his second glass of Belver Bears, his favorite vodka, and was, indeed, feeling enormously relaxed.

He'd spent most of the day working with the acting president, persuading him to make the "right" decisions and assuring him that limiting the American oil supply was, again, a provisional measure. Christopher Theron had also called to share with him their failure up on Jan Mayen Island. Izotov had sent that strike force at Theron's request. What else was he supposed to do? Every order brought with it the promise of extreme pleasure and was too powerful to resist. He was aware that his actions were reprehensible, but he regarded them as a cold intellectual. He'd had the president murdered and had felt nothing.

The door opened, and a shadow passed over him. "Polina, what took you so long?"

"I was preparing the towels. I'm sorry. Are you ready? We'll begin with the oil."

"Oh, yes. I've had a very busy week. This is going to feel very good."

"I doubt that," came another voice.

Suddenly, hands were on Izotov's wrists, binding them to the table with heavy straps. He tried to kick, but his ankles were already being held down, they too bound, immobilized.

And there she was, Viktoria Antsyforov, taking a seat on the floor below the table, sitting cross-legged so she could stare up at him.

"Hello, Sergei."

Izotov swallowed. "Did he send you?"

"Who?"

"Theron."

"No, I've come alone."

She looked rejuvenated, her face fuller and darker, her hair a little longer, her lithe frame poured into a white, long-sleeved top and black slacks. The knee-high boots, too, always the boots, were partially hidden beneath the pants.

"So let me guess: You're looking for work . . . or you're here to kill me."

"Actually, you are my work. Now, don't raise your voice. Polina is with me. The security cameras have been switched off. Your bodyguards are dead, and so are those agents you've put in place around our acting president's house. You can't threaten his family anymore, and when I'm done with you, he'll negotiate a cease-fire with the president of the United States."

Izotov smiled bitterly. "I thought you were tired, Viktoria."

"Exhausted. But I'll get to sleep soon." She narrowed her gaze on him, probing. "Tell me, Sergei, did they put a chip in your eye?"

"You already know the answer."

"Funny, I like you better this way. You'd probably apologize for killing my husband and my brothers."

"You know I didn't. But I would."

"And you killed Kapalkin, didn't you?"

"You should be happy."

She snorted. "You did the world a favor."

"Maybe, but there's always another."

"Like Theron? Who is he? What does he want?"

Izotov winced. The question sent a shock to his brain. "I can't answer that. But let's talk about you. I can have our acting president grant you a full pardon. We can reinstate you with the GRU. You'll direct the foreign service."

"But your friend Theron will have to put a chip in my eye first, right?"

"Viktoria, listen to me. Do what I say, and all the pain will go away."

She got to her feet.

"Wait, where are you going? You won't kill me?"

"I'm sorry, Sergei, I already have."

His mouth fell open.

"Yes," she said. "Your favorite vodka. Every man's vice can be his undoing."

"How long?"

She checked her smartphone. "Another two minutes or so to think about what you've done to me, to everyone else like me. The people you've tortured and murdered. The innocents. There's no repentance now, no place for you in heaven. And the last thing you'll remember is me spitting on you as I leave . . ." She did.

"Viktoria, I never . . . I'm sorry, please!"

* * *

The Snow Maiden left the room, closed the door after her, and fell back against it, eyes hot with tears. She hunched over and retched it all out.

Oh, yes, he'd been wrong.

Only *she* could make the pain go away. Not him. Not anyone else.

Now she was free. Kapalkin and Izotov were gone. The motherland would have new leadership, a new path.

Only two things remained: having the tracker removed from her arm . . . and losing her American escorts.

FIFTY-THREE

DreamRunner Motor Yacht
East of Madagascar
0910 Hours Local Time

Christopher Theron had fallen asleep in his office chair for the second night in a row. He'd been on the phone, repeatedly grilling his sources regarding their failure at Jan Mayen Island. Scouts reported that the submarine had long since sunk, that multiple helicopters had been destroyed on the island, and that the place was now occupied by Norwegian troops who'd captured a small contingent of Spetsnaz operators. The airfield had been cordoned off, and some of the wreckage was being transferred into a C-130 by a team of American Air Force personnel. The Norwegians had no doubt discovered his operating room, along with all of the surgical equipment and supplies.

Even worse, he'd lost contact with Werner, and the media was in a frenzy with reports of Izotov found dead in Moscow.

Theron would continue with his damage control, purging databases and breaking his ties with six different South African aviation companies, along with his shadow partners from India. He knew how to consolidate his operations and shield himself. He'd done it before; he'd do it again.

Business was bad. So was pleasure.

Dennison was nothing but a mannequin to him now, their sex tiresome no matter how hard she tried. Without the challenge, without the hunt, she'd become a toy, half-broken, about to be forgotten. She'd been lying in their quarters, sick with a stomach flu for the past two days, the crew unable to help her.

He rubbed his tired eyes and checked his e-mail account once more. His liaison with the Bilderberg Group had sent him a message: The directors had called for an urgent meeting, in person, no exceptions. He took a long, slow breath. He would not survive that meeting.

Swearing, he opened the desk drawer, searching for his Vektor SP1, not that he planned to kill himself, hardly, but he thought he'd hang off the deck and empty a magazine into the ocean to release some rage.

The pistol was gone. He searched two other drawers, then turned at the sound of the salon's door creaking open.

A male steward barely familiar to him brought in a tray with two glasses of fresh orange juice, coffee, and croissants.

"You've forgotten to knock?"

"I beg your pardon, sir."

"You . . . you came aboard when we stopped in Toamasina, didn't you?"

"Yes, sir." The young man placed the tray on Theron's desk.

"This crew has been with me for years. I trust the captain's recommendations, but if he's hired someone who's forgotten how to knock . . ."

"I haven't forgotten, sir. You simply haven't earned my respect."

Theron frowned. "What does that mean?"

"It means that your captain is a man of conviction who only wants to do his job and obey the law. He may be loyal to you, but he doesn't plan to spend the rest of his life in jail, either."

Theron took a step back, away from the desk. "Who are you?"

"My name is Thomas Voeckler. I'm an intelligence officer from the United States of America. Perhaps you've heard of us. We're a big country with a powerful military." He glanced back to the door, where two men in full scuba gear and clutching military-style rifles stood, dripping all over the floor. "These guys are Navy SEALs, and they've got ten more friends outside. And oh yes, this, by the way"—Voeckler reached into his pocket—"is your gun." He held up the pistol, then tossed it back to Theron, empty of course.

Theron tossed the gun back onto his desk and snickered. "All you are is an inconvenience. I've got my own army of attorneys."

"You'll need 'em. We've linked you back to the

Forgotten Army with a witness named Aslan. We've got you tied to the kidnapping of Dr. Helena Ragland and to that operating room on Jan Mayen Island. We even captured one of your doctors on the island who's confessed to everything. Dennison provides us hard evidence of your chip technology, as will Izotov's body. Oh, and speaking of the Russians, there's an SVR agent up on deck as well. They're interested in what you might know about Izotov's murder—as well as Kapalkin's."

Theron's breath shortened. "Be as smug as you like, little man, but you have no idea who you're dealing with."

Voeckler frowned. "Actually, I looked you up on Wikipedia. They left out the part about you being such a douche, so yeah, I guess you're right."

He gestured to the SEALs, who moved forward, and one of them grunted, "Don't make any trouble, otherwise you *will* get wet."

"Sorry about your girlfriend, too," added Voeckler as they escorted Theron out. "I gave her the stomach bug so she'd be confined to quarters and not recognize me. Kind of thing we spies like to do . . . she'll make a full recovery so we can get that chip out of her eye."

"I don't care. Tell me this, little man, have you found the Snow Maiden yet?"

"Why do you ask?"

"Because if we can't destroy the superpowers, she will."

Voeckler raised his brows. "One woman? I don't think so. Anyway, she works for us now."

Theron felt his temples throbbing, and by the time the SEALs wrestled him up onto the deck, he was cursing and screaming, railing against the audacity and indignity of it all, blasting himself for his failure, and trying to wrench free as the SEALs wriggled him into a pair of zipper cuffs.

"All of you," he shouted. "All of you, look at me. This is what power looks like. This is what success looks like. Not you in your pathetic uniforms, slaves to your governments. Not you, slaves to all the lies. You're being controlled and you don't even know it."

He stood there, panting, and Voeckler came up to him and widened his eyes. "Nice speech. The cuffs kinda ruin the success argument, though. Keep working on it." He slapped his palm on Theron's shoulder, then turned his gaze seaward—

Where a *Virginia*-class nuclear submarine had just surfaced.

FIFTY-FOUR

Lex rented a little one-bedroom apartment not far from Camp Pendleton because he enjoyed the privacy and liked to turn in early without being teased by his colleagues. He was a morning guy, rising at five A.M. to go for his run, hit the free weights, then get on with the rest of his day. Discipline was remembering what you wanted, and living alone kept him focused.

The clock on the TV's channel guide read 10:21 P.M. He was lying there in bed, thumbing through the channels, and thinking about Slava and Halverson.

Yes, that sweet lady who'd saved their lives had bled out before they'd reached Iceland. Holding back tears, Lex had told General Mitchell that if anyone deserved the Medal of Honor, she did, and he planned to initiate the package by gathering witnesses and submitting their written accounts to be passed up the chain of command. Major Stephanie Halverson had, beyond a shadow of a doubt, distinguished herself conspicuously by gallantry and intrepidity at the risk of her life above and beyond the call of duty.

Her boyfriend, McAllen, was still broken up, beyond consoling for now. He'd come around. The Marine Corps Raiders had big plans for him.

After returning to CONUS, Lex had gone up to Sharon Springs, New York, to visit with Slava's parents and tell them what a brave and admirable NCO their son had been and how he'd sacrificed his life doing what he loved. Losing Slava was terrible enough, but sitting there, staring into his parents' eyes, watching them cry and talk about their son, was pure torture, so much so that when Lex got back, he'd remained in his apartment for two days, wishing he'd spoken more candidly with them. Slava was dead, and Oksana was still out there, somewhere . . .

Nothing made sense any more. He'd stopped watching the news. He wasn't sure when he was due back on the base. He wondered if he'd wind up like Captain Willard at the beginning of *Apocalypse Now*, lying there in a hotel room, going crazy, waiting for them to bring up a mission like room service.

At least he'd run out of vodka and was too lazy to buy more. Vlad and Borya had left a few messages that he'd failed to return. Maybe tomorrow he'd feel better. Maybe he was just getting old.

He sighed, lifted the remote toward the TV to change

the channel again—when a silhouette moved into the doorway.

As he reached toward the nightstand to grab his M9 lying in its holster, the light switched on.

She stood in a black leather jacket and matching knee-high boots. Pistol trained on him. Dark eyes riveted on his.

"What the fuck?" he cried.

"Speak Russian only," she said.

He sat up, glanced to his gun, then stammered and began to speak in English. He caught himself and switched to Russian: "God damn it, bitch, what are you doing? How'd you get out?"

"Forget your weapon. Leave it there." She moved into the room, still holding him at gunpoint.

He raised his palms.

She removed one hand from her pistol, reached into her pocket, and slipped out a data card. She tossed it on the bed.

"What is that?"

"The location of your sister, Oksana. She's still in Siberia. They moved her to another *sharashka* farther north. I've confirmed she's there. You can go get her now."

"How do you know about her?"

The Snow Maiden looked insulted. "I used to be an intelligence officer—and I pulled your file from GRU headquarters while I was in Moscow. They know that when you were at Fort Levski, you ran a search for her."

Lex's frown deepened. "Why are you doing this? Why should I trust you?"

"I wanted to pay you back."

He shrugged. "For what?"

"For what you're going to do to me tonight." She raised her palm, then slowly, cautiously, lowered the pistol and placed it on his dresser. She faced him and began unbuttoning her leather jacket.

She wore nothing beneath.

He lost his breath.

"I'm sorry about your door," she said. "I think I broke the lock while I was picking it."

"You're a crazy bitch."

She crawled across the bed and slid on top of him. "I like being a crazy bitch . . . but you . . . you look sad."

"You take the good with the bad, I guess."

"Let me take away the bad."

His fingers went up to the bandage on her arm. "What happened?"

"I did a job for your president. They put a tracker on me. I had it removed. I wanted a little more privacy."

"So they're going nuts, trying to find you right now."

She smiled. "They shouldn't have let me go."

He grabbed her wrist. "I could go to jail for this."

"You won't." She placed a hand on his cheek and began to kiss him gently on the lips. "I heard about the pilot, too. Halverson. She had skills."

Lex closed his eyes. "Yes, she did."

"I know you're hurting. I am, too. That's why I came

back. When you captured me, and I looked into your eyes, I was scared."

He snorted. "Scared of going to prison."

"No, scared because I found someone who really looked at me."

"Well, you got your wish. And here I am, in bed with the world's most wanted terrorist."

"Not any more. I'm just a girl. And we need each other. Will you have me?"

He rose from the bed, crossed to the light switch and shut it off. She lay there in the fluttering light of the TV, her body cast in shadow, her eyes glimmering. "Will you come with me to get my sister?"

"Yes."

"And when we're done, I'll arrest you."

"You won't have to."

With a shudder, he returned to the bed. She pulled him on top. Her hair smelled freshly washed, hinting of jasmine and honey, and for a few seconds he just lay there, breathing her in, feeling the life return to his head and heart. Maybe someday they could work together and help put an end to this war, but for now, she was right. They had each other.